CLOVER
BLUE

Books by Eldonna Edwards

THIS I KNOW

CLOVER BLUE

Published by Kensington Publishing Corporation

CLOVER
BLUE

Eldonna Edwards

JOHN SCOGNAMIGLIO BOOKS
KENSINGTON BOOKS
www.kensingtonbooks.com

JOHN SCOGNAMIGLIO BOOKS are published by

Kensington Publishing Corp.
119 West 40th Street
New York, NY 10018

All Kensington titles, imprints and distributed lines are available at special quantity discounts for bulk purchases for sales promotion, premiums, fund-raising, educational or institutional use.

Special book excerpts or customized printings can also be created to fit specific needs. For details, write or phone the office of the Kensington Special Sales Manager: Kensington Publishing Corp., 119 West 40th Street, New York, NY, 10018. Attn. Special Sales Department. Phone: 1-800-221-2647.

Library of Congress Card Catalogue Number: 2018912557

The JS and John Scognamiglio Books logo is a trademark of Kensington Publishing Corp.

ISBN-13: 978-1-4967-1289-9
ISBN-10: 1-4967-1289-7
First Kensington Hardcover Edition: June 2019

eISBN-13: 978-1-4967-1291-2 (e-book)
eISBN-10: 1-4967-1291-9 (e-book)

10 9 8 7 6 5 4 3 2

Printed in the United States of America

For Brer, my touchstone, my lodestar.

ACKNOWLEDGMENTS

Before publishing my debut novel *This I Know*, I had little idea of just how much happens behind the scenes between completed manuscript and release. I am so very grateful for my supporting cast at Kensington. Thank you John Scognamiglio for honoring my work under your fabulous new imprint. Thank you Lulu, Vida, Lauren, Alex, and all the wonderful people whose names I don't know but who work diligently to ensure that my cover is beautiful, the contents are close to perfect, and the book lands in the hands of influential readers.

Thank you Claire Anderson-Wheeler for always being available to explain, to elaborate, to commiserate and to celebrate. Given Aladdin's magic lamp, you're exactly the dedicated, earnest, meticulous agent I'd have wished for. How lucky am I?

Thank you to all the authors who've extended their hands in friendship and encouragement, especially those who took time out of their busy schedules to read and review *This I Know*. Barbara Claypole White, Amy Impellizzeri, Cathy Lamb, Lesley Kagen, y'all are the best of the best. A very special gratitude to Donna Everhart, who midwifed me through this process when you were going through one of the greatest challenges of your own life. I am so lucky to know you. Thanks also to my fellow debutantes from Authors '18, where we learned that whole first novel thing, sometimes painfully, but mostly joyfully, together.

Thank you Teri Bayus for trusting me with Central Coast Writers Conference attendees and for your voluptuous friendship. You are the definition of what it means to be a champion for writers. Thank you Peter Dunne for your invaluable notes that pushed me to make *Clover Blue* a story that belongs to all of us. Who knew that a young adult watching *Eight Is Enough* and *Dr. Quinn, Medicine Woman* would one day be fortunate enough to have the writer/producer of those shows read her early pages? Your feedback was nothing less than gold, and I cherish our friendship.

I enjoy a petulant relationship with social media; it's difficult not to get distracted from writing and be swept down the rabbit holes of Facebook, Twitter, Instagram, etc. This is partly due to all the wonderful people I've met through these channels. People like Kristy Barrett of A Novel Bee, a veritable one-woman cheering squad for writers and readers who makes a special effort to uplift debut authors. You amaze me, inspire me, and make me laugh. Kudos also to your sidekick Tonni Callan, who is a book-loving Olympian in her own right. Thank you to all the Facebook reading groups and their moderators, too many to mention, who've introduced readers to my books. A special shout-out to the group I Grew Up in Sebastopol in the 70s for the wealth of research information while writing *Clover Blue*. I'm pretty sure a few of you would have lived at Saffron Freedom Community.

Thank you Women's Fiction Writers Association for all you do to inspire, educate, and support writers of women's fiction. Thank you SLO NightWriters for providing a network for local writers. Thank you to my original writing clan, Collective Journey, for all your love and support throughout the years. We've been together for over two decades and I cherish every one of you.

Thank goodness for libraries, librarians, and booksellers. Where would we be without your fierce love of books?

Thank you to all of you who read *This I Know* and shared the book with other readers, for your lovely reviews, for reaching out to tell me how the story touched you personally.

Thank you to my sibs Sharon, Luanne, Mari-Beth, LaVonne, and David, who show up at my readings and shout their adoration from the rooftops. You were my first commune and I'm so grateful for that. Thank you Anita for teaching me to read. I miss you, sis. Thank you to my children, who tell me how proud they are of their mom. A special thanks to my son Jacob, who offered a ton of helpful feedback on the voice of a young male narrator and who came up with the term "growing pleasures" that I used in the book.

Thank you Lorena Rodriguez, "sister" kidney donor for championing my memoir, then my debut novel, and now this book. You are a true "book angel" and a very special person only some of us are fortunate enough to call friend.

Thank you to my beautiful tribe of amazing massage therapists who've sustained Avila Beach Massage while I focused on my writing. I could not have accomplished this without you.

Finally, thank you William "Brer" Braddock, my beloved, for the countless hours, weeks, and months you pored over my words and helped me reshape them into better ones. For inhabiting these characters as if they were your brothers and sisters. For your tender honesty and exuberant praise. As Rumi once wrote, "Every story is us."

AUTHOR NOTES

When I was a teen I briefly "house sat" at a small commune while the inhabitants were away. During those few days I slept in a shack on a pad piled high with musty fur coats purchased at thrift stores. I rode bareback on horses as they grazed between lumps of melting snow. My two friends and I heated up gruel from the local food co-op on top of a cast-iron wood stove. It didn't take long for me to realize that I much preferred my soft bed and the hot, palatable meals I'd enjoyed all my life. However, living in that commune for a few days also planted a seed of wonder. I relished all the earthy smells and sounds living so close to nature. I began to romanticize living in a wilderness community with people who espoused shared ideals.

I never realized that dream except to write about it here in this book. I chose an area near Freestone, California, because of its proximity to Sebastopol, a hub of freethinkers and leftover flower children. I didn't learn until much later while on a research trip that an actual commune existed north of Freestone at one time, apparently a pretty famous one. This is to say that Saffron Freedom Community and her members were borne of my imagination and are in no way a representation of any place or person other than the ones living in my mind. And after reading *Clover Blue*, hopefully in yours as well.

Ever has it been that love knows not its own depth until the hour of separation.
—Kahlil Gibran

1

September 3, 1974

The Olders are letting us watch the birth. Harmony runs down the path ahead of me, her bare feet kicking up a cloud of dust. When she gets to the teepee she turns and yells, "Come on, Blue! Aren't you excited?"

"I'll be there in a minute." I balance on one leg to brush a sharp acorn cap from the bottom of my foot.

"Okay, but hurry up or you're going to miss it." She opens the canvas flap and disappears inside.

Letting us watch is a stretch. More like they insisted. Harmony and I were asleep when Moon was born so we both missed that one. Sirona says we're old enough now. Sirona is the family midwife. She delivers babies in people's houses around Sonoma County. This is only her second birth here at Saffron Freedom Community. The first was when she gave birth to Moon four years ago.

I walk slowly, taking small steps. I might be old enough at ten, but that doesn't mean I'm ready for this. I can't shake the memory of when our nanny goat, Inga, had a baby a couple years ago after one of the neighbor's goats got loose and mated with her. Inga ate the sac around her kid and the other stuff that came out of her afterward. I hope we don't have to eat anything that comes out after Jade's baby is born. We're vegetarian so probably not. But you never know with this family.

I want to be excited, but I'm a little freaked out. I'm worried Jade's baby might not survive, just like the baby goat that got sick and died. Goji forbids doctors and hospitals. We believe in natural medicine. Sirona probably knows what she's doing but what if she doesn't? What if none of them know what they're doing?

When I reach the teepee Harmony pokes her head through the doorway and grabs my hand, pulling me forward. "Come on, slowpoke."

I take a breath and step inside.

Jade is propped on pillows in the middle of the room. Her belly button looks like the tied end of a balloon, one that's about to burst from too much air inside. Willow and Coyote are on their knees near the head of the mattress, each holding one of Jade's hands. Sirona crouches at the other end, her red hair like a lit match piled high on top of her head, softly coaching Jade. The rest of the Olders sit with their backs against the far wall of the musty canvas, quietly chanting the *ohm*.

The minutes drag on for what seems like forever. Harmony paces back and forth behind Sirona. Every time Jade moans, Sirona tells her, "Almost there. Almost there." I'm pretty sure she's been "almost there" for over an hour now.

Jade tilts her head back to look at Coyote, her tired eyes begging for comfort. I hate that she's hurting. Goji often tells us that every light has a shadow, and pain is the price of joy. Goji is the leader, but he doesn't call himself that. He is kind of a guru, though, and everyone looks up to him. Still, this seems like too high of a price if you ask me. I wish Sirona would fix it. I thought that was her job.

Coyote pulls the tie-dyed headband off his Afro and dabs sweat from Jade's forehead. "You're doing great," he whispers.

Another moan from Jade that turns into a howl. I glance at Moon, asleep on a mat on the dirt floor, his head on his favorite blanket. He doesn't move. I can't believe the noise doesn't wake him.

Sirona lays a hand on each of Jade's thighs. "Here we go, sister. Baby's crowning. On the next contraction, go ahead and push."

Harmony hovers behind Sirona, trying to see over our sister-mother's wide shoulders. I stick as close to the doorway as possible. I don't like the noises Jade is making. She sounds like one of the neighbor's dairy cows when they low for their calves after they're taken from their mothers.

Jade lets out a low growl, then holds her breath, straining as Willow and Coyote support her upper body until her face turns beet red. Harmony drops to her knees next to Sirona. She practically has her nose in there between Jade's legs, trying to get a close-up view of the action.

She glances over her shoulder and waves at me. "Blue, get over here! You gotta see this! The head is coming out!"

I stay put.

Harmony rolls her eyes and turns to Sirona. "Can I touch it?"

Sirona nods.

I feel a hand on my back. It's Goji. He nudges me forward just as Harmony touches her finger to what looks like one of those aliens she sometimes draws in her sketchbooks. The head turns sideways. The mouth opens and closes but it doesn't make any noise.

"One more push," Sirona says.

A gush of blood and water, then Jade's baby slips out from

between her legs and into Sirona's hands. I feel like I might pass out. All these smells, like the sea on a hot day.

"It's a girl!" Harmony squeals. "Woo-hoo! I've got a new baby sister!"

Doobie and Wave stop chanting and move to join Goji and the others next to Jade's bed. Jade perches on her elbows, glancing from the baby to Sirona. "Why isn't she crying?"

I take a step backward to watch from a safer distance. Sirona squeezes a funny-looking bulb into each side of the tiny nose. Nothing. She leans over the baby's blue face and puffs into her mouth. The baby makes a squeaky sound, then lets out a lusty wail as she kicks her little legs. Everyone breathes a sigh. Sirona hands the baby to Jade's outstretched arms, a rope-like cord still leading to where she came from. I feel like I'm about to cry but I don't know why.

The brothers slap each other on the backs. Willow and Sirona drape their arms around Jade, crying happy tears, as if all three of them just gave birth. Having been raised equally by all three women, I've been taught to consider each of the sisters my mother. It's never been important to know who actually gave birth to me.

Until now.

"Who did I come out of?"

All heads instantly turn toward me. I look at Willow. "Are you my mother?" Then down at Jade, now clutching the baby to her bare chest. "Or you?"

Harmony stares at me, her big eyes suddenly mirroring my question, the one I'm pretty sure I'm not supposed to ask. Willow glances at Goji. He shakes his head slightly and whispers to Doobie. Doobie takes my hand. "Let's go for a walk."

I pull away from him but he practically drags me out the door. As he leads me farther from the teepee I try to guess his answer to my question. It can't be Sirona. I was five when she joined SFC. As far back as I can remember it was Willow who watched me the most. But Jade's always been nicest, liked to give me baths and tuck me in at night. Which one? Maybe neither. Maybe like Harmony's mother, my mom left Saffron Freedom Community a long time ago and never came back.

Doobie stops and rests both his hands on my shoulders. I close my eyes and wait for him to reveal the name of my mother.

"Goji will talk to you about this later, Blue. Now isn't the right time."

My eyes pop open. "I don't want to wait for Goji. Why can't you just tell me now?"

Doobie glances toward the teepee and back at me. He crouches lower so we're eye to eye. "It's complicated, little brother."

I look away from his face and focus on the peace symbol embroidered on his beat-up denim hat. "Seems pretty simple to me. Just point to her."

He hangs his head and combs through his beard with one hand. "I'm sorry. I can't do that. You'll have to wait for Goji to tell you."

I kick at the dirt with my bare foot. "Can't or won't?"

Doobie stands and motions toward the teepee. "Come on, Blue. Let's go meet your new baby sister."

I give up and follow him. He opens the flap and waits for me to step inside. The room smells like sweat and copper and bread. The Olders are all laughing and crying at the same time. The naked baby is still waxy and bloody as it squirms against Jade's bare skin. I sit on the floor next to Harmony and try not to look at the pink streaks on her legs where she must have wiped her hands. She throws her arms around me and squeezes. "We've got a new sister. Isn't she beautiful?"

The slimy new baby is not what I would call beautiful, but Harmony's arms feel like the only thing holding me together right now so I just nod.

Coyote kisses Jade's cheek and the top of the wet little head in her arms. After a few minutes Sirona wraps the baby in a blanket and hands her to Goji. He holds the bundle high in front of him with one hand behind her head, studying her face.

"She has such a bright glow about her. Like a million stars packed into one tiny being." He lowers the baby and kisses her tiny nose. "We'll call you Aura. Welcome, little sister."

"Welcome, Aura!" everyone says.

One by one they pass the fussing baby from arm to open arm. When Harmony hands Aura to me, she stops crying and stares into my face.

Doobie nudges me, grinning. "She digs those baby blues, brother."

Everyone laughs. Jade jokes that Stevie Wonder is the father but we know it's Coyote. Not just because of the baby's dark skin and black hair. You could see Coyote falling in love with that baby from the instant he laid eyes on her. It's the same way I've felt toward Sirona when she's patched me up after I've hurt myself, or when Willow made sure my bathwater was the perfect temperature, or when Jade used to sing me to sleep. And how Gaia used to twirl me around until the sky and the trees blurred into one. All the sister-mothers feel like moms, which is probably why I never bothered to ask which one gave birth to me before today.

After a celebration dinner, Goji invites me to his tiny shack for a man-to-man talk. "Come for tea after the sun sets," he says, kissing the top of my head.

As soon as the last pot is rinsed and hung up on a hook to dry, I bolt from the community dining area and sit on a big rock near the garden. I've never been inside Goji's house. It's off limits to the Youngers and rare that even one of the Olders is invited inside. I wait for the exact moment the sun disappears behind the surrounding mountains to walk toward Goji's private home and knock on the wood frame.

His voice answers from inside. "A door is only closed to those who see it that way."

I push aside the wool blanket hanging over the opening and stand just inside the doorway of his one-room house. It's even smaller than it looks from the outside. A small fire flickers in a little woodstove at the center of the room with a pipe leading through the roof. Stacks of books line the wall next to a messy table covered with papers and notebooks. Goji's cat, Ziggy, purrs at the foot of a mattress piled with blankets.

"Come here, little brother," Goji says. He's sitting cross-legged on the floor with his eyes closed, naked as usual, same as me. His black hair, just a few inches longer than his beard, is pulled into a ponytail that falls down his thin back. A white headband covers his forehead.

I creep closer, not sure where to stand. I'm not afraid of him. Goji has never been anything but kind to me. But there's something about him that makes you feel reverent, like I imagine people who were around those guys Gandhi and Jesus we've studied about. He's fed me, taught me The Peaceful Way, clothed me—when we wear clothes—and created this amazing place. I know he loves me.

Goji motions toward a pillow across from him, eyes still closed. "Sit."

I sit.

He extends both his hands in front of him, palms facing me. I press my hands against his. He smiles and opens his eyes. "Welcome."

"Thank you."

He drops his hands into his lap and I do the same.

"I understand why you asked about your birth today."

I feel my face grow warm.

"It's okay, Clover Blue. I've been expecting this day."

"I . . . I just wondered . . ." I stammer before starting again. "I'm curious. . . ."

"Go ahead."

I stare at the yin-yang pendant hanging from a thin leather strap around his tanned neck "Who are my parents?"

Goji retrieves a small book from the rickety table next to him and opens it to a bookmarked page. On the cover, a drawing of a turbaned head floats below the words *The Prophet*. Goji clears his throat and begins to read. *"Your children are not your children. They are the sons and daughters of Life's longing for itself. They come through you but not from you. And though they are with you they belong not to you."*

Goji closes the book and sets it on the floor. He reaches for my hands again and this time holds them tightly in his. "We are all family here. The sister-mothers are your mothers. Whether or not you came from them, you come through them. All of them."

"Are you saying none of them are my real mother?"

"I'm saying they are all your mothers."

Goji's taught me that we're all pulled to our destiny and mine was to be part of the Saffron Freedom Community. But I want to know specifically which of the mothers I came out of. I press him for more.

"Yes, but which one actually gave birth to me?"

Goji's face looks pained and a little twisted, like when the sun gets in your eyes on a bright day. "You are the son of life's longing. You understand this, Clover Blue?"

"I know how lucky I am to be part of this family. I just want more details about . . ."

Goji takes a deep breath and lets it out slowly. "Your birth family failed to watch over you but it wasn't their fault. You were seeking something beyond them. Had it not happened that day it would have happened on another day. The soul cannot be stopped from searching for what it desires."

"Failed to watch over me? What do you mean? Where? What happened?"

He shakes his head. "It doesn't matter where you came from, Clover Blue. What matters is only here and now. God—the god *in* you—was seeking home and it is right here. Surely by now you understand that Love is the greatest attraction."

"But it matters to *me*. Why can't you—?"

"Society has their own set of rules, ones that aren't necessarily in alignment with the rules of nature. We took you in because it was destiny, ours and yours."

"So you adopted me?"

Goji sighs again, this time not as slowly. "It wasn't a legal adoption. It was a *love* adoption." He leans in, his dark eyes staring into mine. "If anyone outside of the family finds out, we'll all be separated. You and the other three children would be taken from us, probably put in foster care. Your older brothers and sisters could go to jail."

"And you . . . ?"

"Yes. And me."

My thoughts immediately go to Harmony. The thought of never seeing her again turns my stomach inside out. I suddenly feel cold. My body begins to shiver. Goji pulls a blanket from the chair behind him and drapes it over my shoulders.

"Clover Blue, you were drawn to this family by our loving energy, as we were to you." He moves his hands to my face and holds it tenderly. Tears spill out of his dark eyes. "Your sister and brother were meant to be there at that moment, just as you are meant to be right here, right now, in this moment with me."

"Which sister? Which brother?"

He doesn't answer.

"Will I ever get to know where I came from?"

He moves his hands to my shoulders. "When you're a little older we'll talk more about this."

"How much older?"

"When you're twelve. We'll talk more about it then."

That's almost two whole years away. I open my mouth to protest but he puts a finger to my lips.

"When you're twelve."

Everyone else is asleep. I lie awake in my bed thinking about what Goji said. His answers are like riddles. Maybe my real parents were drug addicts. Maybe they were mean people who hit their children. I should be thankful for my loving family here. Goji teaches us that gratitude is at the center of every experience, good and bad. He's right. He's always right.

2

August 12, 1976

Nobody knows my real birthday. Little by little I've learned bits and pieces about the day I arrived. I don't remember anything because, one, I was asleep and because, two, who remembers anything from their third year of life? All I know is that when Goji asked how old I was that first day I'd shyly held up three fingers. He declared August twelfth as my re-birth date.

Normally birthdays are like any other day because we're supposed to celebrate each day as a new birth. But because I'm turning twelve on the twelfth of the month, we're having a party. Of course this is also the day Goji has promised to tell me more about my past. He hasn't mentioned it since the night Aura was born, but he's taught us that our word is a measure of how evolved we are, so I'm pretty sure he'll keep his. We'll probably chat after the party.

Some of the Olders have decorated the army-green shade that hangs over our dining area with wildflowers and vines. When I walk up to the long wooden table, Willow kisses me and plants a wreath on my head made of clover blossoms. Her wet eyes have tiny lines just starting to grow out of the corners. "This is your day, Clover Blue. I'm so happy for you. For all of us."

Sirona made lasagna with tomato sauce and home-made goat cheese, my favorite meal. She sets the steaming dish in the middle of the table using fuzzy winter mittens for pot holders. Sirona usually wears her long red hair loose but she's braided it along the sides and together in the back, all fancy like a druid queen or something. Goji strides up wearing gauzy pants with a wide sash, but no shirt. He invites me to take his chair at the head of the table and he sits in my usual place. It feels weird, sitting where I face everyone.

Harmony is the last to arrive for my party. Her hair is a mess, like she just crawled out of bed, same as it looked during this morning's meditation. When she sees me she does a fake bow before pulling out a chair next to Goji. "Namaste, Master Blue," she says, giggling.

Doobie sits to my right. He jabs me in the shoulder and grins. "Here, little brother. I rolled you your first joint."

I glance at Goji, who nods his okay, holding up a single finger. "One puff."

I run the joint under my nose and sniff, like I've seen the Olders do, then tuck it behind my ear. "Thanks, Doob. I think I'll save it for later."

He pats me on the back. "That's cool, buddy."

We all gorge ourselves on pasta before moving to sit on the wooden stumps placed haphazardly around the bonfire pit in the center of the compound. It's the middle of the day in August and nearly 100 degrees, and the pit hasn't been in use for a while. Wave picks up his beat-up guitar and starts fiddling with a few chords. He reminds me a little of the cover on our John Denver eight-track, with his curved blond bangs and wire-rimmed glasses.

Wave tunes a few strings, then winks. "I learned to play one of your favorite songs." He says it in a weird gravelly voice that makes everyone laugh. He closes his eyes and strums crazy hard, doing his best imitation of Richie Havens. "Freedom-uh, freedom-uh . . ." over and over, louder and louder. The louder Wave sings, the higher his voice goes until he's practically shrieking.

Coyote claps his hands over his ears and turns his back to the music. "No, no, no, man, please stop." Everyone starts laughing.

Wave grins and goes off on an instrumental bit. Some of the others start humming and dancing playfully around me. I like the attention but it also makes me feel shy. Harmony keeps trying to get me to dance. I'm surprised but relieved when Wave suddenly quits playing. He points with the neck of his guitar to where a blue Volkswagen bug parks just inside the fence at the end of our long drive. "Are we expecting company?"

We all watch as the driver's door pops open and a barefoot woman in cutoffs climbs out. Apparently only one door works because the other person has to slide over and get out on the same side. From where I'm sitting I can see the passenger's blond hair, red blouse, and white pedal-pushers. Definitely not one of us. For one, she's fully dressed, and for two, she looks clean as a whistle in the middle of a dirt oasis.

Doobie stands and shields his eyes with one hand. A smile stretches across his face. He lets out a whoop and races toward the women. When he reaches the car, he hugs the driver so hard her feet lift off the ground. He twirls her around, then sets her down and yells toward us. "Hey, everybody, look who's here!"

My face breaks into a grin when I recognize Harmony's mom walking toward us. I turn to see Harmony's eyes go from wider than I've ever seen to narrowed, furious slits. Gaia and Harmony moved here when I was five. At first Gaia seemed to really dig all of us, but then she started going to Grateful Dead concerts, leaving Harmony behind for weeks at a time while she followed the band wherever they played. Three years ago Gaia left for Seattle to see a concert. Months passed before we eventually realized she probably wasn't coming back. We haven't seen her since.

Everyone waits for Goji's reaction as Gaia and her passenger approach with Doobie in tow. Willow and Wave lean into each other, whispering quietly. Coyote nervously bounces two-year-old Aura on his knee. Jade moves to stand next to Sirona, locking arms as if getting ready to play a game of red rover.

Before anyone has a chance to say anything, Gaia takes the blond girl's hand and pulls her close. "Hey, sisters and brothers. I know it's been a long time and you're all probably ticked about that. But I brought a friend who needs a safe pad while she gets her shit together."

Nobody moves. The girl drops her chin to her chest and stares at the ground.

Gaia drapes an arm around her friend's shoulder. "Her stepfather beats her."

The girl's eyes fly open. She looks at Gaia the same way I look at Harmony when she blurts out something that was supposed to be a secret.

Gaia scans the fire-pit circle like she suddenly remembered something. She catches sight of the tail end of Harmony, who's now booking it in the opposite direction. I know I should chase after my sister, but I'm too excited about seeing Gaia.

Gaia hands off the confused-looking blond girl to Doobie. "Dammit!" Gaia says, and chases after Harmony, who's already reached the tree line. We all know she'll never catch Harmony if she doesn't want to be caught.

Doobie stands with his empty arm still outstretched, glancing back and forth between us and the blond girl. She jerks her arm away from Doobie, looking like she's about to cry. She turns in the direction where Gaia was headed, but Gaia has disappeared into the woods. Her chin starts to quiver.

Goji watches, expressionless, as a tear runs down the girl's flushed cheek. "How old are you, little sister?"

She swallows before answering. "Eighteen?"

Goji nods at Jade and Sirona, who walk the girl away from the main group. The three of them stand together for a few minutes, my sister-mothers patting the newcomer's back as they gently question her. Gaia's friend starts full-out bawling. Jade runs back to Goji and whispers something in his ear. He stands and smiles at me.

"Happy birthday, Clover Blue." He hands me a gift wrapped in plain paper and tied with string. I can tell from the feel it's a book. He lays a hand on my shoulder. "Thank you for shining your beautiful light on our path. I love you, little brother. I'm sorry to leave the party early but I need to deal with this."

Goji's always talking about not getting attached to expectations. I do my best to hide my disappointment. "It's okay, Goji. I'll save you some cake."

He smiles and bows before joining Sirona and the other girl in the distance.

"Maybe we can talk later?" I call after him.

He doesn't answer. The three of them slowly walk toward Goji's shack at the edge of the community. When they reach his front door, Sirona peels off to rejoin the rest of us.

Doobie glances toward the tree line. He and Gaia used to be together before she split a few years ago. "Uh, I think I'll go make sure Gaia and Harmony are cool." He trots off to where Gaia followed Harmony into the woods.

Everyone is suddenly quiet. Willow gently nudges Wave. "Why don't you play your song again?"

Coyote winces. "Please don't." He glances at Wave. "No offense, brother."

Wave grins. "None taken."

Jade squats down and grabs Moon's and Aura's hands. "Who's ready for ice cream?"

The children jump up and down, nearly pulling Jade over. "Me! Me!"

Coyote drapes his big arm around my shoulder and squeezes. "C'mon, birthday boy. Let's go have some dessert."

Our lively gathering has turned quiet. People seem more nervous than excited. I keep glancing toward Goji's shack. I wonder if the crying girl will be allowed to stay. We haven't added any new members since Coyote, Sirona and Gaia showed up over the summer of 1969. But then Gaia took off again four years later, leaving Harmony behind.

The homemade ice cream melts almost faster than we can get it to our mouths. We clean the dishes over two metal tubs of water, one for washing and one for rinsing. I should be happy, but I'm a little bummed. Although I'm glad Gaia is back, she kind of ruined the party. To top it off, the one person I most want to celebrate with has run away. Harmony and I have been like brother and sister since the day she and Gaia arrived. And ever since Gaia left, we've grown even closer.

If Goji does let the girl stay, he'll tell us the new name he's given her. That'll mean he's opened a door for her to join Saffron Freedom Community. Goji is the one who gave each of the Youngers our new names. The Olders aren't supposed to talk about the day I arrived at SFC, but Doobie let it slip that I was sound asleep, clutching a tiny white flower when Goji took me into his arms. "He quietly chanted until you woke up. As soon as he saw the color of your eyes he said, 'Hey, Blue. Hey, Clover Blue,' and it stuck. He told us all that you chose us and it was meant to be." When I pressed Doobie for more details he clammed up.

Goji returns to the dining area with the new girl just as we finish drying the dishes. We all wait for him to speak. He lays a hand on the young girl's head and looks at us. "Everyone, this is Rain."

The girl stares at her tennis shoes. Other than a smeared dirt handprint on the front of her white pants, she looks like a townie; clean like she just climbed out of a bathtub. She's so beautiful I can't stop staring.

Goji puts a finger under the girl's chin and lifts her face. With his other hand he sweeps the curtain of white-blond hair out of the way and looks directly into her bright eyes. I can tell by the blotches on her light skin that she's been crying. I can also see that she's already under Goji's spell. That's just the way it is with him.

"Welcome," he says to her.

We all chime in, "Welcome, Rain!"

She's surprised by our communal greeting and starts crying again. Everyone lines up to give her a hug. Even though I just went through a growth spurt, Rain has to bend down a little when it's my turn. Her cheeks are stained with tears. She smells like soap and something else familiar that I can't put my finger on, but I've smelled it before, I'm sure of that. Maybe at the library or the food co-op.

"Hi. I'm Clover Blue."

Her mouth turns into a pout. "I'm sorry I interrupted your party."

"It's okay."

She gives me a gentle squeeze before moving on to the other Youngers. When she gets to little Aura, she bursts into tears again.

For the rest of the day, the sister-mothers fawn over Rain. They try to distract her by showing her around the land, the lean-to kitchen area and the outdoor shower. They take her to see our goats, Inga and Greta; the chickens; and our huge vegetable garden. The brothers keep their distance but they're all watching, including Goji. Especially Goji.

Of course I'm watching, too. Rain is the prettiest girl I've ever seen in my life. She looks like she belongs on the cover of one of those *Sweet Sixteen* magazines I've seen at Walgreens in Santa Rosa. The ones Harmony always makes fun of.

I wish Harmony would come back. I know she can take care of herself, but I'm starting to worry. I'm pretty sure I know where to find her. When nobody's paying attention, I slip behind the outhouse and over the hill and race toward the woods. Just inside the cover of trees, I hook a quick right along the edge to our secret deer path. I follow it to a wooden bridge that Harmony and I made from a fallen log, and cross the creek. I stop when I get to the hollowed-out trunk. It used to be big enough for us both to curl up inside together and tell stories.

I drop to my knees and poke my head inside. Sure enough, there she is, looking as mean and stubborn as that rooster we had for a while before it got eaten by a bobcat.

"Go away, Blue," she growls.

"Come on, Harmony. You must want to see her after all this time."

When I make a move to join her she glares at me. "No, I really don't want to see her."

"But she's your mom."

"Ruth only gave birth to me. Willow, Jade, and Sirona raised me." Ever since Harmony's mom took off, she refuses to call her Gaia.

I sit back on my heels. "The sister-mothers raised me, too. *Including* Gaia. At least you know who your birth mother is."

She looks up quickly and I know she feels bad. "Sorry. I shouldn't have said that."

"It's okay. I was just giving you a hard time." I eye the spot next to her. "Can I come in? Please?"

She scooches over and I crawl through the opening. We just barely fit inside the burned-out tree together. I sniff the musty air.

"It still smells like fire, doesn't it?"

She wrinkles her nose but doesn't say anything. Harmony's normally the chattiest person I know. I tickle the tops of her feet with a fern frond. I can tell she's fighting a smile. She slaps me on the arm. "Stop trying to make me un-mad."

"I just want you to come home. It's my birthday, man."

She digs her bare toes into the leaves and bits of bark in the soft dirt. "I know. And Ruth screwed it up. Like she screws up everything."

"It won't be screwed up if you come back."

Harmony sighs. "I'll come back only because it's your birthday. But I don't want to see her or talk to her. Will you tell her that?"

I nod. "Deal."

On the way back we make a plan for her to hide in my bedroom until after evening meditation. We take the long way home around the far edge of the property and come out of the woods near the tree house. I try to cover her while she scrambles up the ladder.

When I return to join the others, Goji is waiting for me near the kitchen, eating a piece of my birthday cake. A glob of frosting is stuck in his long beard. He motions for me to come closer, hopefully to invite me to his shack for our long-awaited talk about my birth family.

"Do you know where Harmony is?"

I glance toward the tree house. "I promised not to . . ."

Goji lays a hand on my shoulder and smiles. "Tell her not to worry. We love her and we'll care for her heart."

"Okay."

He goes back to eating his cake.

"Goji?"

"Mmm-hmm."

"Remember that night Aura was born and you said we'd talk again when I'm twelve?"

He licks his plate clean and sets it on the table. "I don't believe I said the exact day you turn twelve."

Ugh, I was sure he meant my actual birthday when he said it. Before I can find the words to ask about setting a day to talk, he spots Rain with Sirona and waves them over. "I'm sorry, Clover Blue. As you're well aware, sometimes the universe has its own plans." Goji drapes one arm around each of the women and guides them down the path toward the meditation area. "Come on, Blue, let's introduce your new sister to The Peaceful Way."

The sun is nearly down when Gaia and Doobie stumble out of the woods together. Gaia stops to pull a burr out of her bare foot before hop-walking the rest of the way across the field. They move to where we're setting up for evening meditation. Gaia's halter top is stuffed in the back pocket of her cutoffs. Both of them have leaves mixed up in their hair and they look stoned.

Doobie smiles sheepishly. "No sign of Harmony, but I found this beautiful lady."

Nobody says a word. Most of the family are already sitting cross-legged on the ground, waiting for Goji to finish explaining our nightly meditation to Rain.

Gaia spots me just as I'm starting to sit. She lets go of Doobie and slaps her hand over her mouth. "Holy shit, is that really you, little brother?" She runs over and throws her arms around me, kissing me about a dozen times on my cheeks and forehead. She pulls back and grabs my hands. "Look at you! I used to carry you piggyback and now you're . . ."

"Twelve, as of today."

"That's right! Sorry I didn't get you anything." She motions toward Rain with her hand and winks. "But I brought us a beautiful new sister, didn't I?"

I blush. Gaia smiles so big her reddened eyes almost disappear. She glances around looking for Harmony, her grin turning into a frown. "My kid still doesn't want to see me?"

I shake my head. "Sorry."

Gaia nods. "Understandable. She's probably freaked out. And maybe a little pissed off." She laughs, her wonderful bubbly laugh that I've missed so much. "Okay, maybe a lot pissed off."

Willow carries the dripping meditation candle she just lit to where Gaia and Doobie are standing next to me. Doobie gets one look at Willow's stern face and backs away, taking a seat behind Moon. Willow straightens her long back and gives Gaia the once-over. "What did you expect, sister? That she'd be thrilled to finally see the person who abandoned her to go play with the other Deadhead groupies traipsing around the country? Harmony's the child, not you. She deserved her mother."

Gaia glances at me and back to Willow. "Do you even hear yourself? You think you're so evolved?"

Rain nervously watches the arguing sister-mothers. Goji moves closer to Willow and Gaia but he doesn't speak. He likes the family to work things out among themselves without his interference. He motions for Rain to sit next to Sirona.

Gaia turns toward Goji. "Am I allowed to join meditation?" He doesn't answer.

"You know what? I've changed my mind." She stomps over to where Rain is sitting and pulls her to her feet. "Come on, sweetie. These uptight people don't deserve you."

Rain's face goes from shy and nervous to panic. Goji steps between Rain and Gaia. Coyote stands and positions himself to Goji's right. My heart feels like it's going to split in half. As much as I miss Gaia, I love Harmony more. I don't know this new girl she brought but I know Gaia. I have a feeling Rain will be safer with us than with her. I move to Goji's other side.

Gaia looks to Rain behind us, then to me and back to Goji. She slowly shakes her head. "I thought we were family. I thought you'd be thrilled for this reunion." She turns to me. "Blue, take good care of your new sister. Tell Harmony that I love her and I'll for sure be back for her."

Gaia turns to leave but stops in front of Willow, who is still holding the candle. The two women stare at each other, the flickering flame reflected in their pupils. After a long moment Gaia shoves her fingers into the wick and snuffs out the flame. "People with secrets should stay hidden." She marches off and

Doobie chases after her. The two of them disappear into the dark.

Everyone is too fidgety to meditate for very long and we break up the circle after a brief chant. Jade gently carries a sleeping Aura toward our massive tree house. Sirona drapes her arm around Rain's shoulder. "You can share Harmony's room. I think she'll enjoy some company. She's been alone ever since her mother . . . ever since Gaia left."

I'm not too sure Harmony will agree. She likes having a room to herself. But then maybe she is lonely. Maybe she just pretends she's happy alone. She's good at hiding things, especially her feelings.

I head up to the second-story room I share with Coyote, where Harmony has been hiding in Coyotes' hammock. She lifts her head when she hears me walk in. "Is Ruth still here?"

"I don't know. I think she's with Doobie."

Harmony spies Goji's present under my arm. "What did he give you?"

"A book."

As I slowly unwrap my gift, she climbs out of the hammock and leans over my shoulder. The moon throws just enough light through the window opening to reveal the familiar cover. I run my fingers over the words *The Prophet*.

Harmony takes the book from me and flips through the pages. "Looks boring." She hands it back.

"Goji's read to me from this one. It might be better than you think."

She rolls her eyes. "I doubt it."

The roar of the VW bug starting up breaks through the quiet of Saffron Freedom Community. The engine chirp-chirps as Gaia shifts through gears and drives toward the road. Harmony moves to the window and watches the headlights flash against the trees then flicker and disappear through the woods. Without turning she says, "Do you think Doobie left with her?"

"I don't know. I hope not."

In the room below mine we hear the new girl sobbing. Harmony flashes a panicked look. "Wait. They gave her *my* room?"

"To share. The other rooms are full."

She sighs. "It's fine. She probably won't stay very long anyway." Harmony cranes her head out the window, trying to look into her bedroom below. "That girl sure cries a lot."

"Maybe you should go talk to her. She seems really scared."

Harmony reaches into her shorts pocket and hands me a glassy black arrowhead. I turn the pointy obsidian over in my hand, rubbing the surface with my thumb. "Wow. It's nearly perfect."

"Happy birthday, Blue." She starts to leave but stops in the doorway. "Thanks for talking to Goji."

I smile. "Thanks for coming back."

She slips out of my room and down to hers. I hear Harmony chattering away to the new girl, trying to cheer her up. I hang my wilting birthday crown on the hook next to my bed. A petal falls and lands square on the nose of the floating face of *The Prophet*. I tuck the book under my pillow and lie back on my lumpy mattress. Below me, the girl's sobs turn into soft whimpers. I suddenly understand why Goji named the new girl Rain.

3

I'm relieved to see Doobie when I pass the kitchen the next morning. I worried that he'd left with Gaia last night. I can tell the Olders are doing their best to lighten things up. Sirona stands in front of the woodstove, humming "Puff the Magic Dragon." When her pancakes are perfectly browned, she flips them one by one to Doobie, who's forced to catch them on the chipped platter he's holding. He carries the towering stack to the community table, where Wave claps him on the back, nearly sending the pancakes into the dirt.

Doobie carefully sets down the plate. When he turns, Wave gives him a big bear hug. "Morning, brother."

Doobie looks like he's about to cry. I don't think he ever stopped believing that Gaia would come back. Not just for Harmony. For him. And now she's gone again.

He wipes his eyes and smiles at Harmony as she walks up to the table with Rain. Our newest sister looks just a tiny bit messier than she did when she arrived, but in the soft light she's even more gorgeous than I remembered. I pull out a chair for

Rain and wait for her to sit before finding a seat across the table.

Harmony sneaks up behind me and whispers in my ear, "Take a picture, it'll last longer."

"I wasn't staring," I whisper back.

She slides onto the bench next to me and kicks me under the table. "Were too."

Goji is the last to arrive. Unlike most days, he's taken special care to look his best this morning. His long dark hair is clean and combed, falling over his shoulders and halfway down his back. He's wearing Jesus sandals below a white embroidered kurta that he got when he lived in India. It looks kind of like a dress. I've only seen him wear it a couple of other times. With all this dirt and only washtubs for laundry, our clothes don't usually get very clean. White rarely stays white for long.

Goji pulls out his chair at the head of the table. The sister-mothers fall into silence, waiting for his greeting. He looks around the table from face to face, spending the longest on Rain's. She blushes and looks away.

"Good morning, family," he finally says.

"Good morning, brother," we say back.

As we pig out on pancakes swimming in maple syrup, Jade invites Rain to tell us a little about herself. "What brought you to Saffron Freedom Community? Besides Gaia, I mean."

Rain dabs at the corner of her mouth with a napkin made from one of our old torn-up sheets. "I ran away from home with hardly any money and no idea where I was going. Your friend Gaia found me sitting on a curb outside the Safeway in Salinas. She just sat down next to me in the middle of town and listened to my story. I mean really listened, like she cared. Then she got really excited and told me about Saffron Freedom Community and insisted that I needed to come here."

At the mention of Gaia, everyone looks at Harmony. She

stabs at a pancake and holds it in front of her, inspecting it carefully and ignoring the attention.

Moon taps Rain on the elbow. "Then what happened?"

Rain smiles sweetly at him. "Gaia said she was on her way to a concert. She couldn't take me here so she drew a map and told me that this place was exactly where I needed to be. I didn't know what else to do so I walked out to the road and stuck out my thumb. Gaia pulled up in her rusty Volkswagen. Said she changed her mind and really wanted to see everyone here." Rain looks at Harmony. "She told me about you, how much she missed you but that the longer she was away the harder it was to come back."

Harmony just shrugs. "Why'd you run away?" she asks, trying to change the subject to anything besides her mom.

Rain glances at Goji, who shakes his head "no" so slightly you wouldn't notice if you weren't watching closely. I'm always watching Goji. I want to be more like him. He's wise and kind and always knows just the right thing to say.

"I was unhappy for a lot of reasons," Rain says to Harmony.

It's a loaded question given my history in this family but I can't help asking, "Won't you miss your family?"

Willow visibly flinches. Rain gets a drifty look in her eyes, like she's peering through a window the rest of us can't see. Her words come out in a near whisper.

"I already do." She shakes her head and bites the corner of her lip as if to rid the thought. "But I can't go back." She studies the food on her plate. "I'm never going back."

"I don't miss Ruth," Harmony blurts.

Goji smiles at Harmony's comment but he looks in my direction as he speaks. "Let's not focus on the past when we have so much to appreciate in the present."

We all go back to eating, but the conversation gets me thinking about all the unanswered questions I have. SFC is my family and I love them. They're everything I've ever known. But once in a while curiosity bubbles up to the surface. What do my real parents look like? Do they have a house? Where do they live? Would they like me? Would they love me as much as this family does?

"Yes, Goji," I say. I swallow the next bite of pancake along with the nagging thoughts about my first family.

Wave and I meet in a clearing for my guitar session. My fingers are barely long enough to stretch to the last two strings on the third fret of Wave's guitar. It makes a buzzing sound when I strum because I can't hold them all the way down.

"Ow." I shake out my hand and hand the guitar to Wave. "I'm no good at this."

He shoves it back at me. "It takes practice. Lots of practice. And these." He turns his left hand over so I can see the calluses on his fingertips. "Cop a feel, man."

I run my finger over the pads expecting them to feel like blisters, but they're more like crusty bumps. He flips his bangs aside and grins. "Pretty soon you won't even feel the strings. You've just got to keep at it."

I try a B chord and it buzzes again.

"Practice, little brother. It's the only difference between what I do and what you do."

"And talent," I add.

"You're a natural, Clover Blue. You need to stop comparing yourself to me. Remember, I started right where you did."

"On a log in the woods?"

"A stool in the basement. Same thing, different setting." He grips my knee and gives it a little shake. "Trust me, this seat is much better."

He takes off his wire-rimmed glasses and wipes them on a faded bandana, then slides them back on his nose. I switch to the easier A and E minor chords, using the blue plastic pick he gave me. He nods his head with each stroke across the strings, wincing just the tiniest bit when I make a mistake.

My fingers start to burn and I stop. "Can I ask you something, Wave?"

"Yeah, man. You can ask me anything, you know that."

"How did you end up here?"

He scratches his chin. Most of the men have beards but Wave's is mostly just soft fuzz.

"You mean here on this log with you or here at Saffron Freedom Community?"

"The second thing."

"How does anyone end up here? It's our destiny."

"Yeah, but was there a specific reason? Where did you live before this place?"

"I grew up in Fresno. My parents weren't bad people, but they were square and wanted me to get a job. I left home right out of high school to move closer to the ocean, where I learned to surf. You already know what that shark did to my leg." He traces the scar on his thigh and smiles. "After the attack I gave up surfing and spent most days outside a coffee shop in Bodega Bay, singing for tips."

"I don't blame you for being afraid of the ocean."

Wave slowly shakes his head. "Respect, not fear. It was a good lesson and I don't need to learn it twice." He strokes the neck of his beat-up guitar. "I taught myself how to play when I was your age. I had big dreams of becoming a famous singer either by myself or with a band. In the sixties, everybody and his brother was a folk singer so it wasn't as easy as I thought it would be."

"You're really good, Wave. You should make a record."

He laughs. "I liked living in Bodega Bay. Lots of surfers and fishermen and beautiful girls in bikinis. It felt right." He stops when a crow caws overhead. We both watch as the bird lifts from a tall branch above us, squawking.

"So then how did you end up at SFC?"

Wave grins. "One day this guy wearing some sort of robe-like getup sits across from me for hours, listens to every song, over and over until the shop closes. When I start to pack up he hands me a ten-dollar bill. Ten bucks! I'm shocked because this guy doesn't look like he had ten cents let alone ten bills. I ask him what his story is and he says . . ." Wave stands so he's facing me. "He bows like this and he says we're brothers. I figure he's high or crazy. But those eyes, man. I couldn't look away, ya know?"

I do know what it's like not being able to look away from him. "It was Goji."

Wave nods. "He had this peace about him and I wanted it. I wanted it so bad. I was hungry and tired and lonely. He asked me if I wanted to join his community. I knew I needed a change in my life, and I definitely needed a place to sleep. I thought, what the heck, and followed him here. Willow was already living at SFC and we immediately knew we were soul mates. She taught me yoga to strengthen my leg where that shark took a chunk. Shortly after I got here, a whole bunch of people left, leaving only Doobie, Jade, Willow, Goji, and myself."

"And then you added me."

He smiles. "Yeah. And then you."

I kick at the log with my heel trying to sneak up on the next question, the one that's been nagging at me more and more. The one I'm not supposed to ask.

"Can you tell me more about that day?"

He shakes his head. "You know we're not supposed to talk about it."

"Goji promised he'd tell me the truth on my twelfth birthday. Then that new girl showed up and he got too busy or something."

Wave sighs. "It was the summer of nineteen sixty-seven. Goji was saying that we were a vortex of love. He told us that others would be swept up into the Love of our community. He promised our small family would expand, including children. It wasn't long after that you appeared."

"Appeared?"

He looks off toward the woods, his eyes watering. "You came out of nowhere, handed Willow a little white flower. We believed it was a sign. When I saw how you were with Goji, with all of us, I was convinced that it was true what he said about how you were seeking us and you found us. We all believed it."

"I came out of the woods? Was I lost?"

"It's all a little foggy now. . . ." He takes off his glasses and rubs his eyes.

"Wave?"

"Yeah?"

"Do you ever think about leaving?"

Wave puts his glasses back on and squats in front of me, looks me square in the face. "Never. This is my home." He flicks his bangs. "Are you unhappy, Blue? Do you want to leave?"

"No. Well, I mean, maybe someday. I'm a little curious about my other family. I mean, if I have one out there. . . ."

Wave takes the guitar from me and leans it up against the log. He lays his big head on top of my knee. "I love you, little brother. You are my family."

"I love you, too." And it's true. I love him so much and suddenly I feel guilty about making him feel bad.

Wave lifts his head. "You ready to split?"

"You go ahead. I'll be along in a bit."

He stands and throws the guitar over his shoulder. "Okay, man. You're doing great. You really are. You'll be playing like a pro in no time."

When he's out of sight I slide off the log and lie on my back on the ground to stare at the sky. I wonder if my birth mother or father is looking up at the same sky right now. I have no memory of anything before here. Sometimes when we're in town at the library or the store, I hear a voice and it sounds familiar. Once in a while a smell reaches into my brain and tries to call up the past, but it's always dark and flat. Maybe I don't want to remember. Maybe it was bad. Or maybe it was so good it would hurt too much to remember.

An ache rises in my chest. I close my eyes and breathe deeply, let it move through me, just like Goji has taught us. *Be with your feelings*, he says. *But don't let the bruises become permanent scars.*

A branch cracks in the huge live oak tree above me. When I open my eyes I can barely make out Goji staring down at me. I worry about how much of the conversation he overheard. Will he be disappointed in me for asking Wave about my past?

Before I have a chance to say anything, footsteps crunch next to my head.

"What are you doing?"

I sit up and turn toward the voice. It's the new girl. "Hey, Rain."

"Are you okay?"

"Yeah. I was just thinking about stuff."

"You looked sad."

"Nah, I'm fine."

She squats down next to me. Her formerly white tennis shoes have turned dirt color in just one day. She leans in closer, her face hovering over mine. That sweet smell again. *Lavender? Wool?*

"You want to help me find kindling? Sirona says she needs it for the cook stove, but I should have someone go with me into the woods until I know my way around better."

I love that Rain has picked me to go with her, but I do my

best to hide how good it makes me feel. "Sure," I say, as casually as I can muster.

The two of us walk farther into the trees. Rain catches me scanning the branches and stops. "What are you looking at?"

Goji puts a finger to his lips.

"Just a bird," I say.

4

Harmony scratches her armpits and plants herself wide-legged, grinning, into what she announces is "monkey pose." Willow throws her a stern look. I try to make eye contact with Harmony, hoping she'll settle down. Instead, she beats her bare chest and grunts. I don't know why she can't seem to keep herself from pushing the Olders to the edge of tolerance of her antics.

Willow frowns at Harmony. "Come on, sister. Rain is here to learn, not to play." She points to Moon. "Even our six-year-old knows that."

Moon stays quiet, preferring to avoid drama, as usual. He's a dedicated little yogi. It's one of his favorite things.

Harmony smiles innocently. "Goji says what we learn with joy we remember with joy."

Goji studied hatha yoga when he lived in India, but Willow learned from some woman down in Redondo. Goji stresses less trying and just simply doing. With him we can get away with giggling. He says the asana are yoga of the body and that laughter is yoga of the soul. Willow has a different opinion about that.

"Goji wants Rain to get used to our community activities. This is my teaching session, not his. Respect, sister."

Harmony drops her arms and sighs. "Sorry."

Willow moves closer to Harmony's reed mat and asks her to step off. When she bends forward her braid falls over her shoulder and sweeps the dirt. She straightens Harmony's mat so it's exactly in line with mine and Moon and Rain's, then walks back to her mat, standing tall in mountain pose to start off the lesson. Willow brings her hands together and touches her fingertips to her chin. She bows slightly toward Rain to my left, then me, then Harmony, and finally, Moon. The three of us bow back. Rain gives us a cautious sideways glance and folds her hands. She interlaces her fingers and bows deeply from her waist.

I step sideways and untwine her fingers so they point upward, flat against each other. "Like this," I say, demonstrating a shallow bow that is more like a nod than a bend.

Rain's cheeks flush.

"Don't worry," I tell her. "Goji's always saying we're all beginners."

Willow smiles at me. "Thank you, Clover Blue."

Harmony mouths, "Thank you, Clover Blue," using her bratty teacher's pet face. I ignore her. I'm on Willow's side for this one. Rain seems really sweet, and I can tell this is a little nerve-wracking for her.

Willow extends her hands toward Rain so she can see them better. "The way we hold our hands is called a *mudra*. This is the 'greeting mudra' meant to show recognition of each other."

Rain nods shyly.

"Okay now, deep breath and raise your hands over your head, tighten your butt, and open your chest." As she speaks, Willow moves into tree pose, arching her back so far she looks like the letter *C*. We all follow suit, including Rain, who does surprisingly well for her first time. "Now exhale and bend forward as far as you're able." Willow blows out dramatically, folding forward until her head is flat against her shins and grabs her ankles. Even after nine years of yoga, I can only bend far enough to grab my calves. Rain has her hands flat on the ground next to her feet. I nudge Harmony, whose eyes go wide.

Willow's brows furrow just the slightest bit. Keeping an eye on Rain this time, she says, "Inhale deeply and move into a lunge, pressing the heel of your foot into the ground and lengthening your spine. Exhale and bring your other foot back. Explore the place between comfort and discomfort, and exist there."

Rain's movements are fluid and her posture is nearly perfect. Willow guides us into cobra, then downward dog and another lunge before coming back to forward fold and finishing in mountain pose. Rain mirrors each pose gracefully, arching, stretching, and breathing as though she's done this a thousand times. Her hands follow each move, curling and unfolding like underwater wings.

Willow bows. "Namaste," she says, then drops her arms and shakes them out.

"Namaste," we say back.

Rain turns toward me and whispers, "What does Namaste mean?"

"It means 'I recognize you as my other,' or something like that. It's a term of mutual respect."

"I get it. Kind of like 'Amen' in church."

Willow moves between Rain and me, still in teacher mode. "Not exactly, Rain. Amen means you agree. Namaste means you acknowledge the Divine in each other."

Rain nods. "Oh. I see."

Willow helps Rain roll up her borrowed mat. "You did really well except for the hands. Try to follow the poses with intention and boldness rather than grace."

"Sorry. Force of habit."

"You've done yoga before?"

"No, but I took ballet and gymnastics ever since third grade."

Harmony playfully slaps Willow on the back. "She could teach us a thing or two!"

Willow's smile takes effort but she eventually finds it. She rolls up her own mat and rests it on her nearly straight hip. "Maybe we'll try firefly pose next time."

Moon jerks his head up from where he was studying an ant hill in the dirt. "Whoa, that's a hard one!"

Rain smiles at Willow. "Thank you for the lesson. I'd love to learn anything you can show me."

After yoga Harmony and I head straight to the community clothing box. We've been planning a long hike for this afternoon. We've grown up running around naked for the most part but we always put on clothes when we leave the community boundary. I'm wearing cutoffs that used to be jeans, but got too short after I shot up two inches over the summer.

Harmony snickers as she picks through the box, looking for something to wear. "Willow is so jealous of Rain."

I scratch a string of bug bites on the top of my foot. "Why would she be jealous?"

"Why do you think? Because Goji pays so much attention to her."

"Because she's new!"

"And young. And gorgeous."

Harmony slips a Jimi Hendrix T-shirt over her head. It fits like a dress on her. She kicks the clothing box back inside the old teepee. "Let's explore the caves we saw last week on the other side of the creek."

I sling my pack over one shoulder, glad she's changed the subject away from Rain. "Maybe we'll find some of those cave paintings Doobie told us about."

She grins. "Or a live bear instead of a dead one."

I laugh and agree, pretending to shrug off her comment, but now I'm having second thoughts about the caves. Sometimes we catch frogs in the creeks and let them go. Sometimes we look for Indian arrowheads. One time we found a dead bear. But live bears could have cubs, and one thing we've learned from the Olders is that this is about the most dangerous situation we could ever come upon. I double-check to make sure I have the safety whistle in my pack. Might not scare off a bear but it could buy us some time if we run into one.

Harmony and I stop to check in with Jade as she hangs laundry on a thin rope strung between two posts near the garden. We pretty much get to do what we want once our chores are done and there aren't any scheduled learning sessions with the Olders. Goji says each day and every single moment is an opportunity for learning and we should always look for the lesson. We're free to explore as long as we tell at least one person where we're going, we're back before sunset, and we contribute a learning aspect of our exploration with the family during sharing time after dinner. This is never a problem because we always learn something and usually have a hard time deciding which thing to share.

Jade waves as we get closer. When she bends to get something out of the laundry basket two-year-old Aura tries to latch onto her mom's dangling boobs for a drink. Jade hands Aura a clothespin to play with and quickly pins a peasant skirt to the line. As soon as she reaches for the next thing out of the basket, Aura does it again. It's pretty funny to watch.

Harmony lifts Aura and props her on her hip. "Blue and I are going to explore the caves on the other side of Salmon Creek."

Jade stabs a clothespin onto a frayed dish towel. A row of copper P.O.W. bracelets slides up her skinny arm to her elbow. She started with just one, engraved with the name of Coyote's brother, Leroy Jackson. Over the years she kept adding more soldiers.

"Okay, but be back in time for dinner." She reaches for Aura, who immediately latches onto the closest nipple.

Harmony and I run past the tree house and scramble up the steep hill behind the SFC boundary. The sooner we're out of sight, the less chance one of the Olders will decide to hold a spontaneous learning session or ask us to help with a chore. I grab Harmony's hand and pull her up the last bit. We wipe the dirt off our hands and start down the path that she and I have created over the past several years. The older we get, the longer the path gets.

We stop halfway to the creek for a pee. I manage to write most of my name in the dirt and she laughs.

"Show-off!" She finishes her pee and stands. "Did you remember the water?"

I open my leather pack and offer her the mason jar. She takes a few small sips and hands it back. I gulp down half the jar. Partly because I'm thirsty and partly because it's less weight to carry. Our pack is already crammed with a notebook, pens, a field guide, a compass, Harmony's sketchpad, a flashlight, two PB&J sandwiches, and the whistle.

It takes us almost an hour to reach the narrow part of Salmon Creek. We leap across stones to get to the other side. Harmony stands on the bank and shields her eyes for a better look at the distant caves. "Do you think there might be bats in there?"

I know she's not asking because she's afraid. She wants to draw them.

"Probably. Hopefully, they'll be sleeping this time of day."

She takes off running in the direction of the dark holes on the side of the rocky hills and I chase after her. I let her beat me because it's too hot to run the full distance and my long hair is already sticking to my back. By the time I catch up to Harmony she's bent over in front of the cave, peeking into the largest opening.

She frowns. "It looked bigger from far away. The dark rocks fooled me."

I drop to my knees next to her. "I think we'll have to go one at a time."

When she doesn't budge I take it to mean she wants me to go first. I pull the flashlight from my pack and crawl through the entrance, leaving my bag outside. I only have to go a few feet before I can stand, but that's all there is, just this little room.

I yell behind me, "Come on in!"

Harmony joins me in the rock-walled space. I shine the flashlight around the circle. "Looks like this is as deep as it goes."

She snatches the flashlight out of my hand and shines it on the ceiling, looking disappointed. "Bummer."

I make a swipe for the flashlight but she holds it out of reach. "Wait!" She aims it at the far corner. "See that? I think we can squeeze through that tall slit in the wall."

I follow the beam of light and measure the small opening against my body size. "Maybe. Maybe if we slide in sideways."

"Try it!"

Harmony's small for her age. If I can fit through, it'll be a cinch for her. I push my left shoulder through the opening. The wall is a little slimy, which helps me slip through. On the other side I find several tunnels heading off in different directions. Light has reached the cave from somewhere above.

I call out to my sister, "You coming?"

She pokes her head in first and slowly rotates it to locate me before squeezing the rest of the way through. It reminds me a little of baby Aura coming out of Jade a couple years ago.

I point out the tunnels, one by one. "Ladies first."

She grins. "Age before beauty."

I'm only a couple months older than Harmony and I rarely

miss a chance to remind her. This is one of those times she gets to use it against me.

The rocks bite into my knees as we slowly crawl forward. Harmony is so close behind me I can feel her breath on my bare feet. And then I fart. Not on purpose, it just comes out.

"Blue!"

The guilt from gassing my best friend passes quickly and I can't help but laugh.

"Rude!" She's trying to sound mad but I hear her giggles. We're used to farts in the community because our diet includes a lot of beans, but they're still funny to us.

Harmony slows her pace and I don't blame her. I crawl around the next bend and run into a dead end. Above us a small beam of light streams into the circular space. There's just enough room for the two of us to sit cross-legged facing each other. Without either saying it aloud, I'm pretty sure we're both thinking the same thing. This is one of the coolest places we've ever found. Much cooler than the forts we used to make under the community table when we were little. And like our favorite hollowed-out tree, this is a place only we know about.

"Far out," she finally says.

We sit quietly for several minutes, soaking in the magic of our discovery. The metallic smell of minerals oozes from the pores of our tiny room. Harmony lifts her arm and strokes the textures of the wall around us, as if she can read its history. She finds a small stone and carves her name into the rock face, then tosses the stone to me. I write mine next to hers. *Harmony Blue*. It sounds like one of those herbal teas Sirona buys from the co-op in Sebastopol.

It's a magical place but there's not much to do in the dark so we make our way back out and into the open, where the sun nearly blinds me and the heat is suffocating.

Harmony finds a flat spot under a willow. "You hungry?"

We eat our sandwhiches and share the apple we picked on

our way here. She chucks the core into the brush and opens her sketchbook. I start turning over rocks and watch as bugs and beetles scatter to find cover while Harmony works on a drawing. On the fifth rock I hit the jackpot.

"I found one! I found a tiger salamander!"

Harmony looks up from her sketch and squints in the bright sun.

"Don't you want to see it?"

She tucks the pencil behind her ear. "Bring it over here."

I capture the salamander and sit next to her. When I open my hand it jumps off and disappears into the grass and rocks. "Bogue!"

Harmony wrinkles her nose. "It was really pretty but it'd probably rather be with its own family than us."

"I know. But I've been searching for one forever."

She reopens her sketchbook. "You'll find another one."

I lean over her shoulder to get a better look at her work. It's a picture of Rain.

"What do you think of her?"

Harmony lifts her pencil from the page. "Who, Rain? I don't know. She seems nice. Almost too nice."

"That's a really good sketch. She looks pretty."

"She *is* pretty. All the brothers stare at her, even Goji. The sisters too." Harmony narrows her eyes at me. "And a certain Younger, who, by the way, can forget about it because she is waaaay out of his league."

I grin. "Are we jealous?"

She frowns at me. "Not jealous. I'm just telling it like it is, man." She goes back to work on the drawing, making sure her long brown hair covers the page so I can't see.

"Hey, Harmony, can I ask you something?"

"Mmm-hmm." She doesn't look up.

"You really don't miss your mom?"

"Nope, not anymore."

I can't tell if she's hiding how she really feels or if she means it. That's always how it is with Harmony.

"Well, I miss her. I get why you were mad at Gaia for leaving but it was nice to see her, even for a little bit."

Harmony closes her pad and stuffs it back in the pack. "What about your parents? You never talk about your first family. Don't you miss them?"

Harmony knows I was adopted by the family but not the part about it not being legal. She's asked for details before but I got flustered and she could tell the subject is pretty much off limits. It's one of the things I like about Harmony. She doesn't try to pick the lock when you close a door. But that doesn't mean she won't knock every once in a while.

"How can I miss what I don't remember?"

Harmony tugs on a blade of dead grass. "Maybe a person can miss what they've never known. I've never been to the circus but I feel like I miss that feeling of being at a circus when I read about it." She turns to look at me. "You wanna know what I really do miss?"

"What?"

"Bacon. I ate it at the shelter once and it tasted so good. When Ruth saw me eating it she slapped it out of my hand. I was only four."

"What did it taste like?"

"She closes her eyes and moans. "Like salty, greasy, chewy, crunchy . . . *everything*."

"I've never had meat and I never want any. The animals . . . I couldn't."

"Like I said, I was four and it tasted good. I'm pretty sure it would gross me out now but I really miss not getting to enjoy the rest of that slice. I miss other stuff, too, like candy and caramel corn. I know the Olders say sugar is bad, but sometimes I want cookies with real chocolate, not carob and honey."

"I bet our neighbor would make you some."

She grins. "Mrs. Fuller? What a good idea! Let's go see her."

"Maybe."

"I'm sorry about . . . you know. The stuff you don't know."

"Goji promised to tell me more, give me more details when I turned twelve. But then Gaia showed up with Rain—"

Harmony throws her hands up in the air. "See? Ruth screws up everything!"

"He says he didn't technically mean *on* my birthday."

She drops her hands and puffs her cheeks, blowing out a sigh. "That's bullshit, man. A promise is a promise." She drops her charcoal pencils into our pack. "You need to hold him to it."

"Maybe I should bring it up at our next writing session."

"Maybe? You deserve to know your history, Blue. You want me to ask him?"

"No!" I blurt it out too loud and too quickly. She looks at me, obviously stung. "I mean, I'll do it. I want to."

Harmony tilts her head to one side and narrows her eyes. "You're braver than you think you are."

I just nod and try to look convinced. She has no idea that most of my courage comes from watching her.

We pack up the rest of our things and walk back toward the creek. When we reach the bank, Harmony and I look at each other and grin. We both jump in, kicking and splashing, then sit on the sandy bottom as the water rushes by and minnows nibble at our toes. Harmony leans back on her hands, grinning. "The water feels sooooo good."

After a few minutes, I climb back up the bank and wait for her to join me. "We should get going. I told Jade we'd be home to help with dinner."

Harmony crawls out of the creek, pulls off her T-shirt, and wrings it out before putting it back on. As we start back down the path I find a stick to use as a hiking pole.

Harmony laughs. "What do you need that for, old man? You blind?"

"I like the way it's bent. Maybe I'll whittle something cool into the handle."

"Hey, Blue, look." She closes her eyes and throws her hands straight out in front of her, teetering forward. "Let's see how far we can make it home without looking. Whoever falls first is the loser."

I squeeze my eyelids shut. "I'm in!" I keep my distance behind Harmony so I don't accidentally poke her with my stick. "No peeking!"

We both laugh as we stumble along, tripping on roots and clunking into branches. Until I hear her scream.

When I open my eyes I spot the small snake, see it lurch backward from her shin. Without thinking I fling the snake with my stick. It flies through the air and lands in the sage several yards from us before scurrying away.

"Did it bite you?"

She points to her leg where two tiny fang marks start to bleed. "I think I stepped on it."

"We need to get you back home. Listen, Wave told me if I ever get bit the first thing is to stay calm."

Harmony looks at me and nods. Tears run down her tanned cheeks.

"You're gonna be okay. We just need to get to SFC so they can take you to the hospital." I pull the water jar from my bag and empty the last few swallows on her leg. She flinches but doesn't make a sound.

"Can you walk?"

"I think so."

"Okay. We probably shouldn't run. Are you calm?"

Her lower lip trembles.

"Take deep breaths."

She inhales slowly, then lets it out even more slowly, just like we learned in meditation practice. I grab hold of her hand and we start back down the path. Harmony limps a bit so I give her my stick to take some of the weight off her leg.

"You're doing great. Just a little farther."

We're almost to the community boundary when she keels over without a word. I drop beside her. "Harmony!"

No response.

I plunge my hand into the leather bag and pull the whistle over my head. I blow as hard as I can. Harmony rolls her head to one side and mumbles but doesn't open her eyes. Her ankle is starting to swell and turn pink. I scoop her up and struggle to run as fast as I can, blowing the whistle with every breath as we race toward home.

5

The sister-mothers take my side at first, offering to drive to the hospital in Santa Rosa. Sirona would claim to be Harmony's mother, since she's the oldest.

Goji shakes his head. "It's too risky. The bureaucrats will take Harmony away from us if they find out Gaia doesn't live here anymore."

I know he's also afraid that if the cops start asking questions, they'll take me, too. And maybe find Coyote, who is AWOL.

Wave carries Harmony over his shoulder up the treehouse ladder and gently lays her on her bed. I sit on the floor next to Harmony's mattress as Sirona works on the wound. She smears a muddy clay mixture over the fang bites, then lightly wraps the leg with clean rags.

"She'll be fine," Goji assures me when I start crying. "You need to have faith in her strong body."

I look up at Goji, hoping to change his mind about taking her to the hospital. "What if she isn't fine?"

He touches me gently on the shoulder. "Sirona's a healer. Your sister is fierce. She'll be okay."

"Harmony isn't just a sister!" I wipe my runny nose on my arm. "She's my best friend."

"And it is that love that will help heal her."

I want to believe him. I want to believe him so badly. But I don't. We're used to dealing with flu and bug bites and poison oak and even having babies. This is way more serious.

Goji squats next to me and twists his long black beard. "You said it was a little snake, right, Clover Blue?"

I nod.

"Baby rattlers store less venom because they're small. And most of the bites are dry."

"But Harmony is small, too."

He stands and gently tugs on a lock of my hair. "Let's go make some herbal tea for when she wakes up."

I don't budge.

"Come, little brother."

He reaches for my hand but I lean away. "I want to stay here."

Goji takes a deep breath. He lets it out slowly. "Okay. Okay, Clover Blue," he says again, nodding to himself as he walks away.

Rain has moved into Jade and Sirona's room for now to give Harmony more space while she recovers. Goji returns after dinner and crouches on his haunches, watching and waiting for instructions from Sirona. Goji might be the head of our family but watching the two of them it's obvious that Sirona is in charge of this.

Sirona's freckled face flushes as she carefully applies another mud pack. She stops just below the knee where a scab has formed from when Harmony and I climbed a tree a few days ago and she slipped.

Sirona steps to the head of the bed. "We need to make sure the bite wound is lower than her heart."

Harmony is like a rag doll, pale and limp, as we prop her upper body with pillows. I'm scared for us. I'm scared for me.

Sirona and Goji sit all night with me, watching over Harmony. I try to stay awake but eventually fall asleep on the floor next to the bed. When sunlight shines into the room early the next morning Goji is gone. Harmony is still asleep. I touch her arm. It's hot.

"Don't wake her," Sirona whispers. "She needs rest. She'll wake when she's ready."

Jade and Coyote trade places with Sirona so she can get some sleep. Jade lays a cool, wet cloth on Harmony's head. Harmony barely opens her eyes before closing them again.

Coyote nudges me with his bare foot. "You should get something to eat."

"I'm not hungry."

"A man needs to be strong for his friends, Blue. Nourishment gives you strength."

I don't answer and I don't move. People come and go all day. They chant, they pray, they sing, and sometimes they even laugh. Goji insists on only positive energy. I don't know how they can laugh when our sister is so sick. I want to yell at them but I don't because Goji will make me leave the room. So I just sit and wait.

I spend most of the day next to Harmony. She makes little noises in her sleep but still hasn't come fully awake. Sirona returns in the afternoon to carefully exchange the clay compresses for herbal ones that smell worse than skunk.

"How long before she'll wake up?"

Sirona smiles. "It takes as long as it takes," she says, sounding more like Goji than the young, dancing, mud-covered woman I remember from Woodstock.

Back then it was just the six of us: Goji, Willow, Wave, Jade,

Doobie, and me. I don't remember much from the first couple years after I came here, but sometime during that summer my memories kick in, as if my brain suddenly threw the switch that saves stuff. Three things stand out: The astronauts landed on the moon. A bunch of hippies murdered some movie stars in Hollywood. And the Saffron Freedom Community attended Woodstock Music Festival in New York.

One of the sister-mothers had brought home a flyer about the concert with a big white bird on it. I sounded out the words, *Peace, Love & Music,* at the top as I colored in the bird using broken crayons. Goji looked at the paper and shook his head. "Why would we travel that far when we already have all that here?"

Around that same time, the townies started getting paranoid, staring and pointing at us when we were out running errands. With his small frame and dark hair, Goji looked a little like the newspaper photos of Charles Manson, although Goji's eyes are much kinder. But the weirdness from locals was enough to change Goji's mind about taking the trip.

The Olders packed coolers with food and a wooden box with water jugs filled from the artesian wells on our property. They tied everything on the roof of the van. It was Wave's van from his surfing days. The seats in the back had been torn out and replaced with a mattress. The inside walls were covered in posters with peace signs and a giant mushroom that reminded me of the *Alice in Wonderland* book that Willow sometimes read to me.

Our family drove three thousand miles across the country to the concert, along with every flower child who managed to find a ride. It took us days to get there; I just remember driving and driving and driving. We bounced around as we listened to music on the radio and from a mound of 8-track tapes stacked in a box between the front seats. It was hot in the back but the windows were open so the air was fresh, if you don't count the smell of pot and all those sweaty bodies laughing and singing and sleeping in a pile.

We got stuck behind what looked like a million cars. We climbed on top of the van and used the coolers as chairs to wait for the line to move. It never did. Eventually the Olders just grabbed everything they could carry, which is pretty much what everyone in line did. By the time we arrived at Woodstock there was no gate. People flooded in and we were just a tiny drop in the wave of hippies washing over the broken-down fences.

We ended up so far back from the stage that we could hear music and some of the announcements on the big speakers, but we couldn't actually see the bands. What stands out most about Woodstock is it was the first time I saw people outside of SFC who were naked. People running around like little kids slipping and sliding in the mud, dancing, and having the time of their lives, even in the rain. My other distinct memory is that I stepped on a bee. Goji carried me, screaming, to a volunteer medical station and that was where we first met Sirona, although she had a different name back then.

There was a long line at the medical tent. By the time it was our turn, my foot had swelled to the size of a lumpy potato. Inside the tent, a lady with red hair and freckles smiled at me. She was tall and round like the old paintings in Harmony's art books. Her boobs, her belly, and her thighs looked like different-sized mounds of rising bread. It turned out she was camped near us and she spent a lot of time talking with Goji after that.

When the music stopped our family trudged back to the road along with thousands of other tired, dirty people to find the van had been ripped off. The tires were gone, along with the music tapes and the posters. A blue truck happened upon the six of us trudging along the road with our thumbs out like so many others. We'd been walking for hours. The driver skidded to a stop and threw open the passenger door. I was so happy to see it was the lady from the medical tent. During that ride, Goji began calling her Sirona, after a Celtic healing goddess. Sirona lived in Vermont at the time, but she drove us all the way back to California. And she's been with us ever since.

Sirona tickles the bottom of my foot, breaking me out of my daydream. "What are you thinking about, Blue? You look like you're lost in space."

"I was just wondering if you miss your home back east."

She glances out Harmony's bedroom window to where several of the others are gathered around the community table drinking lemonade. "Sometimes I miss the snow and the fall colors. That's why I go back to visit every couple of years."

"What was your name back then?"

She smiles. "Eileen. Eileen McQuiddy."

"Do you ever think about moving back?"

Sirona leans backward, resting on her hands. "My parents died in a car accident when I was five. My grandma Lula raised me, taught me most of what I know about midwifery and healing with herbs. She was my anchor. She died three years ago." Sirona sits up straight and looks at Harmony, then back to me. "And when I'm there, Blue, I miss here. I miss all of you."

The cowbell clangs two short gongs followed by a space, then two more. Sirona peers out the window to see who rang the bell. "It's Lois Fuller. Must be a baby coming."

Once word got around about Sirona being a midwife, people outside SFC started asking her to deliver their babies. The only problem is we don't have a phone so they have to call our neighbor Mrs. Fuller, and she runs over here to get Sirona.

Sirona gathers her basket and kisses my head on her way out. "I'll be back soon to check on our little sister."

I carefully climb onto Harmony's bed to try to eavesdrop on Sirona and Mrs. Fuller's conversation, but Sirona is already running toward her truck. Mrs. Fuller looks up and waves at me.

"Hey, kiddo, why aren't you down here enjoying lemonade with the others?"

The Fullers live on the farm just north of our leased land.

Mrs. Fuller is one of the few outsiders allowed into SFC. Most of the locals just know us as "that hippie commune" off Bodega Highway.

I check to see if anyone else is within earshot before answering her. "Harmony's sick. I'm staying with her until she wakes up."

"Is she okay?"

I glance at Harmony and back to Mrs. Fuller. "I don't know. She's pretty sick."

Mrs. Fuller shocks me by kicking off her shoes and climbing up the ladder of the treehouse. When she comes through the doorway she takes one look at Harmony and gasps.

"She looks so pale! Probably the heat. Is she staying hydrated?"

"She got bit by a baby rattlesnake."

Mrs. Fuller drops to her knees and uncovers Harmony's bandaged leg. "Did they take her in for an anti-venom shot?"

I shake my head. "Goji doesn't believe in Western medicine. Sirona's been using herbs and clay and stuff."

"How long ago was she bitten?"

"Yesterday afternoon."

Mrs. Fuller's mouth falls open. "Too late for anti-venom. But she still needs to go to the hospital."

"Goji won't allow it. We tried." I swallow hard, trying not to cry. "Maybe you have something in your medicine cabinet that will help?"

"I have some antibiotic cream. And aspirin to knock her fever." She feels Harmony's forehead, then gently runs her fingers through Harmony's hair. "Let me go see if I can talk some sense into that man." She whirls around and pads back toward the ladder.

"Mrs. Fuller? What are you doing up here?"

I jerk my head toward Harmony. She tries to smile but it takes too much effort.

"Hey! You're awake! How do you feel?" I think about calling Mrs. Fuller back but I want Harmony all to myself for a few minutes.

"Thirsty." Her voice is barely above a whisper.

I grab a mason jar of water off the crate next to her bed and hold my hand over hers so she won't spill it. Together we tilt the glass to her cracked lips. She takes a sip, then chokes when she tries to gulp it.

"Easy," I say, and set the jar on the floor next to me. She curls her finger, signaling for me to come closer. I put my ear next to her mouth.

"I peed the bed." She lets out a faint laugh.

"I'll get you some clean sheets. I'll be right back, I promise!"

I scramble down the tree, shouting toward the others. "She's awake! Harmony's awake!"

Everyone can't fit in the room at once and Goji is afraid the oak tree will weaken on this side so he lets people in two at a time. Once Mrs. Fuller and the family have gotten a peek at Harmony he shoos them away. Everyone but me and Sirona, who's already back from a false alarm.

Sirona hums to herself as she changes the dressing.

I plug my nose. "How can that stinky stuff possibly be helping?"

Harmony holds the sheet over her nose and mouth. "Worse than hummus farts."

Sirona smiles as she clips the bandage in place with a safety pin. "The warm clay helps to absorb any leftover venom near the site. It only works for the first twenty-four hours or so. After that we need to use herbal remedies to prevent necrosis."

I hate when people use words I don't know. "What's necrosis?"

"Death of the tissues."

Harmony bolts upright. "My leg could die?"

Sirona takes Harmony's foot in her hand. "We won't let that

happen." She kisses each toe one at a time. "*I* won't let that happen, sweet girl."

Sirona gathers her basket of rags and herbs. "I need to get more supplies." She nods toward the mug on the crate. "Drink your echinacea and goldenseal tea."

As soon as Sirona is out of earshot I blurt it out. "I'm sorry, Harmony. I shouldn't have played that game of closed-eyes walking with you. I should have known it was dangerous."

"It was my idea, Blue."

"I know but . . ."

"I'm tired. I don't want to talk."

"Would you like me to read?"

"Yes please." Her breath reeks of garlic. Sirona must have added it to the tea.

"Which one?"

Harmony runs her finger over the stack of books we got from the library before our snake encounter. While she was sleeping I arranged them from top to bottom alphabetically, by title, starting with *Charlie and the Chocolate Factory* and ending with *A Wrinkle in Time*. Harmony stops at *To Kill a Mockingbird* and plucks it from the pile. She pats the bed and I climb in next to her. I start reading but she falls asleep before I get halfway through the second chapter.

I put my finger to my lips when Sirona comes back to check on her. She gently unwraps the loose rag and replaces the herbs. Harmony grimaces in her sleep but she doesn't wake. Goji was right about Harmony getting better, but I think it was mostly luck that she survived that bite. We should have taken her to a hospital.

When it's dark outside I climb out of Harmony's bed and creep down the ladder one rung at a time. I'm a little shaky from skipping meals and not getting enough sleep. Halfway across the moonlit compound I stop and pee in the dirt, spelling out her name instead of mine.

6

September 1976

Goji doesn't call them rules. He calls them guidelines because people don't have to abide by them if they have a good reason. All the guidelines are voted on and even if just one person objects we keep talking until everyone can agree. Once in a while we have to change one of them. Like when we added fish as a type of meat after Coyote came home with a trout one time. Goji told him humans evolved from fish so it would be like cannibalism. Doobie ended up using that fish for fertilizer on a few pot plants. Those plants grew like crazy that year.

Birth control is another example. The guideline states that we should avoid Western medicine. The women insisted that the world is overpopulated and that they need to be in charge of their own bodies, so birth control is allowed. Today we made another exception to that guideline; the sister-mothers bought a snake-bite kit.

The community guidelines are written in a huge volume that we just call The Book. It sometimes gets passed around the table during sharing time after dinner. People can write notes in The Book or draw pictures like Harmony sometimes does, or press a leaf or a flower between the pages to remember events. I found a snakeskin last week and I put it in there to remember the day Harmony got bitten. Harmony drew a smiley face on it, which kind of made me mad. It's not funny to me.

Goji keeps The Book in his shack for safekeeping, but we've all had to memorize them:

1. *New people must be unanimously welcomed by all community members.* If someone new wants to join, they have to live at SFC long enough to know they want to stay and the family feels like they're a good fit.
2. *We live in harmony with the earth.* Our water comes from an artesian spring and anything that needs to be kept cold is stored in a metal cistern in the creek. We cook and heat on our propane stove or wood-fired oven. Our shower is a bag of water warmed by the sun, leading to a hose with holes, propped from a tree branch.
3. *The only drugs permitted are marijuana and mushrooms.* These are considered soul medicines. We also don't permit alcohol in the community but I once saw Coyote drinking a beer in a tree.
4. *Chores are divided equally.* Sometimes men do laundry and cook and sometimes the women chop wood. We Youngers are expected to help with the worm bins, sweeping the kitchen area, hauling compost, gardening, gathering eggs, and doing dishes.
5. *We consume a humane diet.* We grow most of our own food and mostly eat fruits, vegetables, tofu, rice, and beans. Eggs are allowed because the chickens are part of our family.
6. *Nonmembers are not allowed inside the SFC boundaries.* We make an exception for Stardust, the tarot card reader from Sebastopol who buys weed from Doobie. Also our neighbor, Mrs. Fuller, who buys our fresh eggs.

7. *We have everything we need to heal ourselves.* Goji believes in holistic medicine. A lot of herbs grow nearby, like arrowroot, chia, and thimbleberry. We use them in our cooking and Sirona grows special plants for her medicines.

8. *Yoga and meditation help expand our minds and our bodies.* Every day begins with sun salutations and ends with group meditation.

9. *Sex is sacred.* It's only supposed to be allowed in the Sacred Space, a yurt that sits kitty-corner from Goji's shack. This is probably the loosest guideline. Over the years people have started crawling into each other's beds or going for "walks" together.

There are more guidelines, but these are the main ones besides the stuff about lessons for the Youngers taught by the Olders. Today's assignment came from Goji. Now that Harmony has recovered, he wants us both to write about what we learned from our experience. Goji is big on these essays. He calls it critical thinking.

I chose fear as my topic because I've never been so panicked in my life as when Harmony got bit by that snake. Goji likes when we write about emotions so I think he'll love it. Harmony's writing a paper about staying aware of your surroundings. Goji uses the word *awareness* a lot so I think he'll dig hers, too.

What I really want to write about is how stupid some of the rules are. The one about no Western medicine scares me. When I think of what could have happened to Harmony I get mad. The new bite kit doesn't have anti-venom. It's just stuff to help until you can get to a hospital. Goji teaches that rules are made to be broken and that mindlessly following the masses leads to destruction of the mind. He tells us we should question authority but he always has an answer that makes sense and it sometimes makes me feel stupid for asking.

Harmony and I sit under a willow tree, her on one side and me on the other, as she dictates her essay. I like writing but Harmony doesn't have the patience for it. She tells me what she's thinking and I put it into words; then she copies it in her handwriting.

She scooches closer to read over my shoulder. "Did you get all that?"

I tuck my pen into the crease of her lined notebook and close the cover.

Harmony frowns. "Hey, why'd you stop?"

"I don't know."

"Something's bothering you, Blue, I can tell. Did you ask Goji about—"

"Nothing's bothering me."

She slaps me on the leg, her way of telling me she knows I'm lying.

I pick up a smooth stone and finger it. "Have you ever wondered why Goji gets his own house while the rest of us sleep together in the tree house?"

"Not really. It makes sense. He needs a quiet place to study and meditate."

"But Goji's the one who says we should be able to meditate anywhere, even in the middle of a crowded city."

Harmony moves so she's facing me. Her two loose braids fall down to her belly. She crosses one leg over the other so the ankle with the bruised snakebite scar is on top. "I think he deserves his own house since he leased the land."

"Okay, well how about the rule that says we're supposed to honor all the creatures? What about the ants we step on every day and the honey we stole from our bee boxes?"

She finds a stone of her own, bigger than mine but not as pretty. Her voice changes to a more serious tone. "We gave the bees a place to live and they gave us honey, right?"

"You already asked him, didn't you?"

She laughs. "Yeah. It was a good answer."

"He has an answer for everything."

"I think we're supposed to just do the best we can."

I toss my stone and it pings off a rock before landing in the brush. "When the queen bee left so did all the others. I suppose if Goji left everyone else here would leave, too."

She looks at me with the same expression Willow gets when she's worried. "Why are you upset? You love this place. Did you see all the kids on the school bus we passed the other day? That could be us!"

"I don't know. I just have questions, is all. I love it here, I really do. But I wonder about the outside world sometimes."

"Me too. But then I remember being dragged all over the place by Ruth and staying in awful places and one time even being forgotten."

"Your mom forgot you?"

Harmony chews on her bottom lip before answering. "She was partying with friends and left. Didn't come back for two whole days. I don't remember much about it, but it was scary being left with strangers. She was more interested in screwing around and smoking dope than taking care of me."

"That stinks. Gaia used to be so much fun to be around. It was almost like she was one of us kids."

Harmony rolls her eyes. "Exactly." She stands up and hands me the rock she's been holding.

"What do you want me to do with this?"

She points to my hand. "Look closer."

I turn the rock over and notice a small vertebrate encrusted on one side. When I try to hand it back to her she drops her hands.

"You keep it."

Sirona drives a few of us to the little store in Freestone to pick up supplies for Rain's upcoming welcoming ceremony.

Harmony and I also need new notebooks for our essays. We buy most of the food we don't grow ourselves from the co-op in Santa Rosa but sometimes we run out of things like baking soda or aluminum foil that we can get here. It's also where we buy our gas.

They only have one person working at the store so the owners let customers fill their own gas tanks. Sirona unhooks a hose from the pump and sticks it in the side of the truck. "You guys go ahead," she says.

Willow, Wave, Harmony, and I head inside to shop for supplies. I choose a black notebook and Harmony picks one with a red cover. She pauses at the candy counter filled with rows of jawbreakers, suckers, and chocolate bars, giving Willow her best sad puppy face. "Can we get something?"

Willow glances at the candy shelf and shakes her head. "You're not eating that crap."

As soon as she turns back toward the cash register, Wave slips us each a penny for the gumball machine and winks. "Spit it out before we get home."

When we come out of the store, two men are standing between Sirona and the truck. She's trying to hold her skirt down in the wind. The driver's side door of the truck is open but the men are blocking her way.

Wave curses under his breath and motions with his hand for us to keep behind him. "Stay cool," he says.

We carefully walk up and set the bags in the back of the truck. The fatter man has one thumb tucked into his waistband above a big buckle that's pushed under his belly. A too-small cowboy hat sits high on his head. The shorter guy is wearing clean black shoes under neatly creased slacks. He leans back against the pump and grins.

The cowboy drapes an arm around Sirona. "Hey, how about sharing some of that free love you long hairs are always talking about?"

Wave looks from one man to the other. His arms are strong from chopping wood, but like all of us, he's taken a vow against violence in all forms, what we call The Peaceful Way. He holds out his hand to Sirona. "Come on, let's go."

The townie pulls Sirona tighter against him. "I think your bush bunny here likes me."

Willow opens her mouth to speak but stops when a cop car pulls up to the other side of the pump. The sheriff gets out and nods at the men. "Freddie, Dale." He senses something's off and looks over the rest of us like he's deciding which side to take. After what feels like forever he moves to our side of the pump. "Leave 'em alone, boys."

Sirona yanks her arm away from the man, who spits on the ground in front of us. "Fuckin' freaks. Go take a bath!"

The fat one laughs. "Stinky-assed pussy, I bet."

The sheriff steps in front of them. He's almost a foot taller than the bigger one, even with the cowboy hat on. "Watch your mouths. There are women and children present."

The three men stare at each other. Harmony runs behind the pump near the two men. My heart speeds up. Knowing Harmony she'll do something stupid like kick or bite one of them.

Willow curls her finger. "Come on back over here, sister."

Harmony stays put. After a long pause the sheriff steps aside and the two men walk back toward the store. The smaller one stops halfway to pull a ribbon of bubble gum from the bottom of his shoe. Harmony peeks out from behind the gas pump and sticks out her tongue to show me her empty mouth. I can't help but grin. I often think about doing brave things but Harmony is the one to actually do the things.

Wave nods at the sheriff as we get back in the truck. "Thank you, sir."

The sheriff gives Wave a long look up and down but he doesn't say anything.

7

Rain sewed her veil for the welcoming ceremony out of eleven pieces of fabric taken from one item of clothing belonging to each of us. Her white dress came from the thrift store. She still doesn't like to be naked except when she's showering, and even then, she hides behind a sheet. Goji says we're clothing optional, which means we have a choice. I can't imagine wearing sweaty clothes on hot days but at least October is comfortable. I put on my best white jeans but they're not very white anymore.

We've all tied ribbons on our upper arms made out of toilet paper carefully braided together to commemorate the day. Aura got hold of the extra roll—a precious item around here—and Moon has wrapped her completely in white. She runs around like a little mummy with trails of tissue wafting behind her. Harmony follows behind Aura, picking up scraps of attached squares and stashing them behind the outhouse until she can hide them better. Knowing Harmony she'll try to get me to trade something she wants when we're out of toilet paper. Knowing how much I hate using newspaper in the outhouse, I'll pay her price.

Jade and Coyote pound out a rhythm on conga drums as Goji leads a barefoot Rain to the center of the compound. It's hard to believe it's been two whole months since she showed up. She looks beautiful in her dress and the many-colored veil strips that dance around her face in the breeze. Goji bows to her before joining the rest of us, leaving Rain to stand alone under an arch made out of walking-willow branches. The tree is named for the way it throws up new shoots when the old one falls over. Harmony and I once counted a walking-willow that wandered a couple hundred feet with nearly twenty baby trees attached to each other.

Rain has written her own vows, with help from the Olders. She turns to face us and says them from memory.

"Dear Family. I promise to honor you, to love you, to respect you, and to cherish the here and now with you. I abandon my former life to start this new one with you. Thank you for welcoming me."

Goji steps forward and lifts the strip of fabric he donated. He kisses Rain softly on the lips and she blushes. The rest of us follow one at a time, each lifting our section until her whole face is revealed. When it's my turn I kiss her on the cheek. She looks happy and relaxed, so different from the day she first showed up with Gaia. She's still cleaner than the rest of us, but her skin is tanned now and her blond hair streaked with near-white strands from so much time outdoors. When I look into her bright eyes it feels like home. Gaia messes up sometimes but today I'm really thankful to her for bringing us our new sister.

Wave rigged a tape player to speakers that hook up to Sirona's car battery. We dance until after dark around a blazing fire, staying up long past our regular bedtimes. Most everyone except Rain has shed their clothes due to wild dancing and the heat of the flames. While Harmony takes a turn whirling around with Rain I head to the john. I'm sitting on the wood bench inside when I hear sticks snap and someone brush against the shack.

"Almost done!"

No answer. I finish up and shovel a pile of sawdust down the hole. When I open the door I expect to see one of the others waiting but there's nobody there. The bushes rustle and a small light flicks on and off.

I call out, "Hey, who's out there?"

Up ahead the light flashes again, and then two men stumble out from the trees. They start whooping and trying to dance with the women. I recognize them from that day at the Freestone store. One of the men grabs for Rain. She screams and everyone stops dancing. The huskier man points at the white cloth tied around Goji's waist and chuckles.

"Oh, look, it's Jesus Christ himself."

The other one laughs. "Faggot Jesus!"

The fat one makes two peace signs as they scan the bodies of the women. "Woo-hoo, look at all the titties on you bush bunnies!" He turns toward Rain. "How come you're still dressed?" He tugs at her buttons, then teeters on his heels and stumbles, catching his balance with Rain's arm. She jerks and fusses but he doesn't let go. The men laugh, backing Rain toward the woods. One of them grabs at her crotch.

I drop to my knees and crawl until I find a rock just the right size. Goji forbids violence but I think this is one of those possible exceptions to the guidelines.

"Please," Rain begs. "Please stop." She bursts into tears. "I'm a virgin."

Wave takes a step forward. "Let her go!"

"Why? So you can pop her cherry?" The smaller man glances between Wave's legs. "With that little pecker?"

Coyote cuts off the music and walks toward Rain. Goji holds his hand up to Coyote, keeping eye contact with the drunken men. "We're peaceful."

Coyote ignores Goji and steps directly in front of the two men.

The cowboy spits on the ground. "You got something to say, Sambo?"

I curl my palm around the rock and stand, waiting for the right angle. I'm just about to let it fly when I hear a metal click and see light from the flames flicker on Coyote's blade as it springs from the handle. He slowly waves the knife in front of them.

"He told you to let her go."

The big one pulls Rain in front of him like a shield. In a flash, Coyote streaks forward and wheels around the townie, pressing the knife to the man's ribs from behind. He jerks Rain away with his free hand. She runs to Sirona, who pulls her close, glaring at the men.

"Geez, we were just havin' some fun," the smaller one says. "We weren't really going to hurt her."

Coyote lets go of the man but he doesn't put the knife away. "Take off your clothes."

The two men look at Coyote then at each other. The smaller one says, "Look, we'll just leave."

Coyote jabs his blade at them again. "You can go after you give me your clothes."

They slowly remove their shirts and pants, stealing worried glances at Coyote and each other, before dropping them on the ground.

Coyote lowers the knife to waist height. "Everything off."

They step out of their underwear.

"The hat too."

The fat one tosses his hat on the ground. His head is mostly bald, with just a ring of thin hair from his ears to his neck.

Coyote calmly waves his knife toward the gate. "Now get out of here."

The men run up the path toward the road, their white butts like uncooked biscuits in the moonlight.

Coyote snaps his knife closed. Goji leans over the pile of

clothes and picks up the hat. He dusts it off and holds it toward Coyote. "It's a good hat."

Coyote pulls the hat over his growing dreadlocks. It looks much better on him than on the cowboy.

The family slowly circles around Rain, wrapping her in a protective embrace. I run toward them. It's not until I join in the family hug that I realize I'm still holding the rock.

8

During our drive to Sebastopol, Doobie asks Goji about putting a lock on the gate at the end of our private road. Everyone's still feeling a little skittish about what happened at Rain's welcoming ceremony last month, especially the women. Goji assured us it was just a couple of unenlightened beings with more alcohol in their system than common sense, but I wonder what would have happened if Coyote hadn't threatened those men? What if they'd managed to drag one of the women into the woods? I'm all for peace and nonviolence but we need to protect the people we love.

I'm sitting in the back of the station wagon between Doobie and Goji. Goji leans forward so he can see Doobie. "That is the opposite message we're trying to send, brother. Saffron Freedom Community wouldn't be free if it was imprisoned by a lock, would it?" He relaxes back in his seat and gazes out the window. "I'll chat with the Czech about putting a sign on the gate to signal that it's private property."

The reason they call our neighbor the Czech is because he's from Czechoslovakia and nobody knows how to pronounce his name, Drahoslav. He owns the land around our leased twenty acres and runs a dairy farm. A single electric fence separates our property from his.

Doobie pulls the flaps of his wool hat down over his ears. The car heater broke last winter and we still haven't fixed it.

I tap Goji on the arm. "Maybe we could take a vote?"

Willow watches for Goji's reaction in the rearview mirror. I get the feeling she'd vote for the lock. He ignores Willow's stare and points to an open parking spot in front of the co-op. "Look there, how's that for serendipity?"

Willow can't parallel park and Goji knows it. The last time she tried it took four attempts back and forth before she finally gave up and parked a few blocks away at a church. She stops and gets out of the car, and Jade slides behind the steering wheel. It takes Jade only one try to slip into the spot. She joins Willow on the sidewalk and they head into the co-op, armed with canvas bags and a wicker basket.

In front of the next store over, the sparkly hippie who calls herself Stardust sits behind a table with a dark blue velvet cape draped over her shoulders. Doobie opens his door and lets me out. "You go help your sisters. I'm going to talk with my friend over there," he says, pointing toward Stardust.

I wait for Goji. He doesn't usually join us on these trips so I'm not sure why he came along. "I've got some private errands to run," he says. "I'll meet up with everyone back here in about half an hour."

Inside the co-op I find Jade scooping oats out of a huge bin into one of our canvas bags.

"Blue, go get a five-pound sack of brown rice, would you?"

I move to the next aisle. From over the shelves she adds, "And some sticks of raw cinnamon."

By the time we check out, every bag is full of food and the basket is overflowing with various supplies thanks to income from sales at our roadside stand and the hours the Olders volunteer here at the co-op. We load everything into the back compartment of the station wagon and slam the gate. Willow nudges Jade and smiles, pointing toward the table where Doobie is still chatting with the tarot card reader. Willow presses a hand into the back of my jacket. "Go retrieve our lovebird, will you?"

I wander over and stand in front of the sign that reads, FOR-TUNES TOLD, PASTS REVEALED. I pretend to look at the trinkets and little statues hoping Doobie will get the hint. A tray with a dozen different gemstones catches my eye. I run my thumb over a glittery purple one that looks like a walnut on the outside. Stardust stops talking to Doobie and picks up the stone. "That's an amethyst. Isn't it pretty?"

I nod.

She holds out her hand. "I've seen you at Saffron Freedom Community but I don't believe we've been properly introduced. I'm Stardust. And you are?"

Her bracelets jangle when she shakes my hand. I can't help but stare at the sparkly red jewel glued to the middle of her forehead.

When I don't respond right away Doobie answers for me. "This is my little brother, Clover Blue."

She leans forward, resting her elbows on the table as she studies my face. "Will you look at those eyes? You, young man, remind me of the Page of Cups."

I imagine a page filled with pictures of drinking cups. It doesn't make sense.

She holds up a card from the colorful deck in front of her. The picture shows a man wearing a Peter Pan outfit with a beret on his head and a goblet with a fish in it. He's standing in front of the ocean. "See how fair and lovely he is? And blue eyes like you."

Doobie takes the card from her and studies it before handing it off to me. "What's it mean?"

"The Page of Cups is a sensitive dreamer. The fish is his inner voice, telling him to listen to the messages he receives."

I hand the card back to her.

She winks at me. "Would you like your horoscope, Clover Blue?"

Doobie grins. "Go ahead, brother. It'll be fun."

Stardust fiddles with a chart on the table. "What's your birth date?"

I shrug.

"Don't be shy."

Goji says never to mention the day I was adopted so I give her one day after my re-birth date. "August thirteenth."

Stardust jerks her head up. Her painted eyebrows knit closer together. The red jewel on her forehead looks like it might fall off.

"Did you say August thirteenth?"

I glance at Doobie, whose smile disappears.

Stardust studies her chart, then looks back at me. It's the coldest November day we've had so far but I'm sweating under my light jacket. I'm relieved when she breaks out laughing.

"Boy oh boy, I never would have guessed Leo. You seem more like a water or earth sign." She thumbs through a book and flips to a page, holding her red-painted fingernail on the words. "Look here. Annie Oakley. Alfred Hitchcock. Fidel Castro. Dorothy Layton. Don Fucking Ho." She closes the book. "Those people were all born on August thirteenth. You must have a strong Cancer moon or Virgo rising."

"What's that mean?" I ask, surprised by my own voice. I've heard the sister-mothers talk about astrology before. All I know is it has to do with stars and planets affecting your personality and stuff.

"Your sun sign is basically your ego. Your moon sign is your emotional self. Your ascending sign is how you present yourself to the world."

Doobie stares at Stardust, taking in every word. I can't tell if he's in love with her or if he's high. Probably both. He picks up the book and fans through the pages without reading. "That's far out, man."

Stardust sees me staring at the gemstone collection again. She reaches into a bag and pulls out a round rock. "Would you like one?"

It's an ugly rock but I don't want to insult her. "That's okay. I don't have any money."

A mustached man wearing high-waisted bell bottom slacks and a shiny half-unbuttoned shirt walks out of the head shop and stands behind Stardust just as Doobie passes her a joint. She stuffs it into the crack between her boobs and grins. "Gotta love the barter system!"

The man behind her reaches into the top of her dress and takes the joint, then tucks it into his own pocket. Stardust lets out a nervous giggle. The man looks Doobie up and down before heading back inside the store.

Stardust hands me the boring rock. "I know it doesn't look like much, but take it home and break it open with a hammer. If you're lucky, you'll find pretty crystals inside."

I fold my fingers over the rock. It feels heavier than I thought it would. "Thank you."

She winks and nods toward Doobie. "Thank your friend here. He's the one who bought it for you."

Willow bounds up to us, tying a wool scarf around her long neck. "Come on, guys! It's time to go. Goji's back and Jade's leaking milk all over the place."

Doobie holds up a finger. "Hang on one more minute. Stardust is about to give Blue his horoscope."

Willow shakes her head. "Aura is overdue for a feeding. We don't have time." She grabs my arm and pulls me toward the car.

Stardust calls behind Willow as we scurry away. "Now *that's* a Leo!"

Goji leans against the car holding a large manila envelope. When he sees us coming he slips several papers inside and climbs into the backseat. Jade sits up front, stuffing a towel inside her sweater. When we're all in the car Willow drops the shifter into first gear and heads toward Bodega Highway. I scooch forward and tap her on the shoulder.

"Hey, Willow, when's your birthday?"

She doesn't answer. Doobie nudges me with his elbow. "Same as yours, buddy, August twelfth. She brought you home on her birthday."

Willow and Jade gasp. Goji jerks his head toward Doobie, who slaps his hand over his mouth. "Sorry, man. It slipped."

As if Goji can sense my next question, he pats my knee. "We'll talk soon," he says.

Willow glances at me in the rearview mirror. When our eyes meet, she quickly looks away.

9

Goji and I usually meet for my learning session in the meadow behind the garden, away from any commotion of our homestead. Last month we studied the poems of Thomas Merton, a Catholic monk who wrote about peace. Now I'm learning about a Persian guy named Shams Tabriz who was a teacher of the famous poet Rumi. Goji loves the Sufi poets but Rumi is one of his favorites.

Goji is already waiting for me when I reach our meeting place after breakfast. He smiles when he sees me. "You have the Rumi book with you?"

I hold out the book and sit facing him but I can't get comfortable. I pull a sharp rock from under my rear and toss it aside. Goji rifles through the pages, glancing at my notes, nodding. "Very good, Clover Blue." He hands the book back to me. "Read a passage that spoke to you."

Sometimes Goji reads but usually he has me choose. I've picked something that might lead to what I really want to talk about today.

"I think this is my favorite: *'Every midwife knows that only pain opens the way for birth. In the same way that scorching fire hardens clay, injury may lead to truth.'* " He's listening with his eyes closed. I pause to make sure he hears this last part. " *'For every seeker is forever changed. Thru quest, hardship leads to understanding. Beloved, breathe thru the pain. Your heart aches to bear fruit.'* "

Goji opens his eyes. "And what is Tabriz trying to teach us?"

"He's comparing the pain that women go through having a baby to how, if we're patient during the hard parts, it will lead us to what we really want."

"Can you think of an example of how an injury could lead to truth?"

"Well, when Harmony got bit by that snake, it made me realize how afraid I was of losing her. Maybe that was the reason it happened. So I could appreciate her more." It's a good answer, but not what I meant to say. I quickly add, "Or maybe it's like the agony of waiting for you to tell me more about my first parents like you promised. Like it's supposed to hurt a lot to make me ready for the truth?"

I brace myself for his reaction but Goji doesn't even flinch. "Tabriz is telling us here that suffering leads to understanding. Kind of like that uncomfortable rock you removed from beneath you." He tilts his head toward one shoulder. "Agony? Are you suffering, Clover Blue?"

Tears well up in my eyes. "Kind of."

"And who is making you suffer?"

I sigh. "I am. It's my choice."

"And can I end your suffering?"

I drop my chin to my chest. "No."

Goji takes the book from my lap and leans in so our bowed heads are touching. "Breathe through your pain, Clover Blue. Be the clay and let the fire make you stronger."

Willow, Wave, Sirona, and Doobie pass Harmony and me on their way toward the Sacred Space, laughing and reeking of pot.

Harmony and I are headed in the opposite direction, toward the manure bin. This afternoon's job is to wheelbarrow poop to the garden area. We'll spread it around the beets and chard, then hoe the rest into the ground for next year's crop of broccoli, beans, potatoes, peas, and tomatoes.

Harmony watches the olders disappear into the Sacred Space as a dark row of clouds edge their way east toward us from Bodega Bay.

"What do you think it feels like?"

"What?"

"Screwing. Fucking. What they do in the Sacred Space."

I don't like to talk about sex with Harmony. One, because she's like a sister and, two, because talking about it is one of the things that gives me a boner. I never used to think about it all that much, like the actual doing it. But lately I pop up at the weirdest times and it's embarrassing. I'm usually able to hide it by turning away and pretending to be interested in a bug or a stone.

I shrug. "I dunno."

Harmony giggles. "I once sneaked a peek when Ruth was still living here. It's bogue. All those bodies slithering around, moaning and pumping."

I'm a little bummed that she's seen inside the Sacred Space and I haven't. Plus that she never told me about it until now.

I pull my work gloves out of my pocket. "Can we talk about something else?"

Harmony sets down her end of the wheelbarrow and hands me one of the shovels that hang on the side of the chicken coop. "Like what? You'd rather talk about shit?" She scoops a pile of composted manure and drops it evenly along the base of several bushy beet plants.

I catch sight of our newest sister coming out of the brambles behind the chicken coop. "Looks like Rain is coming."

"Oh, so now we're going to talk about the weather?" Harmony rolls her eyes. "You are such a prude."

I give Harmony a shove. "Hah, not that rain, our Rain."

I point to where Rain stands holding a basket of fresh eggs. Her hair is mussed and her hands are covered with tiny scratches, some of them still bleeding a little. I'm glad she's not headed to the Sacred Space with the others. The sisters have been very protective of Rain. Ever since she showed up the brothers have been tripping over themselves being extra nice to her. It's kind of embarrassing to watch.

Rain carries the basket toward us. "Those hens sure are good at hiding these things. I just found an egg in the middle of a bunch of blackberry bushes!"

"I once found one under our dining table," I say. "Went right from the floor to the frying pan!"

Rain giggles.

"I found one in my bed. I sat on it every day and tried to hatch it."

We both turn toward Harmony, who's resting her chin on the handle of her shovel, grinning. "Just kidding! But you believed me for a minute, didn't you?"

"Naw." I nudge her. "I knew you made it up."

Rain smiles. "That was a good one, Harmony."

Harmony sticks her tongue out at me before plunging her shovel back into the load of compost. As much as she claims to dislike her mother she sure is a lot like her. Gaia used to love fooling the family with tall tales of her travels. She once told us that Jerry Garcia invited her backstage and she ended up spending three days smoking dope, getting it on with the band, and dropping acid. She said they even let her on stage to play the tambourine for one of their songs.

I miss Gaia. Harmony won't admit it but I think she misses her, too. I know she keeps a picture of the two of them hidden in the back of one of her old books. It slipped out one time when I was looking for something to read to Moon. In the photograph Gaia is laughing, her mouth wide, holding a joint in one hand and a pinwheel in the other. Harmony stands beside her naked mother with her little hands to her cheeks, also laughing, as if they both just heard the funniest joke in the world.

A dry clump of manure hits me in the arm. "You going to just stand there and let me do all the work while you make googly eyes at her?" Harmony juts her chin toward Rain, who's walking down the path with her basket of eggs.

"I wasn't making googly eyes. I was just deep in thought."

Harmony sways her hips playfully and snorts. "I have a pretty good idea about those deep thoughts."

I plow my shovel into the pile. "No you don't."

In truth this is one of those times I wish Harmony could read my thoughts. That she could see what I see and feel safe talking about missing her mother. Maybe then I'd feel safer telling her how much I wish I knew mine. I know she remembers the good times with Gaia, lots of them. She has real memories but I have to make up stories in my head about my birth parents. Sometimes I imagine good ones, where we're a normal, happy family. Though I'm not really sure I'd like normal, whatever that is.

10

The thunder rumbles closer and louder. On nights like this I feel a little sorry for Doobie. He's the only one who doesn't have a roommate in our gigantic tree house. Sirona and Jade sleep in the same room with Moon and Aura. Harmony shares a room with Rain. Willow and Wave have always slept in the same bed, even though it's against the guidelines written in The Book. I think they started before the rule was made or maybe people just ignore it since they've been together for so long. Goji sleeps in his shack but even he's not alone because he sleeps with his cat, Ziggy.

Coyote's army hammock hangs empty across from my bed. He's an insomniac and often disappears on walks at night. On nights like this, you'd think he'd want to take shelter in the tree house, but Coyote loves storms. Nobody knows where he goes but he usually comes back long after I'm asleep.

Blinding light followed by a deafening crack of thunder hit at exactly the same time. A yelp escapes from my mouth. The branches sway with the howling wind and the plastic we tack over the windows every winter, tears off the nails and flaps noisily. It feels like the tree house might just crumple into a pile of mattresses and sleeping bags on the soggy ground. Fear rolls through me and I pull the covers over my head. I'm warm but my body is shaking like a wet dog.

I don't say a word when Harmony climbs in next to me, just like when we were little. She snuggles against my back as the storm moves over us, turning to a steady rain. Within minutes I drift off to sleep. When I wake in the morning Harmony's gone. Her ratty old stuffed bear, Boo-Boo, is in her place. Coyote is back, sound asleep in his hammock. I hide the bear under my pillow and tiptoe down the ladder for sun salutation.

It seems odd to salute the sun on a rainy day, but Goji reminds us that the sun is still there behind the clouds, blessing us, and deserves our blessing in return. We move the picnic table aside so we can do yoga under the canopy, where the ground is mostly dry. Goji faces us as we mirror him through the familiar poses of mountain, downward dog, cobra, and back to mountain. The stretches help to warm my body and stop the shivering.

Coyote and I slide the table back under the canopy while Wave and Sirona make scrambled eggs with spinach and goat cheese. Wave lets Moon break the eggs into the bowl and toss the shells into a pail we'll mix in with the compost. He's pretty good at it for a six-year-old. Sirona hums as she whisks the eggs. We're not supposed to talk before breakfast so that we remain in a quiet, peaceful place until we break our overnight fast. Humming doesn't count as talking.

After breakfast, Rain carries the pail of eggshells and other food scraps toward the compost box. I walk behind her on my way to the outhouse. A branch cracks and I look up to find where it came from. I can't see him but I recognize the moccasined foot disappearing up the trunk. Goji is like a squirrel the way he floats from branch to branch sometimes. He's always loved climbing trees but ever since Rain arrived he's like a shadow over her, watching. I don't think she notices because she wasn't raised to be aware like the rest of us at SFC. But I do.

Harmony knocks on the outhouse door while I'm inside. I know it's her because of the rhythm. We have a code we made up when we were little kids. She taps out four times, the first one the loudest. THUMP thump thump thump. We got it from Doobie, who pounded on Coyote's big drum for one of our dance ceremonies. Doobie said it was an Indian drumbeat. Goji told Doobie that he'd lived in India and never heard it. This was his way of dropping a hint on Doobie. Goji prefers to call the local Indian tribes Native Americans. I thump back with my foot against the floor so Harmony knows it's me in here.

She's waiting outside the door when I come out. "Doobie wants everyone in the pot patch. We need to help harvest and trim before the plants get moldy from the rain."

"Right on," I say, and follow her down the path. Neither of us brings up her snuggling with me during last night's storm.

When we arrive at the patch, the others have already gathered. We grow the marijuana between rows of sweet corn to hide them. Doobie and Wave have cut down all but one of the towering plants.

Doobie wipes his brow with his forearm. He hasn't been the same since Gaia visited. He still jokes around but there's a sadness inside his laughter.

He hands me the machete. "Would you like to do the honor, little brother?"

I almost drop the machete. It's much heavier than I thought it would be.

Doobie steps behind me. "Hold it with both hands. Swing it like a bat."

I've never played baseball but the Olders took me to a drive-in theater a few years ago to see a movie called *Bang the Drum Slowly*, so I get the drift. I heave the machete behind my shoulder and everyone jumps back. I swing and miss.

Coyote laughs. "Easy, Blue. Keep your eyes open or you might cut your foot off."

I try again. This time I manage to topple the plant, but higher than I should have cut it. Doobie lays a hand on my shoulder. "Good job, buddy."

We spend the rest of the day trimming the biggest leaves from the plants and storing them in paper sacks. Doobie and Wave hang the main stalks in the attic of Goji's shack to dry out. In about a week or so we'll trim them again and store the pot in mason jars, hidden around the compound. The Olders usually have enough to last until the next harvest since they keep most of it. Doobie only sells to a few people he personally knows.

Sirona makes a special soap to clean the sap from our hands but we still have to scrub and scrub. I'm the last one still scrubbing when Mrs. Fuller pulls into our driveway. The passenger door opens and Stardust, the tarot card reader from Sebastopol, climbs out. Mrs. Fuller must have picked her up hitchhiking. Or maybe Stardust really is psychic, since she's one of the few people Doobie sells pot to and she just happens to show up on harvest day.

Stardust starts up the pathway toward us, her bangles and bells jangling. The sister-mothers exchange eye rolls as Stardust approaches wearing big hoop earrings, a colorful head-scarf, and a jingly belt on her hips. I've heard the Olders poke fun at Stardust's claims that she can communicate with the dead. Coyote joked that he's heard voices when he does mushrooms but it doesn't make him a psychic. Goji doesn't like us to judge other people, but even he laughed at that.

Moon and Aura race toward our neighbor lady. Mrs. Fuller has been teaching Aura her alphabet. She sometimes brings Moon crossword puzzles and she gave Harmony a set of charcoal pencils. Mrs. Fuller used to be a teacher, but they closed the old Freestone school about ten years ago. She's invited me to come with her to help out in a classroom in Sebastopol where she volunteers. I'm working up the nerve to ask Goji for permission. He's not a fan of the American educational system, says it teaches all the wrong things and leaves out the important ones about philosophy and living in harmony with nature. But I'm still curious.

Stardust plants herself between Goji and me next to the metal water basin. She's wearing a big white flower in her hair.

"Aloha, friends! I just got back from Hawaii. I brought you all some puka shells." She hands a bag to Willow, who peers inside, then looks at Wave. They both shrug. Stardust turns to Goji. "I want to join Saffron Freedom Community. I just love you all and I want to be part of the group."

Goji smiles sweetly. It's obvious he doesn't think she's a good fit but he's the most open-minded person I've ever met.

"Why do you want to become part of this family?"

"My old man apparently found a new girlfriend while I was in Kauai. I need a new scene."

Goji shakes his head. "That's not how it works. Saffron Freedom Community is a home one is called to, not a place to land because you're backed into a corner."

Stardust turns her mouth into a pout. "Well, how does it work then? What do I have to do?"

Goji motions for her to join him. "Come, let's go for a quiet walk."

Stardust breaks into a huge grin. They take just a few steps before Goji pauses and points to her belt. "Please take off the noise."

Stardust furrows her eyebrows but loosens the belt and drops it in her big purse.

Goji doesn't move. "And the jewelry."

She frowns. "Why?"

He doesn't answer. She glances toward Willow, who nods.

Stardust is down to a skirt and sleeveless top when they finally leave for their walk. The two of them amble down the path toward the main gate, then veer off toward Goji's shack.

We haven't added new people in years and all of a sudden we get two joiners in the space of a few months. I liked Rain from the moment she stepped foot into SFC. Stardust, I'm not too sure about. From the shocked looks on everyone else's faces, I don't think I'm alone in my opinion.

When Goji and Stardust drift out of sight, Harmony and I walk toward Mrs. Fuller and the other Youngers, who've gathered at the community table. Harmony stops to stomp in a puddle, covering both our legs with muddy water.

"Stardust isn't one of us."

I step back from the puddle before she completely soaks me. "Goji says we should build doors, not walls."

She stomps again, this time missing me. "Why do you always repeat everything he tells you? Goji also says we should think for ourselves."

"A paradox."

She wrinkles her nose. "A pair of what?"

"*Paradox.* It means two conflicting ideas."

She starts walking again. "Whatever it is, you need to come up with your own ideas once in a while. You're starting to sound like Goji's parrot." She glances at me. "Sorry. That came out meaner than it was supposed to. I'm not as good with words as you are."

When we reach the picnic table Harmony throws her arms around our neighbor's shoulders. "Hi, Mrs. Fuller."

"Hello, dear. How're your charcoal sketches coming along?"

"Pretty good."

Mrs. Fuller squeezes Harmony's hands. "I'd love to see them when you're ready to show me." She glances at her watch. "Oh shoot, I have to run. I've got a pork roast in the oven."

Moon looks up from his crossword. "What's a pork?"

Harmony makes squealing and snorting sounds. "It's a pig, silly."

Moon glances at me to see if our sister is telling the truth. She's known for trying to pull the wool over people's eyes, especially with the Youngers. I nod at him.

Moon looks back at Mrs. Fuller like someone just stole his favorite blanket. "You *eat* them?"

Mrs. Fuller picks nervously at a paint stain on her sleeve. "I'm sorry, honey. I forgot that you're veg . . ."

I quickly move next to her and take her arm. "I'll walk you to your car, Mrs. Fuller."

"Thank you, Clover Blue." She glances back at Moon as we head toward where she parked. Under her breath she says, "That was stupid. I've upset him."

"He'll be okay. We're all about diversity and nonjudgment here. The Olders will explain it to him."

She opens her car door and pauses. "You're such a smart young man. Have you thought about college?"

"I'm only twelve. I don't really know much about college."

She laughs as she settles behind the wheel. "It's where you get to learn a little about a lot of things and a lot about the things you're most passionate about. Do you have any ideas of what you might like to study?"

"I kind of hope to be a writer someday."

She pulls the door closed and rolls down the window. "If you want to be a writer you don't have to wait for someday. Just write."

"I don't know if I'm any good."

"You'll never know if you don't take that risk. And the more you write the better you'll get. That much I do know." Mrs. Fuller starts the engine.

"That's what Goji says about meditation and . . ." I stop myself mid-sentence. Harmony's right. I need to stop quoting him.

"And what?"

"Nothing. I was just thinking about how Harmony's sketches have gotten better the more she draws."

"Exactly!"

Mrs. Fuller's eyes dart around the community, looking for Stardust. "I don't know if that girl needs a ride back to town."

"Don't worry. One of the others will drive her back."

Mrs. Fuller looks up at me. "I hope you'll come to the school in Sebastopol with me next week. Those kids need to meet someone like you."

"I'll ask Goji."

"I already discussed it with him. He said it was fine."

"He did?"

"In so many words."

"What did he really say?"

She grins. "He said it would be good for you to see how lucky you are. I'll pick you up next Wednesday morning. Around eight?"

Before I can answer she rolls up her window and pulls away.

I do my best not to stare at Stardust during dinner. Harmony doesn't even try to hide her staring. She keeps elbowing me, as if I can't see the drastic changes without her making a scene. It's weird seeing Stardust without big hoop earrings hanging from her ears or a scarf on her head. Her thick black hair is tied with twine in a simple ponytail at the back of her neck. She's even washed off the bright lipstick and blue eye make-up. Except for her colorful skirt, Stardust now looks like the Quakers we studied about in our world religions sessions with Goji. The jangling, colorful gypsy is no more.

People are unusually quiet through the meal, mostly looking up from their plates just long enough to make eye contact with another family member before going back to eating. When everyone's finished, I start to clear the dishes but Goji motions for me to sit.

"Let's enjoy some sharing, starting with our visitor." He smiles at Stardust. "As you know, when we strip away ego a person is better able to become authentic and grow into a fully developed being." He lays a hand on Stardust's shoulder. "Everyone? This is Jane." He turns to her. "Would you like to address the community?"

Stardust/Jane starts to stand but Goji gently tugs on her arm, meaning he wants her to stay seated. "We are all equal here. All on the same level, face-to-face, eye to eye."

She slowly settles back into her chair. "Thank you for welcoming me. I hope to prove myself worthy of your community." She glances toward Goji, who nods. "I have accepted this new name as a sign from the stars that . . ."

Keeping his head bowed as he strokes his beard, Goji says, "Please start again."

She clears her throat. "It's a privilege to spend time with you. Please let me know how I can be of service." She starts to say something else but thinks better of it.

Goji leans forward and looks around the table. "Jane would like to learn more about Saffron Freedom Community. Does anyone have any objections to allowing her to stay on for a bit?"

Willow fidgets in her seat. I can tell she has doubts about the idea. But Doobie seems happier than I've seen him since Gaia left. He waits only a few seconds before shouting, "Welcome, Jane!"

One by one the rest of us chime in, echoing, "Welcome, Jane," but not nearly as enthusiastically as Doobie.

11

By the time I was seven years old I knew how to cook, weed the garden, trim pot plants, empty the shitter, milk the goats, gather eggs, wash laundry, and diaper a baby. Rain is starting from scratch learning all our chores. Usually Jade does the milking but Rain asked me to mentor her.

"Can I ask you something?" Rain says, as she gingerly squeezes milk from Inga's teat.

"Of course. You can ask any of us anything."

"Maybe a stupid question, but why is it . . . why are we called Saffron Freedom Community?"

"That's not a stupid question at all. It started out as Sunshine Freedom Community but Goji changed it to Saffron after having a vivid dream around the time a bunch of people left here. In his dream, Goji said the sun turned into liquid gold, like the colorful saffron spice he saw in the open markets of Delhi."

"Delhi?"

"It's in India. He spent time in Asia studying yoga, meditation, chanting, and other spiritual stuff."

"So he's like a guru, right?"

"Kind of, but he'll tell you we're all gurus."

She laughs. "I'm not a guru."

"Guru's just a fancy word for teacher. You taught Willow how to macramé. So that makes you her macramé guru."

She's quiet for a minute. "So other than Goji, who's your favorite of the Olders?"

I never said Goji was my favorite but I let it go. It's obvious he's becoming *her* favorite.

"That's a tough one. I've always loved Gaia. She was so fun and full of life. Most of the Olders feel, well, older. Gaia treated me like she was the same age as I was. Plus, Gaia is Harmony's birth mother so I feel a special connection to her."

Rain laughs. "That girl might be small but she sure makes up for it in spunk." She leans forward. "Willow is your mom, right?"

Before I can respond, our older nanny goat, Greta, tries to step away from me and I nearly spill my pail of milk. I press my head into her coarse flank and she settles down. "They're all my moms."

"Yes, I know, but Gaia said Willow adopted you."

"Gaia told you that?"

"She said it's a complicated story and that I should ask you directly."

Questions about my parents are uncomfortable. Goji still hasn't had "the talk" with me. But he did warn me that people wouldn't understand if the truth gets out about my adoption.

"I'd rather not talk about it."

She throws me a concerned glance. "I'm sorry. It was rude of me to ask." Rain goes back to the other question. "So who do you like next best after Harmony?"

"I dunno. I love them all." I really don't know. They're all my favorites for different reasons.

"I understand, everyone here has been so nice to me. But I still feel like I hardly know anyone and I'd love to know what you think."

I play with a dead twig under my boot, thinking. "Well, Willow holds her thoughts inside. She keeps us on track with things like homework and chores. She taught me to read by the time I was four. Wave is physically strong but he's a very gentle person. He used to be a surfer. They're both really into yoga, so they make a good pair."

Rain stops milking and strums an invisible guitar. "And he plays a mean guitar."

"Right. He writes songs, too. I keep telling him he should make a record. He's been teaching me chords but I'm not very good at it."

"What about Doobie? He seems like such a sweet guy but probably not someone I would have known before I came here. I've never smoked a cigarette, let alone marijuana."

"I kind of figured that. You seem pretty straight edge."

She grins. "Wanna know a secret?"

"Sure."

"I'd never been more than ten miles from home before I ran away."

I like the sound of the word *home* coming out of her mouth. It sounds comfortable, like the houses we pass on our way home after dark.

"Where's home?"

Rain smiles. "It's here, silly."

"I know, but before here."

Her smile disappears. "A few hours south." She changes the subject back to the family. "So, Blue, what's Doobie's story? He seems so softhearted. Funny too."

"People think he's just a pothead but he's a smart guy who loves pretty much everyone. Gaia sort of used to be his old lady. She once told me that Doobie's mom was really mean and that he's been looking for love all his life."

"Aw. That's so sad."

After what Rain had said about her stepfather beating her, I instantly regret talking about Doobie's mom. I glance over at the abandoned bee boxes. "Jade is quiet around people but she has a way with animals. We used to have bees and she'd talk to them when she took out the honeycombs. She never once got stung. She's also a great cook."

"She and Coyote are together, right? What's his deal?"

"You already saw how protective he is. He carves things out of wood and he taught me how to whittle. He and Jade made Aura together. Sirona helped deliver her. She's a really good midwife."

Her eyes go wide. "You were there?"

"Everyone was. Well, Moon mostly slept through it. I don't blame him. I slept through his birth."

"Wow. What was that like, seeing a baby born?"

"I thought it'd be really bogue but it was actually pretty cool. Sirona also knows a lot about herbs and stuff. You saw how she saved Harmony's life."

"That was a miracle. I prayed for Harmony all night after she got bit."

"You did?"

"Of course. Didn't you?"

"I surrounded her in white light and healing. I guess you could call it a prayer. It's just something we do for each other here."

Rain stops milking and looks at me like I'm from outer space. "You don't believe in God? Don't you want to go to heaven?"

I look across the garden to the meadow dotted with redwoods and live oak. I set my pail on a stump and pat Greta on the behind to let her know she's free, then jump onto a low-hanging tree limb. I gently bounce up and down, grinning at Rain. "I think we already live in paradise."

She looks around our property and smiles. "It is really beautiful here. But that's not the same thing as being a good Christian or walking streets of gold after you die."

I leap from the branch and land next to Rain, nearly bumping into her. "I think heaven is more like a metaphor. People want to believe in a peaceful, happy life. Maybe because they didn't get one in this lifetime. Or maybe they did, and they want more of it after they die."

Rain wrinkles her nose. "A metaphor? I've gone to church since I was a baby and nobody ever said heaven was just a symbol."

"We study lots of religions from all over the world. Goji teaches that all the great prophets like Jesus and Mohammed and Buddha pretty much said the same thing."

"And what's that?"

"Be kind. Respect life. Pay attention. And focus on the here and now, not the promise of something better in the afterlife."

Rain gets quiet and goes back to squeezing. The tring-trings turn to sploosh-sploosh as her pail fills. I hope I didn't hurt her feelings about her religion.

"Hey, Rain, you're pretty good at that for a city girl."

"I'm not a city . . ." She trails off and blushes. "Thanks. You're a good milking guru."

"So what about you? Who's your favorite family member so far?"

She winks. "I'd have to say you."

A tingle spreads up and down my spine. I wonder if she knows what a huge crush I have on her. I think she likes Goji, but at thirty-four, he's a lot farther apart in years than Rain and me.

"I've always wanted a little brother," she adds, making it clear it's not a girl-boy thing the way I'd hoped.

Before I can respond Rain starts sniffling. The girl is like a faucet and you never know when she's going to let loose. Her eyes shine through her tears in a way that stuns me. She's so incredibly beautiful. I've never seen *into* anyone like this before. I reach for her arm but she looks away. She picks up her pail of milk and sets it next to mine, smiling at me through her tears. "I win!"

We carry our pails toward the kitchen, where some of the milk will be curdled for cheese and some will be used in whatever recipe Jade and Coyote are cooking up for us today. As we head down the path, Rain playfully nudges me with her shoulder. I nudge her back and we both laugh while trying to steady the milk to keep it from spilling. In the distance Goji waves and her face brightens. I suddenly feel protective of Rain. And envious of Goji. He's taught us that we should turn envy into wishing happiness for the other. I want to be happy for Goji but right now I want Rain all to myself.

By the time we reach the picnic area, her tears have dried. But for some reason I've caught them. It's all I can do to make small talk with the Olders before running off toward the woods. I run until I'm sure nobody will follow me, then drop under an oak tree and cry like a baby for absolutely no reason.

"Blue! Clover Blue!"

The sound of my family calling jolts me awake. I forgot about our trip to the city today. I sit upright and wipe the leaves from my hair. "Coming!"

Every few months the sister-mothers drive into Santa Rosa to get their birth control pills and to look for used clothes and dishes at the thrift store across the street from the clinic. We don't use plastic at SFC and the ceramic plates break pretty often around here. Harmony is working on a mosaic tabletop made from all the broken pieces.

When I reach the others, Harmony hands me a triangle of tin foil. The Olders built a wood-fired oven a few years ago to bake bread. Lately we've been using it to make pizza topped with homemade sauce and oregano from our herb garden. It's my new favorite food.

"You missed lunch," she says. "Where'd you disappear to?"

"Nowhere."

"Goji wants to talk to you when we get back from town.

You're supposed to let someone know when you go somewhere. I mean *nowhere*."

"Thanks for saving me a slice." I unwrap the pizza and shove
nearly half of it into my mouth all at once as we climb into the
back of the truck. Jade lifts Moon onto the tailgate but takes
Aura up front to sit with the sister-mothers. Moon sits next to
me on the bench inside the homemade topper. He immediately
takes out *Frog and Toad Are Friends,* the book I helped him
pick out at the library last week. One of my jobs has been to
help him learn to read since he's having a hard time.

Sirona pulls out onto the highway. Willow opens the sliding
window between the cab and the back so we can hear the radio.
Sirona reaches down to change the radio station. "Fucking
disco."

We're not supposed to use "lazy" swearing words but Sirona
has always had a hard time keeping this guideline. She twirls
the knob past several stations before coming to stop on a song
about fifty ways to leave your lover. All three women start
laughing and singing along until the DJ breaks in to announce
that Jimmy Carter has been officially declared the winner of
yesterday's election.

The sister-mothers stop singing, then start whooping and
high-fiving each other. Sirona honks the horn for at least a mile.
Willow rolls down her window and screams, "Bye-bye, all you
lying warmongers!"

"Bye-bye, assholes!" Harmony yells.

The women fall silent. Jade and Willow simultaneously
swivel in their seats to glare at my sister. When Sirona turns off
the radio Moon pulls his book close to his face, readying himself for the trouble our sister is in. Harmony's smile falls into a
frown.

Sirona stares at Harmony in the rearview mirror. Much to our
relief, a huge grin breaks out over her face. "Bye-bye, mother-
fuckers!" She slaps Jade on the knee and laughs until tears stream

down her cheeks. Willow starts singing "The Times They Are A-Changin'" and the rest of us join in. Everyone knows the song by heart. We sing it over and over at the top of our lungs. By the time we pull into the parking lot of the women's clinic we're all so hoarse we can hardly talk.

"You two go ahead and look around at the thrift store across the street," Sirona says to Harmony and me. "Take Moon with you."

Harmony and I each hold one of Moon's hands to cross the street and push inside the glass doors. I'm hoping to find an army jacket like Coyote wears. Harmony wants hiking boots. She rarely wears dresses, and when she does, she puts pants on underneath them.

We rifle through a row of pants until I find a pair of corduroy bell-bottoms that look about my size. Harmony slides a wool sweater off a hanger and throws it at me. "Try it on."

Moon follows me into the dressing room and sits on the floor with his book. The pants fit perfectly in the waist but drag on the floor. I pull the sweater over my head and step out to look in the longer mirror.

Harmony whistles. "You look snazzy, man."

"They're too long."

"Hem them. Or cut them off." She throws a faded Led Zeppelin T-shirt into our basket and trots toward the shoe aisle. When I catch up, she's on the floor, pulling on a pair of cowboy boots. She stands and struts to the other end of the store. "Whaddya think?"

"Are they comfortable?"

She grabs a wide-brimmed hat from a rack and walks back toward me, exaggerating her hips. "Well, I don't know, pardner. How about you? Are *you* comfortable?"

The oversized hat falls over her eyes. She tips it back with her middle finger and grins at me.

"What do you think, Moon? Is it a good look?" I glance

around the aisle. He must have wandered off on our way to the shoes. I look at Harmony. "We should find him."

She doesn't bother to take off the boots. I check the dressing room to see if he went back to read his book. It's empty. We jog up and down all the smelly rows of clothes but there's no sign of him. I point toward the back of the store. "Try the toys. I'll look in the books section."

Neither of us has any luck. I start to panic. "What if he left? What if he crossed the street? Man, we're going to be in such big trouble."

We race toward the door. An older lady with glasses perched on the end of her nose stops us. "You girls haven't paid for your items yet."

Harmony scowls. "*He* has money."

I'm used to being called a girl because of my long hair so I don't get upset, but Harmony always defends me. I pull a wad of dollars out of my pocket and one falls on the floor. Harmony bends over to retrieve it.

"There he is!" She points to a corner near the front door where Moon blends into a pile of folded blankets. He's reading his book. And he's wearing a huge pair of black horn-rimmed glasses.

"Moon!" I race toward him. "You scared the crap out of us."

He runs his finger under a line of words in the *Frog and Toad* book and starts reading aloud. Perfectly, without stumbling on a single word. My mouth drops open.

Moon adjusts the glasses. "I can see the words!" He points toward a basket brimming with used glasses, some spilling onto the floor. "I tried on every single one. These are the best."

"How much?" Harmony says to the lady.

"Ten cents."

I lay several crumpled bills on the counter. "We've got a pair of cords, two shirts, this sweater and her boots."

The woman fishes around in a green bank bag and hands us

back the change. She glances around the store. "Where are your parents?"

"We're orphans," Harmony blurts out, still holding her grungy old shoes.

The woman gasps. I elbow Harmony, who keeps a completely straight face. "She's kidding, ma'am. Our parents are across the street. Thanks for the stuff."

I grab Moon's hand and pull him out the front door. When we get to the other side of the street Harmony breaks into howls and squeals, slapping her knees. "Shoulda seen your face!"

I don't laugh. "Don't ever do that again, Harmony."

"Oh come on, Blue. It was hilarious. Why do you have to be such a downer?"

"I just worry what will happen to us if someone tries to take us away."

She shakes her head, grinning. "You worry too much, man."

Harmony acts so much like Gaia sometimes it's almost scary. I don't tell her so because she hates when I compare her to her mom.

Before we can climb back into the truck, Sirona, Willow, and Jade stride across the parking lot, their peasant dresses billowing in the November wind. Aura is tucked inside Jade's thick sweater, resting on her mother's hip. When Sirona sees Moon she squats down, so she's face-to-face with him. "What's up with the glasses, little man?"

He lets go of his book and it falls onto the concrete. With both hands, he strokes Sirona's cheeks, her red hair, the paisley print of her blouse before looking her straight in the face.

"I can see your eyelashes!"

12

December 1976

Mrs. Fuller honks her horn from just outside our driveway gate. I wave to let her know I see her. Goji steps onto the stoop of his shack with a wool blanket draped around his shoulders. He looks toward Mrs. Fuller and back to me as I walk down the driveway toward her huge car.

"Morning chores complete, Clover Blue?"

"All done. I did some of Rain's, too. She's not feeling well."

At the sound of her name, Goji's eyes go from sleepy to wide awake. He bows slightly, holding one hand over his heart. I pick up my pace in case he changes his mind about letting me help Mrs. Fuller in her sixth-grade classroom. When I glance back to see if Goji's watching, he's already trotting toward the tree house. For someone who constantly talks about detachment, he sure seems hooked on our newest member.

During the drive to Sebastopol, Mrs. Fuller gives me the rundown about what she does in the classroom. "The government keeps chipping away at school budgets. More kids to a classroom means less one-on-one with students who need extra help. The biggest challenges are reading and math."

"Harmony's better at math," I say. "I help her write essays and she helps me with geometry."

Mrs. Fuller laughs. "Geometry? If you kids are already working on geometry you're a lot better at math than you think." She pats my knee. "Besides, I'd already planned on having you help in the reading group."

She pulls off the highway and makes a couple of turns before pulling into the parking lot in front of the elementary school. To the right of the building, groups of kids chase each other around a grassy playground. Some of the older boys shoot baskets on one end of a basketball court while girls jump rope at the other end.

Mrs. Fuller sees me watching and smiles. "Recess."

"Recess?"

"A break for exercise. Otherwise they can't sit still in the classroom."

I can't imagine sitting all day at a desk, with or without a break. But the idea of having more friends to play with makes me think maybe school isn't all bad. I love hanging out with Harmony but it might be nice to have other friends my age that aren't girls.

"C'mon, kiddo." She lifts a canvas bag stuffed with books and notebooks from the backseat. "Let's get inside before they run us down when the bell rings."

We walk along a shiny floor dotted with scuff marks. The school smells a little like vomit and a lot like Wave's van did when the whole family was crammed inside it. Halfway down the hallway a bell blares and I nearly jump out of my skin. Before I can collect myself, hordes of screaming kids stream through the doors. When they spot Mrs. Fuller, several children swarm around her, jumping up and down, squealing happily and yelling her name. Beaming, she pats heads, squeezes arms, and hugs a few before pushing through the crowd.

"Wow. They really love you," I say above the noise.

"And I love them back." She motions toward a doorway on our left, next to a row of hooks where kids are hanging their jackets and hats. "They'll love you, too."

The noise and chaos follows us inside the classroom. Mrs. Fuller raises her voice above the rambunctious kids finding their way to desks to introduce me to the teacher. "This is the young man I was telling you about, Clover Blue."

The teacher smiles and tilts her head to one side. Her long hair is pulled into a high ponytail. She looks tired for someone so young. "What an unusual name," she says, shaking my hand. "The kids call me Miss S. My last name is Schmeideknecht but they have a hard time pronouncing it, let alone spelling it." She smiles. "Yours is much easier to remember."

She turns to where two boys are shoving each other in the back corner of the room. "Roger! Danny! Hands to yourselves or to the principal's office."

Like magic, the room instantly goes silent. All the kids turn toward the teacher, then stare at the two boys. The larger boy folds his arms across his chest and waits for the other one to back away before claiming the desk they were fighting over.

Miss S. introduces me to the class. "I want you all to give a nice welcome to Clover Blue. He's a friend of Mrs. Fuller and he's going to be helping in the reading circle today."

A few of the kids clap. Some snicker. A red-haired girl in the front row raises her hand.

"Yes, Nancy?"

The girl looks at me and wrinkles her freckled nose. "Where do you go to school?"

Mrs. Fuller answers for me. "Clover Blue is home-schooled."

More snickers. Another hand shoots up in the back corner. Miss S. nods at the big kid. I can sense her holding her breath. "Yes, Danny?"

"Are you a girl or a boy?"

I was prepared for this one since I get it a lot when we're

away from SFC. Miss S. looks flustered as she tries to stutter out an answer but I interrupt her. "A boy," I say. "And you can just call me Blue."

"Maybe we should call you Blue Velvet," he says, laughing. Several of the others laugh along with him.

Miss S. claps her hands. "That's enough."

I'm already doubting my decision to help Mrs. Fuller. She said Goji agreed to let me come so I could appreciate what I have. I'm pretty sure he knew this would happen. It's not too late to back out. I could easily walk home and be back by lunchtime. I take a couple of steps in the direction of the door. Mrs. Fuller grabs my hand before I can get away.

"This nice young man is volunteering his time to help in the classroom. He's a friend of mine. Let's treat him with the same gratitude and respect you give to me." She squeezes my arm and whispers, "They like to test new people. Give them a chance."

Miss S. clears her throat. "Okay, class. Let's break up into our reading groups. I'll take Group One, Mrs. Fuller will lead Group Two, and Clover Blue will be helping those of you in Group Three."

The room fills with the sounds of desks screeching against the floor as they move to form three circles. The students reach inside backpacks and pull out their books. Each group has a different book. Miss S. points to my group. "They're reading *The Lion, the Witch and the Wardrobe* by C. S. Lewis. Have you read it?"

"We got that one when I was seven."

Mrs. Fuller grins proudly. "I told you he was an advanced reader."

Miss S. hands me a tattered copy. "It's a timeless book for all ages, don't you think?"

"I've read it at least a dozen times. My little brother, Moon . . ." I stop myself when her eyebrows go up at the mention of another weird name. "I agree."

She points in the direction of my group. The first face I see is Danny, the bully from the back of the room. He looks older than the rest of his classmates. He looks older even than me. I glance back at Mrs. Fuller, who nods. "Just let them take turns, one paragraph at a time."

I nervously walk toward my group of ten or so kids. "Hi, everybody. Who wants to go first?"

Nobody volunteers.

"Okay, well I'll just pick someone. Where did you last leave off?"

A small girl wearing cat-eye glasses raises her hand. "We're just starting this one."

Danny leans back in his chair. "It sounds like a stupid book."

I take a breath and think about what Goji would do in this situation. He'd probably tell me to "be the mirror" or something vague like that. I turn toward the bully. "What do you like to read about?"

He folds his arms across his chest. "I hate reading except for comic books."

"Okay, well what kinds of stories do you like best?"

"I like monsters."

I'm no good at being the mirror. Harmony's right. I need to come up with my own ideas. But the best idea I have is to imagine what Harmony would do.

I grin. "You're going to love this book, Danny." I grab an empty desk and wriggle it into the group, right next to him. "It has lions and witches and all kinds of magic stuff."

I open his book and hold the left side down with my hand. "Go ahead," I say.

Danny's cheeks go bright red.

I point to the first line. "Just pretend it's a comic book."

He glances at me and back to the page. "Okay, but if one of you makes a peep I'll smash your face." He puts a finger under the first word. "Once there were four child." He stops. "Child.

Ren. *Children* whose names were Peter, Susan, Edmund, and Lucy. This story is about something that happened to them when they were sent away. . . ."

His voice is low and quiet, unlike the noisy outburst from earlier. Each time he stumbles I help him sound out the word, just like I used to with Moon, who now devours books like this in a day or two. Danny reads painfully slow but the other kids stay quiet, not wanting to spark his anger. The longer he reads the less he stumbles. When he moves to the second paragraph, the girl to his right opens her mouth to take her turn, but changes her mind. I glance up to see Mrs. Fuller and Miss S. both smiling as they watch Danny read a full page before stopping. The kids in our group all clap when he looks up from the book.

By the end of the hour, each student has had a turn. They're slow readers and it's a little hard to listen without wondering how they got this far in school without learning to read better. For all the times I've felt embarrassed to stick out like an oddball around other people, right now I feel lucky not to be Danny.

The rest of the day I move around the classroom, stopping to help anyone who raises their hand as they work on their assignments. Everything they're studying I learned several years ago, sometimes from the Olders and sometimes from books I checked out from the library.

When it's time for us to leave, Mrs. S. stops me in the hallway. "I forgot to have you fill out this form. All the volunteers need to register with the office."

I look down at the paper. There are boxes for full name, birth date, and a parent's signature.

"Can I take it home and bring it back next time?" After reading the form, I already know there won't be a next time.

"Sure. I think that'd be okay." She hugs Mrs. Fuller. "Thanks for your help today. And thanks for bringing this guy. I can't believe he got Danny to read aloud."

Mrs. Fuller squeezes my arm. "He's a natural."

On the way home Mrs. Fuller explains that school will be out for the holidays. She asks if I'll join her again in the middle of January when they reopen. I think about Danny and those other kids, how bad they need the help. But then I remember Goji and the rest of my family, and how risky it could be to fill out that form.

"I need to think about it, okay?"

She pulls into our driveway. "Really? It looked like you were having a pretty good time."

"It was okay, but . . ."

"But what?"

"I'm needed here. I have lots of chores and, you know, stuff to do."

Mrs. Fuller frowns. I can tell she's disappointed. "I hope you change your mind. We make a great team." She nudges me with her elbow. "And I think that red-headed girl likes you."

I laugh, but it's a fake laugh.

In the distance, laughing, pulling, pushing, and trying to slow each other down, Harmony and Rain race up our grass driveway to greet me. I hop out and jog toward them, forgetting the paper in the car.

13

Goji takes small, intentional steps with his hands folded in front of him. He chants quietly to himself, almost as if I'm not here. We walk side by side between the tractor ruts left behind by the Czech. The tracks are filled with tread-patterned pools of rainwater. When Harmony and I were little, we used to walk along the edge of the cow pasture after the spring rains. We'd stomp in the puddles until we were both covered in mud. Before going home we'd dunk ourselves in the cattle tank because if we showed up that dirty we'd be given laundry duty for a week. It's our least-favorite chore next to shoveling chicken manure.

I keep to Goji's right, studying him as he walks. He's a small man compared to the other Olders. The older brothers are all taller than him. A couple of the sisters, too. I'll probably catch up to him in height before long.

Goji stops to watch the cows as they feed. "Clover Blue, today you are the teacher and I am the student."

"I am?"

"Yes. What would you like me to know?"

He's always saying there's no wrong answer, but when I search my mind for the perfect response I come up blank. "I can't think of anything."

As soon as it's out of my mouth I feel like an idiot.

"Come on now. You bring dozens of books home from the library. Surely you've learned something worth sharing."

I loosen the wool scarf from around my neck and push the hood off my head, hoping the fresh air will inspire me. *Think, Blue! Think of something impressive.* I glance toward a group of Jersey cows watching us as they chew. "Did you know that cows are color-blind?"

Goji shakes his head. "Hmmm. I didn't know that."

"They can't see the red in the bullfighter's cape. It's the waving that gets their attention."

"And how might you apply this knowledge to your own life?"

I knew it was a trick. He always does this. Everything is a metaphor with Goji.

I give it my best shot. "It means you can't always get by on appearance. You have to actually do something to be useful?"

He huffs a warm breath on his hands and rubs them together. "Are you asking me a question or stating your answer? Give me an example."

I hate these surprise tests. I'd rather write an essay, where I have time to think and work out my answer. I glance over at our station wagon, parked near the fence.

"Maybe like all those bumper stickers against the war. You need more than signs and slogans. You have to act. Like protests and stuff."

Goji turns and hugs me. "You are one in a million, Clover Blue."

It feels good to have beat the game or whatever it is he wants to teach me by pretending to let me be the teacher. We're not supposed to seek validation from others, but I'm relieved by his approval. The other men in the family are like older brothers but Goji is the closest thing to a real father. I wish I knew more about him. He doesn't talk much about his past. He's constantly telling us to stay in the present moment. But I pry a little anyway.

"Goji? What was it like starting this place? I mean, was it just to get away from the crowds and live in nature? I've heard Willow say you all wanted to make a bigger statement about society."

He looks off toward the row of trees at the end of the fence. "It was all of that and more. One of the things I learned during my time in India was that we are so much more than our bodies. We are a vibration of everything around us. If you're surrounded by cars and noise and pollution, by a greedy culture of consumerism, it becomes part of who you are. But out here"—he spreads his arms—"out here it's just us. Just nature." He turns back to me and lays a hand on my cheek. "Just love."

And just like that I feel comforted. By his time alone with me, by his wisdom, and, mostly, by his reassuring hand on my face.

As we turn back, Goji drapes his arm around my shoulder. "I've noticed you seem a little off lately. Between our two new members and needing extra help with the Youngers, it must seem a little like we've forgotten how lucky we are to know you, Clover Blue." He makes a sharp right toward the station wagon. "But I wonder if you might be willing to take on one more responsibility."

I'm guessing he wants me to wash the muddy car, but Goji opens the rusty back gate of the station wagon and reaches for a cardboard box. He hands it to me and smiles. A whimper escapes from inside. My eyes go wide as I tear open the top flaps. Inside, a furry ball of warm yellow puppy stares up at me.

"You got me a dog?"

"Well, it's a family dog to help protect us and alert us to outsiders who . . . who might not have good intentions. But I was hoping you'd be his main caretaker."

"Are you kidding?" I scoop the puppy into my arms. It's the yellowest dog I've ever seen. "Where'd you get him?"

"He was dropped off at the dog pound. Someone found him alongside the road and worried he'd get hit by a car."

I kiss the top of the puppy's head. He smells like peanuts. "What's his name?"

"That will be yours to decide."

"Me? Really?"

Goji nods, smiling.

"Can I go show him to the rest of the family?"

"Of course. Happy New Year, little brother."

I tuck the puppy inside my coat and jog toward the center of our compound. By the time I reach the others I've already decided on a name.

"Hey, everybody!" I hold out our newest family member for everyone to see. "Meet Sunny!"

Half a dozen pairs of hands nearly smother the puppy as they pat and stroke him. "Welcome, Sunny," they all say.

I look up to thank Goji again, but he's gone.

Sunny whimpers and cries next to my bed for a long time. I tried to leave him in the box but he wouldn't quiet down. Luckily Coyote is out on one of his night walks. There's no way I can sleep so I finally let him curl up next to me under the covers. Goji says I need to train him to sleep by himself because he'll grow too big to carry up the tree house ladder. But I can't stand to hear him cry. He probably misses his mother and the other puppies in the litter. Mrs. Fuller told me that people drop unwanted pets in the country all the time, thinking farmers will take them in.

I start to wonder about my own first family again. I wonder

if I cried, too, those first nights after I came to SFC. Was I lost when they adopted me or did someone dump me on the family? I have no memories from that first year, let alone any recollection of my parents or possible siblings. Sometimes I hear or smell something that reminds me of something that I can't name. Like when we first got the goats their baah-ing sounded so familiar, like a bell ringing in my chest. Or that time we were so far behind on the laundry we took our dirty clothes to the Laundromat and I couldn't stop sniffing the box of powdered detergent because the smell was so comforting. The sister-mothers had to pry it out of my hands to pour into the washing machines. I love my life here. But what if I was meant to be with my first family? And what if they're still looking for me?

I wake to Sunny licking my feet and crawl backward under the covers to nuzzle him. He yawns and licks my nose, smothering me in puppy breath. "Hey, boy, how you doing?"

The smallest bits of light are just starting to peek through the branches outside my window. Coyote is back in the room, snoring as usual. It's cold and I don't want to leave the warmth of my bed but I'm sure Sunny has to pee. I set him on the newspaper inside the box next to my mattress and he immediately starts yelping again.

"Shhhh!" I wrap a blanket around my shoulders like a cape and climb down the ladder with Sunny cupped inside my flannel shirt. As soon as I set him down he pees, squatting like a girl. I take him with me to a nearby tree and lift my leg to pee. "Like this," I say.

I hear a giggle behind me. "What in the world are you doing, Superman?"

"Harmony! Don't sneak up on me like that. You scared the crap out of me." I pick up Sunny and tuck him under my arm.

She laughs and points to the lump under my blanket. "Can I hold him?" Harmony opens her hands under my shirt and I let Sunny flop into her arms.

"He's so cute I could scream!"

"Don't. You'll wake everyone. Plus you know we're not supposed to talk before sun salutation. Why are you up so early anyway?"

"Same reason you are." She presses her cheek against Sunny's back and smiles.

We head toward the kitchen to find something to hold us over until after group yoga. Willow and Wave show up as we're looking through the shelves. They're always the first to wake and do their own routines before the family joins together. Willow kindles the coals in the wood stove with some sticks and sets a kettle on for tea. She spoons leaves into a hunk of gauze and twists the top. Wave squats by the firebox and lightly blows until the fire roars.

I point at the jar of goat milk on the table and then at Sunny. Willow shakes her head and motions toward the station wagon, then cups her hand and pretends to eat out of it.

Harmony follows me toward the car to get the dogfood. "Let's feed him inside the car." She rubs her hands together. "It's freezing out here."

"Shhh!"

"Oh, for crying out loud. Nobody can hear us way over here. Besides, it's a stupid rule."

She sets Sunny between our feet as we slide in and close the door. "Man, it's so cold I can see my breath!" She zips her coat and pulls up the hood.

"It'll warm up soon."

"Ha! You talked! You know it's a dumb rule."

"I was just trying to be respectful out there. You should be, too."

I tear open the bag of dog food and pour a handful of kibble on the floor. Harmony shivers and snuggles closer to me. I spread my blanket across both our laps while Sunny finishes eating. When he starts to whimper, Harmony lifts him and strokes his floppy ears. "He's so soft. You could make earmuffs out of these."

"Gross."

"Kidding!" She kisses the puppy on the forehead and he licks her face. "Why do you think he did it?"

"Did what?"

"Gave you a puppy."

"I don't know."

"Goji likes you best."

"Does not."

She kicks at the back of the front seat, leaving muddy skid marks. "Yeah, you're right. I think he likes whoever is the newest best. Do you see how he looks at Rain?"

"Jane is the newest, not Rain."

Harmony makes a *pfft* noise. "Jane's not one of us."

"Not yet."

"She won't last. Trust me."

I open the ashtray on the door handle and peek inside. A stale roach and a penny. The top snaps closed. I pull my hand away and study the dent in my thumb. "Why'd you ask me about Rain?"

Harmony draws a dog with her finger on the steamed-up window. "I don't know. She's not like the others, so quiet and sweet and squeaky clean."

"Rain doesn't mind the dirt. She's a hard worker."

"That's what I mean. She's such a good person. Like almost too perfect. Why in the world would her mom let her husband beat her?"

"Maybe she didn't know."

"She knew." Harmony purses her lips. "She absolutely knew."

"Harmony?"

"What?"

"Did one of Gaia's boyfriends hit you?"

"No."

"Did they . . ."

"I don't want to talk about Ruth."

Harmony opens the broken door handle with a pair of pliers. "Come on. Let's take Sunny for a walk before sun salutation."

We make a loop around the property, trudging over half-frozen grass now dripping with dew. Sunny follows close by our feet, racing to catch up if we get more than a few feet ahead of him. When we get back to the main camp everyone is waiting for us to start yoga. Goji is having Moon lead today. Our little brother stands facing us like a miniature yogi, his hands in prayer mudra as he bows. Goji moves behind Rain, whose cheeks are blushed from the cool air. He loosely circles her waist with his arms as he helps guide her into tree pose. She wobbles and nearly topples when her leg slides off her knee. Her cheeks go from rose to crimson.

Goji steadies her, then moves his hands to warm her face. "Better?" he whispers, breaking his own no-talking rule.

Harmony nudges me and makes a big-eyed face. "Told you so," she mouths.

Harmony was also right about Stardust Jane. After lunch I spot her heading up the driveway toward the road wearing the flashy clothes and jewelry she arrived in. I follow quietly behind her. She stops suddenly and without turning says, "You can walk with me but you can't sneak around behind me. That's just rude."

I jog up next to her and she starts walking again. "How did you know I was there?" I'm pretty sure she couldn't hear me because, one, I was being really quiet and because, two, her jingly jangly things would make it nearly impossible.

"I sensed you."

"Are you really psychic?"

She smiles. "We all are. Some of us are just more tuned in."

"You mean like intuition, right?"

"You can call it that. The universe gives us all kinds of tools. Tarot, a map on our palms, our sixth sense." She waves her hands toward the sky. "The stars and planets."

I study the lines on my palm. "Can you really read people's futures?"

"I can read people." She turns and walks backward, facing me. "You crave knowledge. You like it here but you're curious about the world. You have a crush on a certain girl. And you're starting to question the things you've been told all your life." She stops when we reach the road. "How am I doing so far?"

"Pretty good. Really good, actually."

She sticks out her thumb as a car comes into view. "You're turning the bend between childhood and manhood, Blue. Listen to your gut. You need to be you, not what someone expects you to be or how you think you should be."

"Wait, are you leaving us?"

The car whizzes past us. She drops her arm and hugs me. "I'm not leaving you. I'm returning to myself." She laughs. "And possibly my old man. He broke it off with the new girl and begged me to come back."

She's talking about the man who stole the joint out of her dress that day in front of the head shop. He gave me the creeps.

"Do you love that guy?"

She looks surprised by my question. *I'm* surprised by my question.

Stardust scrunches her face a bit, then recovers. "I love everyone."

Another car approaches and she sticks out her thumb again. The car slows down and pulls over. I recognize the local preacher's wife who buys veggies and pies from us at our roadside stand. She leans across the front seat and rolls down the passenger window. "It's dangerous for a girl to hitchhike, don't you know that?"

Stardust flashes me a smile and opens the car door. "I do know that and I'm so grateful for you to offer a ride." Stardust climbs in and closes the door. "Please tell everyone this nice lady gave me a ride to Sebastopol."

The driver gets a confused look on her face. "But I'm not headed to Sebastopol."

"I know. That's why I'm so grateful to you, ma'am."

Stardust turns and blows me a kiss. "You be you," she says. The last I see of Stardust is her bangled arm waving out the window as they drive out of sight.

14

Goji has asked us to "close the circle," something we do when a person leaves for more than a day or two. We've closed the circle many times. Like when Wave and Willow go to month-long yoga retreats or when Sirona visits family back east. We closed the circle every time Gaia left to chase the Grateful Dead. Today we'll do it for Stardust Jane. The idea is not to close that person out, but to hold space for them inside the circle and inside our hearts.

"Jane has left our home," Goji says during sharing time. "But a part of her remains."

He lights a candle in the middle of the table, then reaches for Willow's hand, to his right, and Sirona's, to his left. The rest of us grasp each other's hands in turn. "Let us send her our blessing and thank her for touching our lives with her spirit. She allowed herself to become vulnerable and we, in turn, opened our hearts to her. Thank you, Jane."

We lift our connected arms in unison, then release our hands, our fingers fluttering like bird wings to signify the letting go. "Thank you, Jane," we all say.

Doobie wipes a tear with his thumb and smiles. First he lost Gaia, who was mostly his old lady when she lived here. It doesn't take psychic abilities to notice that he has a thing for Stardust Jane. They got high together a lot while she was here and I'd seen them coming and going from the Sacred Space sometimes, always smiling, eyes half closed. He's convinced she'll be back, but I have my doubts. She's where she wants to be. And it isn't here.

Doobie twists his beard, then shakes his head, like a dog trying to rid itself of water. He slides a joint from his jacket pocket and lights it with a match. "She'll be back." He takes a long drag, coughs, then drags again and holds it in.

Coyote reaches across the table and pats Doobie's hand. After a quiet minute he says, "Brother, you gonna bogart that joint or pass it over?"

Doobie laughs, spewing smoke, and hands it across the table. By the time it goes around the Olders and gets back to him it's down to the size of a fingernail. He unclamps a roach clip from the rim of his floppy hat before taking the last pull. The joint pops and he jumps back.

Doobie looks at me and frowns. "You need to work on sifting the seeds out, little brother. That's harsh, man."

Sirona slaps him on the upper arm. "Yeah, well your breath is harsh. Blow the other way."

Everyone doubles over laughing at this, not because it's funny but because they're stoned. Harmony and I look at each other and I roll my eyes. She makes the cuckoo sign next to her head.

It's our turn for dishes so Harmony and I start clearing the table. I wash, Harmony dries, and Moon puts dishes away while Aura plays with empty pots on the floor of the kitchen area. Most of the Olders have disappeared inside the Sacred Space. Harmony throws a dish towel over her shoulder and dumps the dirty dishwater into a bush. She turns the bucket over to sit on top of it. "Wanna go spy on them?"

"No way."

"Why not?"

"Because."

"Because why?"

I glance toward the Sacred Space. "It wouldn't be right."

She twists her towel and snaps it at me, hitting me squarely on my leg.

"Ow!"

"Sheesh, Blue. Don't be such a goody-goody. It'll be fun."

"No, it won't. You even said it's gross."

Aura starts banging on a pot with a wooden spoon. Her black curls fall over her face like a wild cub as she beats noisily on the bottom of the pan. I snatch the spoon away from her and she starts to wail.

Harmony glares at me. "Nice going."

I squat down beside Aura. "Hey, sis, wanna help me feed Sunny?" She stops crying and nods her head, sniffling. I glance at Harmony. "You coming with us?"

She spreads her damp towel on our homemade cutting board. "Okay. But it won't be as fun as my idea."

Aura and I feed Sunny while we wait for Moon to finish putting away the silverware. Moon has a thing for order and carefully lays each spoon in the drawer so it nests inside the one below it. He does the same with the forks as best he can for mismatched utensils found at thrift stores. The knives he puts in a separate drawer with the blades and handles alternating so that they fit perfectly into their small compartment. When he's done he slowly slides the drawer closed so that nothing will move out of order.

I pat him on the back. "You ready, little man?" Moon got new glasses at the children's wellness clinic in Santa Rosa last week. He pushes them up the bridge of his nose and nods.

Sirona has never said who Moon's father is. It could be any of the men, but with Moon's green eyes and fair skin, it's probably not Coyote. My guess is Wave. Ever since the day Moon got glasses I catch Willow looking at Moon, then Wave, then back to Moon. It's a sad look.

It's already been dark for over an hour by the time we finish Sunny's after-supper walk. I make sure to take us in the opposite direction of the Sacred Space so we don't disturb the Olders. And also because I don't want to hear the sounds. I've heard moans coming from Willow and Wave's bedroom and other times when the Olders sneak into each other's beds. It doesn't bother me, but the idea of hearing them all at the same time freaks me out.

We take turns at the outhouse, letting the girls go first. Moon and I wait outside. The sister-mothers recently put the kibosh on anyone peeing outside because it was starting to stink like piss. We're allowed to take a leak outdoors only if we're far away from the main grounds. And we're not supposed to go in the same place twice.

I glance toward the Sacred Space, its canvas walls glowing with speckles of candlelight. A Moody Blues tune drifts toward us. I'm pretty sure the Olders will be busy for a while.

"Hey," I say when Harmony comes out. "I just remembered I left my pack by the fence yesterday when Goji and I went for our walk."

Harmony wrinkles her nose. "It's dark. Can't it wait until morning? It's not like the cows are going to steal it."

"I want the book inside it. I'll be back before you know it."

She herds Moon and Aura toward the tree house ladder. "Come on, kids. Let's go play hide-n-seek until Blue gets back."

I trot toward the fence, glancing backward until all three of them disappear up the steps before hooking a right down the path. I stop when I spot Goji and Rain standing in the doorway of the Sacred Space. I take a few steps closer and hide behind a tree where I can hear and see them more clearly.

Goji lays a hand on Rain's lower back. "You don't have to join in. Just sit with me and observe the beautiful expression of love shown to each other."

He holds the curtain aside. Candles line the entire wall of the yurt. The Olders are gathered in the middle of the floor in a linked chain of oiled bodies. Each has their legs curled around the person in front of them massaging the next one's back. Goji moves through the door, still holding the curtain for Rain. She peeks inside, then takes a timid step inside. Goji drops the curtain behind her.

I think about running through the door and rescuing Rain. It's a stupid thought. I'm not allowed in the Sacred Space. Plus it's not like she didn't go in on her own. Still, I'm uneasy. And a little jealous.

I run as fast as I can to the fence and find my pack right where I left it. On the way back I nearly trip over Goji's cat, who is coughing up a fur ball.

"Gross, Ziggy!" He meows and curls himself around my leg. "You shouldn't be out here. The coyotes will eat you in the dark." I carry him to the front steps of Goji's shack and set him down. "Go on back inside, Zig." He sits and looks up at me, blinking. "I'm not supposed to . . ." I glance toward the Sacred Space. "Okay, maybe just this once." I fish the flashlight from the bottom of my pack and pick up Ziggy. I shine the light toward the foot of Goji's bed and Ziggy's favorite blanket, covered in his orange fur. I set him on the bed and pat him on the head. "There you go, old man."

As I turn to leave, the beam of light lands on Goji's desk. I recognize the manila envelope from our recent day at the co-op sitting on top of a pile of books and papers. I start for the door, then tiptoe toward the desk and pick up the envelope. It's addressed to Mr. David Kagen and it has weird stamps on it. I resist the urge to peek inside. The top desk drawer is slightly open, exposing what looks like a half-eaten Zagnut candy bar. I nervously pull the drawer open farther. Beyond the rolling papers and a book of matches I hit the jackpot. There must be half a dozen Zagnut bars along with a pack of Juicy Fruit chewing gum.

I close the drawer and open the one below it, hoping to find more of Goji's secret stash. No candy. Just a pile of letters bound with string. I start to slide the drawer closed when I recognize Gaia's handwriting. I pick up the pile and fan through the envelopes. They're all from Gaia, and they're all addressed to Harmony except the last one, which was mailed to Goji. It's postmarked about a week after she showed up with Rain. I get why he'd hide forbidden candy, but why wouldn't he want Harmony to hear from her mom? Did he think it would upset her?

Outside I hear voices. I quickly switch off the flashlight and close the drawer. It gets quiet again. I tiptoe out the door and wait, my heart banging against my chest. A great horned owl hoots from a nearby perch. No voices and no footsteps. It must have been my imagination. Or maybe my guilty conscience. I jog in the direction of the tree house. Halfway there I nearly slam into Rain running up the path.

"Sorry, Rain! Why are you running?"

She pulls a blanket tighter around her shoulders but not before I see that she's naked from the waist up.

"I'm, uh . . . I need to use the bathroom."

"I have a flashlight. Let me walk you there."

She glances toward the Sacred Space.

"Rain, were you . . . are you okay?"

She nods. "I'm fine. Sorry, I gotta go." She takes off toward the outhouse, her blanket flapping behind her like a cape. I think about chasing after her, but it's clear Rain wants to be left alone.

I find Harmony sitting with Moon and Aura on one of the

beds they share with their mothers. Harmony is telling one of her scary stories.

"And then the ugly old witch looked into the cracked mirror and . . ." When I walk in she stops talking. "What took you so long?"

"I wanted to get this." I hand Moon my copy of *Where the Wild Things Are* from my backpack. It's one of his favorite books and mine, too. I'd borrowed it so many times from the library over the years that one of the librarians gave me my own copy.

Harmony frowns. "I was just getting to the best part of my story."

"I know that story. It'll give them nightmares." I turn to Moon. "Do you want to read?"

He takes off his glasses and hands the book to Harmony. "My eyes are tired from seeing."

She passes it back to me. "You read it, party pooper."

I read the lines from the Max character and Harmony reads the mother's parts. Moon does the monsters, lines he knows by heart, just like I did at his age. Halfway through the story, Rain quietly peeks into the room. She looks tiny beneath a bulky sweater I recognize from the community box.

Harmony pats the bed for Rain to join us. Aura snuggles into Rain's lap and sucks her thumb, worrying the silky edge of a wool blanket against her upper lip. When we get to the part of the story about the wild rumpus, the kids perk up. By the time the sister-mothers appear in the doorway we're all jumping on the mattress, growling and whooping. Moon flops on his back so that our jumping bounces him toward the foot of the bed.

Sirona shakes her head, laughing. "What in the world are you doing?"

He looks at his mother, smiling to show the gap where he recently lost a tooth. "We're rumpusing!"

Willow, Jade, and Sirona break out in big grins before joining

us on the bed, hooting and hollering. Rain seems to have forgotten her earlier troubles, laughing and jumping along with
the rest of us. Even Sunny, who was curled on the rug, starts
barking at us until we all fall down together and laugh like a
bunch of lunatics—the word the townies use when they talk
about us. They say it like it's a bad thing.

15

May 1977

I'm supposed to work on my essay about TV but since we don't own one it's tough to write. Harmony remembers shows from when she was little, living with Gaia in the city.

"What did people watch?"

She blows on her sketch of Willow and wipes away bits of charcoal. "Cartoons, mostly. We lived with people who were usually stoned or tripping so they laughed even harder than I did." She sees me thinking and makes a sad face. "Sorry. I always forget that you've never seen cartoons."

I shrug. "I think I'll write about how advertising makes people buy things they don't need."

"Goji will love that. But someday I'm going to show you Bugs Bunny and Porky Pig and The Roadrunner."

Harmony goes back to drawing. I still haven't told her about what I found in Goji's desk. If she knows about the candy bars she'll want to sneak into the shack to steal one. If she looks in the other drawer she'll find the letters Goji has been keeping from her. Maybe he thought it would be easier for Harmony all these years to forget about the past. She seems content here without Gaia. But I can't help but wonder if she'd be less pissed off knowing her mom has been trying to stay in touch.

Willow stops stirring a huge pot of beans when Jade pulls up in the station wagon and climbs out, carrying a sack of supplies from town. It's hot for May, and she's sweating. Aura starts toward her mom, then stops to chase a lizard around the table until it darts under the stack of logs near the pizza oven. Jade sets the bulging cloth bag on the other end of our long wooden table, which makes my pen bump along the page, leaving a long streak of ink.

Jade straddles the bench and pats between her legs. "C'mere, little girl." She combs out Aura's tight curls with a wide pick and snaps a rubber band over the wad of black frizz. Aura leans back and shoves Jade's blouse up, then pats her mother's face as she nurses.

Willow rummages through the groceries. She sets aside sacks of flour and oats to make her special bread.

"Have you ever noticed we're the only hippies left?" Jade says to no one in particular. "Everywhere I looked today I saw polyester leisure suits, gold chains, and platform shoes."

Willow looks up from the food bag and frowns. "We're not hippies, Jade. We're antiestablishment individuals who refuse to comply with social norms."

Jade laughs. "Isn't that the definition of a hippie?"

Willow moves back to her pot of beans. "We may be a product of the counterculture movement, but our way of life has more to do with community and mindfulness. We're about spiritual evolution, not tagging a ride on the average hippie train."

"Yeah, but it seems like the country is tightening up its collective asshole, you know? People seem cranky, greedier, more self-centered."

Willow takes a sip from a wooden spoon and frowns. "I blame the coke. That stuff makes people crazy."

Jade strokes Aura's back as she nurses. "Have you ever tried it?"

Willow looks up from her pan of soup. "Cocaine? No way. Not my thing. You?"

"Yeah, just once. I didn't like it. Made me itch all over."

Harmony kicks my leg under the table. When I glance up she makes a monkey face and pretends to scratch her armpits. Willow and Jade both look over at us as if they've just now realized we're here, which is probably true.

Willow shakes her spoon at Harmony, trying not to smile. "What are you two up to?"

Harmony flips her sketchbook around so the sisters can see. In the drawing, Willow bends over a pot, steam rising, a scarf tied at the back of her neck.

"That's really good!" Jade says. "You've captured her perfectly."

Harmony closes the pad. "Nah. It's sloppy. I didn't get her eyes right."

"Lemme see," I say. Harmony tries to snatch her notebook away but I beat her to it. "Please?"

"Okay. But they're not very good."

I flip to a page with a drawing of Coyote, a joint in his fingers, blowing a puff of smoke. The next page is filled with various critters including a raccoon, a chicken, and a ground squirrel. On the following page I come face-to-face with myself propped against a tree.

"I look so serious."

Harmony props one elbow on the table and leans into her fist. "You are serious."

"No I'm not."

"Yeah, Blue, you are."

I slide the book back to her. "I'm just a deep thinker."

"More like a deep stinker," she says, laughing.

"Har de har."

Aura pulls away from Jade and climbs on top of the table. She's wearing little brown sandals she found in the community box that are too big for her feet. Harmony pulls Aura into her lap and tickles her chubby legs. "Look at you getting so big you're wearing Moon's old shoes!"

Jade glances at Willow, then at me. "Those were your shoes, Blue. The ones you were wearing when you . . . when we adopted you."

Harmony slips one of the shoes off Aura's foot and hands it to me. "Aw, Bwoo, wook how tiny your widdle feet were."

I grab it out of her hand and study the shoe. I have no memory of the sandals or my feet in them. For some reason I have an uncontrollable urge to sniff it.

Harmony grabs the shoe back. "Ew!"

Goji strolls up and leans forward at our end of the table. The sisters go suddenly quiet and busy, stealing glances in his direction.

"How's the essay coming, Clover Blue?"

He almost always uses my full name except when he calls me little brother.

"It's a hard one since I haven't watched TV."

"Then find a television."

"You want me to watch TV? I thought it wasn't allowed."

"No, I want you to watch people *watching* television."

He turns to Harmony. "What about you?"

"I'm working on my art project."

"Of course you are." He glances at her sketchbook. "May I see?"

Harmony flips through her work and lands on a drawing of Goji meditating. He's cross-legged, a small amulet hanging from a leather thong around his neck. His eyes are closed and his hands rest on his knees, palms upward. Ziggy is curled in his lap.

"Very good, Harmony."

She blushes. "Would you like to have it?"

He pats over his heart with his hand. "I already do."

Goji gently squeezes both our shoulders before moving toward the sisters. He kisses them on the cheek, one at a time, lightly touching Aura on the forehead as she settles back into Jade's lap. "Hello, sisters."

"Hello, brother," they say.

The way the women look at him, it's always the same. Their eyes glisten and they freeze, as if they might miss the slightest glance or word or touch. The brothers show a deep respect in their exchanges with Goji, but with the sisters it's outright reverence. Goji's calming energy is like a peace that washes over us and we all take comfort in it. It's the reason people rarely leave once they join SFC. Maybe Jerry Garcia has the same effect on Gaia as Goji has on all of us. Maybe it was stronger with him because of the music. I don't understand why a person would leave. But I know why they stay.

It wouldn't be that hard for me to leave. I could just wander off when we're in town. Or I could sneak away in the middle of the night. I don't plan to. Partly because I love everybody here and I don't want them to get in trouble. And because when I see other people I assume they're secretly envious of our freedom. Something tells me I have more of it here than I ever would out there.

Mrs. Fuller parks her car at the gate and walks up the path, carrying a box of baby chicks from the feed store. The Fullers always sex the chicks before bringing us just the girls. One time a rooster got through and we kept him. We didn't want to give him back to the Fullers because we knew they'd butcher him. The rooster was very protective of the hens. We had to separate him from the coop anytime we got near it after he attacked Sirona while she was collecting eggs. Then one day he disappeared, leaving behind a mess of feathers in his struggle with the bobcat who took him. I was sad but not too sad because I was afraid of the rooster. I imagine that cat paid for his dinner in scars, though.

Sirona and Willow run to greet Mrs. Fuller, wearing only sarongs tied around their waists. Willow takes the chicks from our neighbor's arms. "Hello, Lois!"

Mrs. Fuller wipes her damp forehead with a hankie. She shoves it back in her pocket, looks the sisters up and down, and laughs. "I'm a little jealous of you naked free birds today. I don't remember it being this hot in May."

Sirona takes Mrs. Fuller's hand and squeezes it. "You know you can be free with us any time, Lois."

Willow hands the box full of peeping yellow chicks to Harmony. Aura jumps up and down as Harmony walks them to the table, where Moon and I are shucking corn. "Lemme see! Lemme see!"

"Hold your horses, Aura. You'll get to see them." Harmony sets the box on the table and immediately reaches inside to pick up a chick.

Aura's lip starts to quiver. "I want one!"

"Okay but you have to be really gentle."

Harmony hands her the chick. Aura squeals and immediately smothers it with kisses. "She likes me!" The chick drops a runny white curl on Aura's hand and she flings the bird to the ground.

I chase after it. "Aura!"

"It pooped on me!"

I set the chick carefully back in the box. "You pooped on me when you were a baby and I didn't throw you on the floor."

Aura starts crying and Harmony slaps me on the back. "Way to go, Blue."

Coyote walks over from where he was chopping wood and scoops up Aura, then sets her atop his shoulders. He trots around the table until she starts laughing, grabbing his hair to keep from falling sideways.

Willow loops an arm around one of Mrs. Fuller's arms. "We were just about to cut open a big fat watermelon. Come join us!"

"I don't know. I should be getting back to my ironing."

Sirona encircles her other arm. "Ironing can wait. It's too hot today anyway."

"But Charlie . . ."

Sirona winks at Mrs. Fuller. "Charlie can wait, too."

Willow drives a knife into the center of the watermelon, then turns it until the two halves fall away. She divides it into enough pieces that each of us gets a wedge, with enough left over for the others when they show up. The goats will get the rinds and the garden will get the seeds for next year's crop.

Doobie and Wave show up just as Mrs. Fuller stands to leave. Doobie has a joint tucked behind his ear that Mrs. Fuller can't stop staring at.

Doobie grins. "Would you like a toke?"

Coyote gives him a look and Doobie shrugs.

Mrs. Fuller smiles. "Maybe another time, but thanks for the offer."

Doobie hands her the joint and winks at her. "Take one for the road."

Everyone's mouth drops open when Mrs. Fuller tucks it inside her blouse. She hugs Willow and Sirona. "Thanks for sharing your delicious watermelon. I'd better be getting back home."

Coyote waits until Mrs. Fuller is out of earshot to read Doobie the riot act. "You're going to get us busted!"

"Nah, she's cool, man."

"How do you know she won't narc us out?"

"Because I sold her a nickel bag last week."

Sirona gasps. "You what?"

Doobie pulls a pack of rolling papers from his pocket and sprinkles it with a thin line of crumbled pot leaves. He rolls the joint tightly and licks the paper to seal it. "You need to give people credit. Not all the townies are as square as they look."

Sirona shakes her head. "I can't believe Lois Fuller smokes pot. She irons her husband's jeans for crying out loud. She goes to mass every Sunday."

"Yeah, but she's also an artist. She protested the war. And she voted for Kennedy. Don't assume you know somebody."

Coyote frowns. "I still think you should be more careful. Growing pot is a crime."

Doobie looks at Coyote and shakes his head. "So is being a judgmental hippie, my friend."

Sirona snickers and hands them each a dripping wedge of watermelon. "He's got you there."

Goji and Rain walk toward us from the direction of Gojis shack. Rain is wearing the plain white dress that Jane abandoned along with her SFC name. Rain still isn't comfortable going without clothes, even on days when it's warm enough for watermelon.

When they get within earshot I overhear Goji say, "Guilt is its own hangman, sister. Don't give him any rope."

I can't imagine what Rain might have done to feel guilty about. She seems like the type of person who'd wrestle guilt from your arms so you wouldn't have to carry it by yourself.

Goji surmises the sweaty, sticky lot of his family and grins. He takes a wedge of watermelon for himself and offers one to Rain.

"No thank you," she says.

I hate seeing her look so down. I reach inside the box and hand her a baby chick.

Her eyes light up. "Oh my goodness, it's so cute." Then she breaks down in tears, dabbing the downy chick to her eyes like a hankie.

"I'm sorry, Rain. Did I do something wrong?"

She smiles at me through her tears. "No, no, Blue, you did

something exactly right. I'm just a blubbery mess today. I'm sorry."

Sirona whispers in Rain's ear. Rain nods. Sirona takes her by the hand. "Let's go make you some moon-time tea."

Rain hands the chick back to me. "Thank you, Clover Blue."

"You're welcome."

Doobie punches me lightly on the shoulder and winks. "Girl stuff."

I nod as if I know exactly what he's talking about. I haven't a clue what he's talking about.

16

The waiting room at the clinic is half full of women, some with babies in their laps. Other than Moon, I'm the only male in the room. I don't like coming here but the sister-mothers told me a TV was installed since the last time I was here and I'd be able to research my paper. It's a small set, hung high on the wall. The TV was off when we got here but the receptionist just reached up and clicked it on because the doctor is getting behind on patients.

As soon as the picture comes to life my gaze goes straight to the screen. It's a show called *Leave It to Beaver.*

"A rerun," Sirona says, as if every episode isn't brand new for me. I've never seen any of them.

Like me, the minute the TV is on, all the women look up from their magazines and drop their conversations in midsentence, as if someone yelled, "Freeze!" in a game of "statue." Even Sirona stops knitting the socks she's working on to gawk at the talking box on the wall. I watch as several stitches fall off one of her needles, leaving a row of suspended curlicues. "I remember this one," she says to Jade. "He gets stuck in the teacup and the fire department has to rescue him."

Jade glances up from a well-read issue of *Mother Earth News*. On the cover photo, a mother and father lean over two boys, one wearing a Boy Scout uniform, as they kneel in the straw near a box of chicks. Jade closes the magazine and sets it on the table. She folds her arms over her chest and leans back in the hard plastic chair. "It was Eddie's fault."

Sirona frowns. "Everything was usually Eddie's fault. I hated that smarmy jerk."

I resist the urge to keep staring at the TV and instead scan the room, where all the women have turned to watch, some with their mouths slack. The two young sisters in the corner stop playing with their dolls, craning their necks to see. Our Youngers know they're not supposed to watch the thing Goji calls "Big Brother in a Box." Aura moves toward Jade, who scoops her into her lap. Moon looks at Sirona, begging with his eyes.

Sirona sighs. "Okay, just this once."

Moon climbs into the chair next to me and takes off his glasses. He hands them to Sirona, who huffs on them before wiping the smudged lenses on her skirt and handing them back.

I continue studying the room, how the nurse now has to call names twice before people hear them and how the women giggle like kids as they watch. The children stare wide-eyed, like those weird little velvet paintings I've seen at the flea market. Every once in a while I sneak a peek at the TV, where a boy scales a billboard with steam coming off a coffee cup. The sound is turned low so I don't hear much except the commercials, which blare louder than the show.

As I watch, Goji's reason for the assignment becomes clear. The TV has sucked the liveliness out of this room. It's like a giant magnet the way it keeps all eyes glued to the screen. Even the receptionist stops filing her folders and stares at the TV until a nurse rounds the corner and tells her to quit watching and get back to work.

I scribble notes as fast as I can so I won't forget anything. And so I can see how the show ends, even though Sirona already spoiled it. Sure enough, the fire department shows up and rescues the boy from the cup. His father waits below, looking worried, then relieved when his son is safely on the ground again.

The nurse reappears in the doorway that leads down a hall. She's holding a clipboard. "Judy? Judy Whitman?"

Sirona nudges Jade. "You're up."

It's weird seeing the Olders answer to names other than the ones I'm used to. I don't know all their old names but now I know one more. When Jade gets up and walks toward the nurse I say, "See you soon, Judy."

She wheels around and glares at me. Sirona starts going a mile a minute on her knitting, her needles clicking together like chattering teeth. Jade walks back and stands in front of my chair. "Don't ever call me that again."

"S-sorry," I say.

When she disappears down the hallway behind the nurse. I turn toward Sirona, who doesn't look up from her knitting. "Respect, little brother."

I pick up the magazine Jade was reading and stare at the cover. The people in the picture look like normal families I see in Freestone and Sebastopol and Santa Rosa. Boys who wear scout uniforms and girls playing hopscotch or jumping rope on the sidewalk in their neighborhoods. Families with dinner on the table and a TV in the corner of the living room. The kind of people who live in regular houses all lit up at night when we pass them on our way home from town.

I wonder what my first home looked like. Was it in the city? Did it have a fireplace? Did I have my own bedroom full of toys and books? I run my finger over the picture of the lady on the cover. She has neatly combed brown hair and she's wearing a necklace. Her name could be Judy. The father, with the bushy mustache, he looks like a Dan or a Steve. I'd name the red-headed boy in the blue uniform Doug, and the younger boy, Ricky. None of them are named Moon or Clover or Jade, I'm sure of that. And I'm betting they aren't sitting in a women's clinic waiting for their sister-mothers to get birth control.

On our drive home I apologize to Jade. "I'm sorry I called you Judy."

She turns in the front seat and tilts her head to one side, her mouth in a pout. "Do you understand why I was upset?"

"Not really. It's your name, right?"

"Judy is the name I was given twenty-eight years ago. I'm no longer that person. Just like you're no longer a baby in diapers."

"I'm sorry, Jade."

She smiles and reaches over the seat to pat my knee. "I know you are. Thank you."

We're almost home by the time I get the nerve up to ask.

"Do you know what my first name was? The one I was given when I was born?"

Jade twists the top half of her body to get a good look at me but I don't meet her eyes. "I don't, Blue. I don't think anyone knows. Does it matter?"

I shake my head no, but inside my head I'm saying yes.

I spend most of Sunday following Willow around, hoping for a moment alone with her. She's elbow deep in the worm bin when she turns and says, "What is it, Blue?"

"What do you mean?"

"I mean you've been like a shadow all day." She uses her hands to gently sift the composted dirt. I know she's trying not to squish any of the worms.

"Have I?"

She twitches her nose, then bends down. "Scratch my nose, will ya?"

I use my index finger to soothe the itch so she doesn't end up with worm poop on her face.

"Thanks. And yes, you have. You know you have."

I kick at the dirt with my heel. "I was just wondering . . . do you know what my name was when you, um, when I first got here? Before Goji named me?"

Willow freezes for a moment. Without turning, she says, "How would I know that?"

"Gaia told Rain that you're the one who brought me here."

Willow removes both arms from the worm compost and wipes them on her dirty bib overalls, her back still to me.

"Is it true?"

She turns, leaning back against the bin with her hands on the rim and nods. "Goji doesn't want us to talk about it."

"I just want to know my name."

"Blue . . ."

"My *real* one."

Willow worries the metal clasp on her overalls. "You know we could be arrested, right?"

I nod. I don't want any of my family to be punished and I don't ever want to lose them. But I don't understand why it's such a big secret. They must have adopted me because I was in danger. They were protecting me.

"Sorry. It was a stupid question."

When I turn to walk away Willow calls me back. "Wait. Look, this is just between you and me, okay?"

I wheel around. "Of course."

"Wave said he thought he heard a girl calling but we were pretty high, you know? He thought he heard a girl calling out the name Noah."

"Like the guy that built an ark?"

"Yeah." She smiles. "Like that guy."

"Where did you find me?"

"I shouldn't . . ." She closes her eyes as if searching the memory on her eyelids. "It was so long ago. We were near a small lake. There was a picnic area."

"Anything else you can remember?"

She opens her eyes. "Only how beautiful you were and how absolutely sure I was that you were destined to be with us."

"Do you still believe that?"

She tosses a long blond braid over her left shoulder. Her eyes glisten then bubble over with tears. She lets go of the worm bin and slides down until her butt hits the dirt. "I'm sorry, Blue. I'm so sorry. I believed with all my being that you were sent to me, my little Buddha child." She buries her face in her hands. "Once you were here it was too late."

"What do you mean? Too late for what?"

She holds her right arm out toward me. "We fell in love with you, so deeply in love with you. Goji assured us it was meant to be and I believe that." When I don't move closer she drops her arm and hangs her head. "But sometimes I have doubts. I lie awake at night and I wonder. . . ."

"Wonder what?"

Willow breaks down into heaving sobs and I feel terrible. But I have so many more questions. *Where did I come from? Why didn't they legally adopt me? Are my parents still alive?* Willow mentioned that Wave was with her. Maybe he'll open up. Or maybe Goji will finally have that talk with me.

I kneel beside Willow and touch her shoulder. "I'm sorry I upset you."

She widens her long fingers and peers through them at me. "I love you so much, Blue. I hope someday you can forgive me."

"I already do. You only did what you thought was right."

Willow throws her arms around me. Her sobs eventually ease but she never lets go. We sit that way until the dinner bell chimes three times, the signal that our evening meal is ready.

During dinner Goji keeps glancing from Willow to me back to Willow again. He's always so intuitive. Nothing gets by without him noticing. When sharing time arrives he asks us if there's anything we'd like to share with the group. Willow looks down at her lap. Harmony practically stares a hole in my left cheek waiting for me to say something.

"Willow accidentally crushed some worms while mixing compost," I finally say.

Willow lifts her head to meet my gaze.

"It was my fault. I startled her when she was working." Willow shakes her head just the tiniest bit.

I look at Goji and my thoughts flash to Gaia's letters, the secret that he's keeping from Harmony. I think about the way he constantly counsels Rain, leaving her doubting herself. Willow had to have been a teenager when I arrived at Saffron Freedom Community. Goji was the Older, the leader. He could have fixed it. He should have fixed it.

I keep the lie about the worms going. "It was probably their destiny, right?"

Willow bursts into tears. Wave throws his arm around her and squeezes. "I'm sure you didn't mean to kill them, sis. I know how gentle you are with those little guys."

Goji glances toward Willow, who buries her head in Wave's shoulder. He looks back at me, expressionless for what feels like an eternity. Finally, a smile breaks across his face and he nods. "There are no accidents, Blue. Everything happens for a reason."

"Everything?" Harmony asks.

"Everything," he says to her, still looking at me.

17

August 1977

Aura runs behind Coyote carrying a basket of wild berries in her chubby arms. She follows Coyote everywhere. Half the time he has Aura's little legs curled around his neck as he moves around the compound with her on his shoulders. She hangs on to his dreadlocks like reins, leaning this way and that as if they're two heads on one body. Coyote often has bits of food in his hair from her munching on apples or carrots while she floats around on his shoulders.

I help load the truck with summer squash, sweet corn, cucumbers, beans, and peas along with Rain's macramé hangers and Sirona's handmade soaps and candles. Willow sets her homemade pies in boxes and slides them onto the tailgate. I was hoping we'd get to eat them, but she's raising money for a yoga retreat that she and Wave hope to attend in Big Sur. She grabs my wrist when I try to break off a piece of the crust. Normally she'd scold me, but ever since our conversation at the worm bin, she's let the other sister-mothers take the lead when it comes to interacting with me.

Willow lets go of my hand. "Sorry, Blue. I'll make some for all of us next time."

When the truck is all loaded up, Coyote drives slowly over the bumps in the long driveway until we reach the roadside stand that Wave and some of the early family members built. A wooden awning swings out and props against the frame, exposing the counter. Along with the pies and homegrown veggies, we spread out bushels of apples gleaned from the wild trees growing in an abandoned orchard behind the redwood grove.

Jade walks off to drop a sign at the corner of the highway. Coyote pulls two stools out from under the counter. He props Aura on one and takes the other for himself. We line the counter with pint baskets of wild blackberries and Sirona's soaps and candles. I hang Willow's and Rain's macramé designs on hooks before placing handwritten sandwich board signs along the road several yards apart. By the time Jade returns, two cars have already pulled up to the stand, both regulars.

The preacher's wife, the one who picked up Stardust from SFC last January, buys a pie and some sweet corn. Her chubby husband waits in the car, fanning his sweaty face with a church bulletin. I help her carry her purchases back to the car. I can tell the preacher doesn't like us. He mutters something about heathens and "filthy lucre." His wife slams the trunk before propping the pie in her lap in the front seat. "We're all His children, Stanley." She turns and smiles at me through her open window. "You're getting to be such a handsome young man. What's your name, son?"

They've bought lots of stuff from us over the years, but she's never asked my name before today.

"Clover Blue."

The preacher rolls his eyes. "What did I tell you?"

She shushes him and points to Jade. "That's a beautiful name. Is that your mom over there?"

"No, ma'am." I blush. "I mean yes, ma'am."

"Well, which is it?"

My mouth suddenly feels too dry for words. She seems nice, but Goji has warned me not to talk to strangers about the family. He says most people don't understand authentic relationships due to cultural brainwashing.

"I . . . I have to go." I make a dash for the back of our stand.

Coyote peers down at me, crouching under the counter. "You okay, brother?"

"Yeah. It's just so hot and the shade under here feels good."

When I hear the car pull away I pop back up from under the counter. Coyote takes Aura into his lap and pats the empty stool. "Pull up a squat, Blue."

I sit on the stool, glad for the soft breeze. It's been over one hundred degrees more days than it hasn't this summer. Mrs. Fuller was so worried about us having heatstroke that she ran a couple hundred feet of hose from one of their livestock faucets to SFC. At first Goji politely refused her offer but then changed his mind after he saw all our faces go from glee to misery. I can't wait to get back to SFC for a real rushing cold shower.

The next customer is a middle-aged man wearing army clothes. Not the faded secondhand ones like some of the family wear. A crisp army uniform. He picks several items from the produce, filling a cardboard box with a carton of eggs, a pint of berries, and a half-dozen ears of sweet corn. He sets the box in front of Coyote.

"How much?"

Coyote scans his box. "Three bucks."

The man pulls a five from his wallet and lays it on the counter. Coyote shoves the bill in his jeans pocket. The army guy watches carefully as Coyote counts out two dollars and hands over the change.

"Thanks, man."

The army guy raises his head to meet Coyote's eyes. "You mean, 'Thank you, *sir*.'"

Coyote doesn't flinch. He's used to this kind of stuff. "Thank you, sir."

The man moves his gaze to the dog tags around Coyote's neck, the ones he got in boot camp before he went AWOL.

"You serve in Nam?"

Beads of sweat glow on Coyote's forehead. "No, sir. I was 4A, sir." He repositions Aura closer to him on his lap. "Flat feet."

The man's army cap falls off when he peeks over the counter to look at Coyote's bare feet. "Don't look flat to me."

I retrieve the hat and hand it to him. "Here you are, sir."

He takes the hat from me and dusts it off on his pants before resting it back on his crew cut. He starts to turn away, then wheels around and yanks the tags off Coyote's neck. "I don't know how you got those, boy, but they're only meant for soldiers." He spits on the ground. "Have some respect."

Coyote hands Aura over to me and slides off the stool to a stand. He's almost a full foot taller than the army guy. Jade hops off the back of the tailgate and runs up behind Coyote.

"Don't," she whispers, smoothing her hands over the back of his cotton shirt. "It's not worth it."

Coyote remains standing, his lips set firm, staring back at the army guy. Aura climbs out of my lap and onto the counter, facing the man. She reaches for his nose with her tiny hand and says, "Boop!" just like in the game Coyote often plays with her.

The man loses his staring contest with Coyote. He backs away from Aura like she's poison and gets in his car. Dust flies from his tires as he peels out, coating our fruits and vegetables with a fine brown layer of dirt.

I look at the dusty pies and pretend to be disappointed. "Guess we'll have to eat these."

Since all the produce is covered in dust we pack up early and head back home. Coyote asks Jade to drive. As soon as we reach the end of the driveway he bolts from the truck.

Harmony looks up from where she's working on her mosaic when Coyote runs past her. She sets a jagged piece of a former plate on the tabletop and makes her way to the truck to help unload our stuff.

"Why is everything so dirty?"

I blow the light layer of dust from a pie and pop a hunk of crust in my mouth, grinning. "Sometimes people try to ruin your day but they end up making it better."

Somebody drove into town and picked up a Slip 'N Slide and a plastic kiddie pool. Thanks to Mrs. Fuller's hose the entire family is sliding and sloshing and splashing around like a bunch of maniacs. Not that their behavior is unusual, only that it's unusual for us to waste a single drop of precious water that we used to carry in jugs from the natural spring. Even Coyote has joined in the fun, his gloomy face of earlier today replaced with wide-open laughter.

Harmony runs up to me and grabs my hand. Locks of wet hair stick to her cheeks.

"Blue! You have to try it!"

I dash toward the long yellow strip of wet plastic. Harmony jumps on the slide right behind me. My body spins in a full circle before I slam into Doobie in a pool of mud at the end of the slide. Harmony smacks into me, then Jade into her, before Goji plows into all of us, giggling like a little kid. By the time we've all taken a few more turns we're covered in mud. As we lie in an exhausted pile at the bottom of the slide I'm suddenly filled with so much happiness I can't contain it.

I look at Goji. "Thank you."

He smiles, his teeth bright white compared to his muddy face. "You see how each day teaches us, brother?"

I know I should answer but all I can think about is that this is the first time he hasn't put the word *little* in front of *brother*.

18

The welfare checks are mailed out on the first of every month. In the early years we refused any government help, but after Aura was born, Goji agreed to let Sirona and Jade apply for aid. His reasoning was that people who raise children to make a positive contribution to society deserve the support of the community.

We stop in at the Freestone Country Store on our way into Santa Rosa. Along with the welfare checks, gardening catalogs, and junk mail is an envelope with familiar handwriting that reeks of patchouli. Jade starts to slip the envelope into her pocket but it falls on the floor. Rain grabs it and reads the address. A big smile spreads across her face.

She holds the envelope toward Harmony. "It's for you. It's from your mom!"

Harmony stands frozen in place. Her eyes dart from the envelope to Rain and back to the envelope. After what seems like forever, Harmony snatches the envelope and shoves it into the back pocket of her jeans. Rain looks confused. Jade looks terrified. I've wondered how they managed to keep the letters from Harmony. It's obvious now that Goji has instructed the Olders to bring any letters from Gaia directly to him. Looks like he forgot to tell Rain.

I wait until we're back in the truck to check in with Harmony. "Don't you want to read it?"

"No."

"Well then can I read it?"

"No."

"Harmony . . ."

She slouches forward, resting her elbows on her knees and her chin in her hands. "Maybe later."

It's the last thing she says between Freestone and Santa Rosa. Jade and Rain are talking a mile a minute up front but the window separating us from the truck cab is closed. Between the sound of the road beneath me and Aura singing "Itsy Bitsy Spider" a million times over, a conversation would be nearly impossible anyway. But I can't take my eyes off the envelope sticking out of Harmony's back pocket and the messy return address in the corner, a post office box in Portland, Oregon.

When we arrive at Sears, Jade asks Rain to find us some new pillows. After a bout with head lice last winter we all had to throw out our bedding and start over. We bought blankets and sheets at the thrift store, but Sirona doesn't trust used pillows. She spent hours combing out the nits and treating all our heads with apple cider vinegar and lye soap, not just once, but three times, to finally get rid of the little buggers. We even had to shave Sunny. He looked like a skinny pig with his pink skin missing all that fur.

Jade hands Aura to Rain. "Take her with you, okay? I need to get some stuff from the hardware department." She turns to Harmony and me. "Here's the list from the others. Get as much of it as you can find and we'll all meet back here by the checkout."

Jade heads to the left and Rain takes Aura toward the right side of the store. I look over the list before handing it to Harmony. "Should we stay together or take half the list and split up?"

She glances at the paper. "I don't feel like shopping. Would you mind finding the stuff and I'll just check it off?"

"Okay, but I might need help with these." I point to the word *Kotex* on the list.

Harmony cracks a slight smile. "At least they're not using sphagnum moss anymore."

I wrinkle my nose. "Eww."

We ride the escalator to the second floor. Harmony leaps off before we get to the last step. She isn't afraid of much, but ever since she got her boot stuck in the escalator when she was seven, she hates the moving stairway. I fake like my shoe is stuck on the top step before climbing off.

Harmony punches me. "Not funny."

I rub my arm. "Sorry."

"Sorry I hit you so hard."

It doesn't take long to find most everything on the list. Back on the first floor, we throw all the items into a cart and start rolling toward the front of the store. Halfway there, a scream pierces the air. Rain is usually so quiet and reserved. Harmony and I glance at each other and tear off toward her voice. When we find her she's hysterical.

Rain races to meet us, her eyes wild. "I can't find Aura!"

Harmony pats Rain's arm. "Calm down, she has to be nearby."

"I lost her! I was supposed to be watching her!" Rain stops an elderly couple walking down the aisle between bins of bedding and bath towels. "Did you see a little girl? About three years old? Curly dark hair?"

The woman glances from Rain to Harmony and me. "I saw a little mulatto child backaways." She points toward the back of the store. "Near the plumbing department."

Rain takes off running. "Aura! Aura, where are you?"

We chase after Rain, trotting up and down the aisles until I spot our little sister at a bathroom display. She's sitting on a toilet, grinning.

Aura sees me and claps her hands together. "I pooped!"

Several shoppers have gathered around the display, some of them laughing, others tsking and shaking their heads. I can't help but snicker. Harmony totally loses it, falling to the floor and howling with laughter.

Rain flies around the corner. She throws her arms around Aura, sobbing. "It's okay! I've got you."

A store clerk with slicked-back hair juts his chin at Rain. "Miss, you're going to have to leave the store. We can't have children soiling the display." He points to the back of the toilet. "It's not hooked up to any plumbing, you realize that, right?"

Rain glares at the man. "She's a little girl! She wandered away and someone could have taken her. The last thing I'm worried about is your stupid display!" She grabs Aura, pulling up her little underpants and smothering her with kisses. "I'm sorry, sweetheart. You must have been so scared."

Aura isn't the one who looks scared. Rain's face has broken out in red blotches.

The greasy-haired clerk calls over a manager, a large woman with blueish hair wearing white nurse-type shoes. She eyes Rain and Aura. "Are you her mother?"

Rain shakes her head. "I'm her sister. I mean her aunt."

"Well, whichever it is you best keep a better eye on her."

This sets Rain off again. The crowd grows bigger as word of a kid shitting in the bathroom display passes through the aisles. Fortunately, Jade shows up after hearing the ruckus. When she tries to take Aura, she can't pry her out of Rain's arms. Aura starts crying, reaching for her mother.

A scowling older man in the crowd grabs his wife and pulls her toward the aisle. "What's this world coming to? That nigger lover raising her child like a jungle bunny, crapping in the store."

Jade is a small person, but when she's mad you'd best stay out of her way. She marches up to the hateful man and stands so her face is within inches of his chin. "Nigger lover? Why yes, I am. I love everyone, including ignorant bigots like you." She rests her hands on her hips and turns to face the other customers. "What's the matter with you people? Don't you have something better to do than upset my sister and my daughter?" She pulls Rain to her feet, then motions to Harmony and me. "Come on, kids. Get your cart."

The crowd parts as the five of us walk toward the front of the store. We're almost done checking out when Harmony runs back down the center aisle. "I forgot something," she calls behind her.

Jade pays for our stuff and turns to me. "Blue, wait for Harmony and meet us at the truck."

I know where I'll find her. I round the corner of the plumbing department just as Harmony zips up her jeans. She looks at the crabby store clerk and shrugs. "Sorry, I just couldn't hold it."

On the way home, Aura falls asleep in Rain's lap. Rain has stopped crying but every once in a while she does this hiccup-sniff thing, several short gasps, followed by a shudder.

Jade pats Rain's leg. "Don't be so hard on yourself."

"You trusted me and I let you down."

"No you didn't. If anything you proved your fierce loyalty to this family. I love you for that."

Rain looks up from Aura, whose sleepy face looks like a little lion cub. "Really?"

Jade shifts down to low gear as we pass the Fullers' house and turn down the bumpy two-track toward SFC. "Really."

* * *

I find Harmony hiding in the old teepee that the original members built in the early days of SFC. The outside has peace signs painted on it and the words *One Love*. It smells smoky and a little moldy. Gaia and Harmony lived in the teepee for a while, but when Gaia left, Harmony moved into the tree house with the rest of us. We've used it for a lot of things, including Aura's birthing room, but now we just store stuff inside. It's become a great hiding place when we're trying to dodge the Olders or need some space.

I stand just inside the flap opening. Harmony's cowboy boot sticks out from behind several boxes of rice and bags of beans.

"Okay if I come in?"

"I guess so."

I push aside an old rolled-up rug and sit next to her. She keeps turning the envelope over in her hand.

"Are you gonna read it?"

She hands me the letter. "You read it. You like her more than I do."

"*Love* her."

"Whatever."

I tear open the envelope, being careful not to destroy the return address. The letter is written on lined yellow paper in sloppy cursive loops with circles for dots over every *i*. A kidney-shaped splotch of coffee marks the bottom of the page. I start reading aloud:

"'Dear Annie Bananny Harmony Boo. I'm sorry it's been a while since my last letter.'"

Harmony snorts. "A while? Hah! Her last letter was four years ago. She wrote one time after she left to say she'd be back in a couple of weeks. I think the drugs have killed her brain cells."

I want so badly to tell her about Gaia's other letters, but I resist the urge. Goji and the Olders must have a good reason for keeping them from her. I take a deep breath and keep reading:

" 'I'm no longer traveling with The Dead. I met some really cool people who invited me to a Rainbow Gathering. These meetings happen all over, on national forest land where hippies like us share stories, dance, listen to music, and commune with nature. It's so beautiful! I think you'd love it. I can picture you dancing wildly like you did when you were a little girl.

" 'It was difficult to get a glimpse of you but not talk or spend any time together when I dropped in with the girl I picked up in Salinas. Is she still there? Has she told you her story?

" 'I understand how angry you must be with me for not coming back sooner and then showing up unannounced. The thing is, I know you love Saffron Freedom Community, and it wouldn't have been right to drag you all over the place with me these past four years. You hated it when we moved around all the time. I feel blessed to know that you are in a safe place with people who care about you.

" 'Hopefully you'll forgive me for not being a better mother. Maybe one day you'll realize I did what was best for you by leaving you there. I hope the money I've been sending has helped you get by.' "

Harmony leans over the page in my lap. "What money?" She grabs the envelope and turns it inside out. "There's no money in here. She's such a liar."

"Maybe she's been sending a little to Goji or the Olders to help cover your expenses?"

"Why wouldn't they tell me?"

I shrug, playing dumb, and go back to reading Gaia's letter.

" 'Anyway I hope you are happy and healthy. I promise I'll be back to visit soon. I have a very special gift for you! Please give everyone my love. I miss you so much. Love, Momma BoBomma Gaiaaroo' "

I hand the letter back to Harmony. She wads it into a ball

and tosses it where the fire pit used to be when she and Gaia lived in the teepee years ago. "What a crock of shit."

"It sounds like she might come back for another visit."

Harmony throws her head back and laughs. "You don't actually believe that, do you? She's gone for years, shows up for a few hours, then splits again."

"You made it pretty clear you didn't want her here."

"Well, she didn't try very hard to change my mind. Ruth only cares about Ruth."

"You said she was only seventeen when she had you. Maybe she was too young to do the mom thing right."

"Pfft. I'd be a better mother at thirteen than she is at thirty."

"Will you write her back?"

"Are you kidding?"

"Do you care if I write her?"

She looks at me like her heart just broke in half. "Of course I do. But I won't try to stop you."

I hate seeing her so sad. "Hey, Harmony, can you keep a secret?"

She jerks her head up and her eyes grow wide. Harmony loves secrets.

"Goji sneaks candy."

She slaps me on the leg. "No he doesn't."

"Yeah he does. He's apparently crazy for Zagnuts."

Harmony shakes her head. "No way! You're making this up to try to cheer me up."

"Saw it with my own eyes when Ziggy wandered off one night. I was afraid he'd get eaten by a coyote or bobcat so I brought him inside Goji's shack."

"You went in there by yourself without being invited?"

I nod.

"What took you so long to tell me?"

"I've been waiting for the right time."

In the distance the conch shell blows, signaling the call to

Aura's birthday celebration. Harmony leans back against burlap sacks of rice. "I'm not going."

"Aura will be really sad if you don't show up."

"I don't feel like a party."

"This isn't about you."

She wipes her eyes with the back of her arm and stands. "Fine. I'll go."

I wait for Harmony to walk ahead of me toward the circle that's already forming around our youngest sister. Aura is turning three, the same age I was when I first came to SFC. She claps her hands as we dance around her. Sirona hands her a teddy bear she hand sewed out of a fur coat she got from the thrift store. We had to throw away Aura's old bear during the lice invasion. Aura jumps up and down, hugging it to her chest. Coyote lifts her onto his shoulders and we all march behind them, singing and clapping.

Goji stands apart, leaning against a tree, waiting to be last. He sometimes does things to purposely show he's not the leader. He smiles at each of us as we parade by. When Rain is directly in front of him, Goji takes a step forward and hands her something. I lean over Rain's shoulder to get a look.

She turns the carving over in her hands. "It's an owl. Am I supposed to give it to Aura?"

I glance toward the tree where Goji stood just a minute ago. "I'm pretty sure he made it for you."

She blushes. "For me? But why? It's Aura's birthday, not mine."

"I think it's supposed to be a totem. Harmony and I learned about them last year."

"What does it mean?"

I hold out my hand and she drops the wooden bird in my palm. "An owl can mean different things. Some cultures see it as a bad omen."

"Oh no!"

"But it also represents wisdom and intuition. Maybe he's just trying to tell you he's watching out for you. He seems very protective."

"He does?"

I hand the owl back to her. "Yeah. He definitely does."

Rain smiles and cranes her neck toward the back of the line to try to meet Goji's gaze. "Thank you," she mouths.

Girls say boys are so blind but I swear it's the opposite.

19

October 1977

Coyote taps my leg as we begin my driving lesson. "Don't ride the clutch, Blue. Use the brake and wait until you're ready to shift."

I step on the brake. The engine lurches and kills.

"Well you got to use the clutch to shift down, just don't keep pressing on it when you're not using it."

I start the truck back up and shift into first gear. "I think it'd be easier to learn if we could go out on the road."

Coyote laughs. "Easier for who?" He points to a flat area in a warren near the woods. "Stop right over there."

This time I'm careful to shift down and push in the clutch before turning off the engine. Coyote takes the keys and starts to get out of the truck. "Good job."

"Wait a sec, Coyote. Can I ask you something?"

"Make it quick. The firewood isn't going to collect itself and I'm already hungry."

"I have a question about the army."

"The army? What about it?"

"Well, I was just wondering if you ever wish you didn't go AWOL. I mean wouldn't it have been easier to just do your stint and be done? Or turn yourself in and take the punishment now that the war is over?"

Coyote lets the truck door gently swing back closed. He looks me up and down while he chews a little on his lower lip. "You know we live in a bubble here, right? Things are crazy different out there in the real world. They sent all the brothers to Nam, put 'em on the front lines. Most of them came home in body bags. My 'stint,' as you call it, meant I'd have to kill people, you realize that?"

"It was a stupid question."

"No, it's not. You need to know this. That war was for the military industry. Most are. But the war against the black man is far from over. What they most want to take away from us is our dignity and our freedom."

I look away from Coyote and drop my head. "What if someone outside of here finds out about me?"

"What do you mean?"

"Like how I was adopted."

"That happened before I got here. All I heard was that Willow and Wave brought you here after you were abandoned by your parents."

"Did they say anything about who my parents were or where I came from?"

"No. I never asked. Figured it was none of my business." He nudges my arm. "You thinking of leaving?"

"I don't ever plan to leave. It would put everyone at risk. Especially you, being AWOL. I could never live with myself if anything bad happened to this family because of me."

He's quiet for a minute but finally says, "You can't let fear keep you from enjoying the freedom you deserve as a human being. Always remember you *can* leave. Don't let concern for someone else's actions become your prison."

"That sounds like something Goji would say."

"Well, I'm saying it now." He cranks open the handle and kicks the stuck door open. "Should we get to work?"

I fidget in my seat.

"Spit that other question out before you choke on it."

I feel my face flush.

"Blue, out with it."

"Umm, do you think Rain is pretty?"

Coyote breaks into a grin. "Ha! And here I thought you had a crush on Harmony."

I jerk my head toward him. "She's practically my sister!"

"They're all your sisters, Blue."

"I know. But I don't think about the others that way."

Coyote slaps me on the knee, still grinning. "Let's go work off some of those hormones."

When we get back to the compound the truck bed is nearly full of wood, mostly live oak and redwood branches. Rain crosses in front of us carrying a pail of chicken feed. Like an idiot, I immediately stall out the truck. Coyote snickers, trying to stifle a laugh. He motions toward Rain with his chin. "Why don't you go help your sister feed the chickens? I'm going to dump this wood in the meadow to chop up later."

I climb out of the truck. "I already promised Harmony I'd go hiking with her today."

He slides over into the driver's seat and restarts the engine. "Suit yourself."

Harmony stands behind the outhouse with her arms across her chest. "You're late. What took you so long?"

"Sorry. Coyote and I had to gather wood and then I helped Rain feed the chickens."

She rolls her eyes. "I'm sure she needed your help."

We start our hike along Salmon Creek. Moon wanted to come along but we bribed him with our portions of bread pudding to let us go without him. Harmony wants us to be alone so we can make a plan to sneak into Goji's shack to steal a candy bar. We've hiked the creek lots of times before, but this time we're walking in the opposite direction, toward town instead of away from it. We want to see how far we can go without running into people.

We've made it about a mile when Harmony stops. Sunny races into the water ahead of us, then tears up the bank before splashing back into the creek. I dig inside my pack and pour out some kibble I brought for Sunny and take out a sandwich for me. I hold out half toward Harmony. "You hungry?"

"Not really. I have a stomachache."

"Wanna take a break?"

Harmony nods and climbs up the bank ahead of me.

"Hey, did you cut yourself on that branch back there?"

She turns. "No. Why?"

I point to her leg, where a bead of blood is making a path from under her T-shirt to her knee. Harmony looks down and turns her leg outward. She wipes the blood away. "Ugh. I think I started my period. That explains the stomach cramps."

"Aren't you too young for that stuff?"

"I'm thirteen as of this month, same age as you. In case you haven't noticed, I'm getting boobs."

"Of course I noticed."

"You noticed my boobs?"

"Not like that. I mean, I noticed the changes. But I didn't pay much attention."

"So you don't notice Rain's boobs?"

"Stop it, Harmony."

I can tell she's enjoying this. I try to change the subject back to her problem. "You wanna head back so you can take care of that?"

She stands with her hands on her hips, thinking. I keep my gaze on her face so I don't have to see the blood on her leg.

"Nah. Can I have your bandana?"

I hand her my headband. She ties the long T-shirt between her legs like a one-piece swimsuit, tucking the bandana inside. I can't help but laugh. "Uh, you can keep that."

"Shut up." She parks herself on the bank, her knees to her chin, and curls her fingers over her toes. "Let's work on our secret plan. I overheard Goji say he's taking Rain to a Kirtan meditation or something next week. We could sneak into his shack then."

"I don't know, Harmony. What if we get caught?" I'm more worried about her finding the letters from Gaia than getting caught.

"We won't get caught."

I reach into my leather pack until my fingers find the tiny pocket Wave sewed into the side. The crayon-shaped lump is still there. I hold the joint toward Harmony. "Maybe this will help your cramps."

She takes it from me. "Whoa! Where'd you get this?"

"From Doobie. On my twelfth birthday. Remember?"

She laughs. "I can't believe you never lit it!"

"I was waiting for a special occasion. This seems like a good one."

Harmony turns the joint over in her fingers, then sniffs it. "You think it's still good?"

"It's an herb. I don't think they go bad, do they?"

She shrugs and hands the joint back to me. I fish around in my pack for matches and peel one off. I steady the flame under the end and watch as Harmony takes a puff.

"You have to hold it in," she says, in that weird choky voice, just like Doobie when he tries to talk without using any breath. She lets out a small cough, then blows a puff of smoke in my face. "Your turn."

"You act like you've done this before."

"I lived with Ruth, remember?"

"She let you toke?"

"No. But our room and our car would be so filled with smoke I *felt* like I was smoking it. I always got sleepy."

I take a pull on the joint and instantly my lungs feel like they're burning. I end up in a coughing fit that makes Harmony laugh so hard she rolls down the bank, nearly sliding into the creek. I take advantage of my hoarse throat to compete with my own best imitation of Doobie, squinting my eyes and shaking my head. "That's harsh, man."

Harmony climbs back up the bank and takes another toke. My throat feels so gross that I don't inhale my next puff, just hold it in my mouth for a while before blowing it out. I don't think she notices but if she does she's being kind. Normally she'd tease the crap out of me for being a wuss.

"Don't tell the others about my period, okay? They'll want to have a big party or some sort of womanhood celebration."

"You don't want a party?"

"Not for this."

"Okay. It'll be our secret."

Harmony hops back down to the creek and wades in. She looks up at me, grinning. I slide down the bank and join her in the cold water.

We never make it to town. Backtracking our way to SFC along the creek, we pick wild blackberries along the way, filling our bellies. I don't feel high. Maybe pot doesn't work on me. But Harmony has been giggling all afternoon and claims her cramps are better. She laughs when I poke myself on a thorn. She laughs when she trips and lands on her butt in the creek. She laughs for no reason, like she's got an inside joke going in her head.

"What's so funny?"

"Nothing." She snickers again. "Everything."

When we reach the hill behind the tree house, Harmony suggests we raid Goji's shack.

"Now?"

"I want one of those candy bars!"

"Bad idea. We'll get caught. You need to trust me on this one."

We stop under a tree, not wanting to end what feels like a perfect day. Harmony lays her hand on my cheek, studying my face the way she does before she starts making a drawing. Her bloodshot eyes crinkle at the corners when she smiles. "I trust you, Blue." She keeps staring until it starts feeling awkward. I gently pull her hand away and lead her over the hill. She trips and we tumble down the last few yards. She lands with her head in my lap at the bottom of the hill. Her laughs turn to giggles, then to quiet breathing.

"Harmony?"

She doesn't budge, even when Sunny licks her face. I think about waking her, but knowing Harmony, she'll get us into trouble for being stoned. This seems like as good a place as any for her to sleep it off. Sunny settles in next to me, panting. I lean back on my elbows and watch Harmony breathe. She looks so peaceful, like one of the Youngers when they fall asleep in the car. I feel suddenly protective of her. I wish I'd never seen Gaia's letters. There's gotta be a way to convince her not to raid Goji's shack.

20

November 1977

Rain and I take a break under a willow after cleaning out the coop and replacing the straw in the nesting boxes. It's hard to believe it's been over a year since she arrived. In that time, she's slowly become more like the rest of us here, less like the fresh-faced girl who stood sobbing on my twelfth birthday. Rain's favorite chores are with the animals: milking the goats, gathering eggs, and brushing the burs out of Sunny's fur. She eagerly soaks up Goji's teachings over their long, private walks. They even spend time alone in his shack, something pretty much no one else does. I'm envious of her time with Goji but I'm also jealous of him for the time he gets to spend with Rain.

"I think I'll make some tea," Rain says as she twists her hair into a loose knot on top of her head. "You want some?"

"Sure."

I stand and offer my hand but I'm distracted by the sound of a car in our driveway. This isn't our usual town day. I glance to where our truck and the station wagon are parked near the garden before spotting a black and white car slowly creeping up

the drive, followed by a dark green one. Whenever we see a police car or a cop while we're out and about, I feel a small ripple
of panic run through the family. But out here on our private
property, we mostly feel safe.

My first thought is that someone has vandalized the fruit
stand again. When I turn back toward Rain she's crawling into
the chicken coop, sending a bunch of squawking hens scattering out the door.

I poke my head inside the coop. "Rain?"

"Shhh!"

"What are you doing in there?"

"They might be looking for me."

"Why? Did you do something bad?"

"I ran away from home."

"But you're an adult. You can do anything you want."

She doesn't move. "I fibbed so Goji wouldn't send me away.
I won't be eighteen until next month." She grabs my arm.
"Please don't tell anyone."

I crawl into the coop and crouch beside her. "I won't. Besides, I'm the one who's supposed to hide."

"You? How come?"

"It's a long story."

We hear a commotion near the center of the community.
Through the tiny henhouse window I spot a local cop and another man in a military uniform talking with Sirona. She shakes
her head when they point toward Coyote splitting a pile of
wood near the edge of the woods. The men push Sirona aside
and walk toward our brother, calling out an unfamiliar name.

"Duane? Duane Jackson?"

Coyote stops chopping and slowly raises his head. It's November, but he's been working in the sun and has stripped
down to just his boots. Sweat glistens on his chest.

The cop draws his gun from the holster and aims it at Coyote.
"Drop the axe!"

Rain pushes her head next to mine and gasps, then coughs,

breathing in the dust kicked up by the scattering chickens. With our cheeks pressed together, we watch Jade run toward Coyote, her long braid bouncing behind her. The cop turns the gun toward Jade, then back to Coyote. Jade throws her arms around Coyote's waist. He drops the axe and wraps his arms around her.

The military guy draws his gun, too, and points it at Coyote. He takes a step forward, dangling a set of dog tags in his left hand. "These yours, Private Jackson?"

Coyote looks down at Jade and kisses the top of her head. Even from this distance we can see her body trembling with sobs. Coyote raises his hands and locks them behind his head. Jade drops to the ground crying, clinging to his leg as he surrenders. The cop quickly handcuffs Coyote's hands behind his back while the other man keeps his gun trained on our brother. When they lead him away, Sirona and Wave run to Jade and blanket her with their bodies.

Willow drops the sheet she was hanging on the clothesline and chases after Coyote, screaming, "No! No, you can't take him!"

The cop wheels around. "Stop right there, lady, or I'll arrest you, too."

Wave has already caught up with Willow. He touches her elbow. "Let him go, sis."

Goji emerges from his shack. The cops size him up as he and Coyote stare at each other for a long moment before Goji raises his hands in a prayer mudra in front of his face and bows. Coyote's hands are cuffed behind his back but he dips his head. The man in the green uniform drapes a blanket around Coyote's naked body and lowers him into the back of the military police vehicle.

As they turn and drive down the dirt driveway, Harmony rounds the corner of the field near the Czech's pasture. She's pulling Aura in a rusty wagon. Moon trudges along behind, poking the air with a stick like an imaginary sword. Sunny runs circles around all of them. When Harmony sees Coyote she drops the wagon handle and runs behind the car, trying to bang on the trunk and make them stop.

I crawl out of the coop and race toward her, catching up just as both cars reach the road. Coyote turns toward us and throws a peace sign as they make a right turn onto Bohemian Highway. Panting, I grab Harmony from the back to stop her from chasing the car farther down the road. She turns and throws her arms around me, sobbing.

When Goji steps lightly behind us, Harmony raises her head and stares at him with reddened eyes. She jerks away from me. "Why?" she chokes out. "Why did you let them take him?"

"Every choice has a consequence, little sister."

She starts beating his bare chest with her fists. "You didn't fight for him! You're supposed to protect us!"

Goji doesn't move, barely flinches with each fist landing on him. I happen to know Harmony packs a mean wallop even when she's kidding, and I'm sure some of those have got to hurt. But he just stares into her eyes until she tires herself out.

Goji rests his hands on Harmony's shoulders. "Coyote is still here." He gestures toward the trees above us, the meadow, and the communal living space. He moves his hand to her heart. "And here."

Harmony crumbles to the ground and breaks into sobs. I rush to her side. I want to be strong for her but my heart feels broken, too. When Goji walks away I wrap my arms around her, holding her until we're both exhausted from crying.

Nobody has much of an appetite at dinner. Goji sets The Book on the table and looks around at all our faces, most with reddened eyes.

"Perhaps we could use this time to share stories and our favorite things about Coyote."

Sirona, who sits to Goji's right, is the first to speak. "The first time I saw him I thought, 'Oh my God, it's Otis Redding.' He not only looks like him, he has that smooth, sexy voice." She looks across the table toward Jade. "He'll be back. I just know he'll be back."

Jade nods, her chin trembling.

Willow tells a story of how she once followed Coyote to see where he went after dark. "I just couldn't figure it out, why he'd leave his warm bed to walk around in the middle of the night. I lost him, of course, and I was about to turn back when I heard him." Her voice breaks. "He was talking to his mama. Sitting on a log over by the fire pit, as if she were right there with him."

Harmony leans forward. "What did he say?"

Willow smiles at Harmony with watery eyes. "He was just telling her about his day. It was the sweetest thing."

Jade says through tears, "His mother died pretty young."

Wave comforts Jade, gently rubbing her back. "That reminds me of this one time we were at the veggie stand together and this woman stopped by with a carload of kids and a screaming baby in her arms. Coyote offered to hold the baby so she could buy the stuff she wanted. At first she hesitated, but then she handed the kid to him and I'll be damned if that baby didn't immediately stop crying. Coyote cooed and sang as if he'd gentled babies all his life. By the time that lady paid for her items, the baby was sound asleep in Coyote's arms."

When it's my turn I can only think of what Coyote said last month during our driving lesson. "He told me what he most fears is losing his dignity and his freedom. I know I'm supposed to talk about a good memory but this is what sticks in my mind." I look toward Goji. "They won't take that from him, will they?"

Goji's eyes look tired. He waits a long time to answer. Finally, he says, "There's a beat between what happens to us and our reaction to it. Inside that tiny beat, we have the opportunity to consciously choose how we're going to react. Coyote's response to whatever they do with him is the key to his freedom and I think he understands that. Just like how we've chosen to celebrate our love for him instead of wallowing in grief."

He makes it sound like you can't do both, celebrate someone and be sad that the person is gone. I'm not ready to let go of my grief. But Goji's words are a comfort.

"You mean like free will?"

Goji breaks into a sad smile. "Exactly. Coyote is the author of his life, just as we all are." He nods at Moon. "Your turn, little brother."

Moon tells about the book Coyote gave him called *The Snowy Day*. It used to be one of Coyote's favorites when he was a boy, living in Chicago. Harmony is next. She tears a page out of her sketchbook and passes it around. It's her drawing of Coyote dragging on a joint with smoke curled around his face. We're all silent while everyone takes a turn holding Harmony's sketch. When it comes back around she quietly tucks it into The Book without a word.

"Aren't you going to say anything?" Moon asks her.

"I think she just did," Goji says, smiling at Harmony.

Doobie says he'll never forget the time he and Coyote did mescaline together and Doobie was convinced that they had exchanged bodies. "I was all freaked out and Coyote was like, aw, you're beautiful, man. I looked at Coyote and I said, 'Yeah, but now you're me and you're ugly,' and we both started laughing so long and hard I thought I was gonna piss myself. My sides hurt for days. Best trip I've ever had."

Rain is seated next to the empty place where Coyote usually sits. She looks down at the chair and fights back tears, which everyone knows is a battle for her. "My first day here, everything was so, I don't know, *different.* I was scared. Coyote sat here on the other side of me. My hand was shaking so bad the food kept falling off the fork. He put his hand over mine and held it. He said, 'It's cool, sister. Everyone here is your friend.' His words calmed me down. I'll never forget that."

Jade smiles, her eyes still leaking tears. "I remember that. I remember feeling a little jealous and worried that he'd fall in love with this beautiful young girl who'd shown up. But that's always the way it is with Coyote. He loves everyone and everyone loves him. He can act like a badass when he wants to but he's one of the gentlest people I've ever known. It's why he deserted. I think he would have laid himself down in front of the enemy before killing anyone."

Sniffles and soft crying erupt around the table. Goji closes The Book and stands. "Shall we close the circle?"

We move to the fire pit, where Wave lights a candle and sets it on a stump. He reaches for Willow's hand on one side and mine on the other. The rest of us grasp each other's hands in turn.

Goji tilts his head toward the sky. "Coyote has left our home, but he has not left us. Let us send him our blessing and thank him for touching our lives with his spirit. Thank you, Coyote."

We lift our connected arms in unison. "Thank you, Coyote."

When Jade starts sobbing, Wave begins to hum "No Woman No Cry," one of Coyote's favorite songs. We all join in, singing. I imagine Coyote dancing in the middle of the circle. The love I see and feel toward Coyote from everyone is so powerful that I start to believe the words that everything actually is going to be all right.

21

Mrs. Fuller rolls up the driveway in her old man's Buick while I'm taking a speedy winter shower. I quickly turn away and cover my waist with a towel. Our neighbor strides past me, ducking under the canopy where it droops between two poles, to where Jade and Sirona are standing in the kitchen. The sister-mothers' eyebrows lift in surprise as Mrs. Fuller yanks open a couple of drawers before finding a spoon hanging from a hook above the woodstove. She starts stirring their steaming pot of soup. Mrs. Fuller has never helped with meals, let alone acted like it was her own kitchen.

I move closer and stand just within earshot to eavesdrop. Sirona sidles up next to Mrs. Fuller. "You okay, Lois?"

Mrs. Fuller keeps stirring. She takes a sip of the broth from the spoon. "Where's the salt?"

Jade moves to her other side, looking concerned. "Hey, what's going on?"

I creep closer toward the kitchen, tightening my towel at my waist, and listen in.

Mrs. Fuller shakes some salt into her hand, then drops it in the pot. "I want to help. That's how it works, right? Everyone does their bit. We all work together."

Jade touches the older woman's arm. "Well, of course, but you don't need to help. If you're hungry we're happy to feed you."

Mrs. Fuller stops stirring and bursts into tears. "I've envied you all for years. So free and so full of love and, well, just such a beautiful family. I want to be a part of it."

The sister-mothers circle their arms around Mrs. Fuller's waist. Sirona rests her head on the older woman's shoulder. "Oh, hon. What about your family? Your husband?"

Mrs. Fuller wipes her eyes with the sleeve of her sweater. "I don't have any kids and my family lives on the East Coast. I married Charlie when I was only twenty. Shortly afterward, his parents died in a car accident so we moved here to run the family farm. Then they took my classroom away and closed the school. I want to go back to college and get my art degree but Charlie thinks I'm being ridiculous."

Harmony sneaks up behind me and puts her hands over my eyes. "Guess who?" When I reach up to pull her hands away my towel falls off. Mrs. Fuller hears the commotion and turns toward us. I feel my face go hot. Harmony and I both lurch to pick up my towel. She hands it to me and winks before joining the women in the kitchen.

"Hey, Mrs. Fuller! What are you doing here?"

Mrs. Fuller drops her head over the soup pot so Harmony doesn't see her tears. "Oh, I'm just helping the girls cook dinner. How're those charcoal sketches coming along? Did you try the shadowing technique I showed you?"

"I did and it's so cool! What about you? Have you started painting again?"

Mrs. Fuller shakes her head. "Not yet. But go look in the backseat of my car. I brought some things."

Harmony motions for me to follow her. I step back into my jeans and throw on a flannel shirt. We peek through the car windows to find the seats filled with canvases, an easel, boxes of paints and brushes.

"She wants to move here," I whisper.

Harmony spins around to look at me. "She what?"

"I heard her tell Jade and Sirona. I think she's leaving her husband."

"Wow. Why would she do that? They have such a nice house and all that land."

"She wants to go back to college to study art. Her husband won't let her."

Harmony peers over my shoulder toward the kitchen. "That's so messed up. Do you think Goji will let her stay?"

"I don't know. He's pretty particular about accepting new members. She doesn't exactly fit the profile for SFC."

"What profile?"

"You know. Hippies. Yogis. Philosophers. And then there's the age range. She's gotta be almost fifty."

Harmony frowns. "Lois is exactly the kind of person Saffron Freedom Community needs. She's friendly, creative, and she knows all about homesteading. Doobie said she even smokes pot."

"Maybe. But I feel kind of sorry for her husband."

"Not me. I feel sorry for her. She's obviously oppressed." Harmony gathers up the art supplies and drops them into a grocery sack she finds in the backseat. She points to the wooden easel. "Help me with that, will ya?" She turns to walk back toward the women.

I drop the three-legged frame over my shoulder and follow her. In the distance, Goji and Rain walk toward the woods. Harmony juts her chin in their direction. "That's getting a little creepy. He's got to be twice her age."

I watch Rain and Goji disappear into the trees. "Maybe it's just a learning session."

"Right. I have a pretty good idea what he's teaching her."

"Harmony!"

She rolls her eyes. "You're so naïve." We start down the path but Harmony stops and whirls around. "Wait, Blue! This is our chance to get some candy!"

"In broad daylight? No way."

"The sisters are busy with Mrs. Fuller. Willow and Wave took the kids into town to shop for supplies."

"I don't know. . . ."

She empties out her bag under a tree. "Fine. Just tell me where they are and I'll get them myself."

I was hoping she'd forgotten about it. I still haven't gotten up the nerve to tell her about Gaia's letters. I don't have the heart to hurt her.

Maybe it's better if she just finds them herself. I glance toward Goji's shack. "In his desk drawer. Right side."

She grins. "I'll be right back. Whistle if you see someone coming."

"Okay, but hurry up."

She dashes up the path and disappears behind the blanket that hangs over the doorway. I lean on the easel like a crutch under my arm and wait.

It's taking Harmony forever and I'm starting to regret letting her go in there. By now she's either sobbing over the letters she's found or she's breaking stuff. I hear a cough and follow the sound to where Doobie is sitting on the ground behind the shack. I whistle a Hermit Thrush imitation, mine and Harmony's secret alarm signal.

Doobie turns toward the sound and waves before I have time to hide. He jumps to his feet and walks toward me, dusting the back of his pants. Harmony flies out of the shack and runs smack-dab into Doobie, nearly toppling both of them.

"Whoa, sis! Hey, what're you guys up to?"

She glances in my direction. "Nothing. We . . . we were just looking for Goji."

He grins. "He and his old lady went for a stroll."

I frown. "Rain's not his old lady."

"Whatever you say, brother." Doobie slides a joint from behind his ear. When he pulls a lighter from his pants pocket, a Zagnut wrapper floats to the ground. He grins. "Busted!"

Harmony frowns at the wrapper. "Where'd you get that candy bar?"

"Same place you were hoping to find one." He lights the joint and offers it to me.

I shake my head. "No thanks."

"Suit yourself." He hands the joint to Harmony, who takes a puff and hands it back. Doobie sucks in a long drag and holds it. He pinches it off and tucks the roach into the top pocket of his shirt. He drops the peace sign and walks up the path toward where Mrs. Fuller and the sister-mothers are now hunched together at the community table.

Harmony sighs. "I have some bad news."

I brace myself for the worst.

"No candy. I looked in every drawer."

"*Every* drawer?"

"Yeah. He must have eaten them. Or maybe Doobie did."

"Did you find anything else?"

"Like what?"

"I don't know. Anything cool or interesting?"

Harmony gets quiet and just stares at me without saying anything. She turns away and crouches in front of the tree to refill the paper bag with the art supplies. "We'll try again later."

"Why?"

"Maybe he moved them to a different hiding place."

I can tell she's getting off on sneaking behind Goji's back. As we walk back toward the community table I keep glancing at her bag. Maybe she hid Gaia's letters in there. Maybe she thinks I didn't see them when I was snooping and doesn't want me to know she stole them. Maybe she's just waiting until after she reads them to tell me. Or maybe she knows I betrayed her and she's planning to pummel me with the easel when I'm asleep.

Over dinner Mrs. Fuller states her case for wanting to join SFC.

"Look, I know I'm a lot older than all of you, but I've been every age you are." She turns toward Goji, who listens thoughtfully. "Every time I set foot in this community it feels like coming home to that idealistic version of myself, the dreams I lost somewhere along the way."

Goji leans forward, resting his elbows on the table and his chin on his hands. "You are like a flower, opening. So very beautiful. I think we should call you Lotus instead of Lois."

Harmony can't contain herself. "I vote yes!"

Goji laughs. "Well, it looks like one of us has initiated a poll." He glances to his left, at Sirona.

She smiles. "Yes."

"Yes," Wave agrees, turning to me. Harmony nudges my side with her elbow.

"Ouch. I mean yes."

Four more yesses until Goji's turn. He looks directly at Mrs. Fuller. "How about we just take it one day at a time?"

Mrs. Fuller nods. "I won't change my mind, but sure, I can do that."

Goji smiles. "Welcome, Lotus."

"Welcome, Lotus," we repeat.

Aura tugs on Jade's sleeve. "Can she sleep in our bed?"

Wave clears his throat. "Actually, Willow and I have been meaning to ask if we could take over the old teepee. Maybe Lotus could have our room."

Everyone looks toward Goji for his reaction. He doesn't hesitate. "It'd be good to have more people on the ground, another set of ears, just in case. ... ." He turns toward me. "While we're on the subject, maybe someone should take Coyote's place with Clover Blue."

Doobie raises his hand, looking at me. "It would be an honor to share a room with you, brother. If you'll have me."

I'm unsure what to say. On the one hand, it's nice having a room to myself but I do miss Coyote's presence, even though he slept there only half the night.

When Doobie sees me pause, his smile disappears. "It's okay, man. I know Coyote's shoes are hard to fill."

"No, no. I think it'd be great."

"Yeah?"

"Yeah, of course, Doob."

Goji looks at Mrs. Fuller, who's been soaking up every word like a sponge. "Perhaps you'd like to share Willow and Wave's room with Harmony? Our little artist would do well to have a mentor by her side."

Harmony pumps her fist. "Yes!" When she sees Rain's confused look she lowers her hand. "Wait. What about Rain?"

Goji smiles at Rain. "A young woman needs her privacy."

Rain blushes. "Thank you," she says.

Goji leans forward, addressing our neighbor. "This is how Saffron Freedom Community works, Lotus. We are each notes of a symphony. And we're pleased you're joining our little orchestra."

Lotus folds her hands in her lap. "Thanks, all of you, from the bottom of my heart. I promise I'll do my best to prove my worth here."

Sirona slurps a spoon of soup and groans happily. "This soup is a good start."

As we're getting ready for evening meditation, a truck speeds down the driveway and skids to a stop at the gate. A chubby man with graying temples gets out and stares at us over the driver's-side door.

Doobie walks toward the man. "Can I help you?"

The man ignores Doobie and shouts past him, "Lois, have

you lost your mind? Get your things and come home this instant."

Mrs. Fuller doesn't answer him.

"Lois, please. For the love of God."

Doobie tells Mr. Fuller to relax. "I'm sorry, man. I feel your pain. But maybe wait a couple days while you both cool down, ya know?"

When he doesn't answer, Doobie returns to the group and sits on the ground next to Mrs. Fuller. He whispers, "You okay?"

She shocks us all when she crosses her legs, propping one foot on her thigh. "I'm fine."

"Wow, man. You're pretty flexible for . . ."

"For an old lady?"

"No, no I didn't mean that. I just didn't expect you to be so limber."

She pats Doobie on the knee. "Believe it or not I do stretches every day. And I've studied Transcendental Meditation."

Goji smiles at this. "Are we ready to begin?"

We all close our eyes. I peek over toward the gate, where Mr. Fuller's sad face looks like a kid who just dropped his ice cream cone. He gets back in the truck and pulls the door closed. I think for sure he's going to punch it and burn rubber on the way out but he doesn't. The truck slowly moves down the driveway and out of sight.

22

Sirona drops the four of us Youngers at the library while she runs errands. Moon and Aura run to the children's section and snuggle into an overstuffed chair. In his wire-rimmed glasses, Moon looks like a smaller version of Wave, right down to the long bangs that fall over his eyes. Every once in a while he swings his head to one side, flipping the hair out of the way before it falls back over his glasses again as he reads to Aura.

We're not supposed to think of any particular family member as the son or daughter or a specific person. The whole idea of SFC is freedom from those kinds of social norms. But it's natural to sense their connection when you see Aura and Coyote together. And if you stand Moon next to Wave, he's basically a smaller version with a few of Sirona's freckles thrown in.

"You guys stay here," Harmony says. "Blue and I need to study."

Harmony and I delve into our projects. Since moving into SFC, Lotus has become Harmony's personal art mentor. She wants Harmony to learn about famous artists along with studying technique. Over the years we've both learned quite a bit about art history but Harmony is hungry for more. The librarians love helping her find the big bulky books filled with pictures of paintings, etchings, and sculptures.

Harmony points to a photo of a dark-eyed woman in her book. "I really want to go to art school someday. I'm going to be like Frida Kahlo."

I lean over her book. "You're going to grow a mustache?"

Harmony shoves me but I can tell she's trying not to laugh. "Shut up, Blue. She was a brilliant artist."

"Wasn't she married to that Mexican painter?"

"Yup. Diego Rivera. Look here; it says they lived in separate houses that were connected to each other."

I snicker. "Huh. Maybe that's why Goji lives in his own shack."

"Maybe it's the other way around. Maybe the sister-mothers wanted their own space and that's why he lives alone."

I raise my eyebrows. "Maybe . . ."

"Well, I love the idea. If I ever settle down I'm just going to live next door to my old man instead of with him." She glances over at my notebook. "What're you working on?"

"Goji wants me to learn about how Catholic priests colonized Native Indians."

"Why?"

"Because I asked him which religion is the truest one."

She laughs. "Big mistake."

"It's actually kind of crazy how the religion spread. It says here that there're over twenty Spanish missions in California."

"I remember visiting one once with Ruth. It felt like being in the Wild West. I think it was named San something."

I stifle a laugh. "I'm pretty sure they all start with San. San means saint."

Harmony opens her next book and pretends to be absorbed in a painting.

"I didn't mean you're dumb or anything."

She ignores me.

I stand up. "Okay, well I'm going back to my own house now."
Harmony smacks me on the leg. "Cut it out."

"Kidding. Sirona said the reference librarian might be able to find articles on something called microfish."

Harmony bursts out laughing. "It's pronounced micro*fiche* not microfish."

I feel my cheeks blush hot as I slide out of my chair next to her at the varnished wooden table. I head to the reference desk, where a new young librarian directs me to the film cabinet. The drawers are listed by years and publications. Rows and rows of envelopes line every drawer, each envelope containing a plastic film card. I carry my list of missions to cross-reference the area, looking for local newspapers starting with the *San Francisco Chronicle* and working my way down to the *Los Angeles Times* and the *San Diego Union Tribune*. I take a couple film cards from the middle including one each from San Luis Obispo and Santa Barbara newspapers.

I love this machine. I've probably spent an hour spinning the slides, zooming, and printing articles about the missions. Curiosity about their history is overtaken by my interest in the architecture. My favorite mission is the one in San Miguel, just north of a town called Paso Robles. Compared to the photos of current cathedrals, these little buildings all seem plain and understated. I pull up more photos and print them out. Not just for me, but because I think Harmony might like to draw them.

I drop the cards in a basket for the librarian to refile and start to carry the printed papers back toward my sister. Halfway there the thought hits me like a rock. I stop at a huge California map on the wall and trace the roads until I find Freestone. Remembering Willow's words, I look for lakes near the center of the coastal region. Lopez Lake. Santa Margarita Lake. Lake Nacimiento. Atascadero Lake. These are the only bodies of water anywhere near Highway 101 that Willow and Wave would have driven past on their way back from Santa Barbara that day.

My heart pounds in my chest as I retrace my steps. I find the card for the *San Luis Obispo Telegram-Tribune* dated 1967–1968 and slide the film under the lens. I scroll through the dates until I reach August 12, 1967. Nothing about a missing child. Most of the stories feature the upcoming county fair. I move to the following day, August 13.

As soon as I see the tiny picture on the third page in I know it's me. Under the photograph of the smiling boy is the name Noah Michael Anderson. The headline reads: "CHILD GOES MISS-ING AT ATASCADERO RECREATION AREA, PRESUMED DROWNED."

Beneath the title it says, "A search party was called but the child has not been found. Police ask anyone with information to contact them." The story describes how the family was at-tending a church picnic when their little boy wandered away from the group. I zoom to the next page. A smaller headline, further in, reads, "DIVERS SEARCH FOR TODDLER'S BODY." I scan the next few days and find one more story: "BOY'S BODY POSSI-BLY TAKEN BY COYOTES." The last article includes a photo of Howard and Delores Anderson staring blankly into the cam-era. Howard and Delores. *My parents.*

They look tired. And sad.

My hands tremble as I hit the print button and watch the pa-pers slowly inch out of the machine, facedown, one on top of the other.

"The library's closing."

I nearly jump clear out of my seat at the sound of Harmony's voice behind me.

"Sorry. I didn't mean to startle you. Didn't realize you were so engrossed in . . ." She leans over my shoulder to read. I grab the film card and stuff it back in the envelope.

"Yeah, the stories are pretty interesting." My hand is sweat-ing so badly the envelope nearly slides out of my fingers.

"Right on. I'm sure one of the Olders will bring us back to the library again so you can finish your research."

"Yeah, no big deal."

She points to the slot on the side of the machine. "Don't forget your papers."

I pull the pages off the tray and shove them inside the book I'm checking out.

She narrows her gaze. "You okay?"

"I'm fine. Just tired from squinting at all that fine print."

She reaches for my book. "I'll check our stuff out while you get Moon and Aura."

I pull the book away. "I've got it."

Harmony throws up her hands. "Sheesh. You don't have to be so crabby about it."

"Sorry. I just want to be sure I get an extended checkout on this one in case I need more time."

"Fine. I'll collect the Youngers. Sirona's probably already waiting in the parking lot."

"Okay, I'll meet you out there."

As soon as she's out of sight I fold the papers and slip them inside my jeans pocket. I return the microfiche and walk toward the front doors, three words swimming over and over in my head.

They kidnapped me!

It's all I can do to keep it together over dinner. I have so many questions. Goji has always told me that being here at SFC was my destiny. But how does a three-year-old purposely get himself lost and wander into the arms of a couple of tripping yogis? There must be more to the story. There has to be.

I stare at the flowers in the middle of the table, trying my best to act normal. Mr. Fuller leaves a bouquet at the gate every day for Lotus. Tonight it's red roses. Wave told Mr. Fuller to "be the honey instead of the bee" if he wants her back. Mr. Fuller has obviously taken Wave's advice to heart. I know it's selfish, but I'm hoping he fails. Lotus is the wise and gentle Older I didn't know we were missing.

Lotus passes a huge bowl of brown rice to Goji. "You should teach classes," she says to him.

Unlike the rest of the family, Lotus doesn't get stars in her eyes when she's around Goji. She listens intently but she never loses herself to him like the others do, especially the women.

Goji waves off the idea with a swipe of his hand. "Saffron Freedom Community attracts those who are looking for freedom and individuality. You are the perfect example. I have no desire to try to convert the world."

"But people need to be exposed to the spiritual connection between humans and nature like you've created here. They're not going to find it at a PTA meeting."

Willow scoops a mound of rice onto her plate. The muscles in her long arms bulge as she balances the bowl; the same arms that probably carried me to Wave's van that day at Atascadero Lake.

She smiles at Lotus. "You mean like an ashram for the community?"

"Maybe. Or just offer classes through community education. I think people would be really interested."

Goji slowly chews his food before responding. "We're already a spiritual community. You can call it an ashram or a commune or some other name, but I'm not interested in being anyone's guru." He turns to Lotus. "Thank you for your affirmation, sister. I don't care to call more public attention to our family. The reason we've been together for so long is because we've created a safe haven undisturbed by prurient curiosity in our open lifestyle. We don't need people showing up with stars in their eyes, hoping for a panacea to fix all their problems."

Lotus nods. "I understand. Maybe you could write a book of essays on various topics instead. You could publish under an alias if you don't want to attract attention."

I wait for Doobie to pass the veggie stir-fry. He definitely has stars in his eyes. Not for Goji but for Lotus. He hangs on to her every word. Wave finally taps him on the shoulder to get his attention. "Oh, sorry man. Here you go, Blue."

The conversation moves to our studies when Goji asks about my research at the library earlier. My heart beats so hard I'm convinced everyone can hear it thumping like a drum against my chest.

"I learned that Catholic priests monitored the American Indians and extinguished their languages."

Goji nods. "It's true. Many tribes no longer have members that speak the native tongue. It's lost forever."

Rain's mouth turns into a pout. "That's so sad."

Goji pats her hand in the way you would a kitten and turns back to me. "I look forward to reading your essay, Clover Blue."

I feed most of my dinner to Sunny, who always waits under the table for one of us to drop a scrap of food. The printed newspaper articles are practically burning a hole in my pocket. I just want to go hide somewhere in private where I can read them again.

Goji stands and carries his plate toward the dishpan. "Let's have a fire tonight. These winter evenings are getting so cool."

I help Doobie start the fire, but when Wave asks me to play a song I shake my head. "My throat's a little dry. You go ahead."

Sirona rushes toward the kitchen, probably to make tea to soothe my throat. Goji drapes a wool blanket around Rain's shoulders, rubbing her back with his hand to warm her. Rain smiles, little flames reflected in her blue eyes. Harmony sits next to me on a log, leaning against my shoulder for warmth. Her hair smells good, like the outdoors has planted itself in every strand. I never get tired of smelling her hair.

"You're shaking," she whispers.

"Yeah, it's pretty cold."

Wave sings a Harry Chapin tune, his newest favorite. All the Chapin songs are stories. This one is about a little boy who changes schools and his new teacher makes him paint flowers in perfect rows of red and green instead of all the colors the boy loves. The song brushes against a growing sadness that I've felt ever since reading the newspaper stories about my disappearance. I take a sip of the tea Sirona made and swallow the cry in my throat.

Harmony nudges me. "You wanna go for a walk?"

"No thanks. I think I'll go to bed early. I might be coming down with a cold or something."

"Can I walk with you to the tree house?"

"Sure."

As soon as we're out of earshot of the others she pulls me to a stop. "What's going on with you? You haven't been yourself since we were at the library this afternoon."

It's nearly impossible to hide anything from Harmony, but I try. "Nothing's going on."

She dips her chin and purses her lips. "If you say so."

"I say so."

I head up the ladder to my bedroom. Now that Doobie has moved in, I rarely have any privacy. I need to be back for evening meditation so I only have a few minutes to myself. I carefully unfold the papers to read the articles more thoroughly.

> Pastor Reed was quoted as saying that a sibling lost track of the toddler, who was last seen playing in the sand between the lake and the nearby woods. Witnesses report that it was a very busy day at the lake with temps hovering in the high nineties. While there is no evidence of foul play, police have not ruled it out.

I run my finger over the word *sibling*, again and again. Seeing the photo of the three-year-old me I suddenly feel caught between two worlds. In the past I've tried to brush aside my curiosity about finding my former parents. Over the years I've accepted living here as a gift, reminding myself how lucky I am to be surrounded by people I love and who love me. I belong here but maybe I belong there, too. Or maybe I don't belong anywhere. Maybe everyone who once knew me has long forgotten Noah Michael Anderson.

"Blue?"

It's too late to hide the papers and it wouldn't do any good anyway. She's already seen me crying over them. I don't say a word as she picks up the wrinkled pages and reads. When she looks up, her eyes overflow with love. She hands me the blurred copy of the little boy's photo.

"Is that . . . is this you?"

I nod. "I think so."

"I thought you said you were adopted by SFC?"

"I was. After Willow and Wave brought me here."

Still gripping the newspaper articles, Harmony looks out my window, toward the others sitting around the fire. "You mean *took* you here."

"Apparently Wave and Willow were tripping on 'shrooms. Willow thought I was sent to her or something. After they brought me here Goji declared that I was seeking them. That I was meant to be here."

Harmony crawls on the bed and faces me, sitting on her feet. "What are you going to do?"

I gather up the papers and stuff them in one of my books. "Nothing."

"Nothing?"

"I can't. If anyone finds out what happened, everyone here will go to prison."

"Everyone?"

"Except maybe Rain, since she doesn't know. And Lotus, of course. I'm not sure how much Sirona or Coyote knows since I was already living here when they joined."

Harmony crosses her arms across her chest. "I'm too young to go to prison."

"That's the thing. They'd probably take you and Moon and Aura, put you all in foster care. I can't have that on my conscience."

"But your parents! What about your parents? Don't they deserve to know you're alive? And your sisters or brothers?"

When I don't answer, she grabs my knees and says, "Blue, look at me."

I raise my head and look into Harmony's face. For the first time I see her for the wise human being she's become instead of the little girl I grew up with.

"I can't, Harmony. I can't lose you. Or them. Or any of this. I love you all so much."

"But aren't you even a little angry? They *stole* you. It's not right!"

"Of course I'm angry. But that doesn't change how much I love them. They were only a few years older than we are now. And they were tripping."

"That's not an excuse."

"I know. But I can't. . . ." I gather up the papers and slide them under my pillow. "I just can't."

The light burns out on my headlamp and we're left with a small beam of moonlight gently lighting my tiny room. Harmony leans forward and kisses me on the cheek. It feels different, this kiss, different from the hundreds that have gone before.

"I understand," she whispers. "But it's still messed up."

We climb down the ladder and head toward the meditation circle. I don't need to tell her to keep this between us. I already know she'll protect my secret like she protects everything that's dear to her, fiercely and with the loyalty of a faithful warrior.

23

January 1978

Sirona sold us on the idea of building a sauna. She says it will detoxify us from all the pollution we breathe but can't see. We built it with boards from the Czech's old barn that blew down and paneled the inside with cedar. My job is to help gather rocks for the wood-burning heater. Our property is peppered with rocks so they're not hard to find. What's hard is wheelbarrowing them back. If I load too many, the tire goes flat and I have to refill it with the bike pump. It feels like I've already made a hundred trips. I'm sweating so bad you'd think I just came out of a sauna.

I'm glad winter is here. Not just for relief from overheating but because I don't feel as comfortable being naked around the others as I used to. I've noticed that Harmony has started covering herself with a towel when she finishes a shower, so it's not just me. I don't get how the other guys can walk around naked all the time around naked women without getting boners. I guess you grow out of it. I hope I grow out of it before summer gets here again.

Wave laughs from the roof of the sauna when I accidentally tip the wheelbarrow too far to one side and the whole pile of rocks tumbles out on the ground. "I think we've got enough, Blue. How about you come up here and help me with the shingles?"

I climb the ladder and join him up top. "What do you think of this sauna idea, Wave?"

"I like it. You know we used to have a sweat lodge back in the early days."

"What's a sweat lodge?"

"It's kind of like a tent with a dirt floor and a pile of rocks near the door. We brought hot rocks inside with a shovel and ladled water over them to create steam."

"Just so you could sweat?"

Wave carefully lays a shingle, overlapping the one above it. "Sweating was a by-product but it wasn't why we did it. The lodge was more of a spiritual thing. We chanted and prayed inside."

"Didn't it stink in there with all those sweaty people?"

Wave points to a pile of shingles next to the ladder. "Give me one of those, will ya?"

I peel off a shingle and hand it to him.

"I imagine if I walked into a sweat lodge in the middle of a sweat it might stink, but when you're in it, I mean really *in* it, you're not focused on smells."

"What are you focused on?"

He smiles. "Connecting with everyone. Connecting with yourself. Getting that hot is a transcendent experience. Sometimes I hallucinated or had visions."

"Were you stoned?"

"Occasionally. But the deepest experiences I had in the lodge, the memorable ones, were when I was completely straight."

I hand him another shingle. "Can I ask you something, Wave?"

He presses the shingle into place and sits back on his haunches. "Sure you can, brother."

"What's it like to be stoned?"

He laughs. "You still haven't gotten high?"

"I tried but it didn't work."

Wave grins. "It feels happy. Peaceful. Introspective. Sometimes it takes a few attempts."

"Can I ask you something else?"

He nods. "Go ahead."

"What was it like back then, when there were more people here?"

Wave shakes his head slowly. "It was crazy, man. So many drugs. A lot of sex. Complete chaos. Goji wanted this to be a spiritual community but it got out of hand. People kept showing up that didn't line up with his ideals. He was very welcoming and open-minded and always gave others the benefit of the doubt. But when people started OD'ing and stealing shit from each other, getting all jealous and not sharing the workload, he finally gave them an ultimatum. Most of them split. Some started a new community a little farther north. I heard it only lasted about six months."

"How did you and Willow get together when there were so many people back then?"

"Willow was really into yoga. She was always doing all these crazy-hard poses. I was still healing from the shark bite and she told me that yoga would speed up the process. The more she shared, the more I wanted to learn. I guess you could say we connected on our mutual interest in yoga but it was more than that. We just clicked."

"Are you still in love with her?"

Wave sets down his hammer. "Still? I will always love her. Love isn't something you fall into. It just is. I love everyone here."

"Yeah, but it's different between men and women, right?"

"If you're talking about intimacy, then yes, it's different for sure. But that's just one way of expressing love for another human being."

He slides another shingle into place and tacks it in. I try to picture what he might have looked like ten years ago, when he and Willow brought me to SFC. He would have been the about the same age as Rain is now. I can't imagine her taking someone else's kid. I pick up the hammer and fondle the handle, tap it lightly against my other palm. A kernel of anger lodges in my chest and swells. I love Wave, and yet after reading those articles I feel like I don't really know people as much as I think.

As if he can read my mind he keeps talking. "Willow can't have kids, you know that, right? She got pregnant when she was a teen and ran away from home. She had an abortion and they botched it."

I set the hammer down gently between us. "Is that why she, why you and Willow brought me here that day?"

He lets out a sad sigh. "We were tripping on mushrooms. She convinced me that you were her unborn child and that you'd come to reunite with her. You were about the age her baby would have been if she'd carried it to term."

I feel the blood run out of my head, making me a little dizzy. I don't know what to say. I want to stay mad, but after hearing about Willow's botched abortion the acid in the back of my throat loses some of its bitterness.

The dinner bell rings, interrupting our conversation. Wave unties his nail apron. "You hungry, Blue?"

Food is the last thing on my mind right now, but I'm relieved not to have to spend any more time in my mind. As we walk toward the kitchen he drops an arm over my shoulder and squeezes my arm. "I was young and stoned and neither of those things are a good excuse. I want to tell you I regret it, but I don't, not really. I love you, brother. I can't imagine my life, *our* lives, without you in it."

Doobie thinks I'm sleeping when he tiptoes out of our room after midnight. I wait until he's down the ladder before peeking out the window. He walks toward the center of the community. I assume he's got the munchies and he's going to raid the kitchen. Through the holes in the blurry plastic sheeting over my window opening, I spot Lotus walking toward him. They exchange a long hug and sit on a log near the fire pit. A match glows bright before the familiar scent of pot drifts through the air and into the branches of our tree. I hear them giggling and talking softly. Lotus hangs on Doobie's arm as they stand and stroll toward the Sacred Space.

I lie back on my mattress and think about how I'll tell Harmony tomorrow, the way her mischievous eyes will light up when I share this juicy secret.

Hours later Doobie trips over my shoes and falls on my bed, waking me from a deep sleep. "Sorry, man!"

"It's okay. I shouldn't have left my shoes there."

I wait for him to get up and climb into his hammock but he doesn't move. He smells like sweat and tree leaves with a layer of skunky marijuana. His breaths come deeper and I know he's asleep. Unlike Coyote, Doobie doesn't snore but sometimes he moans. I never know if he's in pain or just having a bad dream.

Doobie turns and curls into a ball on his side. I can't see his face but I can feel him smiling. As I drift back off I realize this secret isn't going anywhere. Not even to Harmony.

24

Doobie seems more like his usual self, grinning all through morning yoga. Lotus looks different, too. Her dark hair that's usually pulled into a bun or clipped at the back of her head now falls in bushy waves over her shoulders. Streaks of silver line the strands closest to her face. Her eyes have a sleepy look but she doesn't seem tired. More relaxed, maybe. During the final savasana pose the two of them interlace their fingers at the edges of their straw mats. Looks like this thing with Doobie and Lotus won't stay a secret for very long.

As we gather around the breakfast table, Sirona whispers in Goji's ear. I assume they're about to make an announcement about the new couple in our midst. Goji pulls his wool cap lower over his ears against the cold. Puffs of steam follow the words out of his mouth.

"Sirona has suggested we go on a family outing tomorrow night to watch a double feature at the drive-in."

Lotus immediately brightens. "What a lovely idea! You know I haven't been to a drive-in since Charlie and I were dating." Her smile disappears for a moment but she quickly finds it again. "What's playing?"

Sirona tousles Moon's hair playfully. *"Pete's Dragon."* Moon's eyes grow wider. He loves books about dragons. "The second movie is *Up in Smoke*."

Wave chuckles. "The Cheech and Chong flick?"

Jade puts a finger to her lips. "I'm sure the Youngers will be asleep by the time the second feature starts."

Goji plucks a glob of oatmeal from his beard, examines it, then pops it into his mouth. "Sounds like we have a plan. Do we have enough reserve funds for all of us to go?"

Sirona frowns. "The kitty is a little dry. We just bought a bunch of warm coats and hats."

"Let me treat," Lotus says. "I'm eating food that you all planted and worked and harvested before I got here. It's the least I can do."

I love the way Lotus rushes in with help when we need it. She's given Harmony more confidence in herself as an artist and encourages Wave to get back out there and surf. After she read some of my short stories she urged me to submit them to magazines.

Sirona hugs Lotus. "That's so generous of you!"

Rain raises her hand, as if she were sitting at a school desk.

Goji smiles sweetly. "You don't need permission to speak, sister."

She folds her hands in her lap. "What about the animals? That's a long time to be away."

Doobie pats Rain on the back. "I'm sure they'll be fine for a few hours, sis."

Rain starts to raise her hand again, then lowers it back down. "May I stay here? I don't really like the cold, but I love the animals."

Sirona shakes her head. "You can't stay here by yourself, hon. It wouldn't be safe."

Goji clears his throat. "I think it's best if I stay behind with Rain. I need to work on some writing anyway."

Harmony kicks me under the table. I kick her back and mouth "I know."

"I also have an announcement." Jade looks at Harmony and smiles. "Our little maiden has become a woman."

Harmony jerks her head toward me, her cheeks burning red with anger or embarrassment, I'm not sure which. "You told! You promised not to tell!" She pushes away from the table and runs off before anyone can stop her.

"It wasn't Blue! He didn't say anything!" Jade calls behind her. "I'm sorry, Harmony!"

Jade slaps her hands on both sides of her face and drops her head. "I found blood in her sheets. I thought it was a happy thing. I even made her a cake." She lifts her head and looks at me. "Please go tell her I'm sorry."

I glance toward Goji, who nods. I slip out of my seat and head in the direction she ran, carrying a piece of carrot cake and the knowledge that it'll probably end up being eaten by whatever critters are nearby when she flings it. I find her in a small clearing surrounded by a group of redwoods, their branches like women's skirts ruffling in the breeze. When she sees me coming she turns her back to me.

"I didn't tell them, Harmony."

"Then how did they know? You were the only person who knew."

"Jade found blood on your sheets."

She snorts angrily and wheels around. "It's nobody's business. Why do they have to make such a big deal out of stuff like this? It should be private."

I shrug. "Not much is private, here. You know that. We're a family."

"Well, it would be nice to have *some* privacy once in a while, you know?"

"Yeah, I know. But Jade had good intentions. She feels really bad for upsetting you."

Harmony spies the dish in my hand. "Is that cake?"

I grin. "Carrot cake."

We take a few steps toward each other, me hesitant, knowing how unpredictable and stubborn Harmony can be. When she reaches for the cake, I brace myself. She shoves most of it in her mouth and chews dramatically. "Oohh. It's really good." When I laugh, she grinds what's left of the cake in my face, pushing it into my mouth. "What do you think?"

I wipe a bit of frosting off my cheek and pop my finger into my mouth. "Yum."

Harmony leans forward and licks my face. "You missed some." She holds her head right next to mine. I feel her breath on my cheek and I don't know whether to back up or stay still.

After a long, awkward moment she pulls away and stares at me. The corners of her mouth break into a wide smile. "I'm not a maiden anymore," she says, mocking Jade. She twirls around, clutching an invisible gown. "Look at me, I'm a woman! A queen! I'm a fucking goddess now simply because I can have babies."

I watch her quietly, being careful not to smile because I'm not sure if she's serious or just making fun. I think about Willow as a pregnant teen, not much older than Harmony and I, and how scared she must have been.

When Harmony sees my frown, she drops her hands. "Come on, Blue. I'm just kidding."

"Oh, good. For a minute there . . ."

She tilts her head toward one shoulder and grins. "We girls need our secrets."

"Maybe. Seems like for such an open community we actually do have a lot of secrets."

"Like the way Goji spends so much time with Rain, following her around like a sneaky cat? And don't think I don't see the way you look at her."

"I do not."

Harmony looks off toward the main compound and narrows her eyes, as if she can see Rain in the distance. "She's really pretty. I wonder what her secrets are?"

Other than the fib about her age, Rain seems pretty much like an open book. "Probably not many."

"She writes in a diary every day, did you know that?"

"You didn't . . ."

"Of course not. I would never invade someone's privacy like that."

"I know. You're a good sister."

She throws her arm around my back as we walk back toward SFC. "I'm a good *friend*."

We all spend most of what's left of the morning and early afternoon focused on chores before packing the truck for our group adventure. Doobie and Wave lift the camper off the truck so we can sit in the back of the truck to watch the movie. Lotus, Jade, Sirona, and Willow cram into the cab. The rest of us climb in back with snacks and bags of popcorn. We're layered in winter coats and scarves and snuggled under piles of blankets. Sirona's old truck crawls down the driveway, six heads bouncing around the back as we drive over ruts left from recent storms.

Rain and Goji wave at us from the gate. Aura tries to climb out of Harmony's lap when she sees them. "Stop! Wait for Wain!"

Harmony pulls Aura back into her lap and snuggles her. "Rain's staying behind to look after the animals." Harmony winks at me. "And Goji is staying to look after Rain!" Wave and Doobie laugh at Harmony's remark but I don't think it's funny.

We head east toward Santa Rosa and the Star-Vue Drive-In. Sirona drives slow enough so we don't all freeze but not fast enough for the cars that honk before whizzing past us. Fortunately, it's a pretty warm day for January. We arrive early and we're first in line, waiting for the gate to open. Lotus and the sister-mothers join us in the back for an impromptu picnic. We're just finishing up our sandwiches when a tiny man not much taller than Moon walks up to take our money.

Lotus pulls a billfold out of her purse. "How much?"

"One dollar for kids twelve and under, three dollars a head for the rest." Lotus counts out twenty-six dollars and hands it to the man. He steps on the tailgate and studies the pile of blankets. "You aren't hiding anyone in there, are you?"

Lotus laughs. "I don't think we could fit another body back here if we tried."

The man doesn't even smile. He steps on the bumper and lifts the corner of a blanket to reveal ten pairs of legs. "Park next to a speaker and don't forget to turn your lights off." He hops down and moves to the car behind us.

Sirona backs into a center spot, two rows from the front. Over the next half hour, one by one we're surrounded by dozens and dozens of cars full of moms and dads with excited kids in flannel pajamas, and young couples on dates. Doobie and Lotus wrap themselves in a wool blanket. Willow and Wave do the same. Sirona pulls Moon into her lap.

"I'm cold," Jade says. "We're moving up to the cab. She takes Aura, who stands backward on the seat to watch the movie.

Harmony snuggles in close to me as the pictures light up the huge screen. "This is the best thing ever," she says.

Moon hushes her. "Shh! It's starting."

About an hour into the movie the blankets start to feel damp and the screen is getting harder to see. The sound on the little speaker is clear but we have to kind of guess what's on the screen through the fog. An announcement comes through the speakers telling us that anyone who leaves will get a free pass for another night.

Sirona looks around the truck bed at the rest of us. "Shall we try again some other time?"

Moon kicks at the blankets. "No! I don't want to go!"

As always, we take a vote. Either everyone wants to stay or nobody has the heart to disappoint Moon. We end up listening to the movie we can no longer see. By the time the credits roll, most of the cars have already left. The ones that remain have more fog on the inside than outside.

We pull back into our driveway a couple hours earlier than expected, since we didn't stay for the Cheech and Chong movie. Sirona switches off the headlights so we don't wake Goji or Rain. We creep slowly past Goji's lightless shack. The whole place is eerily dark and quiet except for a tiny flicker of light dancing across the canvas ceiling of the Sacred Space.

Willow's hand goes to her mouth. "Uh-oh."

Doobie snickers. "While the cat's away . . ."

I crane my neck in the direction of the Sacred Space. "It might not be what it looks like."

Harmony laughs and slaps me on the leg. "Oh, come on, Blue. I doubt they're doing yoga in there."

Lotus shushes us. "They're adults, people. Let them be."

We park at the far end of the community, beyond the tree house by the lean-to filled with stacks of cut wood. Sirona shuts off the engine. A sliver of a moon hangs directly above us. An owl hoots from the edge of the woods.

Moon and Aura have fallen asleep in the cab, their heads clunked together like a couple of drunks. Jade lifts Aura from the front seat. Moon wakes and rubs his eyes, knocking the glasses from his face. Sirona tucks them into her coat pocket. "Time for bed, little man." She takes his hand and leads him toward the tree house. Sirona glances back at the rest of us, who are all looking toward the Sacred Space. "Come on, you guys. It's late. And it's none of our business."

Nobody misses morning salutation. Usually at least one of us oversleeps or chooses to skip out but not today. I'm pretty sure I know why.

Goji calls Rain to the front of our group. "I think it's time we let our sister Rain lead us in greeting this beautiful morning."

Rain reluctantly trades places with Goji and slowly tiptoes to the edge of his mat. With her palms together, she takes a long breath. She looks at us, glowing, beautiful as always.

"Don't be shy!" Sirona says. "We all had our first time."

As soon as it's out of her mouth Sirona gasps. Jade laughs and Rain blushes, her chin dipping to her chest. She peeks out from behind a curtain of white-blond hair toward Goji.

He nods, smiling. "Go ahead, love."

Rain finishes another slow, deep breath, then lifts her hands over her head before leaning into a forward bend. We all follow along with her. One by one we move through the poses together, breathing in unison. There's a sort of reverence among us that I haven't experienced since the early years. Even Harmony, who almost always makes a joke, and Doobie, who is often the first to laugh at Harmony's jokes, are completely silent.

We finish in mountain pose, pausing an extra beat before the sister-mothers gather around Rain, praising her with quiet hugs and long stares into her aqua-blue eyes. As they lead her toward the kitchen to start breakfast, Rain glances back at Goji. I know that look. We all know that look.

25

Wave looks nervous but happy as he ties a surfboard to the roof of the truck camper. Lotus talked him into going surfing and we're all coming along to cheer him on. The sister-mothers packed a huge picnic lunch. Sirona gave Moon and Aura pans and spoons to make a sandcastle. I'm bringing a Frisbee I got at a yard sale the last time we were in Sebastopol.

With the camper attached there's not much fresh air so it's hot and stuffy in the back of the truck. My leg keeps sticking to Harmony's leg. She leans over and tugs at a blond hair below my knee.

"Whoa, you're getting furry."

I pull my leg away.

She crosses her bare leg over one knee to inspect her own leg. "At least yours are blond. I'm getting brown ones. I hope I don't end up looking like a gorilla." Harmony grabs my hand and puts it on her leg. "See?"

None of the women at SFC shave so I'm used to being around

hairy legs. The downy hairs are barely noticeable against Harmony's tan skin. Her leg feels smooth to me.

She knocks my hand away. "That tickles."

I spend the rest of the ride trying not to look at Harmony's legs. Fortunately, it doesn't take long to get to Bodega Bay. As soon as we're parked, everyone but Wave runs down to the ocean while he changes into his wetsuit. We wade into the chilly water at the edge of the breaking surf. I carry Aura on my shoulders to keep her dry. Sunny races into the water, barking at the waves as they chase him back to the beach.

With his board under one arm, Wave slowly walks toward us. He stops when he reaches the water. Willow zips up the back of his wetsuit and kisses him on the neck. He smiles, but it's a lukewarm smile. Lotus puts a hand on his shoulder and tries to make eye contact with him. "Stare your fears straight in the face. Otherwise they'll own you the rest of your life."

Wave barely nods, just keeps looking straight out to sea, as if frozen in place.

"You've got this, brother," Goji says. "And we've got you."

Goji's words seem to be the thing that trips the switch. Wave takes off his glasses and hands them to Willow before racing into the surf. He lays on the board, paddling like he's on his way to the other side of the ocean. A few other surfers bob in the water on either side of him. When the next big one rolls in, he paddles to match the speed of the wave and jumps up to surf position. He wobbles unsteadily before the board shoots out from under him and up into the air.

Moon shields his eyes with his hand. "Where'd he go?"

It feels like forever before Wave pops up and swims toward his board. He paddles out beyond the break again. He gets turned around just in time and then he's on his feet again as another big wave comes in. We all hold our breath as the hump of water builds and builds. But this time he stays upright, catching the curl of water at just the right moment. He sails toward us with his arms to his side, tipping this way and that as he glides toward the shore.

We all let out our breaths in a collective "whoo-hoo!" as he triumphantly punches the air with his fist. He runs toward us and shakes his hair out like a wet dog. The sun catches the droplets on his tanned face and his bright white teeth glow when he grins. He wraps his arms around Willow and Lotus. The rest of us throw our arms around the three of them. He kisses Willow, then turns to Lotus and kisses her, too. Her grin is almost as big as his.

Wave breaks the hug and races back toward the water like he's being chased. We watch him take a few more spills and catch a couple of good rides. After a bit, Moon and I walk farther up the shore to look for shells together. Along with some smaller shells and a couple of polished pieces of sea glass, I find a sand dollar completely intact. I wrap it in a bandana and tuck it into my shorts pocket.

Sirona waves to us from where the others have spread out a blanket and filled it with food. We gorge ourselves on apples, nuts, and peanut butter sandwiches, then spread out lazily in the sand. The water is still too cold to swim in without a wet-suit. Harmony is wearing a bikini she bought at the thrift store. It's weird how seeing girls in bathing suits is more of a turn-on than seeing naked people all these years. I roll onto my belly to avoid embarrassment.

Harmony kicks at my leg with her bare foot. "Let's go build a sand castle."

"Maybe in a bit," I say.

She frowns. "Why are you being such a dud?"

I just shrug.

"Be that way." She walks off with the pans and spoons. I prop my chin in my hands and watch Moon and Aura chase Sunny up and down the beach at the water's edge. Harmony scoops sand into the pans and dumps it out in a circle of humps.

The Youngers drop next to her, patting the pan-shaped lumps into smooth mounds.

When he's finally tired out Wave takes a break from surfing to join us. He stands at the edge of the blanket, dripping water all over us, and plunges his board into the sand like a tall tombstone. "I'm starving!"

Sirona jumps up and wraps her arms around Wave. "I'm so proud of you!"

Willow throws Sirona an odd look, but Sirona doesn't see it. Wave definitely sees it. He squats next to Willow and kisses her on the neck. She hands him a sandwich and he wolfs it down, then takes off running back toward the ocean with the surfboard under his arm.

Willow watches him disappear in the water. "I think we've created a monster.

Lotus winks at her. "I think we killed the monster."

By the time we load into the truck to go home, the sun has baked most of us into burnt toast. Harmony's brown hair looks a shade lighter against her tanned face and the humidity from being at the ocean has made it wavier. Her mom claimed to be one-eighth Cherokee. Harmony definitely looks like she could be an Indian princess.

Harmony catches me staring. "What are you thinking about?"

"Just stuff."

"Good stuff or bad stuff?"

I grin. "All good."

Willow cooks a celebratory curry with rice and flat bread. Everybody seems especially happy tonight. Maybe it's the exciting day at the beach or maybe it's just one of those days when everything feels right. Whatever the reason, the whole family is in a really good mood. As we mop up the last of our curry with the bread, Goji rings a small bell, signaling a special announcement. Everyone falls silent.

"My beautiful brothers and sisters," he starts. "I need for you to open your ears and your hearts. I've spent a lot of time meditating on this and I believe it's time to heal a wound that has prevented our family from experiencing wholeness." He looks from face to face, with a pained smile. "I've been communicating with our sister Gaia. She sincerely desires to heal this deep wound, and so do I. She's requested a visit to Saffron Freedom Community."

Harmony stiffens next to me as Goji makes eye contact with Willow to start the voting.

"Yes," Willow says after a long moment.

"Several more yesses echo around the table. When Goji gets to Lotus she says, "I always liked that girl." She turns to Harmony. "Your mom used to remind me a little of myself at that age."

Goji looks at me. "Yes," I say. He turns to face Harmony, who, just moments ago was laughing so hard she nearly choked on her tea. Now her mouth is set firm, her eyes unblinking.

"Beloved sister, I know that you have suffered the pain of abandonment, but it is suffering that cracks us open so that we can let in the light. I beg you, please, help this family heal."

I expect Harmony to dart from the table and make for the woods or the tree house, but she stays put. And then she shocks us all by slowly nodding her head. "Okay," she says.

Goji smiles. "Okay?"

She nods again. Half the others wipe tears from their eyes. I'm one of them. I grab Harmony's hand under the table and squeeze it. She doesn't squeeze back but she doesn't let go either.

Goji hands Lotus a slip of paper with numbers on it. "Do you think Charlie would let you use the phone to call our lost sister?"

26

When we stop to pick up the mail in Freestone, our box is jammed full. Sirona hands Lotus a fancy envelope with familiar handwriting. Mr. Fuller stopped coming around after seeing Lotus and Doobie holding hands by the fire pit about a month after she moved in. I thought he'd given up but he's taken his efforts to win Lotus back to the next level. His new tack has been to entice Lotus with tickets to plays and art shows that he mails to our P.O. box.

Sirona leans over Lotus's shoulder. "What is it this time?"

Lotus opens the envelope. "A catalog of art classes at Berkeley." She slides an extra sheet of paper from inside the brochure. "And an enrollment application."

"You should apply!"

Lotus shoves the envelope in her purse. "Don't be silly. I'm too old to get into the program."

Sirona touches Lotus's arm. "No you're not. You of all people should know that. How many times have you encouraged every one of us to follow our dreams?"

"Bah! I've made peace with not going back to school." But as soon as Sirona looks away Lotus disappears down the dairy aisle of the Freestone Country Store to read the catalog more thoroughly.

Sirona thumbs through the rest of the mail pile. "Mostly junk. Let's go."

The store owner calls after us. "Wait, there's a package for one of you. I couldn't fit it in your slot." She bends over behind the counter to retrieve a box. She reads the label, then smiles at Harmony. "It's for you, sweetie."

Harmony stares at the box without changing her expression. The store lady shakes it at her. It makes a jingly sound. "Well, here, aren't you going to take it?"

Harmony snatches the box and heads to the car, letting the screen door bang behind her. I chase after Harmony and join her in the backseat of the station wagon.

"I'm not opening it," she says before I can ask.

"Can I?"

She doesn't answer.

"Okay," I say. "Whenever you're ready."

The minute we pull in the driveway, Harmony hightails it for the tree house, probably to hide her package.

Rain and I are on ash duty so we head for the fire pit. Every week we shovel the ashes and add them to the compost. I water down the ash bed with the hose so they won't fly back in our faces as we work. Rain and I take turns stabbing our shovels into the pile and tossing the soggy ashes into the wheelbarrow. When it's full, Rain starts to roll the wheelbarrow.

"Let me take it," I say.

Rain pushes a lock of hair out of her face, leaving a smudge of gray on her cheek. In her tattered apron and mud boots she looks a little like Cinderella. "I can do it."

I grab the handles of our rusty wheelbarrow and smile at her. "You can take the next load."

Rain walks alongside me as we make our way toward the compost pile next to the garden. When we get to the edge of the last row of squash, I flip the wheelbarrow to dump the ashes and start raking them into the mixture of leftover veggies and chicken poop.

Rain stands with her hands on her hips, watching me. "Do you like living here, Blue?"

I stop raking to consider my answer. I've learned that when my sisters ask questions, they aren't necessarily looking for the truth as much as wanting you to agree with them.

"That's a strange question. Why do you ask?"

"I don't know. Seems like a guy your age might rather be in school, playing sports, meeting girls, going to the movies. You know, normal things."

"This is what I know, so it's normal for me. I'm not interested in sports or sitting in a classroom."

She smiles. "You left out meeting girls. You're such a handsome guy. They'd go gaga for you."

I feel myself blush.

"I didn't mean to embarrass you. I just feel like I can be completely real with you."

"What about you, Rain? You could be out working at a regular job, meet a guy, get married, have a family."

It's her turn to blush. "I suppose I could."

"But you've already met someone, right?"

"Blue . . ."

"Yeah?"

"Do you think the sisters resent me? For being with Goji, I mean."

I drop my rake and right the wheelbarrow. "Nah. They seem happy for you. For him too."

"But they're used to sharing. I don't want to share. I don't want to be with the other men here in that way."

"I don't know what to tell you about that. I did ask Coyote about the Sacred Space one time and he said nobody has to do anything they don't want to do with anyone. He told me that it used to be kind of a free-for-all but then people started pairing off and it just kind of settled out. That sometimes they'd be together in the space but they don't trade off like in the old days."

"What about you? Do you approve of me, of . . . ?"

"Goji?"

She nods. "He's a good person, right?"

I'm not sure how to respond. I've had mixed feelings about Goji ever since reading those newspaper articles. Everything I believed about him has slowly started to unravel. But I don't want to break Rain's heart, so I give her a nonanswer.

"He's really smart and always has a way of explaining things from a different perspective. And he's super peaceful. I've never seen him get mad. Ever."

She takes a step forward and kisses me on the cheek, and there it is again, that wonderful smell beneath the smoke and ash. "Thank you for being so open with me."

Flustered, I turn back toward the wheelbarrow and accidentally step on the front of my rake, popping the handle straight up and into my forehead. It makes a loud *clunk* when it nails me between the eyes.

"Blue!"

I lean forward for a second, holding my eye and wincing. "I'm okay." I quickly stand up with only one eye open and grab the handles of the empty wheelbarrow.

She wrestles it away from me. "That had to hurt." She kisses me again, this time on the spot that's already welling up into a big knot on my brow. "Let's go see what Sirona has that we can put on that."

As I follow behind her, I can't help but think about how much she must be missed by those she left behind, what they might say if they could see her now. And I wonder how bad it must have been for her to decide to leave.

*   *   *

Harmony doesn't let me open the package until after evening meditation. She comes into my room while Doobie is still downstairs and tosses it onto my mattress. I look at the box, then up at her.

"Go ahead."

Before she can change her mind I rip through the tape and brown paper, once again being careful to preserve the address in case Harmony changes her mind about writing Gaia back. I pull a wadded-up newspaper out of the cardboard box before reaching inside to retrieve Harmony's gift.

"It's a tambourine."

Harmony stands next to the bed with her arms folded across her chest. I jump onto the mattress and jingle it above my head.

She rolls her eyes. "It's stupid."

I drop the tambourine to my side. "Aw, you hurt my feelings."

"Not you, the tambourine. Why would she send me that?"

I hold it out to her. "Because she misses you?"

She shakes her head. "You keep it."

"Oh come on. She misses you. Look, she even signed it." I trace my hand over the writing. "Wait. Oh, man, you've got to see this."

Harmony doesn't budge.

"Why are you being like this? She's coming for a visit. You gave your blessing."

"I said it was okay for her to visit but I still hate her."

"No you don't. You're just mad at her. Come look at this."

Harmony drops onto her knees next to me and silently reads the signature.

I grin. "Jerry freakin' Garcia! She was telling the truth."

Harmony rocks back to sit on her feet. "She probably wrote that herself."

I shove her backward onto the bed and start tickling her. "Would you lighten up? I'm supposed to be the serious one, remember?"

She kicks at me, trying not to laugh but she can't help herself. I grab her flailing arms and hold them together at the wrists. She's laughing so hard she starts crying, except it isn't funny anymore and she's crying for real. I let go of her arms.

Her bottom lip quivers. "I do miss her sometimes."

It hurts to see the pain in her face and not be able to fix it. "I know," I say.

And then without thinking I kiss her. Not like a sister. Like a girl. She doesn't move when I break away. Our faces hover just inches away from each other.

She reaches up and lightly touches the bulge on my forehead. "What happened to your head?"

"I got into a fight with a rake."

"Did it hurt?"

"A little."

She lifts her head and kisses the bruise. The feelings in my head move into the rest of my body. I want to kiss her again but I'm afraid of breaking this spell.

"You should go back to your room," I whisper.

She nods but doesn't move.

I climb off of her legs. Harmony rolls off the bed and stands. I hand her the tambourine. She holds it against her chest, staring at me in a half-child, half-woman kind of way.

"Night, Blue."

She backs slowly out of the doorway. I listen to the jingle of tiny cymbals as she tiptoes down the hall.

27

July 1978

Willow and Wave cleaned out the teepee and patched the leaky spots with duct tape and garbage bags. The outside is ugly but the sisters have gone crazy on the inside. A small stove sits on a brick platform smack-dab in the middle with a pipe leading up through the opening at the top of the teepee. Everything else looks like something out of those Arabian Nights fairy tales with tapestries attached to the canvas walls and mosquito netting draped over a bed smothered in colorful pillows. Lotus donated a colorful oriental rug that she took out of her house while Mr. Fuller was in town. Everything else came from thrift stores or yard sales, right down to the ceramic bodhisattva on top of a wooden crate. I half expect Willow to come dancing through the doorway wearing finger cymbals and a veil.

Harmony peeks her head in just as I'm piling a stack of wood in the corner of the teepee. "Whoa, this is far out!"

At the sound of her voice I drop the log I was about to plant on the pyramid of wood. The whole pile tumbles into a mess in front of me. She runs over and starts picking up pieces of wood. "Sorry I startled you. Here, let me help."

"It's okay, I've got it." I take a small log from her. "You don't have gloves on. You'll get slivers."

She turns in a full circle, studying the new decorations. "This is so much cooler than when Ruth and I lived in here." Harmony missed most of Willow and Wave's move-in because she and Moon spent the afternoon running errands with some of the Olders in town.

"Yeah, they did a great job." I finish stacking the wood, being extra careful to set the last log lightly on the top before moving toward the door.

"Hey, where you going in such a hurry?"

"I need to feed Sunny."

"I'll go with you."

I pause a moment too long and she feels it.

"You don't want me to come along, do you?"

"No. I mean yeah, sure I do."

She sets her mouth in a tight line. "Look, whatever that was last night, let's not make it weird, okay?"

"I'm not making it weird."

She pushes past me, opening the flap and stepping out of the teepee. When I join her outside she smirks at me. "Yeah, you are."

I shrug my shoulders. It does feel awkward. *Why did I kiss her like that?*

"Come on. Let's go feed Sunny."

She walks toward the shed where we keep the kibble, her ponytail swinging like a hypnotic pendulum with each step as I follow.

Before our family dinner Goji leads a blessing ceremony for the newly refurbished teepee. Chanting, he carries a large owl feather to fan the smoke in every direction of the room from a burning bundle of sage. Afterward we follow him up into the tree house, where he does the same for Willow and Wave's old room that Harmony and Lotus now share. We all start back toward the stairs.

Doobie clears his throat. "Do you think you might bless me and my buddy's space, too?"

Goji looks at the bundle of sage. All that's left is just a stub with a blackened head. Doobie pulls a joint from behind his ear and smiles. Goji lights the joint and takes a drag, then blows the smoke into our room before passing it to Wave, who does the same. The joint travels down the line until it reaches me. I take a puff and blow it out without inhaling. Harmony snatches it from me before anyone can stop her and takes a final pull, before heaving into an insane coughing fit. I slap her on the back and she drops to her knees.

Sirona rushes past us and hovers over Harmony. "Are you okay?"

Harmony looks up, grinning. "Yeah, I was just messing with you."

She takes another puff, inhaling deeply, then blows out three perfect little o's. When she sees us all staring at her she laughs. "What's the big deal? You all know I grew up with a pro."

Sirona takes the roach from Harmony and stabs it out on the trunk running through the middle of the tree house. "Just because you can doesn't mean you should."

Harmony joins me in my room, where she lounges in Coyote's hammock with her sketchbook while I read from a book of poems by Hafiz that Goji assigned. Just before sunset she jumps up and runs to my window. We both watch as Gaia's faded blue VW bug rumbles into the main compound.

Gaia climbs out and stands in front of the car. The hood has a huge yellow peace sign painted on it. Her hair is twisted into dozens of long braids, half of them piled high on her head and tied with a long scarf. With her long ruffled skirt and bare feet she looks like something straight out of *National Geographic.*

Gaia looks around until she spots most of the others gathered near the fire pit. When Goji sees her walking toward them, the Olders instantly turn to gauge his reaction. They fall away when he moves toward Gaia and opens his arms.

"Welcome home," he says in a voice much louder than his usual, measured tone. He whispers something into her ear before stepping away.

I nudge Harmony. "Should we go down?"

She shakes her head. "I've waited years. She can wait until I'm damn well ready."

Harmony disappears into her own room. I'm torn between following her and seeing Gaia. I feel bad for Harmony but I really miss Gaia and I'm hoping we can all start over. As the family gathers around our long-lost sister-mother, I hesitate for just a moment before climbing down the stairs and running toward them.

Gaia turns toward Doobie and playfully sticks out her bottom lip. "I've really missed you, brother." When she takes a step toward him he flinches and she feels it. She glances down to see Lotus holding his hand. "Hey, sister, I'm Gaia. And you are . . ." Her forehead crinkles as she suddenly recognizes the woman standing next to Doobie. "Wait, *Mrs. Fuller?*"

Lotus lets go of Doobie's hand to embrace Gaia. "Hello, Gaia. I go by Lotus now."

Gaia throws back her head, laughing. "Holy shit! Nothing is permanent but change, right?"

Rain steps forward. "Do you remember me?"

Gaia stares into Rain's face and smiles. "Of course I remember you. But you looked really different then. Straight-laced and baby-faced. You cried most of the way here. Your name is—"

"Rain. It's Rain now."

I edge my way forward. When Gaia sees me, she slaps her

hand over her mouth, tears spilling out of her eyes. She lunges toward me. "Whoa, look how tall you've gotten!"

Gaia wraps me in a bear hug, nearly smothering me in patchouli-scented kisses. I'd forgotten how much I love her hugs. She pulls back, holding my hands. "Look at you all grown up. Ha! And so handsome." She glances behind me. "Where's Harmony?"

I look up toward the tiny light coming from Harmony and Lotus's side of the tree house. "I think she just needs a little more time."

"It's okay. She's probably as nervous as I am."

One by one the rest of the Olders embrace Gaia. To each of them, she holds her hands in the prayer mudra and says, "I'm sorry for the pain I've caused you." By the time she gets to Willow, everyone has tears, including me. Willow hesitates a moment longer than the rest before leaning in to embrace Gaia.

Goji motions for Gaia to follow him toward his shack. "Let's you and me chat for a bit while we wait for Harmony."

Doobie builds a fire and we sit around on stumps passing the time. I poke at a flaming log with a stick. "Do you think he'll let her stay?"

Wave pats me on the knee. "We'll all decide together, you know that."

"Yeah, but he has a way of deciding what we decide."

Wave is tuning his guitar when Gaia and Goji return. Wave smiles and starts singing a John Denver song. We all know this one so everyone starts singing. Gaia turns her face away from us, but the longer the song goes the more her tears flow. The main lyric goes, "You fill up my senses," but most of the others probably don't realize the actual title is "Annie's Song." Or remember that Annie is Harmony's real first name.

I move next to Gaia and lightly touch her arm. "Do you want me to try to convince her to come down?"

She glances toward the tree house and shakes her head. "She'll come to me when she's ready."

28

I don't expect to see Harmony at sun salutation but Lotus has coaxed her down. Lotus has one arm draped protectively over our sister's shoulder as they walk toward the mats. Harmony keeps her head down in an attempt to avoid eye contact with her mom, but it's not necessary. Gaia has overslept, something she often did when she lived here. Goji let Gaia sleep in the Sacred Space last night. Rain offered to share her room but Gaia didn't want to crowd Harmony, who'd be just a few feet away in her room with Lotus.

It isn't until after breakfast that Gaia shows up while Harmony and I are washing dishes. She sits at the empty table and rests her chin on her hand, watching us.

"Hey, little angel."

Harmony ignores her.

"I know you're pissed, honey, but believe me, you were better off here than traipsing all over the place with me. I've settled down now. I'm living outside Portland, in a really nice place. I think you'd love it there."

Harmony glares at Gaia. She clenches the dish towel in her

fist. "You're right. I'm better off here. You can go back to wherever you live now."

"Harmony . . ." I say it under my breath.

Her green eyes are fierce below a fringe of long bangs. "What? I should just forget that she abandoned me like so much garbage?"

Gaia stands. "That's not true and you know it. I love you with every cell in my being. Love is why I chose to let you stay here."

"Let me? Like I had a choice? You took off and never came back."

"I came back. . . ."

Harmony snorts. "Three years later! And then you left again. Am I supposed to be all grateful? Pretend that it didn't hurt? That I didn't cry myself to sleep for six months after I realized you weren't coming back? I was nine years old. Nine fucking years old!"

I look around to see if anyone heard Harmony cuss, but everyone seems to be giving her space. Or hiding.

"I know. I'm sorry for the pain you're feeling."

"You don't know. And you're not sorry. Not for me. You're just sorry for yourself. It's always all about you."

Gaia takes a step toward us. "I planned to leave you alone. I didn't expect you to forgive me. But Jade forwarded a letter to me. From the government. I've been using the Freestone address here so SFC would get the welfare checks and the food stamps. They need me, need *us*, to come in to verify that—"

"Let me guess. You want me to lie for you. Tell them you were here being mommy."

"God, Harmony, don't make this harder than it already is."

"If I do it, you'll leave?"

Gaia wipes her eye with the back of her hand. "If that's what you want, yes."

Harmony tosses the towel on the ground. "Fine. I'll do it." She marches off toward the path behind the garden.

Gaia watches until Harmony is out of sight. "She hates me."

I shake my head. "She doesn't hate you. She's just mad."

Gaia tries to smile but it breaks on her face. "She always had a temper. She's passionate like me."

"Give her time."

"Will you talk to her, Blue? If she doesn't come with me to Social Services they'll show up here. They could decide it's not safe for her or Moon and Aura. And it could be bad for you, too. For everyone here."

"When do you have to go?"

"They set the appointment for two o'clock this Friday in Santa Rosa."

"I'll try." Three days from now . . . that's way too much time for Harmony to change her mind. "She's pretty stubborn."

"I know. But I see the way she looks at you. She loves you, Blue. She'll listen to you."

"Maybe. But maybe not."

I find Harmony under our favorite willow tree, hovered over her sketch pad. Sunny sits beside her, his tongue hanging out, panting. The two of them probably ran the whole way. More like she ran and Sunny tried to keep up with her.

I drop next to her. "Hey."

Harmony has her finger on the lead of the pencil, scrubbing the page furiously as she shades the area around Gaia's portrait. She doesn't try to hide her sketch from me like she usually would. Lotus has given her more confidence, but I'm pretty sure she's more driven by emotion than boldness right now.

The drawing perfectly captures Gaia's high cheekbones, wide forehead, full lips, and hooded eyes. Gaia claims to be one-eighth Native American, which would make Harmony one-sixteenth, I guess. They both have darker skin than me, but when you live like we do, it's hard to tell how much is actual skin color.

Without looking up she says, "She asked you to make sure I'd go to social services with her, didn't she?"

"Yeah. You gonna go?"

"I said I would, didn't I?"

"She's worried you'll change your mind."

Harmony closes her sketch pad. "Did you hear what she said? She didn't just put *me* at risk. She jeopardized the whole community by gaming the system."

"She wanted the Olders to have money and food for you. She was looking out for us. She didn't have to do that."

"But it's illegal. She could go to jail. And if they start nosing around, so could Willow and Wave and most of the rest of the Olders. And then what would happen?"

I drop my head. "I don't want to think about it."

"Me neither. Which is why I'll go to the damn appointment with Ruth."

I run my thumb over the back of Harmony's hand. She leans into my shoulder and sighs. I want to protect her. I want to believe that Gaia wants to protect her. And that Goji will protect all of us from the peering eyes of nosy social workers.

While we were gone, Gaia prepared an amazing meal of sweet-and-sour veggies, pineapple fried rice, and her famous kickass salad. Harmony sits on the same side of the table as Gaia so she doesn't have to make eye contact with her mother. But the only person Gaia is looking at is Doobie. And he's looking back. It's an oddly quiet meal with everyone looking around at each other while they quietly chew.

Finally, Gaia stands and carries her dish toward the washtubs. "You all go take it easy. I'll clean up."

This makes everyone's eyes go wide. First, she made dinner.

Now she's offering to wash and dry dishes. Gaia used to make excuses not to cook *or* do KP duty.

Doobie jumps to his feet and starts clearing dishes. "I'll help you."

I wake to footsteps next to my bed. When I open my eyes, a pair of bare feet slip past my mattress and through the doorway. As soon as he's out the door I peek out the window. Doobie tiptoes down the path toward the Sacred Space. He stops to pee along the way, then disappears out of sight. I listen for Lotus but she must have left before him. I picture the three of them, Lotus, Gaia, and Doobie, and immediately try to erase the image. I put my pillow over my head and eventually fall back asleep.

Doobie and Gaia are missing from sun salutation. Lotus moves through the poses like thread through a needle. Her breathing is slow and even. When we finish morning yoga she makes us all apple pancakes. Gaia and Doobie show up halfway through breakfast looking like a couple of rumpled scarecrows with their hair all mussed and wearing nothing but crooked smiles. They both reek of pot.

Lotus smiles at the giddy couple. "Have a seat. There's plenty more." She slides a stack of pancakes onto their plates, then sits on the other side of Doobie.

He giggles nervously. "Thanks, Lotus. I'm starving."

Gaia shovels a forkful into her mouth. "Whoa, sister, these are amazing."

Lotus pats Moon on the arm. "Since you've cleaned your plate so quickly, would you take your little sister to look for eggs? I used up the last one making breakfast."

"Sure. C'mon, Aura."

When the Youngers disappear toward the chicken coop, Lotus gently sets her fork on the table. "Look, I knew what I was getting into. Free love. Free spirits. Free from expectations." She turns to Doobie. "You're free." She stands and walks toward the counter with her plate. "And so am I."

Doobie chases after Lotus as she heads up the path. When she reaches the outhouse she turns and holds her hand up. Doobie turns and slowly walks back toward the table.

29

On Friday morning Gaia trades her hippie clothes for a plain white blouse and black slacks from the thrift store. Willow pins Gaia's braids into a bun, then wraps her head with a scarf and tops it with a big sun hat. Harmony is wearing a sleeveless dress with her hair pulled into a high ponytail. I hardly recognize the two of them as they walk past me toward the VW bug for their social services appointment.

I catch up to them just as they're getting into the car. "Hang on!"

Gaia leans Harmony seat to look at me through the passenger window. "What is it, Blue?"

"Can I come along?"

"I don't think that'd be a good idea. If they start asking questions . . ."

"I'll just say I'm a friend."

"You need to check with Goji." Gaia pats the front seat. "C'mon, Annie."

Harmony turns to me. "We're practicing our real names so I don't mess up."

"Goji's not here. He and Rain went somewhere on an errand."

Gaia looks from Harmony to me. "Okay. But you'll have to stay in the waiting room." She glances at my bare feet. "And you need to put on some shoes."

I hold up the sneakers I was hiding behind my back and grin.

"Lean forward, Har . . . Annie. He'll have to sit in back."

I squeeze into the tiny backseat. Gaia shifts into gear and the VW putt-putts through the gate and onto the road. As we tool along Bodega Highway, Gaia turns up the radio. With the windows down and all that wind I can't make out a word. I push a pile of clothes aside to make room so I can put on my shoes. A syringe rolls off the seat and onto the floor. I pick it up and inspect it in front of my knees, out of their line of sight. I pull out the plunger, then push it in again. When we go over a bump I accidentally stick myself in the finger.

"Ow!"

Gaia turns to try to see me. "What's going on back there?"

I drop the syringe and kick it under the seat. "Nothing. I just bumped my head on the ceiling."

Gaia laughs. "Yeah, not a lot of room in these things. But I love this ride. Traded half a pound of weed for it from some freak in Humboldt County." She glances at Harmony. "Don't worry, that was a long time ago. I'm not a pothead anymore."

I suck a drop of blood from my finger and stare out the window at the apple orchards and pastures. As we get closer to Sebastopol, the farms get smaller and the houses get closer together. On the east end of town where Bodega turns into Highway 12, we cross Main Street and from there it's just ten minutes before we pull into the social services lot.

When Harmony bends her seat forward to let me out, the syringe comes into view. I quickly extract myself and slam the seat back into position.

She catches me frowning. "What's wrong?"

"Nothing. I think the exhaust fumes just made me a little sick to my stomach or something."

Harmony steals sideways glances at me as the three of us walk into a room filled with metal chairs lined up against one wall, most of them filled with mothers and kids. Cheerful posters decorate ugly beige walls covered with scuffs and patches. A couple of toddlers sit on the floor next to a box of books and junky-looking toys. The women all look tired.

Harmony and I stay near the door while Gaia checks in at the window.

I tap Harmony on the arm. "Are you nervous?"

"Stop it. I'm only nervous if you keep asking if I'm nervous."

We wait in uncomfortable steel chairs for our turn. Gaia's foot is kicking a mile a minute. In her polished black flats and stiff, boring clothes, it's like somebody switched out a real flower with a fake plastic one.

A heavyset woman with short hair appears, clutching a green folder. "Ruth Porter?"

Gaia jumps to her feet and motions for Harmony to follow her. Harmony glances back at me from the doorway. I throw her the peace sign and smile before they disappear down a fluorescent-lit hallway.

They're gone for what feels like hours. I spend most of the time meditating. I can feel people staring and hear them whispering, but I don't care.

When they finally return, Gaia's voice is crabby. "Let's go," she says. One look at Harmony's face, and it's obvious the meeting didn't go well.

As soon as we're outside Gaia starts yelling, "Fucking bureaucratic bullshit!"

I lean toward Harmony. "What happened in there?"

She looks like she's about to cry. "They need to do an inspection. To verify where I live. Where she and I *both* supposedly live."

My stomach sinks. Goji's not going to like this. None of them will.

Gaia throws her arms up in the air, still cussing up a storm. "Fuck them! That's it, I'm done!" She tears up the stack of papers in her hands and tosses them in a nearby trash can along with her hat and scarf. When we reach the parking lot she yanks open the car door. "Come on. Let's go get some lunch."

Gaia stops at a hole-in-the-wall bar for sandwiches. The room is dark and hazy and filled with smoke. The only people besides us are a waitress and a couple of men at the bar, smoking cigarettes. We sit at one of three wooden tables covered with overlapping water stains. The waitress laughs at me when I ask if they have any veggie burgers.

"This ain't no hippie kitchen. I can bring you a salad, blue eyes." She looks at Harmony and raises her painted eyebrows.

Harmony closes her menu. "I'll have a salad, too."

The waitress wipes a glob of something brownish off the table with a napkin while she waits for Gaia to order.

Gaia fans herself with the menu. "Bring me a bacon burger. Extra mayo."

Harmony and I both drop our jaws. Gaia looks at us and laughs. "What? I need protein. That bitchy caseworker drained all my energy."

When the food arrives, Gaia is no longer at our table. She left to put change in the juke box and started talking with one of the guys at the bar. They both disappeared down a hallway toward the bathroom.

Harmony keeps looking toward the red EXIT sign over the hallway entrance. "What's taking her so long?"

I shrug. "Maybe she had to take a crap."

Harmony punches my arm. "Gross."

We eat our salads, which are just brown-edged iceberg lettuce and flavorless tomato slices. I bury my plate in croutons to soak up the giant lake of ranch dressing.

Harmony picks at her salad with a fork. "What do you think is going to happen?"

"I don't know. Maybe Goji will have an idea."

"I'm worried, Blue."

I set down my fork and grab her hand. "Don't worry. They'll take care of you."

She glances up from her plate.

"*I'll* take care of you."

By the time Gaia stumbles back to the table, her burger is cold. Her hair has fallen out of the bobby pins and her blouse is untucked. She takes one bite of her sandwich and tosses it back on the plate.

Harmony stares at her mother's feet. "Where are your shoes?"

Gaia wiggles her toes and laughs. "Fuck fucking shoes. Let's get out of here."

I glance toward the bar. "What about the bill?"

The man at the end of the bar waves at us and winks at Gaia.

"I already took care of it. C'mon."

Gaia hands me the keys when we get to her VW. "You drive."

"I don't even have a permit yet."

"I'm giving you permission. That's your permit." She pushes the seat forward and climbs in the back. "I'm gonna take a nap."

Harmony frowns. "Blue and I are almost the same age. I thought you were a feminist. You don't trust me to drive?"

Gaia curls up and rolls so her back is to us. "I don't give a shit, you two figure it out. Leave me alone."

I hold the keys toward Harmony. "Here you go." We both know she's a better driver. Sirona took over our driving lessons after Coyote left and she sometimes lets Harmony drive her all the way to the Freestone Store.

Harmony climbs into the passenger seat. "I don't want to drive. I just want her to know that I'm capable." She glances toward the backseat and growls a little under her breath. "Unlike her." She looks back at me. "Can you get us back to SFC?"

"I think so." I turn the key and crank the engine. "Pretty sure."

It's a straight shot on Highway 12 to the turnoff toward SFC. I grip the steering wheel with both hands. I'm terrified of getting pulled over or doing something stupid and getting us hurt.

Harmony pats my leg. "Relax, Blue. You're doing great."

Trucks, cars, and eventually even a school bus passes the bug and pulls in front of us. The kids in the backseat stick out their tongues and stretch their faces, pointing. Harmony makes a piggy face back. One of them cranks a fist up and down, the signal for a semi truck to honk. Harmony reaches in front of me and makes a short beep-beep with the horn. They all start laughing.

Unfortunately, the horn wakes up Gaia. I glance at Gaia in the rearview mirror. She sits up in the backseat, staring out the window like a lost kid. Her eyes are so dilated there's almost nothing but pupil. She mumbles, sounding completely out of it. "Sacred Space, my ass. He doesn't fuck anybody."

Harmony wheels around to face Gaia. "You're not making any sense. Go back to sleep."

"He calls it sexual transmal . . . transmittal . . . transmutation or some shit. Supposed to make you more enlightened or something if you don't come." She exaggerates Goji's soft voice: "Hold that energy and funnel it inward." Gaia flutters her fingers in the air in front of her and makes a ghost sound. "Wooooo . . . can you feel my energy?" She laughs but it's more like a cackle than her usual full-throated laughter. "Orgasms are a good thing. I prefer to let the love out, not hold it in."

Harmony turns back toward the front window. "We don't want to hear about your sex life. Really inappropriate, Ruth."

"Hah! Get real. I see the way you look at each other, flirting. And the way Goji looks at your blond sister? I bet he fucks that one."

My face goes hot. I stare straight ahead. But if what she says is true, maybe Goji hasn't actually had sex with Rain.

Gaia's words are slurred but deliberate. "He blew it. He had a way to make things right and he fucking blew it."

Harmony spins around on her knees and peers over the seat at her mom. "What are you talking about?"

"She's my ace in the hole to get you back, kiddo."

"Who is? I don't want to go back, not with you. I'm right where I belong."

Gaia starts to cry. "No, you're not. Blue neither. Or Rain, for that matter. A kid should be with their family. It's fucked up, man. Totally fucked up. I tried to convince them, but nobody would listen."

Gaia mumbles something else before passing back out. All that's visible in the mirror is her slack mouth, tilted down on one side.

Harmony turns back around in her seat. "Do you think she tried to convince them to take you back home?"

"She's messed up on something. I wouldn't take anything she says too seriously."

"But maybe she found out about you. I remember her loudly arguing with Goji one night about you. It was shortly before she took off that last time."

I glance in the rearview mirror but all I can see is the long row of cars behind us. "Doesn't matter now. Let's just get her home."

We drive the rest of the way in silence. It takes almost twice as long on the way back as it did to get to Santa Rosa. I keep thinking about the letters in Goji's shack. Maybe he was afraid that Gaia would tell Harmony about how I ended up here.

As we approach the Fullers' house Harmony points toward the driveway. "Hey, that's Lotus's car."

I slow down even more than I was already going. "She's probably picking up some more of her things."

Lotus stands near the back of her car. She slams the trunk closed while balancing a cardboard box in her other arm and carries it toward the farmhouse.

Harmony sticks her hand out the window and yells, "Hey, Lotus!"

Lotus walks through the open doorway and disappears.

"Looks like she's bringing stuff *to* the house, not the other way around."

"Your room isn't very big. Maybe she's trading it for other stuff she needs."

We turn down our long drive and through the gate, past the hand-lettered Saffron Freedom Community sign. I park the bug under a willow tree near the garden. Harmony and I both jump out, leaving the doors open so Gaia has fresh air. I pull my T-shirt over my head and tuck it into my back pocket. Harmony strips down to the cotton slip she had on under her dress.

Jade runs up to greet us. She looks from the car to me. "You drove? Where's Gaia?"

I nod toward the backseat, where Gaia is curled in a fetal position, snoring. Jade reaches in and tugs on Gaia's bare foot. "Hey, sister. How'd it go?"

Gaia doesn't respond.

"I think it wore her out," I say. "Maybe we should let her sleep."

Jade looks suspicious of Gaia's condition.

"Where is everybody?" I say, changing the subject.

"They drove into town to hear Wave sing at that pizza place, to take their minds off . . ." She looks at the car. "Off everything. I stayed here with Aura because she's not feeling well. They should all be back soon."

Harmony kicks off her shoes. "We saw Lotus on our way in. She was at her house."

Jade glances nervously toward the road. "Yeah, I think she

was going to drop off some of her things before joining the rest of them."

I suddenly feel exhausted. "I think I'll go for a walk. My legs are cramped from sitting all day."

Harmony turns to me. "I'm going with you."

Jade calls after us. "Wait, so you don't know anything more?"

Harmony keeps walking, leaving me to answer. I turn and shrug. "We'll be home before sunset, okay?"

Jade glances back at Gaia curled in the backseat of the bug. "Okay." The look on Jade's face says anything but okay.

As soon as we reach the path beyond the edge of SFC Harmony stops and grabs my arms. "What are we going to do? We can't have county services sticking their noses into the community. We don't have electricity or plumbing and none of us are in school."

"I know. I'll think of something."

She let's go of me and hangs her head. "I wanted to believe she'd really changed. All that stuff about starting over in Portland with a real job and not smoking so much weed."

"You need to think about yourself right now. Gaia is an adult."

Harmony crosses her arms in front of her chest. "What if she screws everything up? If they try to put me in a foster home I'll run away."

"Nobody's going to put you in a foster home."

"How do you know that, Blue?"

I look into the eyes of the girl I've known since we were five, running around like a couple of wild cubs. "Because I won't let them."

She smiles. "Blue?"

"Yeah?"

"Are you going to kiss me again?"

"Do you want me to?"

She nods.

I lean in to kiss her but stop myself.

"What's wrong?"

"I don't know. It's weird. I've always thought of you as my sister."

"Always?"

"Always before lately."

"I'm not your sister, Blue. I'm your best friend."

She tilts her head so her mouth is just inches from mine. I can't help myself. I kiss her, longer and more intensely than I'd meant to. When I pull back her eyes open and I feel like I could swim away in them.

"Still feel weird?"

I smile. "No. Yes." I brush the hair away from her face. "A little. But it feels right."

We walk farther, hand in hand, until we reach one of our favorite live oak trees. It's huge, almost as big as the one we built our tree house in, with low limbs and a wide spray of branches that nearly sweep the ground. I sit and lean against the trunk. The grass is warm beneath me. Harmony scooches between my legs with her back against me. I wrap my arms around her arms and kiss her lightly on the back of her neck. A tingle runs through my entire body.

I want to tell her I'll protect her, but I don't want to ruin this moment with a promise I might not be able to keep. "It's going to be okay," I say, as much to myself as to her.

She softens in my arms. We watch as the sun lowers itself under the tree line on the far side of Salmon Creek. In the distance the cowbell rings for dinner and we ignore it.

30

Gaia slept all night in the back of the bug. She's still there when I come down the tree to pee just before sunrise. She looks pale and it scares me. Her head is in a weird position, halfway off the seat. I touch her toe. I'm relieved when she moves her foot. She makes a whimpering noise, but she doesn't wake.

"Gaia? You okay?"

She rolls to face the back of the seat and pulls her knees to her chest. "Go away."

It's not until we're halfway through sun salutations that Gaia finally shows up. She stretches a mat out in front of me next to Doobie and steps into tree pose. She immediately loses her balance and nearly falls backward on top of me.

"Sorry," she whispers.

Goji throws her a stern look for speaking out loud.

Harmony is unusually quiet through our morning meal. Jade cooked grits with eggs and hash browns, one of Harmony's favorites, but she hardly touches a bite. The others make small talk about anything and everything except Gaia and Harmony's appointment. We haven't told anyone about the county inspection. And it doesn't look like Gaia is going to fill them in.

When Goji finally speaks, I hold my breath. I expect he'll have something to say about my driving home yesterday. I'm relieved when he addresses Gaia instead.

"Obviously yesterday must have been a difficult day. Perhaps it might be easier to discuss privately."

Gaia looks up from her plate. Her skin has a grayish cast and she looks older than her thirty-two years. "It was awful." When she starts to cry, Doobie tries to comfort her.

Goji stands and walks behind Gaia. "Let's go for a walk, sister."

She takes his outstretched hand and they amble off together toward the shack.

An hour later Goji calls us all back to the table with the cowbell. As soon as we're seated he reaches for Rain's hand to his left and Doobie's to his right. We all reach for each other's hands and wait.

"Our sister has some news she would like to share."

Gaia raises her head. Her normally cheery face has been replaced with bloodshot eyes. "I have to leave. Those food stamps and the checks I was forwarding were illegal because I was living out of state. I could be charged with fraud. Social services wants to come to SFC and do an inspection. They need us to prove that Harmony and I live here."

Willow opens her mouth to speak but Goji shakes his head. "Let her finish."

Gaia takes a shaky breath. "You'll all be at risk, especially the kids. I can't let that happen." Her eyes fill with tears. She looks at Harmony. "If they find you here, they'll take you." Her eyes flick in my direction. "And the more they go looking, the more they might uncover."

"Like what? We're not hurting anyone," Rain says.

Goji glances at Rain, then looks away quickly. "They'll force us to get permits, or, more likely, shut us down. The Czech might sustain fines. They could claim neglect and take the minors into custody."

Sirona makes a pfffft sound. "Neglect? These are the best-educated, most well-fed children within miles."

Goji nods. "I know, sister. But that's not how they'll see it. By law, the children have to be enrolled in school. All of our structures would come down, including the tree house. Everything would be condemned." He smiles at Lotus. "We've been very lucky that our neighbors support us and the locals tolerate us. If the government gets involved, it's over. But Gaia isn't making this decision alone. If you all want to take that risk, we'll ask her to stay."

Gaia looks around the table. Nobody says a word. I feel Harmony trembling next to me before she stands.

"I don't want to go! This is my family."

Gaia's face pinches into a pained look of guilt. "I know. I'm so sorry. It would only be for a little while until they're convinced that we've left. Then you can come back."

"They'll just come looking for me up there."

"Highly unlikely. But if they do I'll say you ran away. Nobody will care, trust me. They're understaffed and underpaid. We're just a small bug in their huge web of bureaucracy."

Harmony sits back down and buries her head in her hands. Sirona puts an arm around Harmony and pulls her close.

I set down my fork. "There has to be another way. Why can't Gaia leave and we can hide Harmony?"

"No. It's too risky," Willow says. She looks at Gaia. "When do you have to leave?"

"The sooner the better. This weekend."

Harmony pulls away from Sirona and rubs her eyes with her sleeve, then slowly gets up and walks away from the table. When I start to stand Goji stops me.

"Let her go. She needs to walk this out. We'll be here for her when she's ready to process."

I'm worried about Harmony but he might be right. I sit back down.

Gaia drops her head to the table. I feel bad for her, I really do. She was always my favorite sister-mother. But it's no wonder Harmony doesn't trust her. For all the fun she brings, it comes with a price. Usually a big one. We've always been taught to re-channel our anger into love. Right now it's all I can do not to scream at Gaia for being so selfish. I can't imagine not having Harmony here. Not even for a few days, let alone weeks or months.

Several hours pass and Harmony still hasn't come back. She's not in her room or anywhere nearby. Not in our hollow tree. Not under her favorite willow. I even checked the chicken coop and Sunny's little house. By dinnertime, people start to worry. Gaia finds me cross-legged in my room trying to vibe Harmony into coming home.

She sits on the edge of my mattress. "Will you go look for her?"

Anger and frustration overtake any desire to be kind to Gaia. I open my eyes. "Why? So you can take her away?"

"I'll bring her back in a few months."

"How do I know that? Or that you'll take good care of her?"

She touches my knee. "Of course I'll take good care of her. I love her."

"I found your needle, Gaia."

"What are you talking about?"

"In your car. I found a syringe. I accidentally stabbed myself with it."

She rolls her eyes. "Must have been that hitchhiker I picked up. I knew he was bad news. I gave him a ride because I needed gas money."

I just stare at her.

"Look, I know I screwed up. But it'll be much worse if they take her. She'd be in foster care until she turns eighteen."

"You've really changed, Gaia. I don't trust you anymore."

"I promise I'll take care of her, Blue. Please give me another chance to prove it."

I can't bear the idea of Harmony in some terrible foster home with strangers. As much as I hate the idea, leaving with Gaia now would be better than losing Harmony completely.

I'm pretty sure I know where to find Harmony. I wait until no one's watching and grab some food for her, then head out on the trail along the creek. I walk past our favorite oak and beyond the redwood grove through the abandoned apple orchard. When I reach the cave entrance I fish the flashlight from the bottom of my pack. I crawl through the opening and turn on the light.

"Harmony?"

I shine the beam toward the far tunnel, crawling on my hands and knees until I reach the spot where there's room enough to stand. "Harmony? Are you in there?" I point the light toward the crack in the wall. "Please answer me."

I listen for her but all I hear is water dripping from the wall to a small puddle on the ground. Turning sideways, I push myself into the opening. For a second I panic, thinking I'm stuck, but then a hand reaches for mine and pulls me through to the other side.

"Why didn't you answer me?"

"Because I don't want to leave."

"I don't want you to leave either. But if you don't . . ."

She slides down the wall and hugs her knees to her chest. "I know."

"Your mom promised me she'd bring you back in a couple of months."

"Ruth makes a lot of promises she can't keep."

I move next to Harmony and squat beside her. She takes the flashlight from my hands and shines it on the wall next to the opening where we squeezed through. Our names are still there.

"Seems like forever ago," she says.

"Just a little over two years."

"Sirona told me you tried to carry me half a mile after I got bit by that snake."

"You passed out. I was so afraid of losing you."

Harmony starts to cry and I take her hand. "Look, I hate that the only way to fix this mess is for you to go with Gaia. I swear if she doesn't bring you back by fall I'll come get you myself."

She turns off the flashlight and rests her head on my shoulder. "I love you, Blue."

My heart feels like a rock in my chest when Gaia and Harmony pull away in the rusty VW bug the next morning. Harmony watches from the back window as the rest of us gather around each other, weeping. We close the circle right there and then. With our arms around each other's waists, Goji starts the blessing.

"Thank you for the privilege of including Gaia and Harmony in this family. We infuse our sisters with Love and Light. We surround them in a shield of protection. And although we understand that it is not ours to map their individual journeys, we look forward to the day we widen this circle to welcome them once again. Thank you, Gaia. Thank you, Harmony."

We answer together, "Thank you, Gaia. Thank you, Harmony."

Despite all the promises of her return, each one of us understands very clearly that there's a chance we could never see them again. They've taken many risks here at Saffron Freedom Community, the greatest one being the day of my arrival. But this day feels harder than any other. Harder than when Coyote was captured. Harder than when Gaia left the first time. Harder than I think I can bear.

31

It's only been a week since Harmony and Gaia left and already we're losing another member. On the day of Gaia's appointment at social services Lotus had planned to tell us she was leaving SFC, but she didn't have the heart.

"Berkeley accepted me." Lotus tucks a college brochure into The Book and passes it to Doobie. "I'm going back to school to get my art degree."

Sirona claps her hands together. "That's wonderful news, sister!"

Doobie's face drops. No sooner had Gaia left than he'd tried to get back into Lotus's good graces. Doobie is a patient man and I think he figured he could wait out her jealousy. He tries to smile but ends up looking like a sad clown. "Good for you, Lotus."

Doobie passes The Book to me without adding anything to it. I open to the back page and find Harmony's last entry. It's a detailed drawing of shapely lips, dated the day of our first awkward kiss. I feel my cheeks blush and quickly close the cover. I'd give anything to relive that kiss. I've played it over so many times in my head. The second one, too. I can't stop thinking about her.

Moon pushes his glasses up his nose and sighs. "Why is everybody leaving?"

"Life isn't static, little brother," Goji says. "It's constantly shifting and moving. Our job is to learn to dance with the changes and alter our lives accordingly. If everything stayed the same we'd never grow."

Aura wiggles in her seat. "I like to dance."

Jade kisses the top of her head. "You're a beautiful dancer."

We build a big bonfire to honor Lotus. I sit on the sidelines and stare into the flames, kicking at the dirt with my bare feet. People start twirling and singing along with Van Morrison, Janice Joplin, the Rolling Stones, and CCR. Harmony would have loved this. She lived for our bonfire dances, where she would rock out, dancing like a crazy person with her hair over her face and her arms flapping like a fledgling bird.

Rain takes one of my hands and tries to pull me to my feet. I shake my head.

"Come on, Blue. She wouldn't want you to be moping around during the party."

"I'm sorry. I don't feel like dancing."

Rain sits next to me on the log and drapes an arm over my bare shoulders. "She'll be back."

"I know."

But I don't know. I have no idea if they made it to Portland or, knowing Gaia, got side-tracked along the way.

Goji skips over to where we're sitting and pulls Rain to her feet. They dance away, leaving me to sulk alone. The party goes past midnight until "Going Up the Country" starts playing and everyone dances around Lotus. She looks at me from the center of the group, her long gray-streaked hair like billows of smoke around her face. She curls her finger, inviting me to join them.

When I shake my head she puts her hands on her hips and shimmies, just like Harmony used to do. I can't help but grin. I walk toward the group and slowly join in. Closing my eyes, I imagine Harmony dancing wildly beside me and lose myself in the music.

In the morning we close the circle for a second time in as many weeks. I'm tired of all the good-byes. I'm tired of feeling sad. I go through the motions with the rest of them but quietly leave the group before Lotus drives away. I climb up the tree house ladder and sit in the room that Harmony shared with Lotus. It's empty except for a mattress, some art supplies, and a few scattered books. I pick up a dog-eared copy of *A Wrinkle in Time* and fan through the pages. Harmony loves this book even more than I do.

We used to imagine ourselves soaring through time and space, looking down on our family. We'd pretend we were invisible, hiding and watching from every nook and cranny we could find. A slip of paper falls out of the book. Harmony has sketched the Black Thing from the story, blotting out the stars. The features are distorted but I easily recognize the high cheekbones and toothy smile of Gaia. It hurts my heart to see how much Harmony resented the person who gave her life. I tuck the drawing back into the book and shove it between the mattress and the wall. As I do, my hand makes contact with Boo-Boo, the soft bear she carried on the day she arrived.

Gaia and Coyote both showed up after our trip to Woodstock. I don't recall which one of them got here first, but I remember Harmony running out from behind her mother's legs to give me a hug. Unlike me, she was used to being around strangers. She grabbed my hand and said, "Let's go play!" so I took her to see our new chickens. She wasn't the least bit afraid. She cornered one of the hens, picked it up, and kissed it. "I love you!" she said, and squeezed the squawking bird before letting it go and chasing after the next one. From that day on I've spent as much time as possible trying to absorb her courage, her bright fire.

I stare out the window toward the path behind the tree house where Harmony and I set out on hundreds of adventures over the past nine years. Holding the tattered bear under my nose, I breathe in a decade of her smells. I can't believe she left her beloved Boo-Boo behind. Maybe she stashed him here knowing I'd find him. Maybe this is her way of promising she'll be back. I listen for sounds of anyone else in the tree house, but other than the breeze rocking the creakiest boards, the rooms are silent. I carry the bear back to my room and hide it under my pillow.

A shrill scream wakes me from a colorful dream and I bolt upright in my bed. The sun hasn't set yet but the light is low. I must have napped for a couple of hours. It takes me a moment to get my bearings. The cowbell clangs over and over like an album stuck in one groove. This is not a dinner gong. I've learned from past drills not to come running without first assessing the danger, so I hunker down by my window and slowly inch toward the frame to see what all the commotion is about.

Willow and Sirona are jumping up and down, hugging each other as Willow jangles the cowbell above their heads. In the distance I spot Jade's small frame running toward the road. Her bare feet kick up dust behind her long skirt as she races toward the gate. Aura chases close behind her. I climb down the ladder just as Wave approaches from the east side of the sauna, where he was stacking wood. Goji appears in front of his shack. Even from here I can see the smile spread across his face. Rain stands in the garden next to Doobie, one hand over her brow trying to see what the commotion is about. Doobie let's out a whoop and chases behind Aura. Maybe Gaia has already brought Harmony back.

Please let it be true.

I scramble down the ladder and run behind Doobie. And then I see him, all six feet two inches, as Coyote lifts Jade and twirls her around and around. When he sets her down she pats his face, her hands shaking.

"It's really you. Aura, look, he's back! I told you he'd be back!"

Coyote scoops up Aura and presses his face to her cheek, then throws her up on his shoulders. Her grin broadens as she latches onto his hair. "Yo-Ye!" she shouts, the name she's called him from the time she first learned to speak. Coyote playfully pinches Aura's bare feet one at a time and kisses her toes. With one arm around Jade and one holding Aura's right leg, he walks toward the family that has gathered to greet him.

We all have a million questions, but he answers them patiently.

"Did they let you off for a visit? Do you have to go back? Did you escape?" So many voices I lose track of who asked what.

"They sentenced me to five years. President Carter pardoned draft dodgers shortly after I went to Leavenworth. But I did eight months before they let me out." He turns toward Goji. "Thank you for the letters you wrote. Maybe your lawyer daddy was right about you shoulda gone to law school. Whatever you wrote, it worked."

Goji embraces Coyote. "Welcome back, brother."

I know so little about Goji's past. Only that he's from the East Coast and traveled to India. I can't picture him as a lawyer. I can't even imagine him wearing a suit.

After evening meditation we surround Coyote, chanting. He turns to face each of us one at a time. With our right hands over our hearts we press our left hand against his, one by one. When he reaches the end Goji opens the circle. Coyote take's Goji's hand on the left and Jade's on the right.

"Welcome home," Goji says.

"Welcome home," we all say together, closing the circle once again.

Rain has taken Aura for the night to give Jade and Coyote some privacy. Doobie is already asleep in his hammock in our room. I envy his easy peace. As I lie in the darkness, quiet conversation turns to soft moans coming from Jade's room. I turn toward the wall, shielding myself from the sliver of jealousy for Jade and Coyote's happy reunion. In my head I chant the om over and over until my mind settles down. The family is finally quiet except for Doobie's deep-sleep breathing.

32

It's been a month since Harmony and Gaia left and still no word from either of them. Every time we go into Freestone for supplies or gas I make sure to tag along so I can check the mail. I don't understand it. Harmony promised to write. Either something is wrong or Goji is intercepting their letters. I've already decided that if I don't hear from one of them by next month I'll go look for her myself.

"Blue!" Wave's voice startles me. He runs up behind me and flips the lever on the pump. "We only have five bucks budgeted for gas this week."

I look at the numbers on the pump: $7.43. "Sorry."

Wave playfully yanks a fistful of my hair. "Where were you anyway?"

"What do you mean?"

"I mean you were staring off in space so far I thought you were searching for the man in the moon."

"I was just thinking."

Wave grins. "I'll bet you $2.43 you were thinking about a certain sister and her mother."

I plug the gas handle into the slot. "You got it half right."

I walk toward the store to check the mail. I've saved it for last in order to hold off more disappointment. Sirona stops me on her way out of the store. "There you are! I have a letter. . . ."

I snatch the envelope out of her hand before she can finish.

"Hey! That was rude."

"Sorry." I turn the envelope over to read the return address.

"There isn't one. I already looked."

But the handwriting is familiar. Not to mention little hand-drawn paw prints tracking to the back side and a drawing of Sunny. I sniff the envelope. It smells like weed and patchouli. I want to tear it open right there in the store but I play it cool and stuff it in my jeans pocket.

Sirona's eyes widen. "Aren't you going to open it?"

"Maybe later."

As soon as we're back at Saffron Freedom Community I make a lame excuse about having to use the bathroom and pretend like I'm headed to the outhouse. I know it's too dark to read inside so I sit behind it, leaning up against the back wall to read Harmony's letter. I carefully tear open the end and slip out a folded sheet of sketch paper with handwriting on it. When I unfold it a wilted flower falls out. Clover. I tuck it behind my ear and begin to read.

> *Dear Blue,*
>
> *I'm sorry it took me so long to write. Ruth brought me to a Rainbow Gathering where people camp out in the wilderness and we stayed a while. I think she figured nobody would find us in the woods. This is the first time we've been near a place to mail you a letter.*
>
> *The Rainbow thing was actually kind of fun. I*

met some really cool people but also a few weirdos—mostly Deadheads. People were tripping their heads off. I ate mushrooms (don't get mad!) but only a tiny bit and holy mother of mermaids you would not believe the art I made while I was tripping. I didn't tell Ruth of course because she'd have been pissed off, but I was bored and figured it might be fun to find out what everyone raves about. All I can say is it's no wonder Willow thought you were her unborn child. I saw things I've never seen in real life. Like, people's cells inside their bodies and the brilliant colors and I saw YOU. Crazy I know but it turned out to be this guy who kind of looks like you but (obviously) wasn't. Anyway it made me happy to see the not-you because it reminded me of the is-you. Does that make sense?

We're in Portland finally. I hid our address inside the envelope flap so nobody but you would see it. Ruth says we can stay here with her boyfriend until enough time has passed for things to have settled down. Her old man seems nice, believe it or not. He owns an import business. The outside of our apartment building is really ugly but he decorated his place with all this rattan and totems and stuff so it feels like an island cottage. There's a padded chair shaped like a bowl called a papasan that two people can sit in at the same time. He has a black cat named Rita that he found by a parking meter. HAHA!

I have my own bedroom and Mark—that's Gaia's boyfriend—took me to JC Penny's and bought me a bunch of clothes. He took us to a fancy Chinese restaurant and I ate like a pig. I

*can tell he likes me, but I don't plan on staying
here long. It's nice and all but I miss all of you.*
Especially you.
Xoxo,
Harmony
PS: Did you find Boo-Boo?

I fold up the letter and slide it back into the envelope. I try to
imagine Harmony in an apartment with walls, a flush toilet,
and a warm heater. My memories of her are so different; running around naked as kids, climbing trees, the two of us barking together along with the distant coyotes under a full moon.
The Harmony I know has tangled hair, dirt under her finger-
nails, and a smile that always makes you wonder what she's up to.
She would hate living in an apartment surrounded by pavement
and traffic. And she would miss us so badly she'd be begging Gaia
to take her back home tomorrow, not a month from now.

On the other side of the outhouse, a door swings open then
bangs shut. Inside, I hear someone puking. Listening to other
people throw up always makes me feel like throwing up, too,
so I jump to my feet to get some distance. I stuff Harmony's
letter in my pocket and start to walk away until I hear crying
along with the heaving and I instantly know who it is. I look
around to see if anyone else is close enough to help, but everyone is out of sight.

I walk back toward the outhouse and knock on the door.
"You okay in there?"

The door opens and Rain stumbles out. She wipes her mouth
with the back of her hand.

"Are you sick?"

She looks at me and blinks away tears. "I'm pregnant."

I don't know what to say so I don't say anything.

Rain grabs my arm. "Walk with me?"

We start toward the tree house, but when we get to the ladder she looks up and shakes her head. We keep walking, past

the tree, past the chickens, into the field beyond the boundary of our property. When we get to an outcropping of boulders she sits on one of them, and folds her hands in her lap. I sit on a rock facing her. I'm afraid of saying something stupid so I wait for her to talk first.

Rain looks away then back to me. "Blue, I lied."

"Wait. You're not pregnant?"

"No. I mean yes, I'm pregnant, but I lied about other stuff."

"You mean about your age? I don't think that matters. Goji says age is relative. He's treated me like an equal from the time I was able to talk."

At the sound of Goji's name she flinches, just a little. She sits up straight, tilting her face toward the sun, eyes closed. The circles under her eyes look like little shadows.

"We're all about truth here but my stories are all lies. I'm not from Salinas."

"I don't care if you came from the North Pole. Why does that even matter?"

She opens her eyes. Her lower lip starts to tremble. "There's more. My stepfather didn't beat me. I don't even have a stepfather. Gaia blurted that out to cover for me. The truth is, I did a bad thing and I ran away from it."

"I can't imagine you doing anything that horrible. You're the nicest person I've ever met."

Rain shakes her head slowly. "I killed somebody." She takes a deep breath and lets it out slowly. "Wow. That's the first time I've said it out loud."

I reach for her hand. "Are you serious?"

She nods. "Yeah. It was an accident but I killed him."

"Do you want to talk about it? I mean, if it would make you feel better to let it all out I'm a really good listener."

She smiles at me through tears. "I've already said too much."

"You said it was an accident. We all do stupid things. We all make mistakes."

"But I keep on making them."

"What do you mean? You're part of our family now. That's not a mistake."

"I told Goji I was on the pill. But I didn't take them. I wanted to get pregnant. I wanted a baby. I want to be loved."

"I don't get it. We love you. Why would you . . ."

"Betray him? Because I'm stupid, that's why. It was selfish."

"Does he know about the baby?"

"I've been throwing up every day for a week. I think he's just waiting for me to say it out loud."

"He'll forgive you. I know him."

"Maybe." She stands and looks toward the community. "But I'm not sure I deserve it."

33

I'd written Harmony back immediately after the last letter to say how relieved I was to hear she was safe. Rain swore me to secrecy about her pregnancy so I didn't share that bit of news in my letter. Or how badly I've missed her. I was afraid of sounding clingy or desperate. Mostly I tried to get her to ask Gaia for an actual date they'll return. Things just aren't the same without Harmony around. Less shenanigans. Less laughter. Less of all the things I look forward to when I get up every morning.

I read her new letter in the back of the car on our way home from Freestone. It's hot so we have the windows down and I have to grip the page so it won't blow away.

> *Dear Blue,*
> *Since my last letter things have changed. For*
> *one thing I'm a lot cleaner. HaHa. You don't real-*
> *ize how good other people have it until you soak*
> *in a steaming bath on a cool night or turn on the*
> *air conditioning during the hot afternoon. Crazy,*

right? Ruth says she might marry this cat. I'm not convinced. The other night we were eating pizza in front of the TV and she passed out. Not like falling asleep, she was out cold and drooling. I'm pretty sure she's still using behind Mark's back. I think he knows it, but he pretends everything is cool so she won't leave again.

I'm starting to get bored. I asked Ruth if she'd take me back to SFC. She said I need to enroll in school this month. Like that will happen in a million years. Mark is being all fatherly like and it's sweet, but he overdoes it. When he put his arm around me on the sofa the other night I moved to the chair. I'm not looking for a father. I probably hurt his feelings. Not even close to the hurt Ruth will put on him the next time she goes full gypsy on him. Pretty sure it's just a matter of time.

Anyway I'm going to keep working on her. If she doesn't agree by the end of the month I'll just borrow some money from Mark's wallet and take a bus back. I can't wait to see everyone again.

Xoxo,

Harmony

PS: Happy Belated 14th Birthday! I have a gift for you but I want to give it to you in person.

On the back of the letter she drew a cartoon-like picture of Gaia sleeping on a sofa with her arm hanging over the edge, still holding a slice of pizza. If it weren't so sad I'd have laughed.

"Why don't you read it out loud?" Willow asks from the front of the station wagon. She's leaning back against the ripped front seat with her bare feet sticking out the window.

Wave adjusts the rearview mirror and grins at me. He's been spending a lot more time at the beach now that he's surfing again and his tan makes him look handsome but crinkly from so much sun.

"She just says she'll be home soon."

He turns to glance quickly at the page in my hands. "She uses a lot of words to say so little."

I don't answer him. If she wanted me to read it out loud she'd have addressed it to all of us.

When we get back home I walk toward the Czech's fence, where I can get some privacy to reread Harmony's letter. I stop when I get near the Sacred Space. We should start calling it the Wasted Space. Ever since people moved into shared bedrooms nobody goes in here anymore. Willow and Wave sleep in the teepee. Coyote moved into Jade's room. Even Rain spends more time in Goji's shack than in her room.

I look around and I don't see anybody so I sneak through the door. The wood floor is covered in rugs and pillows. Half-melted candles, some stuck into wine bottles, line the curved wall. I try not to think about Harmony's description of all the grunting and humping, but it's pretty much all I can picture now that it's entered my mind. I wonder how many of them did it at once, how often they switched partners, and what the women did together. I know the biology of men and women and I can imagine what it might be like for two men but I'm too embarrassed to ask how it works with two girls.

I shake the thoughts from my head and sit cross-legged on the cleanest rug near the far end of the yurt. I wonder if Goji would let me take over this space. I could get a dresser and a desk at the thrift store. Maybe a new bed and a bookcase. I'd finally have some privacy instead of sharing a room with Doobie. I love Doobie but he smells like BO. And he mumbles in his sleep. Even if Goji is okay with it I'd need the whole family's permission. And sacred or not I'd definitely want Goji to sage the place first, knowing its history.

I've just finished reading Harmony's letter for the third time when I hear someone calling me. I slip through a tear in the canvas on the back side of the Scared Space and dart into the woods. When I'm parallel with the dining area I walk out from under the trees.

Jade approaches, holding a small bag of flour. "I've been looking for you."

"I went for a walk."

She balances the bag on one hip. "I need some milk for the recipe I'm making."

"I thought Rain milked this morning."

"She started to, but she got sick. I think she has the flu or something."

Rain obviously still hasn't told her secret. "I'll do it."

"Thanks, Blue. You two always get the most milk from the nannies."

I grab a bucket and follow the sound of Inga's and Greta's belled collars. I find them in the field behind the chicken coop. Rain sits nearby, watching them graze.

"Sorry I couldn't finish milking. I feel better now."

I cluck my tongue and Inga walks slowly toward me, her bag nearly bursting. "Don't worry about it. You just relax."

Rain draws her knees upward and leans back on her hands. Her white-blond hair is swept up with a few stray hairs falling down around her face. She may be a pregnant teenager, but she still looks like an angel to me.

I easily fill half a bucket after relieving Inga's overfull bag. She skips off and I move to Greta, who impatiently marches in place as I tug.

"I wonder what it will be like?" Rain says.

"What will be like?"

"Being full of milk like that. Feeding a baby."

I pat Greta on the rump and throw a towel over the bucket

to keep the flies out. She leaps onto a boulder and "bahs" before springing away.

"You're asking the wrong person. Sirona and Jade both nursed their kids. Sometimes each other's kid. You should talk to them."

Rain folds forward and drops her head to her knees.

"You still haven't told anyone you're pregnant?"

She shakes her head without lifting it. "Sirona probably has figured it out by now. I've been wearing baggy clothes and I haven't asked for her special moon tea in months."

"Do you want me to tell them? I could make an announcement at dinner."

She looks up, propping her chin on her knees. "Would you?"

"Do you know when you're due?"

"Early December, I think."

I do the math in my head. "About four more months."

"Give or take," she says, smiling for the first time since we ran into each other.

When she stands, the light shines through her thin sundress, highlighting the swell of her belly.

"Have you been to a doctor?"

She shakes her head. "I want to do this alone."

"You won't be alone. Sirona's a good midwife. She'll take care of you."

The dinner bell rings in the distance. I carry the pail in one hand and hold Rain's hand in the other as we walk toward the others, gathered around the table.

When everybody's seated I clear my throat. "I have an announcement."

Goji smiles. "If you wouldn't mind waiting, Blue, I have one I'd like to make first." He raises his glass of lemonade and smiles at Rain. "Saffron Freedom Community is expecting a new addition to the family."

We all turn and look at Rain. Her mouth drops open. "I'm sorry, I was going to . . ."

Goji raises his glass of lemonade higher, cutting off Rain's apology. "Rain and I are excited to welcome a child, sister or brother to all of us, a new being created with love."

Everyone clinks glasses, hooting and cheering as Rain's cheeks blush a bright pink. Jade and Sirona surround Rain, patting her stomach and hugging her. I look across the table at Willow, who smiles weakly. Wave pulls her close. He playfully nibbles her earlobe and whispers to her. She moves to join the other women. "I'm happy for you," she says to Rain. "For all of us."

We noisily finish our meal before passing The Book around the table. I hand The Book to Rain, who writes, *Goji and Rain's baby conceived in deepest love.* The Book makes it back around to Goji and he reads her words, his brows furrowed. A tear spills out of his left eye onto the ink, blurring the words on the page. He looks up and holds his arms out. Rain joins him at the head of the table. He leans his head into her belly and sobs like a baby.

Doobie elbows me and whispers, "What was your announcement?"

I wave him off. "It can wait until tomorrow."

34

This is the fifth time I've tried the sweat thing, hoping I get to that place the others talk about where all the toxins leave and you feel rebirthed. So far I only feel hot and it's hard to breathe. I'm completely drenched and the sweat is starting to drip off my nose. I study Goji's face, his eyes closed, sweat glowing on his skinny body. If he weren't sitting up I'd think he was asleep.

I know I'm supposed to be meditating but thoughts keep interrupting my mind. Thoughts about Harmony. I've written several letters with no reply. Nobody has heard from Gaia either. Gaia has a history of making poor choices. I keep reminding myself that Harmony is a warrior, and she'll fight her way out of any bad situation her mother might put her in. But the waiting is agony.

I wonder if my first family felt like this, not knowing if their child was dead or alive. How long did they suffer? Did I eventually fade from their memories? The newspaper articles made it sound like my parents accepted my death, but maybe they still hold out a sliver of hope that the worst hasn't happened. It must be a living hell if it's anything like the dread I feel at the thought of losing Harmony.

I fidget on the hot planks under me. "Do you think Harmony is okay?"

Goji doesn't answer. He's probably deep in meditation. Or maybe he really is asleep.

After what feels like several minutes, he says, "I think you worry too much. She'll be back or she won't. Focus on the joy, embrace your grief, and move forward with love and without expectation."

"How can I move forward when my best friend is missing? Gaia said she'd bring her back after the summer."

"Does your frustration or worry bring her home?"

"No."

"Does it make you feel better?"

"Not really."

"When you are worrying or missing her, is there room for joy or peace?"

"I guess not."

"Have you tried communicating with her in other ways?"

"We don't have a phone. Even if we did I don't know the number where they're staying."

"No, Clover Blue. I meant with your mind, your spirit."

Maybe the heat is getting to him. I'm pretty sure if I could call her with my mind she'd be back by now. I think about her day and night. But if anyone knows how to dial up another human being on the mind-line it's Goji, so I bite. "How would I do that?"

"Picture your sister. Where is she?"

"In an ugly apartment building in a cloudy city with a strange man and her drugged mother."

Goji's eyes open. He frowns. "I've never heard you speak

with such disdain and judgment. How did your lovely heart become so stained?"

"I just miss her, that's all."

"I know. I do too. We all do. But remember it's our suffering that shapes us, makes us stronger." He grins and adds, "They don't call them growing pleasures."

"But I have this bad feeling. Like something is wrong."

"Good. Pay attention to that. Let your feelings guide you."

I close my eyes and try to picture Harmony sitting on a sofa in front of a TV surrounded by vinyl furniture and knick-knacks. *Let your feelings guide you. Let your feelings guide you.*

And I suddenly know what I have to do.

"Sorry, Goji. I need to get out of here. I'm too hot."

He nods. "Each time a little longer. You're doing very well. I suspect your mind will feel clearer today."

I wipe the sweat off my face with a frayed towel. "It already does."

Back in my room, I stuff a few things into my backpack, then tear a sheet of paper out of my notebook. I watch through the window as four-year-old Aura chases Sunny around the compound, curls bouncing around her head like little springs. Jade and Coyote smile at her from the table, where they're huddled together over cups of tea. Every time Aura passes, they high-five her and she lets out a happy scream.

I scan my room, the familiar books and blankets, my guitar, Doobie's hammock. The tree house creaks in the fall wind, a sound that has become so constant in my life I sometimes wonder how people sleep without being rocked to sleep every night. Below me laughter bubbles up to my ear. Willow? Sirona? Or maybe Rain, who, now that everyone knows she's pregnant, has worn a smile that seems to have extinguished all her former tears. I hope my leaving doesn't make her sad again.

> *Dear Family,*
> *I've gone to find Harmony. I need to know*
> *she's okay. Please don't worry. I'll be careful.*
> *Love, Clover Blue*
> *PS: Moon, will you please take care of Sunny*
> *until I get back?*

It's not that difficult to disappear into the woods unseen. I wait until I'm even with the Czech's farmyard before stepping out and jogging toward the road. I've walked only half a mile when the sky opens up, pouring pockets of rain in short blasts until I'm drenched. With my head down and my thumb out, I keep walking. Bodega Highway isn't a busy road. A couple of cars slow down then keep going, parting streams of water in their wake. I don't care if I have to walk the whole way to Portland; I'm not stopping until I find her.

An empty lumber truck slows down, then stops in the lane with its blinker flashing. I run toward it, convinced he'll pull away before I get there. The door swings open as I get closer. I pause near the metal step and look up.

Her voice startles me. "Well, don't just stand there, climb in."

I heft myself onto the seat and pull the door closed. The driver rolls down her window and tosses a cigarette into the rain. Her curly brown hair is clipped short above broad shoulders. The sister-mothers cut wood and help with building stuff but I've never seen a woman driving such a big truck before.

"Where you headed, kid?"

"North."

She lets out a throaty cackle, a rougher version of Doobie's laugh. "North to the North Pole or north as far as the next town?"

"Portland, Oregon."

"Portland? That's gotta be six hundred miles from here!"

I drop my hood to wring out my wet hair.

She gives me the once-over. "Shit, you're one of those hippie kids, right? Livin' off the land, doing drugs."

"I don't use drugs, ma'am."

She laughs again. "Sure you don't. But I bet your friends do. Your parents kick you out or something?"

"No, ma'am."

"Stop calling me ma'am. My name's Paula. And you are?" She takes her hand off the shifter and offers it to me.

"Blue. Clover Blue."

This gets her laughing again, so hard she goes into a coughing fit. "Nice to meet you, Blue. Your sister's name Pink?"

I've learned that no answer is sometimes the best answer to questions like these. I stare straight ahead. The view from up here is amazing. I never knew the truckers were up so high.

"Pretty good handshake for a skinny kid." She reaches over and squeezes my upper arm. "Shoo-wee! I could use a helper like you. Are you looking for work?"

I've never thought about getting a job. We raise most of our own food and I can't imagine getting up and going to work for someone else, or what I'd do with all the money, for that matter.

"No, ma'am."

"Paula."

She pulls out another cigarette and offers me one. "No thank you, Paula."

She flicks the lighter and draws deeply. Her upper lip has crinkles in it, though she's probably younger than Lotus, based on the photographs of two little girls taped to the dashboard.

She catches me looking at the pictures and smiles. "That's Andrea and Angela. They're twins."

"Cute."

"Cuter than me. The girls just turned thirteen. I only hope they don't get involved in drugs or get knocked up. The world has changed a lot since I grew up."

I don't know how to answer that so I just nod and change the subject. "You don't happen to have a map, do you?"

Paula points to the visor above my head. "I got Sonoma County, California, and western United States. Take your pick."

I spread the map of the western states across my lap and trace Highway 29 East, over to Interstate 5, all the way up to Portland.

Paula glances at my finger on the map. "I told you it was a long way. I'm going as far as Redding. We have a mill up there. You're welcome to ride along."

"Thank you."

She tosses the crumpled pack of Salem's on the dusty dashboard and squints as she takes a drag. When she blows out, the smoke fills the cab. I crack my window. Taking the hint, Paula cracks hers and blows the next puffs outside the truck.

She leans forward to get another look at me. "Anyone ever tell you that you look like Leif Garrett?"

"Who's that?"

"Ha! Only the face on every cover of every teen magazine. All the girls are gaga over him."

"We don't get any magazines."

"He's also on TV and he has a record album."

"We don't have TV. I mostly listen to music from the sixties. We're pretty laid back."

"That's a shame. You ought to head the other way, toward Los Angeles. With that blond hair and blue eyes they'd make a star out of you. Can you sing?"

"Not really. My older brother gave me a guitar but I'm not very good at it."

"I don't think the majority of those kids can sing. Probably lip-sync most of it. No way that Partridge Family sounds that good."

"Partridge Family?"

She jerks her head toward me. "What planet are you from, anyway?"

I study the map, hoping she won't ask any more questions. It's bad enough sticking out like a sore thumb in my long hair and thrift store clothes, but I feel lost when it comes to stuff like current events or famous people.

Thankfully she doesn't push it. "You got somewhere to stay tonight?"

"I'll probably camp at one of the state parks along the way."

Paula glances at my feet, taking in the size of my pack. "There a pup tent in that bag?"

"I don't need a tent. I'm used to sleeping under the stars."

"Well, if you change your mind between here and Redding I've got a motel booked for tonight. You're welcome to sleep on the floor."

"I'll be all right. Thank you, though."

The slap-slap of the windshield wipers makes me sleepy and I nod off. When we pull off the road a couple hours later I've forgotten for a moment where I am until Paula pats me on the leg. "C'mon, kid. I need some grub."

We walk toward a small café surrounded by eighteen-wheelers, many of them filled with redwood logs. The rain has finally stopped but the sun is hidden by clouds. Judging by where the light shines through, I'm guessing it must be about five o'clock. I wonder if they've noticed me missing at SFC yet. Maybe when they call me to help with a chore. Maybe not until they sit down to dinner. I hate that they'll worry.

I glance at a pay phone next to the diner.

Paula follows my gaze. "You want to call home?"

"We don't have a phone."

"A neighbor maybe?"

I picture Lotus on the other end of the line. She'd try to con-vince me to come back. "I don't have the number."

She stops outside the café and crosses her arms. "You didn't tell them where you were going, did you?"

I shake my head.

She sighs and opens the café door. "I'm starving. C'mon, kid."

Paula orders a hot pork sandwich. The waitress turns to me. "What'll you have, miss?"

Paula stifles a snort. I order a cup of soup. When the waitress hears my voice, she looks at my hair, then back at my face. "Sorry. I thought you were a girl."

Paula peers over the top of her menu. "You're going to need more than a measly cup of soup to keep you strong for the trip. Order a burger. My treat."

"No thank you."

"BLT?"

"I'm vegetarian."

The waitress chuckles. Paula ignores her. "For Chrissake, at least order a *bowl*."

I hand my menu to the waitress. "I'll have a bowl of soup, please."

When the waitress disappears Paula leans forward with her arms on the table. "So you ran away from home, right? You know how worried your folks will be? Hippies or not, they'll be worried as shit, I can tell you that."

"I know. But I need to do this."

"It's a girl, isn't it? You got the look of a broken heart in those beautiful blue eyes of yours. Well, let me tell you. If she moved away with her family, they ain't comin' back. You might as well turn around right now."

The waitress returns with our food. I slurp a couple spoons of minestrone. It's actually pretty good. I didn't realize how hungry I was.

"I'm going to visit my sister," I finally answer.

Paula's eyebrows go up. "Your sister?" She wipes her mouth with a paper napkin, then pokes a fry into a mound of ketchup. "Ah, now I get it. Your parents split up and Mom moved away with your sister. I'm sorry, kid. You must really miss her."

"I do."

"And your mom, too, I bet."

Two truckers sitting at the counter drop a few bills next to their empty plates and stroll toward the door. One of them yanks on my hair on the way out.

"Hey!" Paula says.

"Just seeing if this girly boy was wearing a wig, that's all."

The other man laughs, staring at me. "You're awfully pretty, aren't you? You one of those fairies from San Francisco?"

Paula glares at the men. "Go on now. I'm sure you have better things to do than pick on a boy half your size."

They head toward the door, laughing. "Get a fucking haircut," one says. "Or a tutu," the other one adds.

I wad up my napkin and throw it on the table.

Paula rests her roughly chapped hand on top of mine. "Don't pay any attention to them. All talk and no balls."

Paula pays our bill and we get back on the road. She fishes around behind the seat and comes up with a cassette tape. She pops it in and cranks the volume, singing loudly with "Yellow Submarine," slapping me on the arm until I finally join in. We sing along with the next three songs, bouncing around like a couple of joyful idiots until "All You Need Is Love" starts up and gets to the lyric about being where you need to be, and the tears start. It's no use trying to hide them. I try singing louder but end up choking on my words.

Paula moves to eject the tape.

I touch her arm. "Please. Leave it going."

She gives me a look that says everything without saying a word. When the song finishes I turn off the player. Paula swipes at the corner of her eye with the cuff of her jacket, then ruffles my hair. "I'm sorry, kid."

Three hours later we pull into a motel and Paula parks the truck. "This is it for me. You coming in?"

I retrieve my bag from the floor of the cab and throw it over my shoulder. "I think I'll keep moving."

"Suit yourself. I'll be in room number eleven if you change your mind. Right down there on the end. I always get the same one."

"Thanks for the ride and the soup."

"Thanks for the company." Paula pulls me in for a half hug. She smells like cigarettes and French fries and everywhere I've never been. She reaches under her seat and hands me a baseball cap with their company logo on it. "Take this. Less trouble for you, I promise."

I tuck my hair up under the hat. She flashes a thumbs-up and grins. I climb down from the cab and walk back toward Interstate 5.

35

The traffic on the highway at night is crazy-fast. I've had my thumb out for over an hour but every single car and truck whizzes past me. At least it's not raining anymore. This thought is immediately followed by lightning and a crack of thunder that nearly startles me out of my boots. I was just starting to feel dried out. I turn and run back toward the motel.

I'm about to knock on the door with the big number eleven painted on it, but try the handle just in case. It's unlocked. Either she's very trusting or she knew I'd be back. I slip inside and stand until my eyes adjust. Paula is snoring louder than Coyote ever did. I step quietly toward the bathroom to take a leak. With the door closed I flip on the light. A cockroach scurries under the sink cabinet, leaving a couple of dead ones behind. To the right of the toilet sits a gaudy pink bathtub with a tiny white rug in front of it.

I push the plug into place and turn on the water, hoping the sound doesn't wake Paula. Sinking into the steaming tub I think about all the times I've nearly frozen under cold "showers" made from plastic bags with holes in them or washing in the creek before Lotus brought us the hose. The closest I've ever come to a real bath was the metal washtub Willow used to bathe me in when I was little. It's never seemed like a big deal. Until now.

I soak until my eyes start to droop and I nearly slip under the water, which is a lot dirtier than I imagined I was. I towel off and creep back into the bedroom. The loveseat is too short for my long legs, but nearly as comfortable as my mattress at home. I doze on and off, my mind wandering between SFC and Harmony. When the sun peeks through the blinds, I slip out before Paula wakes and walk back toward the freeway.

It takes me all day and three more rides before hitting the Oregon border. A vinyl siding salesman drove me to Legget before a couple of stoned Humboldt College students took me as far as Arcata. I walked to Highway 199, where another trucker picked me up at the I-5 on his way to Eugene, Oregon. He's not much of a talker and I'm glad for that. I lean back and marvel at the size of the redwoods as we pass through Klamath National Forest. I thought we had big trees in Freestone but these are giants.

The trucker slows down, edges onto the shoulder of the highway, and idles. I don't see any truck stops or weigh stations and the last sign said the interstate is twenty miles away.

"We got us a bear," he says quietly. "Best you keep quiet and let me do the talking." I start to turn around but he stops me. "And don't turn around! Don't even look at him. Just be invisible."

I stare straight ahead, except for a quick glance in the side mirror as a cop walks from his cruiser toward the driver's side of the truck. My heart races, knowing that if he finds out who I am it'll start a huge snowball of bad things, beginning with the arrest of most everyone at SFC. In my mind I hear Goji's voice when he was trying to explain to Harmony how Coyote getting arrested was the result of his prior actions. *Every choice has a consequence.* I didn't think this idea through. And I've just stupidly put my entire family at risk.

When the cop reaches us, the driver, who never told me his name, rolls down his window and hands the officer his license and other papers.

"Afternoon," the cop says. He looks down at the license. "Kenneth," he adds.

I forget about the stay-invisible rule and follow the cop's voice. He's an older man, freckled, with a reddish white mustache. The officer catches my movement and cranes his neck to get a look at me. "Who's that you got with you?"

"Just giving the kid a lift."

"Hitchhiker? Where'd you pick him up?"

"Crescent City. The on-ramp for the one ninety-nine."

"You brought a juvenile across state lines?"

Kenneth glances at me, then back at the cop. "I don't know how old he is. It was raining and he needed a ride."

The cop takes a long look at the papers. "I'm going to check these and come back. You boys just hold on, okay?"

Kenneth nods.

When the cop is out of earshot the trucker growls under his breath. "How old are you?" he asks.

"Fourteen."

"Shit. Shit, shit, shit."

"I'm sorry."

"It's not your fault. It was stupid of me to pick you up."

"It was actually very kind of you."

He looks at me and smirks. "Kind of stupid."

The officer comes back, this time on my side of the truck. "I'm going to need you to step out, son."

I freeze. This cannot be happening.

"C'mon now. You're not in trouble. I just need to know who you are and where you belong."

I look back at Kenneth, who just shrugs.

The officer hands the papers back to the trucker. "Slow it down, buddy."

"Yes, sir." Kenneth hands me my pack. As soon as I take it he pulls the door closed and shifts into gear without a good-bye. He's already in third gear by the time I reach the police cruiser.

The officer surprises me by opening the front passenger door of his car instead of the back. "Take off your cap."

My hair falls down my back when I remove the trucker hat Paula gave me. I expect a rude comment but he just motions for me to get in. He slides in the other side and closes the door.

"What's your name, son?"

Something about the way he says the word *son*, a tenderness beneath the authority, hits me square in my chest. My throat feels suddenly dry, like I've swallowed every drop of saliva in my mouth.

"Look, I see your type every day. I've heard every story, some true and some flat-out lies. But what I do know is that we've been getting reports of young people like yourself being picked up and disappearing. I'm not going to arrest you. I've got kids, and if they ran away I'd be sick with worry. I just want to return you to your parents."

For half a second I consider giving him my real name, Noah Anderson. In a heartbeat, the whole charade would be over. What if my birth parents got that call today? Would they even believe it? Would it make life worse for them after finally moving on and starting over with their lives only to have a teenager dumped back in their lives?

Thoughts of Harmony keeps my tongue locked in place. I glance at the name on the officer's pocket badge: Christopher J. O'Brien.

"Tommy McQuiddy," I say, choosing the name from my library card with Sirona's last name on it.

"Where you from, Tommy?"

"Freestone."

"Never heard of it."

"California. Near Sebastopol."

He shrugs.

"Not far from Santa Rosa."

"All right. Here's what we're going to do. You're going to call home and tell them you're okay. Then I'm going to put you on a bus back home. If I don't hear from your parents within twenty-four hours I'm going to start looking for you. And I won't be as nice as now."

"We don't have a phone."

"You lying to me, Tommy McQuiddy?"

"No, sir. We live kind of in the boonies."

He opens my pack and removes my flashlight, a pair of dirty socks, two bruised apples, a bag of raw nuts, and my notebook. When he gets to the whistle his eyebrows go up. "You in the marching band?" he says with a laugh.

"No, sir. It's for if I'm ever in trouble. I've . . . I've had it since I was a kid."

He sets the whistle on the seat. I cringe when he pulls out a tiny pair of brown sandals. He looks at me, waiting, the shoes dangling from his fingers.

"My little brother's. He died when he was three years old."

The officer frowns and gently returns them to my pack without a word. He starts flipping through the pages of my notebook, reading bits and pieces of my stories, poems and essays. "You're quite the prolific writer."

"Yes, sir. I like to write."

He stuffs everything back into my pack and hands it to me. "I've usually got a pretty good feeling about people and my gut tells me you're a decent kid. Am I right?"

"I try to be."

"Everything okay at home?"

"Yes, sir. I wasn't running away. I went to look for someone."

"Hundreds of miles away?"

I nod. I already know what he's thinking.

"I chased a girl when I was your age. Never caught her. But you know what? The next one I hooked was even better. You don't believe me now, but you'll see. Be patient."

"Yes, sir."

He calls my name into the radio, checking to see if I'm registered as a missing person. I resist the urge to bite a hangnail while we wait for an answer on the police radio. The name Tommy McQuiddy finally comes back unreported.

The cop drives me to a bus stop in Medford, Oregon, where he buys me a Greyhound ticket to Santa Rosa.

"Your parents will have to pick you up from there. Maybe call your minister or a teacher."

"Our neighbor has a phone. I'll call her as soon as I get in."

"I'm going to take you at your word, son. No funny business. We Irish have to stick together, right?"

I nod.

"And remember what I said." He claps me on the back and winks, pointing to the row of darkened windows. "She might even be on that bus."

I climb the steps and find an empty seat on the opposite side from where Officer O'Brien stands. I feel ashamed. I hate that I lied to him. The driver closes the door and off we roll in the opposite direction of where I need to go.

36

It takes fourteen hours to reach Santa Rosa. If not for the money Paula sneaked into my coat pocket I'd be half starved. The bus makes stops at McDonald's and Burger King so the only food I've had is French fries and milkshakes other than candy bars and chips from the machine in a bus depot along the way. My body isn't used to eating junk food. I've had diarrhea for the last two hours. I feel sorry for anyone who goes into the bathroom in the back of the bus after me. I'm sure they're all scowling at the back of my head right now.

I think about getting off several times along the way but the fear of being picked up by another cop stops me. The next one might not be so nice. Maybe by the time I get home there'll be a letter from Harmony. Maybe she went to another one of those Rainbow Gathering things with Gaia. But part of me wonders if she likes her new life and has decided to stay and just doesn't know how to tell me.

When the bus finally pulls into the Santa Rosa depot I walk across the parking lot and stand in front of a map hanging inside a glass display. Fourteen miles to Freestone.

"You need a lift home?"

I turn to find the older woman who sat behind me on the bus. She's holding a flowered suitcase.

"Nah, that's okay. I'll just walk. Thank you, though."

"I'm headed to Sebastopol. Which way is home?"

I glance at the dark sky. It looks like more rain. Sebastopol would save me seven miles.

"Actually, that's exactly where I'm headed. You sure you don't mind?"

She smiles. "You look like my grandson. Blue eyes, blond hair." She looks me over more closely. "Not as long as yours."

"Let me carry that for you." I take her suitcase and she smiles even bigger. "Polite like my Jeremy, too."

On the way to Sebastopol she asks a million questions, all of which I dodge by saying I'm here to visit my older sister who lives on a farm. When she offers to take me directly home, I turn her down.

"But it's getting dark!"

"I've been sitting on a bus for fourteen hours. I could really use a walk."

"Well, if you're sure." She pulls into a Zephyr gas station. "It was nice meeting you . . . what did you say your name was again?"

The lie is out of my mouth before I can stop it. "Tommy Mc-Quiddy."

She nods, her smile fading. "Don't recall any McQuiddys around here."

I open the door and climb out of the car. "Thanks again for the ride."

As I head out on Bodega highway the rain lets loose. After hearing from that cop about boys getting picked up I decide to walk instead of hitchhike. I've gotten a couple miles when a car zooms past, then hits the brakes and does a U-turn. The car passes me going the other way then turns again and pulls be-hind me. They flash their headlights. I look over my shoulder, but the blinding lights keep me from seeing the driver. I don't know anyone who drives an orange Vega. It might be someone who recognizes me but it could be someone who assumes I'm one of those commune hippies and sees an easy target.

I turn around and keep walking toward home. The car crawls up beside me and honks. I ignore it. They pass me and park just ahead, throwing the passenger door open. I stop walking and look up. A small figure sits hunched over the wheel. When I don't move the driver climbs out, seemingly oblivious to the rain, and leans against the trunk. She crosses one foot over the other and grins. "What's your problem? You waiting for a lim-ousine?"

At the sound of Harmony's voice my heart nearly leaves my chest. I want to run to her but my feet might as well be ce-mented into the shoulder of the road. She uncrosses her ankles and walks toward me. "Hey. Hey, you okay?"

I nod my head. Apparently my mouth isn't working either.

Unfamiliar smells hover in the air between us as she walks toward me. She stops in front of me and smiles, raindrops col-lecting on her eyelashes. And then there it is, under all that soap and city, the earthy girl I love more than anything in this world. I bury my head in her hair, holding her close until there's no rain, no cars, nothing but the two of us and our breath moving in and out together. I pull my head away and kiss her on the mouth for the third time in my life. I'm no longer planning the next one. This kiss will always be the best of my life.

She grabs my hand and tugs me toward the car. "Let's get out of the rain. Do you wanna drive home?"

I follow her toward the ugly orange car. "Where did you get this? Please tell me you didn't drive here all the way from Port-land."

She just shrugs and flings her hands upward, grinning.

I get in the passenger side. As far as I'm concerned I'm already home.

Harmony turns off Bodega down a tiny dirt spur and parks under the shelter of a group of redwoods. I'm soaked to the bone and the warmth pouring out of the car heater feels amazing. She leaves the engine running and the heater going so we can dry out. The rain has turned from a downpour, to showers, to a steady sprinkle on the windshield.

Harmony adjusts her body so she's mostly facing me. She looks older than when she left, older than fourteen. I want to ask her so many questions.

"Why did you stop writing me?"

She glances down at her jeans and picks at a rip in the knee before meeting my gaze. "I was afraid you'd be mad."

"I wasn't mad, I was worried."

"I didn't write because I started thinking about staying for good, maybe going back to school. I needed to take a break from SFC and figure out what I want."

"So you just stopped missing me?"

"No, Blue. Never." She looks back up at me. "I met this guy at a park near the apartment. We started hanging out and I liked him."

My heart sinks. I don't want to hear this, but I can't find the words to tell her to stop.

"He was super straight-laced. I hoped maybe he could offer me something I never got from Ruth or SFC. When I told him about our family and the Rainbow Gathering and stuff he acted like I was a complete weirdo. I thought it'd be nice to hang with someone normal, but it turned out he was just a judgmental jerk."

I like to believe that I'm not the jealous type but the idea of her with some other guy makes me a little nauseous. "You could have just told me that. I'd have understood."

She smiles. "Really? You'd be totally okay with my new boyfriend and possibly moving out of state for good?"

"Well, maybe not for . . . it doesn't matter. You came back. End of story."

"I'm not finished. There's more to the story."

"Sorry. Go ahead."

"It's about Mark, Ruth's boyfriend? At first he seemed like a regular guy, all fatherly-like. He paid for new clothes, all our food, my record albums, and whatever else I wanted. After growing up here, with cold showers and thrift stores and a diet of beans and rice it kind of felt like hitting the jackpot. Not like a millionaire, but way more conveniences and money than Ruth ever had. But then . . ."

She stops and looks out the windshield. "I've missed these trees."

I take her hand and kiss it. "But then what?"

She sighs. "He was spying on me. He cut little holes in the bathroom and my bedroom walls."

"What a creep!"

"I know. I found a camera on his side of the bathroom hole."

"Did he . . . ?"

"He never touched me. I think he was too chicken shit for that. Just liked watching. When I told Ruth, she didn't believe me so I showed her the holes. Her response was to OD on heroin."

"She overdosed?"

"I took her to the hospital. I hung around until they told me she'd be okay. When they started asking questions I gave made-up names for us. Then I stole Mark's car and left. I'm done taking care of her."

I pull her to me. "I'm so sorry. You're home now. We'll take care of you. *I'll* take care of you."

Harmony cries quietly in my arms. "I hate her. I hate her stupid boyfriend. I hate that I was stupid enough to hope she'd change."

After a few minutes she lifts her head and looks at me, wiping away her tears. "Why were you out walking the highway just now? Did something happen at SFC?"

"Nothing happened. I mean, Coyote's back and Lotus left."

"I figured Lotus would leave. We saw her packing that day we went to Santa Rosa. Wait . . . Coyote is back?"

"Yeah. They let him out after President Carter changed the law or something."

"I can't wait to see him!"

"Oh, and Rain is pregnant."

"Whoa, that's radical, considering what Ruth said about . . . I mean if it's Goji's." She gives me a sideways glance and I know what she's thinking. My crush on Rain was obvious to everyone. "It is Goji's, right?"

"Harmony, I was coming back from trying to find *you*."

"You went to Portland?"

"Not quite. I never made it. It's kind of a long story."

She smiles. "Aw, you were coming to save me?"

"Like you need saving. You've never needed saving. I just needed to be sure you were okay."

She rests her hand on my arm. "Blue?"

"Yeah?"

"What do we do now?"

I tuck a lock of hair behind her ear. "We can leave, go somewhere together."

She frowns. "I feel like I just did that."

"Or we can go home."

Harmony takes a deep breath and lets it out slowly. She shifts into reverse. When we reach the road, she drops the shifter back into PARK and reaches into her canvas bag. She hands me a cellophane package.

"What's this?"

"A Moon Pie. You used to stare at them at the grocery store when we were little."

She sees my face fall, having no idea how sick I just got on that kind of food.

"Trust me. You'll love it. I have a stash of crap food to last for a year in the trunk, including Zagnuts, which, by the way, aren't that great." Then she laughs, that laugh so deep and full that I've missed even more than I knew.

Harmony puts the car back into gear. The car starts to move then rattles a little, and the engine dies. She turns the key again and again but the engine won't restart. My eyes go to the gas gauge.

"Oh shit, I forgot how low it was. We probably shouldn't have left the engine running." She smiles her devilish grin.

We push the Vega off to the side and leave it. The rain has let up by the time we walk down the drive toward Saffron Freedom Community. Although it's our usual dinnertime, the community table is empty, as is the kitchen. The tree house, Goji's shack, the teepee, and the Sacred Space are all dark. Sunny bounds toward us up the driveway, barking. When he recognizes us his tail wags so hard I think it might fly off. He runs in excited circles around us, panting. I bend down on one knee to hug him. He slobbers all over my face.

"It's okay, boy. I'm home."

"Where is everybody?" Harmony whispers.

A small glow quivers on the east side of the property, most likely from a fire. I point toward the light. "Maybe over there?"

We walk toward the soft flickering near the yoga and meditation arbor. A quiet hum fills the air. The closer we get the louder and clearer it gets. Our family is huddled together, each person holding a candle, eyes closed, chanting in deep meditation, even Moon and Aura. I put my finger to my lips and signal for Harmony to follow me. Making a wide circle around the group, we stop and drop to our knees, silently crawling the last few feet. Harmony and I sit several feet behind Moon and Sirona, crossing our feet over our folded knees.

Harmony closes her eyes, resting her hands, palms open on her thighs. Willow and Rain both have wet tears on their cheeks. Moon's face is strained, as if trying to reach a high note.

From the looks of them, they've just closed the circle. They must have waited a couple days after discovering my note, assuming I'd change my mind and come back.

I study their faces as they haunt the night air with their eerie voices. And that's when I realize that it's not the om they are chanting, it's my name. *Bluuuuuuuue* . . . deep breath . . . *Bluuuuuuuue* . . .

I suddenly feel ashamed for putting them through grief and worry. I should have told them instead of sneaking away. Goji has always spoken of free will and the ability to carve out our own paths, but with me, there's so much more at stake.

Harmony reaches for my hand and squeezes, a smile spreading across her face. I know that smile. She's about to do something or say something irreverent, probably make me uncomfortable. And there is nothing I can do to stop her. As the first few words of "Song Sung Blue" leave her lips, people begin to stir, as if waking from a deep sleep. Then Aura squeals and jumps to her feet. She runs to Harmony, pulls her into the middle of the circle.

"It worked! Yo-Ye, look! We called her with our minds!"

Coyote opens his eyes and grins. He nudges Jade, who looks up from her candle. Her hand instantly goes to her mouth. One by one they all open their eyes. Doobie joins Harmony and Aura, throwing his arms around the two of them. "Welcome home, little sister!"

In a matter of seconds they're all gathered around Harmony. Willow holds Harmony's face in her hands. "I'm sorry, sweetheart, Blue went to look for you. He's not here."

Harmony turns and points to where I'm sitting quietly on the ground. "He found me."

"We found each other," I correct her.

Aura runs to me and throws her arms around my neck. "Because we called you! You must've heard us, right?"

I look up at Goji, who has one arm draped around Harmony and the other around Rain. I lift Aura and hold her high in the air. Happiness radiates from her smile.

"I heard you loud and clear."

Harmony breaks in, wearing that mischievous grin again, "You did great, Aura. We just need a little bit more help with something."

The Olders instantly look serious again. Coyote speaks first. "What do you need?"

I hold my breath, waiting for Harmony's answer.

She stands and looks toward the road. "Does anyone have a gas can?"

37

I lay in bed last night thinking about how weird today might be. I feel bad for running off and I'm nervous about seeing everyone in full daylight. The relief that Harmony and I are safe will wear off and could turn to resentment for scaring them like that. I wait until everyone else is up before quietly climbing down the tree to join the family for yoga.

But it's just like any morning as we move through sun salutation. Everyone seems happy, giddy even. I can't take my eyes off Harmony. Something about her is different but it's her sameness that I find so reassuring; the arch in the small of her back as she moves from mountain into cobra with an exuberant exhale; her voice as she patiently answers everyone's questions over breakfast; her smile, and the brief glances in my direction that warm me from the inside out.

"What's her boyfriend like?" Jade asks Harmony over a feast of blackberry pancakes with homemade butter and maple syrup. "Is he a good person?"

"He's a salesman," she says, answering and not answering at the same time. "I think—"

Doobie interrupts. "Is Gaia coming back?"

Harmony shakes her head. "I doubt it. The nurses said as soon as she's well enough they'll move her to a rehab to help her get clean."

Harmony talks about her mother without emotion in her voice but I can see the hurt in her face. I, for one, have lost my faith in Gaia. I realize she's an addict, but not protecting Harmony is more than I can forgive right now. And if I ever meet that Mark guy I don't know if I could restrain myself from violence.

The rest of the day is mostly normal, filled with chores and hugs and lively chitchat. But a current of nervousness rides beneath the joy. Up until three days ago I've never tested the limits of my free will. The truth is, leaving to find Harmony put them all at risk. Nobody brings it up because then they'd have to explain that risk to Rain and possibly Sirona and Coyote, too. But there's an air of mistrust that wasn't there before. Maybe they think now that I've had a bigger taste of the outside world I'll want to go back out there.

Their anxiety feels like a balloon floating over all our heads, ready to pop at any moment. I need to let a little of the air out. "I want to apologize to all of you," I say as we ready to reopen the circle after dinner. "I should have talked about what I planned to do instead of sneaking away like that. You must have been worried."

Willow reaches across the table and squeezes my hand. "You scared the shit out of us, if you want to know the truth. I'm just so glad you're okay." She turns toward Harmony. "Both of you."

I put my other hand over Willow's. "I'm sorry I made you guys suffer. I didn't think it through."

"You got that right," Wave says.

Coyote shakes his head quietly. When he speaks, his words surprise me.

"I would have done the same thing in your shoes. Nothin' more important than loyalty. You followed your heart and it led you to search for one of our own." He looks around the table, stopping when his gaze meets Goji's. "We should have done more to ensure that our little sister was safe. Blue here showed us what it means to be a man."

"To be *human*," Sirona corrects him. "But you're right. I'm sure all of us worried that Harmony was at risk."

Goji listens quietly. He looks older than his thirty-four years and more tired than I usually think of him, especially next to Rain. Ever since he and Rain got together Goji started investing less time opening discussions or teaching. It's almost like he forgot why he's here other than to be with Rain. He rarely lets her out of his sight.

Goji slowly stands and takes Rain's hand to his left and Sirona's to his right. The rest of us all join hands. He lifts his face toward the trees and closes his eyes. When he speaks it's as if he's talking to someone else or something else.

"Thank you for this family, *my* family, a tribe of beautiful souls connected hand to hand and heart to heart. We welcome Harmony and Clover Blue back into our loving arms as we celebrate their inward and outward journeys."

"Welcome home," everyone says.

I wait for him to open his eyes but he keeps them tightly closed, tears running down his cheeks and into his beard. We stand like that for several minutes before Aura breaks the silence.

"I have to pee." She pulls away from between Jade and Coyote and runs toward the outhouse. The rest of the family slowly drop each other's hands.

One by one we drift away leaving only Goji, still silent in his otherworldly prayer, and Rain, looking awkwardly confused as she watches him and waits.

*   *   *

I spend most of the rest of the day expecting Goji to call on me for a private talk. But it's Wave who invites me into the teepee for a meeting after closing meditation. When I step inside, Harmony is already there, along with Willow, Jade, Coyote, Sirona, and Doobie. Willow motions for me to join them in a circle of pillows on the floor. When I glance at Harmony she just shrugs.

I choose a pillow from a pile near the door and purposely drop it in a space that's not next to Harmony. Maybe this meeting is about the two of us becoming too close. I want to keep our deepening friendship private—as private as a person can in a place where everybody talks openly about everybody's business.

"I think we're ready to start," Wave says.

Harmony glances around the room. "What about Goji? And Rain?"

Willow lights a candle and sets it in the center of the circle. "Goji retired early and Rain is with Moon and Aura in the tree house. I asked her to read them a bedtime story so we could all talk."

Harmony doesn't give up on her willingness to wait for everyone. "But we can't have a meeting without Goji, can we?"

The Olders trade pained glances. Sirona fusses with her Tree of Life pendant. Doobie picks at a broken toenail. Jade leans over Doobie's foot as if she's suddenly interested in the disfigured toenail.

Wave and Willow both start talking at once. "He's not . . ." They stop and look at each other. Wave nods to her. "Go ahead." Willow takes a deep breath and begins again. "We asked him about the meeting and he told us to go ahead and talk amongst ourselves. He wants us to function more independently of him. But he was in agreement on the topic."

I'm confused. "What topic?"

"Well, for starters, who does that car belong to?" Wave says.

I look at Harmony. Trying to read her response is like working a puzzle without the cover of the box. You just never know with her.

"It belongs to Ruth's boyfriend," she blurts out. "And yes, I stole it."

"Then we need to get it back to him," Coyote says. "We can't have the police showing up here."

Harmony shakes her head. "I don't think he'll report it. It was more like a trade."

Coyote's forehead creases. "A trade? For what?"

I shake my head the slightest bit but Harmony ignores me. "For naked pictures he took of me without my permission. Through a hole in a wall he made to spy on me."

Willow gasps. "He what?"

Harmony turns toward Willow. "I destroyed the film but I kept the pictures I found in his sock drawer. I'm guessing he's more worried about those photos than his ugly old car."

Jade pulls Harmony toward her. "Oh, sis . . ."

Doobie stands and starts pacing around the teepee. "I knew I should have gone after her. He's probably the reason Gaia OD'd."

Harmony tilts her head backward so she can see Doobie. "In a way, yeah. But Ruth has been using for a long time. And she was more upset about the possibility of losing another shitty boyfriend than her own daughter."

Doobie sits back down on his pillow and drops his head to his chest. "I'm so sorry that happened to you."

Willow touches Harmony on the knee. "We don't care about the car. We care about you and Blue. Which is why we want to protect you from social services or the police. We're asking that from now on you stay on the property. We don't ask this lightly. You know we're all in jeopardy if you get picked up."

I glance nervously at Sirona. She's bound to get suspicious with all this talk about the authorities and us getting into trouble.

"You mean about his adoption?" Harmony asks. For such a smart girl she's really good at playing dumb.

Sirona looks at Willow. "Was there a problem with Clover Blue's adoption?"

Willow swallows and stutters, "Well, no. I mean yes, but . . ."

Wave chimes in. "It wasn't exactly legal. Blue was left by his parents and we rescued him."

As I listen to their messed-up version of the facts I wonder if they actually believe this story. Maybe over time they've convinced themselves that I was lost or that Goji was right about me seeking them. Just like he convinced me.

Sirona looks confused. "So what you're saying is if he gets picked up you'll be in trouble?"

Willow bites her bottom lip before answering Sirona. "We'll all be in trouble, except you, and Coyote. Accessories just for knowing about it."

Coyote glances at Jade, shaking his head. "Holy shit, *illegal* adoption?"

"But we all love him so much," Willow says, looking at me. "And you love us, too, right, Blue?"

I lift my head and look from face to face, ending with Willow's. Deep inside me, bottled anger for taking me that day argues with my undying love for this family. I stare into her eyes, my jaw trembling with words that fight to find their way to my tongue. I think about my other family, the one who thinks I drowned in that lake and the brothers or sisters I never got to know. My head feels like it will explode.

I slowly stand up. "You made me love you!" I blurt out. "I didn't have a choice because you took that choice away from me. And now you're trying to take away my freedom, too?"

I kick my pillow as hard as I can. It flies over Willow's head and knocks over a bouquet of wildflowers on a table behind her. The jar rolls to the edge and shatters on the floor. Willow doesn't even flinch, absorbing the full force of my anger as though satisfying a years-long craving for punishment.

Wave stands up. "Blue! You need to calm down."

I glare at him. "Calm down? Really? You want me to calm down?"

Willow holds her hands out toward me. "We're your family, Blue."

"No, you're not!" I sob. "You stole me!" I back slowly toward the door. "You may be my tribe. But that other family? Those were my people. You earned my love. They *deserved* it."

Wave takes a step toward me.

"Don't. Just . . . don't." I turn and walk out the door.

Harmony follows me out of the teepee and catches up to me near the fire pit. "Do you want to talk?"

I shake my head.

"We could leave, Blue. Go find your first family."

"I don't know. I need some time to think. I feel all mixed up right now."

Tears bubble up in her eyes. "You're not going to leave without me, are you?"

I lean in and kiss her forehead. "Never. I just need some space to sort things out."

She nods. "Okay," she says, biting her lower lip as I run toward the woods.

I wait until evening meditation to slip into my bedroom, leaving my boots near the base of the tree, where everyone will see them. I pretend to be asleep when Doobie pads past my mattress and climbs into his hammock. I hear other footsteps pause near our doorway, whispers, and then, finally, silence.

My mind keeps racing from anger to guilt to sadness. If not for Harmony, I'd throw my pack back over my shoulder and set out to look for my first family tonight. But I can't leave her now. And if she came with me we'd get caught, I just know it. Like Gaia, she's not the kind of girl you slip past the law unnoticed. With her big personality and fearless daring she'd surely get us into trouble. It's the thing I love most about her and also the thing that scares me the most.

38

November 1978

Nobody has brought up my angry outburst in the teepee last week, not even Goji. I'm sure he's heard about it by now but either he doesn't care or he's waiting for the perfect moment to have a talk. I'm hoping it's the first reason. The closest he's come to addressing the topic is over lunch, talking about this Rajneesh guy he studied with in India.

"The most important thing I learned from him is that truth isn't something you discover outside yourself, it's something inside of you." He looks directly at me when he says it.

Doobie scratches his beard, deep in thought. "So what you're saying is that a lie is only a lie if you believe it?"

Coyote shakes his head. "My mama was a good woman. She taught me that a lie is a lie is a lie."

Rain looks uncomfortable, shifting in her seat. Maybe it's because of the growing baby. Or maybe because of the stuff she shared with me about how she lied about her age, the stepfather, and about the birth control pills. And that she killed someone, but that it wasn't her fault. Is that a lie, too?

Goji leans back in his chair and smiles at Coyote. "That was your mother's truth. Perhaps it's your truth as well." He drapes an arm around Rain and pulls her toward him. "Sometimes we bend the truth for love's sake. Who has the power to judge actions that come from such a deep place of devotion?"

Listening to Goji, it's all I can do not to start yelling again. My teeth hurt from clenching my jaw. Harmony senses my uneasiness.

She stands and picks up some of our plates. "I love you guys, but you're so full of shit."

She walks toward the kitchen laughing and shaking her head. Some of the others chuckle, but it's a nervous laughter, not the full-throated joy of the past. There's no hugging or shared high-fives or jostling of shoulders. We clear the rest of our dishes and everyone quickly heads in different directions, as if someone planted a time bomb in the middle of the table.

I keep to myself for most of the day, trying to avoid everyone. Not just because of what Goji might have to say; I'm worried about blowing my friendship with Harmony. We've always done everything together, but what if this new thing between us ruins it? Since she got back, we've hardly had a private moment together for talking, let alone anything else. I don't know if I should keep her closer or give her more room.

Harmony startles me as I come out of the outhouse. "Hey! You want to go for a hike later?"

"Yeah, sure. I mean, if we have time. I promised Sirona I'd help her can milk."

"Are you avoiding me?"

"What?"

She pulls her coat tighter around her. "I asked if you're avoiding me."

"Of course not. There's just been so much to do, and after what I said in the teepee I thought maybe I should lie low."

"You spoke up for yourself. I was really proud of you."

"You were?"

"A little surprised, but yeah, definitely."

"I surprised myself. I probably shouldn't have said all that."

She grabs my upper arms and gives me a shake. "Are you kidding? They need to be called on their BS when it stinks."

"Yeah, but Sirona . . ."

"Sirona hardly even flinched. She bought their story—hook, line, and sinker. It's like nobody ever challenges anyone or anything anymore. Remember when we used to have all those amazing philosophical discussions around the dinner table? Why don't we ever do that anymore?"

She's right. Goji used to throw out a question and we'd debate for hours, sometimes until after dark.

"I don't know. Maybe they all got bored with that game."

Harmony turns toward the empty community table. "It wasn't a game. It was how we learned to reason out answers instead of just swallowing what we're told. You want to know what I think?" She doesn't wait for my answer. "I think they got complacent. We used to be this big happy family and now it's more like mini-families within the family, everyone more interested in themselves, their kids, their personal agendas. The Olders have divided up into couples. Nobody uses the Sacred Space."

"But isn't that what happens in normal families? Kids grow up, get married, have kids of their own."

"We're not supposed to be normal! Goji has always taught us to challenge norms."

I put my finger to my lips when I spot Goji and Rain walking toward the outhouse, arm in arm. Harmony glances behind her, then turns and rolls her eyes. "See what I mean?" she whispers. "He's like a little puppy around her."

"Hello, children," Goji says as he approaches. "Is everything okay?"

Rain stands with her legs firmly planted, hands resting on

her bulging belly. Harmony starts to answer him. "We were just discussing—"

"Goat milk," I say, interrupting before she opens another messy can of worms. "Sirona needs help canning all Inga's surplus."

Goji smiles. "The closest thing to human mother's milk. It'll keep us all healthy this winter." He pats Rain's belly. "Especially those who need the extra protein."

Rain points to the outhouse door behind me.

"Oh, sorry." I move out of the way, then take a few more steps backward. "We'll see you at dinner, I guess."

Goji nods and I jump at the chance to get away, heading down the path toward the kitchen area. Harmony trails behind me. "Let's help Sirona together so we can go for a walk before dinner."

She can't see the big smile stretched across my face at the suggestion of some alone time together.

"Sounds good." I say it all matter-of-fact, but absolutely nothing could make me happier right now than Harmony and me alone together.

It takes hours to boil down the goat milk and put it up in jars. Harmony runs off to change her clothes after spilling some on her pants. By the time she gets back it's started raining. I glance at the darkening sky. "Maybe we should wait for tomorrow to take a walk."

She sighs. "Okay. But you're not going to weasel out of it, are you?"

I reach for her hand and pull her onto the bench next to me. "Not a chance."

Harmony sneaks into my room before the sun is up, waking me from a dream about a car crash where we tumbled over a hill and I was searching for survivors. She wipes my forehead with the edge of the sheet. "You're all sweaty."

I struggle to get my mouth to work, still dry and my mind half in the dream. "What are you doing here this early?" I whisper.

"You want me to leave?"

"No, I'm just . . . I'm not very awake yet, sorry."

She glances over at Doobie, sleeping peacefully in his hammock. "He sleeps like a rock, doesn't he?"

"Yeah. He really does."

Harmony sits on the edge of my mattress. "I was hoping we could get an early start on our hike."

I stretch my arms over my head and yawn, then quickly close my mouth. My breath is probably terrible. "Okay, sure. When do you want to go?"

"Right after breakfast." She winks. "I have a little surprise for you. For us."

"A surprise? What kind of surprise?"

Harmony grins. "Your belated birthday present."

Doobie makes smacking noises with his mouth. Harmony jumps off my bed and stands in the doorway. "See you at sun salutation." She darts down the short hall before I hear her boots clunking down the steps of the tree house.

I expected resistance but it doesn't take much convincing to get permission from the Olders for Harmony and me to go on a picnic together. Willow even packed us a lunch. They probably figure neither of us is apt to run off knowing Rain is less than a month away from having her baby.

Harmony finds a dress in the clothing box and slips it over her head. I remember the first time I saw Rain in that dress, how I thought she looked like an angel floating around the compound in her bare feet and near-white hair. I half expected to see wings sprouting from her back, she was that beautiful. On Harmony the dress looks more like a nightgown the way it clings to her new curves. She resembles Gaia more and more every day. She'd clobber me if I ever told her that.

We climb over the hill and set off down the well-traveled path toward our favorite grove of redwoods, about a mile from SFC. Today is one of those summer-in-November kind of days. Our weather can suddenly go from cold and rainy to hot for no reason. One day you're wearing a winter coat and the next you're running around shirtless and barefoot.

As soon as we're out of earshot Harmony stops and fishes a small baggie out of her dress pocket. "Open your hand."

"What is it?"

"Don't ruin the surprise. Just open your hand."

I offer my palm and she shakes a bunch of small brownish chunks into it. She sees my blank stare and grins. "They're magic mushrooms. Psilocybin."

I take a sniff. They smell like moldy bark. "Where'd you get these?"

"From that guy at the Rainbow Gathering I wrote you about. I saved some for us."

"I don't know, Harmony. . . ."

She pinches half of the crumbs between two fingers and drops them in her palm. "It'll be amazing, I promise."

"Is it scary?"

"No, it's really cool. You'll see." She pops her portion into her mouth and starts chewing. Her face scrunches up. "They taste terrible but it's worth it. Go ahead."

I look at her, then down at the mushroom bits.

She holds out her hand. "If you don't eat them I will!"

I don't want to look like a chicken and I don't want her to OD just to prove a point. I dump them in my mouth and start chewing. "Ugh! Can't we just swallow them?"

"I know they're gross, but it's supposed to be better if you chew them first."

I wait for her to swallow before doing the same. When I start guzzling water from my canteen, she snatches it out of my hand. "Don't!"

"Why not?"

"Because you're probably going to barf. Most people do. It's better to have less in your stomach."

"Is that why you hardly touched your breakfast?"

She grins.

"Now you tell me."

"Sorry. If I'd told you, you'd have gotten suspicious."

"So how long before it kicks in?"

"Not long." She takes my hand and pulls me along. "Let's keep walking so we can get to our spot before we come up."

"Come up?"

"Before we start tripping."

As we walk our hands start getting sweaty but I don't want to let go because she might think I don't want to hold her hand. As if she can read my thoughts she drops my hand and wipes hers on her dress.

By the time we reach the redwood grove I'm feeling nauseous. No sooner do we spread out a sheet than I have to run behind the tree and throw up. When I return she hands me the water.

"Just rinse, don't swallow. You feel anything yet?"

I swish the water around in my mouth and spit. "Yeah. I feel a little tingly."

She giggles. "Me too. Feels good, huh?"

"Yeah. Just now when the water was in my mouth it felt weird, like it was alive, swooshing around my tongue and my cheeks."

"Cool." She pats the sheet next to her. "Take a load off."

We stretch out with our arms behind our heads. Yesterday's clouds have broken into small puffs of white against a sky the color of Stardust's sapphire gemstones.

"I'm so happy." I hear my voice in my ears but I'm not sure I said the words aloud. *Did I just think it?* "I'm so happy."

"You're two happy. Like *t-w-o*, not *t-o-o*." Harmony giggles at her own joke. She jumps up and starts twirling around, holding her dress like a ballerina. Her movements create a smear of color in the same shade of yellow as her skirt, her hair floating around her head like a lion's mane. "Look, Blue! I'm tu-tu happy." This cracks her up and she falls back on the sheet in hysterics.

Her laughter sounds like Aura's when she was a baby, sweet and gurgly. This makes me laugh, and the more I laugh the more she laughs until she grabs at her sides. "Stop, stop! I have to pee."

Several Harmonys follow close behind her like pages of a fanning book until she disappears behind some bushes. I go back to watching the sky, where tiny crystals shift in unison as if the whole of it is breathing above us. The clouds form and re-form to create different shapes. Everything is in a warped speed, as if time has slowed while turning up magnification of each particle. The beauty is stunning. ·

Harmony stands near my feet, smiling. "What are you looking at?"

"Everything."

"Everything?"

"Yeah. It feels like I've been seeing the world through a smudged window and now the glass is clear." I turn my head and suddenly every single needle in the redwood tree comes into sharp focus. "This must be how Moon felt when he tried on the right glasses that first time."

She kneels beside me and starts combing her fingers through my hair. "I love your hair. Can I braid it?"

I roll onto my stomach and prop my chin in my hands. When she tugs at the separated strands I close my eyes and follow the prickling sensation down the follicle, into my brain, and out my fingers and toes. The earlier tingles have intensified and become contagious, spreading through my body until goose bumps break out on my arms and legs. I open my eyes and study the patch of grass along the edge of the sheet. Each stalk is like a tiny tree, each grain of dirt separate from the one next to it.

Harmony flops the braid over my shoulder. "Let's walk down to the creek."

I follow her to where the water roars past after last night's rain. We sit on the bank and watch for what seems like an hour or a minute, I'm not sure. All I know is that I'm mesmerized by the sound of it rushing against the rocks, the way the sunlight sparkles off the surface. Even the smell of it. Everything stretches toward me, encapsulates me.

"Harmony?"

"Yeah?"

"My butt feels like it's part of the earth beneath it, like I'm growing out of the dirt."

Harmony unfolds her fingers, her hands hovering just above the surface of the ground next to her legs. "I know what you mean. I feel it, too. Like I'm part of everything." She stands and twirls, then starts skipping back toward our tree. I run behind her, stopping to jump because I feel as if I could leap high into the air, higher than the trees, maybe as high as the birds. I've never felt so free and happy in my life.

When I reach our spot she's naked, stretched out on her belly with her feet in the air. I step out of my jeans and lie beside her. She turns and rests her head on my chest. "You know how people talk about being sun-kissed? I feel the sun kissing me for real. Teeny tiny kisses on every inch of my skin. It feels amazing."

I run my hand gently over her shoulder, her waist, the curve of her hip. I feel her shiver beneath my touch.

"Are you cold?"

"No."

"God, Harmony, you're so beautiful."

I feel her cheeks move into a smile on my skin. I roll her onto her back and kiss her. Our mouths feel like one mouth sharing a single tongue as we move between gentle and hungry kisses. She lets me touch and touch and touch. She touches me back, then stops.

"I don't want to—"

"I know," I whisper. "Me neither. This is enough. More than enough."

Our breaths match the wind ruffling the grass around us. The love I feel for Harmony moves through me like a ghost. We hang out in our little paradise for hours; listening, breathing, playing, feeling until the tingling sensation gradually wanes, but the glow remains, an aching sort of tenderness. I don't remember getting dressed or even deciding to. The sun is setting as we float back down the path toward SFC, exhausted but happy.

Neither of us is hungry despite our untouched picnic lunch that we left for the birds and other critters. Harmony and I steal glances across the dinner table as we push bits of food around our plates. I hear the others talking, but the words bounce off my ears like bits of foam. When evening meditation comes I sink deep inside myself and find that place under the redwoods, the closest I've ever felt to home.

39

December, 1978

Rain and I hunch together over mugs of steaming cocoa under the dining canopy. The weather has turned cool again, almost overnight. Jade and Coyote left with Aura early this morning to visit her family in the Bay area. The compound is eerily quiet, but in a good way. I've missed my time with Rain almost as much as my time with Harmony.

"This is the best hot cocoa I've ever tasted."

She puts a finger to her lips and whispers mischievously. "That's because it's real chocolate, not carob. I bought some cocoa powder at the county store."

"Goji let you buy commercial chocolate?"

Rain grins triumphantly.

"He'd fly you to the moon if you asked. He's head over heels for you."

She dips her head and blushes.

"I didn't mean it was a bad thing, Rain. I know you love him."

She raises the mug to her mouth and sips. A soft moan escapes from her mouth.

I nudge her. "Yeah, I know what you mean. It's so good."

Her hand freezes, holding the mug, halfway back to the table. She's so still she looks like one of those beautiful mannequins in the department store windows in Santa Rosa.

"You okay, Rain?"

She takes a deep breath and sighs it out, setting her cup back on the table. "I'm fine. They're just fake contractions."

"Fake contractions?"

"Sirona calls them Braxton Hicks. False labor that prepares you for the real thing."

"Do they hurt?"

"Not really. It's more like a tightening. Uncomfortable but not painful."

We go back to sipping. She catches me staring toward the path leading to the meadow where Harmony and I spent that day tripping on mushrooms.

"What . . . or should I say who . . . are you thinking about, young man?"

Rain is the one person I trust not to make a big deal or tease me, but I'm suddenly feeling very self-conscious. I'm pretty sure Rain knows that I had a crush on her and that I was jealous of Goji. I trust her, but I'm not ready to talk about Harmony and me. I glance down at her swollen belly, pushing the limits of the buttons on her wool coat. I think everyone is hoping a new baby will bring life back into the community. I know I am.

"I was just thinking about names. Have you chosen any for the new baby?"

She strokes the fur over her bulge and smiles. "Goji will name him or her."

"Don't you want a say in the matter? I mean, it's your kid, too."

"I'm sure he'll pick a good one."

"Okay, but just for fun, what name would you choose?"

She chews on her bottom lip. "Well, I love the name Heidi

for a girl. It was one of my favorite books growing up. Boys' names are harder. Maybe something biblical."

"A Bible name? Why?"

Rain holds up a finger to signify another fake contraction. She unbuttons her coat and places my hand on her belly with her hands over mine. It feels hard at first, then gradually softens.

"Wow. That's amazing."

She smiles and lets go of my hand. "My parents were pretty religious. I have . . . I had a biblical name."

"Can I ask what it was?" I hope she doesn't get mad like Jade did when I found out her real name is Judy.

Rain grins. "Promise you won't laugh?"

"I promise."

"Bethany. I went by Beth, but Bethany is my legal name."

"Why would I laugh at that?"

She giggles. "I don't know. I've gotten so used to my new name that it sounds silly now."

"I like them both."

Rain drops her head to my shoulder. "Thanks, Blue."

"I used to have a Bible name."

She lifts her head and turns toward me. "You did?"

"Yeah. Noah."

Rain draws in a sharp breath. Her face goes pale and she looks like she's going to pass out. I hold her arm to steady her. "Another one?"

She clutches her big belly. "Oh. Oh no."

"What? What is it?"

She tries to stand, then sits again. "Help me away from the table."

I hold my hand on her back as she slowly swings her legs, one at a time, over the bench. The wood seat is wet and there's a puddle on the ground underneath where she was sitting.

"Don't be embarrassed. I pissed myself once when I was sick."

She shakes her head. "I think my water just broke."

I feel like an idiot for accusing her of peeing. "I'll go get one of the sister-mothers!"

"No, stay with me!" She takes a deep breath, tears spilling out of her eyes.

"I thought you said they don't hurt?"

She grabs my arms and pleads. "Please don't leave. Walk with me to Goji's place."

"Are you sure?"

She nods. "I'm sure."

We slowly amble toward the shack. Halfway there Rain doubles over and throws up. When we reach Goji's front step she winces.

"I thought you weren't due for another three weeks."

Rain takes a deep breath. "I might have miscalculated. Or maybe this baby is just sick of waiting. I've had a backache all morning and these contractions. I just figured they were more of the fake kind."

"If your water breaks I think it's real."

She forces a smile and drapes her arm around my shoulder to steady herself. I call out for Goji as we close in on his shack, but he doesn't seem to be around. Except for the night I sneaked Ziggy in and found the candy bars, I've never entered his home without being invited.

Rain doubles over again, steadying herself against a post near the front step. I wait for her to catch her breath. "Are you going to be sick again?"

She shakes her head. "I need to lie down. I'm feeling faint."

I hold her arm as we climb the step, glancing around behind me in hopes of catching someone, anyone. Off toward the garden I see Sirona running toward the shack. She must have heard me yelling for Goji. When she reaches us, she tries to lead Rain toward the bed in the corner but Rain flops in an overstuffed chair near the door. She clutches the worn arms that have stuffing coming out where Ziggy has clawed his way through the fabric. "I just need a minute."

Sirona holds Rain's hand. "When did this start?"

Rain leans forward, parting her knees to make room for her belly. "I don't know."

"About half an hour ago," I say. "We were sitting at the table when she started having contractions. Her water broke as soon as she stood up."

Sirona squats in front of the chair and lays her ear against Rain's belly. I move behind the chair and rest my hands on Rain's shoulders. Rain grabs both my hands.

"She threw up on the way here. Is that normal?"

Sirona holds one finger up. "Shh! I need to listen."

I stand perfectly still. Ziggy leaps from Goji's desk, scattering notes and papers. "Shh!" I say to Ziggy.

Sirona lifts her head. "Blue, I need my stethoscope. Will you run and get my midwifery bag?"

I have to unfold Rain's tight grip on my fingers. I race to the truck and grab the familiar satchel from behind the front seat. By the time I get back, Rain is in the middle of another contraction. I stand in the doorway of the shack and watch her and Sirona breathe through it together before handing Sirona her bag. She digs a stethoscope from inside and places it on Rain's belly.

Feeling a bit useless, I tiptoe over to clean up the mess of papers Ziggy scattered. When I pick up the manila envelope, two crisp airline tickets slide out and onto the floor. They're dated for January to Bombay, India. The names printed on the front are "David Kagen" and "Bethany Kagen." I peek inside the envelope to find two passports with Goji's and Rain's pictures on them with the same names. He and Rain never mentioned anything about getting married. Goji has always insisted that marriage is a government institution that bastardizes love.

My hands shake as I stuff the passports and plane tickets back into the envelope. I look toward Rain, my mouth half open, wanting to ask if she knows that Goji is planning to take her to India. She lets out a low moan, then takes a deep breath and slowly lets it out. My questions are the last thing Rain needs right now.

Sirona lifts Rain's hair away from her face. "We need to move you to a bed, sister."

Rain knits her brow. "I thought you said it was better to stay active during labor? I'm in labor, right?"

"Yes. But we need to get your blood pressure up before you can be upright and move around." Sirona glances in my direction. "Blue, what in the world are you doing over there? I need your help."

I drop the envelope and move next to Sirona. She motions for me to stand on the other side of the chair. "You hold her on the left and I'll take the right."

Sirona and I steady Rain as she lifts out of the chair. The three of us move awkwardly toward the mattress on the floor against the wall. A stream of pinkish water runs down Rain's bare leg and into her wool sock. Rain lowers herself onto the bed, waiting for Sirona to prop pillows behind her before lying back.

Sirona pulls a latex glove from her bag. "I want to check your cervix. Would that be all right?"

Rain's eyes go wide. "Is my baby okay?"

"The heartbeat is strong. I just want to get a baseline on dilation so we can keep tabs on your progression."

I'm feeling uneasy, like she needs a better helper than me. "Should I go find Goji? Or the other sister-mothers?"

Rain grabs my arm. "Please stay!"

I take her hand and sit on the floor next to the bed. Sirona taps Rain's leg. "Bend your knees, hon. This will probably make you have another contraction. Look at Blue. Just breathe through it like we practiced, okay?"

I turn away from Sirona and stare directly into Rain's face. Her hair looks like corn silk against the grungy gray pillowcase. She smiles at me through watery eyes. "Namaste," she whispers. She starts to say something else but winces instead when Sirona checks her. Together we deep-breathe through three long breaths before Sirona snaps the glove from her hand.

"All done. Three centimeters, fifty percent effaced."

"What does that mean?" I say.

"It means that she's going to have a baby. Probably today. Tomorrow at the latest." She smiles at Rain. "I want to send for Goji now, okay?"

Rain grimaces through another contraction, crushing three of my fingers together. When it passes, Sirona nods at me and I start to stand but Rain won't let me go.

Sirona glances toward the door. "Okay, I'll go find him. I'll be right back. I promise."

As soon as Sirona is gone, Rain yanks on my arm. She grabs for my face, my hair, lingering with her trembling fingers. "She knew. Gaia knew! No wonder he didn't want her to stay."

"Rain, what are you talking about?"

She points to a cupboard. "Top shelf."

I open the cabinet. "What am I looking for?"

"A bag. A small canvas bag."

I feel around on the shelf until I find it. Inside, a tied batch of envelopes. The same ones I'd found the day I discovered the candy bars, all but one addressed to Harmony.

Another contraction grips Rain. I rush to her side, hold her hand. When it passes she pulls me close. "I thought Goji was protecting Harmony from Gaia, but he was protecting himself. You need to give the letters to Harmony."

Goji bursts through the doorway with Sirona. I quickly stuff the envelopes in my overalls' pocket.

He rushes to Rain's side. "How's she doing? Is she okay?"

Rain looks at me, then back at Goji. Tears flood her eyes. "Why?" she says, panting through a contraction. She tries to sit up but the color runs out of her face and she faints, falling back on the pillows. Her hand slips out of mine like a loose glove.

40

Harmony paces in circles around the community table. "What do you think is taking so long?"

"I don't know." I pat the bench next to where I'm sitting. "Would you please stop? You're making me dizzy."

She glances at my hand but sits across from me instead. With both elbows on the table she leans into her fisted hands, glancing toward the Sacred Space, where they've moved Rain to labor so they'll have more room. Harmony's long brown bangs nearly cover her big eyes. "I don't remember Aura taking this long to come out. Why did she faint?"

"Sirona said Rain was dehydrated. She gave her some juice."

Harmony bites a fingernail. "Do you think they'll take her if she needs to go to the hospital?"

I've had the same thought and it worries me. I think back to the snake bite and Harmony's coma and how I worried that she might die.

"I'll drive her to the hospital myself if she needs to go."

Harmony lifts her face from her hands and smiles weakly. She glances toward the tree house.

"Hey, we should go read Rain's pregnancy books. Maybe there's something in there about how long labor should last."

I reach inside the large pocket of my overalls and lay the bound letters on the table.

Harmony looks at the pile of envelopes. "What's this?"

"Rain gave them to me when we were in the shack. They're from Gaia. Your mom's been writing to you for years but Goji—"

Harmony fans through the stack. "He . . . he hid these from me?"

I nod. "I'm so sorry."

Tears flood her eyes.

"Maybe you should—"

Before I can finish my sentence she stands, dazed, and walks away clutching the letters to her chest.

Outside the Sacred Space I hear Rain's long moan followed by Sirona's soothing voice. The smell of incense follows Willow as she bursts through the doorway carrying a bucket. The way she holds it away from her I'm pretty sure it's not water. When she sees me she sets the pail in the dirt.

"Don't you want to go in?"

I do and I don't. I want to see with my own eyes that she's okay but I'm afraid of seeing her in pain. It tears me up inside to see her like that.

"I'm not allowed in the Sacred Space."

"That was before. We're her family and she needs our support. And she's asking for you."

When I don't move Willow holds the wool blanket aside and nods for me to go in. I take a deep breath and walk through the doorway.

Everyone looks tired but focused as they sit cross-legged on pillows scattered around the room. Candles burn on a table to one side of the door. A mattress heaped with sheets and pillows lies empty in the center of the room. Rain is squatting over a towel with Goji supporting her. Sirona kneels behind them, rubbing Rain's back. It's the first time I've ever seen Rain without clothes.

"Easy breaths," Sirona says. "When the next one comes I want you to take a deep breath. Hold the breath but push, okay?"

Rain nods. Her hair is stuck to the pale skin of her back. I take a few steps forward. Rain turns, and as soon as she sees me she starts crying, reaching for me. I start to back up, but Wave runs up behind me and rests his hands on my shoulder.

"I've upset her," I whisper.

"No, brother. Those tears aren't because of you. They're *for* you."

"She was fine until she saw me."

"She's still fine. She's happy you're here. Trust me."

"Come, Blue," Sirona says. "Help me catch this baby."

I shake my head. "That's okay. I'll just stand over here."

"Now, Blue!" Sirona isn't asking, she's insisting. "Wash your hands in the bowl, then come over here."

I scrub my hands and dry them on the towel that Willow hands me. When I get next to Sirona I crouch on my knees. "What should I do?"

"The baby's head is crowning. I'm hoping it'll come with the next contraction."

I look toward the doorway. "Somebody needs to get Harmony. She's gonna be really bummed if she misses the birth."

Wave gives my shoulder a squeeze. "Doobie went to look for you and Harmony before you got here. He'll probably be back with her any minute."

A low growl starts in Rain's chest, then bubbles to her throat. It sounds a little like Greta when she's calling for Inga.

Sirona reaches beneath Rain. "Okay, this is it. I'm going to massage the perineum so she doesn't tear. Your job is to make sure the baby's head doesn't hit the floor."

I feel like I'm going to pass out. "Shouldn't we get her to the bed?"

"This is better. We're working with gravity instead of against it."

I glance at Goji. He's kissing Rain's shoulder over and over. "I love you," he whispers. "I love you. I love you. I love you."

His words seem to fuel the next breath that Rain takes. Her face turns redder and redder as she stares into his eyes.

"Push, push, push!" Sirona says. She grabs my hands and centers them under Rain's bottom. I feel the slippery bulge of the baby's head in my hands. I start to pull away but Sirona stops me. "She asked for this. For you."

The language that explodes from Rain's mouth is foreign to me, a string of syllables followed by a scream as the head becomes shoulders, hips, and finally, two tiny feet in my hands.

Sirona leans in and kisses Rain's between her shoulder blades. "Good job, sister!"

I cradle the slippery baby as Sirona ties two pieces of cloth around the umbilical cord and snips between the knots. "You did great, Blue." She swipes the baby's mouth with her finger and uses a small rubber syringe to clean out the tiny nose.

Rain's legs start shaking. Goji catches her as she wilts to one side and lays her gently on the floor, using his hands as a pillow beneath her head.

Rain cranes her neck toward the baby. "Is he okay? Is my baby okay?"

Sirona flicks the bottom of the baby's foot with a finger. It takes a sudden breath, then lets out a cry. She thrusts a towel around the baby, wiping the face as she takes the squirming baby from me. Wave tucks a pillow under Rain's head, relieving Goji's hands.

Sirona gently hands the baby to Goji and smiles. "She. It's a girl."

Goji stares into the blue eyes of his tiny child, weeping. He lays her across Rain's chest, where the baby nuzzles her way to Rain's breast and immediately latches on.

"A good eater," Sirona says. "That's a great sign." She throws a worried glance between Rain's legs. "We've got a little blood here so your placenta has detached. I'm just going to help you deliver it and then we can move you to the bed, okay?"

Rain nods without looking up from her baby.

I look away when Sirona drops the bloody blob into a pan. Rain starts to shiver. Her skin is so pale it almost looks translucent. I grab a blanket and drape it over her and the baby. Rain looks around at all the faces hovering over her. She stops at mine and smiles through her tears. "I'm going to take the best care of her, little brother. I will never let her out of my sight."

Rain looks so peaceful and happy compared to just a few minutes ago. She clutches the baby and falls asleep, exhausted.

Outside the Sacred Space, Harmony's loud voice feels like a brutal intrusion on the quiet beauty of this room. I probably screwed up, giving her those letters today. I hear Doobie trying to quiet her before Harmony bursts through the door. Her eyes are wide with anger or fear or both.

I jump to my feet. "Come on, Harmony. Rain's really tired." I gently touch her arm.

Harmony glances down at Rain, then turns back to me. "Rain is your sister, Blue."

"Our sister. She's your sister, too."

"No, I mean your *real* sister, one you're related to."

She narrows her eyes at Goji. "You stole Ruth's letters to me because she figured it out." Harmony's eyes dart around the room. "You used me and you used my mom to keep her from telling everyone."

Sirona turns away from the basin where she was washing her

hands. With her arms dripping she says, "You people need to take this outside right now."

Goji stands. "Sirona's right. This isn't the time or place for these questions. We're celebrating a new life here."

"What about Blue's life? The one you stole from him?" Harmony shoves a notebook toward me, her finger pointing toward handwriting at the top of a page. It's dated August 13, 1976. "You have to read this."

"Is this Rain's diary? Harmony, that's private."

Sirona takes a step toward us. "Whatever this is will have to wait until—"

Harmony ignores her. "Damnit, Blue, just read it."

Goji moves quickly toward Harmony, swiping at the diary, but Harmony is too fast. She glares at him, eyes wild, her hand like a crossing guard in front of us. She shoves the diary toward me.

Stunned, I take it and start reading.

"Out loud, Blue."

" 'I wonder if God will ever forgive me. Goji says God is in me, that I need to forgive myself for losing track of my little brother at the lake. He makes it sound so simple but it's not. Every time I looked into my mom's face I saw her pain. Dad didn't talk about it but his silence about Noah was almost worse. I'd give anything to go back to that day and start over.' "

I close the journal and look over at Rain, still sound asleep. My whole body is shaking. I feel like I'm going to explode.

Harmony reaches for me. "Blue, I'm sorry. I know I shouldn't have read her diary but . . ."

Sirona turns on her heels to face Goji. "What on earth are they talking about?"

Harmony moves closer to Sirona. "Willow and Wave stole Blue from a park when he was three years old. Rain was just a kid at the time, and Blue disappeared while she was supposed to be watching him."

Willow breaks into sobs. "We were tripping. I . . . I . . . it just happened. I thought he was my baby. I was so scared."

I turn to Wave, who slowly shakes his head from side to side as he comforts Willow. "It was a terrible mistake. I'm so sorry, Blue."

Harmony pulls the letters from her pocket and holds them up for Goji to see. "Rain felt responsible. She ran away because she couldn't forgive herself. My mom brought her here on purpose when she realized Rain was probably Blue's sister."

I turn to Goji. "You robbed me of my family *twice*? Rain thought I was dead. All this time she believed it was her fault. You could have helped her—you could have helped both of us. . . ."

Goji shifts his weight from one foot to the other, glancing toward the door.

I take a step closer to him. "You were afraid she'd leave. That we'd leave together."

Sirona's chin trembles as she takes everything in. "Goji? Is this true? Is Rain really . . ."

"And he's taking her to India." I glare at Goji. "Tell them."

He grimaces, but doesn't answer.

Sirona looks down at Rain. She gently stokes her leg then takes in a sharp breath and throws the blanket aside. "We've got a little problem here. She's still bleeding."

I race to Rain's side and drop to my knees. Sirona starts furiously massaging Rain's belly. Next to me a pool of blood spreads beyond the rug and across the wood floor. I lean down and put my mouth next to Rain's ear. "Hey," I say, squeezing her limp hand. "Hey, Rain, wake up."

Nothing.

"Bethany? It's me."

Rain's eyes flicker open, then close again. When she tries to speak I move my ear to her lips.

"Noah," she whispers.

Her arm falls away and I catch the baby before she rolls to the floor.

I look around the room at the others. "We need to get her to a hospital!"

Sirona nods at Goji. "He's right. She's lost a lot of blood. She needs a transfusion and medicine to stop the bleeding."

Goji collapses next to Rain and lays his head across her chest. His body heaves with sobs. "Take her," he says.

41

Wave wraps Rain's limp body in a blanket and scoops her into his arms. I'm still holding the new baby. We all race after Wave as he carries our sister toward the truck. Sirona lowers the gate and quickly lines the camper with blankets. She climbs inside to care for Rain on the way to the hospital. The baby starts crying, her little head arching back against the crook of my arm. Willow offers to take her from me. I take a step backward.

Sirona shouts from inside the truck. "Boil the baby goat bottles and nipples! Give her fresh milk if she gets hungry!"

Doobie and Wave get into the cab and wait for Goji to join them.

Goji shakes his head. "I'm going to stay here with my daughter. The rest of us need to meditate and surround our sister in healing white light."

Sirona slaps the inside wall of the truck. "We need to go!" she yells. "Now!"

Wave pulls the door closed. When Doobie turns the key, a weak buzz sounds followed by a series of clicks. Doobie's jaw drops as he looks at Wave. "Dead battery," he mouths.

Jade and Coyote are using the station wagon so Doobie jumps

out and runs toward the Vega. He grabs a key hanging from a nearby tree and hops in the driver's seat. We haven't driven it since the day Harmony came back.

The thought of losing my sister again seems impossible. *Please let it start. Please, please, please.*

Doobie cranks the starter. The engine roars to life on the first try. Harmony raises her fists in the air. "Yes!"

The motor sputters and dies.

I hand the baby to Willow. "I'll be right back."

I take off running toward the Fullers' house. They have a phone. And a car. I race through the middle of a herd of Jerseys, who flee in every direction to make way for me, lowing noisily. By the time I reach the Fullers' yard my bare feet are covered in mud and cow muck.

When I spot Lotus's car parked in the driveway my heart nearly leaps out of my chest with relief. I climb the steps two at a time. Through the door I see Lotus from the back, standing at her easel, paintbrush in hand. A naked Mr. Fuller lounges on an overstuffed sofa. I only hesitate for a half second before pounding on the door. I'm crazy out of breath but when Lotus sees me she squeals. "Blue! It's so good to see you." She glances down at my filthy feet. "Maybe you want to . . ."

"Rain needs to get to the hospital. Can you call an ambulance?"

"Rain? Is she in labor?"

"She had the baby. They can't stop the bleeding."

"Oh no. Oh dear." She fishes a set of keys from her purse, calling out behind her, "Charlie, send an ambulance to Saffron Freedom Community!"

She races toward the car and motions for me to get in the other side. I look down at my feet and shake my head. "I can go faster if I run. I'll meet you there."

When I reach SFC Harmony races up to me, tears streaming down her face. "Blue . . ."

"No. No, don't say it."

"I'm sorry, Blue. I'm so sorry."

"No, no, no . . ." I push past Harmony just as Lotus pulls into the driveway. I follow the wails of my family toward the Sacred Space. In the center of the room, the others are gathered around the wool rug where they've carried Rain back to where she labored. Goji is crouched over Rain's head, crying into a fistful of her hair. I don't want to believe it. I can't believe it.

I walk slowly toward Rain and kneel at her blood-spattered feet. They're cold in my hands. I take her feet into my lap and close my eyes. The other voices are a blur in the room. It's just Rain and me drinking cocoa together. Rain and me milking the goats. Rain and me gathering wood, working in the garden, carrying water.

I finally break under Lotus's hands on my shoulders as she peels me away from my sister and into her arms. I cry harder than I've ever cried in my life. Lotus stands strong against my grief, my rage, my disbelief.

"Let it out," is all she says. "Let it out."

Sobs of grief give way to dawning fears of what will happen to Rain's baby. They'll take her. And once the pieces come together, they'll take everyone here to jail.

I pull away from Lotus to face the others, my cheeks soaked with tears. "I loved you. I loved you so much. How could you . . ." I take a long look at the beautiful and kind sister he kept from me, now pale as a ghost on the floor. I think about the relationship we had but mostly about the one we might have had, if she'd been given the chance to find me before Wave and Willow that day. "It's over. I won't cover for you anymore."

I walk over to Willow and hold out my arms. She clutches the baby to her chest and shakes her head. "Don't, Blue. Please don't."

"Give her to me."

Willow looks back at me, her eyes begging for mercy. She glances toward Goji, still weeping over Rain. And then her shoulders drop, just like that, and she hands the new baby to me.

Goji lifts his head. He suddenly seems small and weak instead of the brilliant philosopher I'd grown to love so deeply over the years. I look at the baby in my arms, and anger dissolves into action. I move swiftly toward the doorway.

"My daughter," Goji says softly. "My beautiful Valkyrie."

I stop. Without turning I say, "Heidi. Her name is Heidi."

We load up the back seat of Mark's Vega with bottles of goat milk and a few of our things. Lotus charges up to us as Harmony pours gas from a can into the Vega. She points to the bundle in my arms.

"Kids, you can't take that baby. You don't know how to care for an infant."

Harmony tosses the rusted can in the dirt and screws the gas cap back on the tank. "We took care of Moon and Aura all the time. We rocked them, burped them, changed their diapers. We did everything but nurse them. We've got milk for her. We'll stop for bottles along the way."

Lotus shakes her head, her eyes misting with tears. "Honey, she belongs here, with her family."

I step in front of Harmony. "I'm her family."

Lotus eyes the baby nervously. "In essence, yes. But Goji is her father."

"Listen, I realize that this is going to come as a shock, but Rain is my actual sister. By blood. We're not taking her. We're bringing her where she belongs."

She glances toward the Sacred Space and back to us. "What are you talking about?"

I worry what will happen if we don't get out of here before the ambulance arrives. In as few words as possible, I tell Lotus how I came to SFC.

"They *kidnapped* you?"

"It's a long story. We need to get free of here before the cops start asking questions." Harmony climbs into the front seat and

I hand her the baby. "All three of us could end up in foster care. Moon and Aura, too."

Lotus peers inside the car. "You can drive?"

"Yes," we both say.

She bites her bottom lip. "You need to promise you'll call me when you get there."

Harmony looks up at Lotus. "Promise."

Lotus leans over and kisses the baby's head. "Good-bye, angel." She closes Harmony's door and hugs me, then pulls a wad of bills from her handbag and stuffs them in my coat pocket. "Be careful."

A siren wails in the distance and Sunny howls as he paces near the car. I let him into the back seat and jump into the driver's side. When I start to back out, Harmony points to where Doobie is sobbing at the community table, all by himself.

"I don't think Doobie knew the whole truth. He seems as shocked as Sirona."

I look at Doobie and back to Harmony. "He didn't ask, though, did he?"

She starts to cry. "But the pot. If they find his crops he could go to prison for life."

I stop and roll down the window. Lotus bends down to meet my gaze. I motion toward the picnic table. "You might want to get him out of here."

She glances toward Doobie and runs in his direction. In the rearview mirror I see her pulling him toward her car before we make the curve in the driveway. We drive past the Czech's farmhouse, past our dilapidated fruit stand, over the Salmon Creek Bridge, and head toward the highway. We don't make it far before an ambulance and police car fly past us in the opposite direction, lights flashing and sirens wailing.

I grip the steering wheel.

"Stay calm," Harmony says. "We'll be long gone by the time they figure out she gave birth."

"What if we get pulled over for driving a stolen car?"

Harmony reaches into her pack and pulls out an envelope.

"What's that?"

"Insurance," she says, fanning through the naked photos of herself before stuffing them in the glove compartment.

My hands are still shaking as Bodega Highway becomes Highway One becomes US 101 south. The picture of Rain's face keeps swimming in front of my eyes, like a movie playing over and over. I want this to be a dream. I want to go back to sitting at the table drinking cocoa and laughing, only this time she tells me I'm her brother and she's taking me back home.

I wipe the corner of my eye with my sleeve and glance down at the sleeping baby in Harmony's arms. She still has bits of whitish wax on her ears and a smear of her mother's blood in the swirl of blond hair at the peak of her head.

Harmony follows my gaze, lifting a tiny hand that instantly curls around Harmony's finger. "She's so little. Do you think we were ever this small?"

"I don't know. Maybe."

Sunny pokes his head between the seats, sniffing at the bundle in Harmony's lap. The baby throws her arms up, then shudders. Her berry-colored lips make a perfect O. Harmony's mouth drops open. "Oh my God. She just peed. Right through the blanket. We need to get diapers. And some real baby bottles."

A few miles more and Harmony points to a tall Kmart sign off an upcoming exit. I turn off the highway and pull into the shopping center. Harmony finds an extra blanket in the trunk and wraps it around baby Heidi, who doesn't make a peep, before handing her to me. "You carry her, I'll find the stuff."

Inside the store, Harmony scoops up a box of Pampers.

"Shouldn't we get the cloth kind?"

She shoots me a look. "You want to wash poopy diapers?"

I don't answer.

"I didn't think so." She grabs a yellow baby blanket from a

shelf, along with a tiny kimono with a matching knit cap and a couple of baby bottles. "Let's get out of here."

On our way to the checkout we pass a row of television sets. Harmony pauses and points at the screen where a weird-looking cartoon bird races away from a skinny coyote right before a rock falls on his head, smashing him flat. The bird races back and faces us. *Meep-meep.*

I look at Harmony. "Road Runner?"

She smiles. "Yup. And Wile E. Coyote, who never catches him."

We throw a map on the moving belt along with the other stuff. The cashier, an older lady with curly gray hair, glances at the baby in my arms and gasps. "That little one looks brand new!" She looks from Harmony's face to mine. "You can't possibly be . . . you're too young to . . ."

Harmony pulls out a twenty-dollar bill, compliments of Lotus. "How much?"

The woman turns back to the register, flustered. "Fourteen dollars and eighty-six cents."

She hands Harmony the change. "Take good care of . . . boy or girl?"

"Girl," I say.

"You need to sterilize those nipples!" she shouts behind us.

Back in the car, Harmony retrieves a funny-looking plastic-coated diaper from the box and fits it around the baby in her lap, taping the sides together. She pulls the kimono over Heidi's head, being careful around the bloody stub of the cord in her belly button, then slides the cap over her head and wraps the new blanket around her.

"Blue, look at her. She's so beautiful."

At the sound of Harmony's voice the baby's eyes come open. She blinks several times, as if the light is too bright.

"Hey, Heidi," I say. "I'm Clover Bl . . . your uncle Noah."

Harmony flinches, just a little. "I'm not used to that name. You'll always be Clover Blue to me."

I lean in and kiss Harmony lightly on the cheek. "I can be both." I turn my attention back to the baby's gazing stare. "And this is your auntie, Harmony. Or Annie. Or whatever you decide to call her."

The baby pulls her fists close to her face. She turns her head and starts sucking on her knuckles.

"Blue, I think she's hungry. Can you put some milk in one of those bottles?"

"That lady said we're supposed to boil the nipples. And don't we need to warm the milk?"

Harmony glances toward the backseat. "I don't see a stove back there, do you?"

I fill up a bottle, unable to get the picture of Rain milking Inga and Greta, possibly even this batch. I remember how she'd wondered what it would be like to nurse her baby. I remember her hair glowing around her face, her cheeks blushed in the cool air. I roll the bottle between my palms, trying to warm it, even just a little.

Heidi's cry startles me. I hand the bottle to Harmony. "Here you go."

The baby's head swims side to side, desperately trying to take the nipple, which seems too big for her tiny mouth. Harmony puts her pinkie into the corner of the baby's mouth and as soon as she starts sucking, replaces it with the bottle—a trick we learned with Aura. Harmony smiles triumphantly as she folds the fuzzy new blanket around Heidi and reclines the seat.

The sun sets as we pass through Salinas. I pull into a filling station that doubles as a taqueria. While the gas tank fills I slip inside the phone booth near the air pump. "Operator, can you look up an address for me?"

"What city please?"

"Atascadero, California."

"Name?"

"Anderson. Howard and Delores."

"One moment please."

I glance toward the car, where Harmony is outside walking in circles, bouncing the baby in her arms as Sunny pees on a lamp post.

"Four one four four Old Railroad Avenue. Would you like the number?"

"Um, yeah. Sure." I don't have anything to write with. "One sec."

I open the booth and holler toward Harmony. "I need a pen!"

She shrugs and turns her back to me.

I step back inside the phone booth and pick up the dangling receiver. "I'm sorry, operator, I don't have a pen."

Silence.

"Operator?"

The line has gone dead. I hang the receiver and out of habit check the change return, but it's empty.

I order two burritos and deliver them to Harmony through the back window, where she and the now-crying baby have re-settled. Sunny is in the front passenger seat, sniffing at the air when he smells the food.

"I'll be right back. I gotta take a leak."

With the bathroom door locked, I lean on the sink to catch myself as waves of grief wash over me. The weight of Rain's death takes me down to my knees in howling sobs. It's so unfair. Unfair to her, to me, our parents, that innocent baby. Someone knocks on the door and I ignore it, letting the loss move through me until I feel empty.

By the time I stand back up the sadness has turned to anger. I never knew a love so deep could turn to a fury so strong; all that trust shattered in an instant. Why didn't Goji make Wave and Willow return me to my family? He robbed us. All those years I could have had with my sister, and then when he had the chance to do the right thing, he robbed me again. I look at my reflection and scream at it. I want to break the mirror but hit the wall with my fist instead, leaving a powdery dent in the plaster and my knuckles bleeding.

I fish a pocketknife out of my pocket, the one Coyote gave me when I turned twelve. I think about how he stuck up for me, told me I deserved my freedom. I turn the smooth handle over in my hand, remembering how Coyote protected Rain from those bad men that night in the woods. He didn't know the truth about me, I'm sure of it.

I open the blade and run my finger along the flat edge, then grab a wad of my rib-length hair, slicing through it in a single swipe. I chop at the rest haphazardly, cursing Goji as I cut away chunks until my hair is the length of my collar. By the time I'm done the floor around me is a nest of blond. I shove the knife in my pocket and walk back to the car.

Harmony watches me, her eyes widening as I close in on the car. I climb into the front seat and wait, but she doesn't say a word. I start the engine and pull back onto Highway 101 south.

Behind me the baby makes soft gulping sounds as Harmony gives her more milk. I glance at the rearview mirror and watch her move the bundle over her shoulder, gently patting like we did hundreds of times with the Youngers. The tears come rushing back when I think of Moon and Aura and how we'll probably never see them again. I pull over under a streetlight in the town of Atascadero and fold my face into my hands.

"You okay, Blue?"

How does she do it? How does Harmony stay so strong?

"I'm fine. I just need to check the map." I pull my flashlight out of the glove box and point it at the streets until I find Railroad Ave. "Got it."

I take a couple more turns. We wind our way past a subdivision, then a few miles down a country road that turns from asphalt to gravel.

"I think this is it," I say, reading the numbers on a steel mailbox in the headlights.

We creep slowly up the driveway past a paddock dotted with

goats and sheep. A ripple of something like a memory or a dream passes through me. I remember that first day meeting Rain, how she smelled so familiar, like a sun-drenched pasture. She smelled like *home*.

The headlights brush the side of a two-story house with a long front porch and a wreath on the front door. I shut off the engine. Inside, a woman moves a curtain aside, peering toward our car in their driveway. An outdoor light comes on and the front door opens. A tall man steps into the light, holding a newspaper in one hand. The woman appears behind him.

My heart nearly folds over on itself.

Harmony taps me on the shoulder. "Are you nervous?"

"A little."

The couple moves farther onto the porch, letting the door close behind them. I slide out from behind the wheel and walk around the car to open Harmony's door. She hands me the sleeping baby. Sunny sniffs the air and whimpers, begging to be let out. "Stay there, boy," I say.

I stand frozen in place, unable to move as my parents watch our every move from several yards away.

Harmony gets out of the car and closes the door. "They're gonna love you."

"I'm bringing them terrible news."

She lays her hand on my back and gently nudges me forward. "You're bringing them twice as much good news."

42

Heidi sits at the dining room table, papers and brochures spread from one end to the other. She's incredibly beautiful, like her mother, with high cheekbones and fair skin. Although a brunette, she has Bethany's crystal-blue eyes.

I peer over the top of the manuscript I'm editing. "You need any help with your essay?"

"No thanks. I want to do this myself." She must see a flash of hurt on my face because she quickly adds, "I mean the first draft. I'd love to have you proof it."

"I'd be honored."

"Uncle Noah, do you think they'll take me seriously with a name like Heidi Rainbow Anderson?"

She knows about my past. Having missed so much myself, I was determined to share every single memory I have of her mom so that she'd know what a beautiful human being gave life to her. We chose Heidi's middle name to honor Rain, the new baby a ray of light in the darkness following her death.

I set down my book and join her at the table. "Probably more serious than they would Clover Blue."

Heidi laughs. "You're probably right."

Heidi chews on her pen and looks up at me, grinning. "I've heard Annie call you that before."

"She calls me a lot of things."

"Yeah. But every once in a while she calls you Blue. Mostly when she's happy."

It's true. Although we abandoned the names Goji gave us out of principle, they're the names we knew each other by, the names we had when we fell in love.

Annie walks in carrying a handful of brushes, her oversized white shirt covered in so much paint it's a work of art by itself. I wink at Heidi and put my finger to my lips. She giggles.

Annie raises her eyebrows. "What are you two up to now?"

Heidi holds up the form. "Working on my college applications."

"Honey, you already know more about animals and farming than most of the instructors. Why spend all that time in school when you could be outdoors, doing what you love?"

"Because I want to become a veterinarian."

Annie turns on the kitchen faucet. I sneak up behind her and circle my arms around her waist, trying to nibble her earlobe. She wheels around and dabs a glob of yellow paint on my nose. I wrestle a paintbrush from her hand and whisk streaks on either side of her mouth like cat whiskers.

Heidi laughs from the table, shaking her head. "You guys are crazy."

In the other room, three-year-old Henry wakes from his nap singing, just like always. Heidi leaps from the table. "I'll get him!" She races out of the room and within minutes I hear them laughing and singing together. The back door slams as they head to the wooden play yard Dad and I built, before he started forgetting the difference between a nail and a screw.

Standing at the kitchen window, Annie and I watch Heidi

push Henry on the swing. He tilts his head back, gripping the chains, his curls glowing in the summer light. Our son is the same age I was when Willow and Wave took me from a church picnic at Atascadero Lake, changing the direction of my life forever. The thought of anyone taking Henry terrifies me.

Annie wipes her hands on her jeans and leans back on the counter. At thirty-two, she looks more like Gaia than ever, deep-set eyes, wild wavy hair, and still that impish smile.

I've been waiting for the right time to tell her my plans. We've promised never to keep secrets. I remove the private investigator's letter from my jeans pocket and hand it to her.

"What's this now?"

"I found him."

Annie unfolds the letter and scans the page. She looks up, wide-eyed. "You know they won't extradite him; there's no reciprocity between the U.S. and India, and besides, the statute of limitations has expired."

"I don't want him arrested."

"Then why bother looking for him?"

"I just want to talk to him."

"Why? Why let that man poison our lives with his toxic bullshit or poor excuses? Her death was his fault. Not growing up with your family was his fault. If not for him . . ."

"I would never have met you."

She takes both of my hands in hers. "Don't torture yourself like this. We have a good life, a beautiful son, and Heidi is getting ready for college. Please. Just let it go."

When I don't answer, her eyes fill with tears. She drops my hands and walks back to her studio without another word.

She's right. I should let it go.

But I can't.

It didn't take long to find him. The private investigator called back within three weeks to say he'd tracked David Kagen to the northern part of India where he's teaching English to Tibetan refugees in a small village north of Dharamsala. I immediately booked a flight to New Delhi. I wasn't worried about the twenty-hour trip or confronting the man who kept me from my family for eleven years. I worried about how to tell Annie, who had long ago forbidden even speaking Goji's name in her presence.

Forgiveness doesn't come easily for Annie, who remains steadfast in her sense of right and wrong. But for some reason she was able to forgive the rest of our SFC family, even joining me for prison visits with Willow and Wave. They were both released on parole after serving half of their eight-year sentences. Doobie and Jade pled guilty to harboring a minor and spent just six months in jail. Coyote and Sirona were found innocent, thanks to Gaia's testimony that neither of them knew I was abducted. It was during their trial that Annie finally accepted the olive branch from Gaia.

Annie doesn't view herself as a victim, far from it. She's a survivor. She survived her mother's abandonment and drug abuse, nine years without running water or electricity, no formal schooling, and more cards stacked against her than any kid should endure. Not to mention taking in Heidi after my mom died from breast cancer, and helping with Dad after he was diagnosed with Alzheimer's.

I pour a cup of coffee and carry it toward Annie's art studio, her refuge, where she spends most of her days. I watch from the doorway as she works on a painting of a teenaged Rain for Heidi's graduation gift. Heidi is almost the same age as her mother was when she died after giving birth to her.

I take a deep breath and move behind my wife. She sighs in a way that usually precedes gearing up to win an argument. But then her shoulders soften and she turns to look at me.

"I promise never to bring him up again," I say. "I don't know if I'll find the answers I'm looking for, but I have to go. And I want your blessing. I need it."

"Okay," she says finally. "Okay, Blue."

* * *

After more than twenty hours on the plane to New Delhi it's another eight hours by train to the foot of the Himalayas. I spend the night on the floor of the train station in Dharamsala along with a multitude of other travelers before finally boarding a bus to McLeod Ganj. The narrow roads are rutted and rocky, nearly throwing passengers into each other's laps as we chug up the rugged switchbacks. Other than me, there's only one other person on the bus who isn't either Indian or Tibetan, a young French woman who speaks heavily accented English but appears to be fluent in Hindi and Tibetan.

I lean back in the seat and try to relax as we bump along the mountain road. I retrieve a Polaroid of Goji from my shirt pocket. In the picture, he stands with his arm around Rain, one hand on her protruding belly as he smiles into Jade's camera. It was taken just a few days before she went into labor, before the world I'd known for most of my life came crashing down, before we drove three hundred miles with baby Heidi in a beat-up Vega.

We stayed up most of that first night answering my parents' many questions, and them, mine. Mostly they wanted to know if anyone had hurt me or Bethany. "Not physically," I'd said. Mom vacillated between grieving the news of her daughter's death and the shock of my return, eleven years after I'd disappeared. "We never gave up hope," she kept saying as she ran her hands through my choppy hair, weeping. "Never."

By the time the police arrived the next morning, Mom was busy boiling baby bottles and Dad was dozing in the recliner with the new baby asleep on his chest, rising and falling with each of their breaths. The police took our statements. Harmony swiped the Polaroid photo before handing Rain's diary to the cops. She threw a fit when they brought a woman from social services to take her to a foster home. My parents convinced the woman to let her stay with us. Gaia showed up three months later, clean and sober, and rented an apartment nearby for her and Annie.

The bus lurches around a sharp bend, pitching everyone forward. I drop the photo of Rain and Goji. A monk sitting across the aisle picks it up. When he starts to hand it to me I point to Goji. "Have you seen this man?"

He stares at the yellowed photograph without recognition, then shows it to the elderly woman next to him. I study the deep lines carved into her round face as she traces the figures in the picture with gnarled fingers. She shakes her head and passes it the French woman.

"I've seen this, this necklace." The French woman taps on the yin-yang pendant around Goji's neck. A flicker of hope rises before I realize that there are probably millions of similar pendants in this part of the world. "Not him," she says. "A much older man."

"He'd be fifty-two now."

She studies the photo again. "Maybe it's him. He took the robes for a while but ended up leaving the monastery."

My heart sinks. "He left?"

"No. He's still here. He married a Tibetan woman. They have a small farm outside the village. He also teaches English."

"Can you take me there?"

She points to a much younger monk sitting three seats over. "Tashi can."

I glance at the dark-eyed child swathed in a maroon robe. He looks no more than ten years old. His head is shaved and his round face punctuated by two prominent dimples.

"His student?" I ask.

She smiles. "His son."

Tashi runs ahead of me in dirty tennis shoes, his robe billowing like a cape. I do my best to keep up with him. We follow a well-traveled path under trees strung with hundreds of colorful flags, flapping their prayers as we pass. My shirt is drenched with sweat by the time we round the last corner before coming to an opening. Below us, a plump woman stands in profile in front of a cement block house with a metal roof.

Tashi runs toward the woman, who kisses the top of his head. He points to me and she shields her eyes, squinting.

The boy waves toward me, shouting, "De sho! Come!"

I walk slowly down the hill. As I do, three more children appear, and it's then that I see the woman is not plump, she's pregnant.

The boy says something to his mother. She points to a field. A man wearing a pointed straw hat stands and rubs his low back. When he sees me, he sets down his basket and walks toward us. His hair is graying and his skin is darker than I remember, browned by the sun.

"Welcome," he says, extending his hand. "My name is—"

"Goji," I say.

His arm freezes in midair, his eyes widening with fear. He glances behind me, then speaks to his family in Tibetan. They scurry into the small house.

We stare into each other's face in silence. All the words I brought with me, the whys and the why-nots, suddenly vaporize in my throat.

"Blue?" he says finally.

I nod.

He looks behind me again. "Did you bring her?"

"Who?"

"My daughter."

I shake my head.

"The feds?"

"No."

His shoulders relax just a bit. "Then why?"

"I thought, I believed . . .

"Yes?"

"I wanted to tell you how much I hate you for destroying my life. How angry I am. But now . . ." I glance toward the doorway, where his wife and children are huddled together.

Goji takes both my hands in his. "Say what you need to say."

I try to pull my hands away but this only makes him grip them tighter. He's stronger than I remember, his dark eyes kinder. I search my mind for the unhealed wounds that propelled me halfway across the world. I think of how he kept Rain from me, kept me from my family, kept Harmony from her mother.

"I need to tell you . . ."

He nods, his dark eyes burrowing into mine as he braces for my words. "Say it."

"I . . . I forgive you."

Goji's eyes brim with tears. "That's what you came all this way to tell me?"

"No."

A stifled cry escapes my mouth, choking me. I pull my fists in toward my chest. He wraps his arms around me and we both crumble to our knees, sobbing.

In the morning, Tashi sets a cup of butter tea on the table in front of me. Goji and his wife, Pema, are already in the field. Their three other children watch me drink, giggling and whispering to each other. When I've finished the tea, Tashi hands me my pack. "I can walk you back to the bus station."

Outside their small house, I scan for Goji but I don't see him. Pema stands at the edge of a row of buckwheat, dwarfed by the huge mountains in the distance. She waves at us, or maybe she's just waving to Tashi; I can't be sure. We both wave back.

As we approach the village, I retrieve Heidi's senior picture from my wallet and hand it to Tashi. He turns it over and reads the inscription—Heidi Rainbow, age 17—then hands it back to me, confused.

"Your sister," I say.

"Sister?"

"Give it to your father."

Tashi looks at the picture again, then me, his eyes nearly disappearing when he smiles. He tucks it into the sash tied around his waist. "Okay," he says, then runs toward a group of boys in matching garnet robes. The boys surround him, their joyful faces bursting into laughter as they playfully knock into each other. An older monk arrives and they grow suddenly quiet. I watch as the Youngers line up, hands in prayer mudra, chanting, as they follow their teacher up the road.

Clover Blue

ABOUT THIS GUIDE

The suggested questions are included to enhance your group's
reading of Eldonna Edwards's *Clover Blue*.

DISCUSSION QUESTIONS

1. *Clover Blue* opens with a birth. What significance do you think this has to the story?

2. Goji claims he's not a guru, but SFC members appear to revere his wisdom and seek his guidance. Do you think Goji's intentions are generally honorable?

3. Who was your favorite character and why? Your least favorite?

4. Did Gaia do her daughter, Harmony, a favor by leaving her at SFC?

5. How would the book have been different if it were set in present time? In the future?

6. SFC exists without plumbing and electricity. What conveniences would you be willing to give up in order to live a utopian life in nature?

7. The children are all home-schooled. Do you think they received a better education than their peers?

8. How might Blue's life have been better if he'd grown up with his family of origin? How might it have been worse?

9. Do any of the characters in the book remind you of people you know or have known in real life?

10. Nudity is commonplace at SFC but sex is considered sacred. Are these two tenets contradictory?

11. Early in the book Goji claims that Clover Blue was seeking Saffron Freedom Community and that it was his destiny to end up there. Toward the end of the book Blue

tells Harmony that if not for growing up at SFC he'd never have met her. Do you believe in destiny? Do ends justify the means?

12. Goji never apologizes to Blue. Why do you think this is?

13. Blue ultimately forgives his abductors. Would you be able to do the same in this situation?

14. What is the difference between family and tribe?

15. What message do you think the author is trying to convey in *Clover Blue*?